Legacy

Legacy

ALAN JUDD

ALFRED A. KNOPF   NEW YORK

2003

THIS IS A BORZOI BOOK
PUBLISHED BY ALFRED A. KNOPF

Copyright © 2001 by Alan Judd
All rights reserved under International and Pan-American
Copyright Conventions. Published in the United States
by Alfred A. Knopf, a division of Random House, Inc., New York
Distributed by Random House, Inc., New York.
www.aaknopf.com

Originally published in Great Britain by
HarperCollins Publishers, London, in 2001.

Knopf, Borzoi Books, and the colophon are
registered trademarks of Random House, Inc.

Library of Congress Cataloging-in-Publication Data
Judd, Alan.
Legacy / Alan Judd.—1st ed.
p.   cm.
ISBN 0-375-41484-3
1. Intelligence officers—Fiction. 2. Russians—Great Britain—Fiction.
3. Fathers and sons—Fiction. 4. Cold War—Fiction.
5. England—Fiction. I. Title.

PR6060.U32 L34 2002
823'.914—dc21   2002016262

Manufactured in the United States of America
First American Edition

To Bim

BERLIN, 1945

EXTRACT TO PF 48/78/76 FROM GEN 100/472 (RUSSIAN
INTELLIGENCE SERVICE [RIS] OPERATIONS AGAINST
BRITISH AND ALLIED SERVICE PERSONNEL OVERSEAS).

BER/1 minute 51 to H/BER, p.2 cont.

4. They left the café at about 2125hrs. Subject
paid for both. He is described as about 5'10''
with light brown hair, centre parting, clean
shaven, ruddy complexion as if used to living in
the open, aged 28-30 approx. No obvious distin-
guishing marks. His uniform was clean and pressed
and he wore the crown on his shoulders. His beret
was blue.

Comment: MORNING LIGHT is still confused by
British uniforms and insignia. When shown examples
and questioned again, he was certain that subject
was wearing battledress and was a major. It is
probable that he was attached to a headquarters
but was still wearing divisional flashes (uniden-
tified), and possible that he was Royal Engineers.

MORNING LIGHT was sure he was not a Gunner (the only cap badge he recognises).

5. The woman was about 5'7'' with shoulder-length blonde hair which shone as if washed. She wore a cream shirt or blouse and a loose, floral-patterned skirt. They were smart and clean, as if new. She had black shoes with heels and nylon or silk stockings with no ladders or holes. She carried a black handbag and wore make-up and nail varnish. MORNING LIGHT could not say whether she wore any rings. Her German was native Berlin, her English fluent.

Comment: MORNING LIGHT's own English is such that almost any other German he hears speaking it sounds fluent to him. Asked to describe the woman's features, he stressed that she was beautiful ("bild schon") and that her teeth were very good ("ebenmassige Zahne") but was vague on particulars.

6. They continued to talk animatedly when they left the café and turned right before crossing the road into Bernauerstrasse. MORNING LIGHT followed them as soon as he had settled his bill but did not regain sight until he saw them turn into Friedrichstrasse and into the Russian zone. He did not follow them in. Although they did not touch each other or walk arm-in-arm, they gave the impression that they would be more than friendly ("mehr als Freunde"). Subject appeared to hesitate as they entered the Russian zone and she went a few paces ahead before stopping. They both laughed, and the British officer followed.

Comment: MORNING LIGHT believes the woman was of good background ("aus guter Familie") because she

naturally paused for subject to open the door for
her on leaving the café, which, "being a British
officer," he naturally did. She was not the usual
Nazi Party/Communist Party call-girl. Asked why he
was sure this was a controlled operation rather
than a girl operating on her own—or not operating
as a tart at all—he insisted that no woman in
Berlin can now dress and look like that without
support and protection. There are no "nice rich
girls" left in Berlin, he says, and her returning
to the Russian zone is, in his eyes, conclusive.
There were also two men at a nearby table who
appeared to take an interest in the couple. He
could not describe them, beyond saying they were
middle-aged and ordinary ("unscheinbar"). An interest in the girl was natural enough but he had a
feeling ("das Gefühl haben") that they could have
been surveillance (SV).

7. Action: Given that we now know MORNING LIGHT's
wartime reporting to have been accurate, his
judgement on such apparently trivial matters is
worth taking seriously. It should be possible to
identify the erring major by checking army headquarters lists of field officers, concentrating on
those recently detached from fighting divisions
and starting with Sappers. Although this may well
turn out to be a straightforward security matter,
we should not bring in the Military Police at this
stage but, with the new GADFLY programme in mind,
we should look first for any opportunity for
development. Army Intelligence Corps representa-
tion has recently been beefed up and I suggest we
start with them. If this is to become the first
GADFLY case, we need to act a.s.a.p.—this day if
possible. May I go ahead?

RH

BER/1.

CHAPTER ONE

LONDON, MID-1970s

IT WAS A WARM summer when Charles Thoroughgood left the army and joined the Secret Service but politically the world was deep in the Cold War. He moved to London and rented a basement flat in Kensington with a view of sodden detritus in the well of the building and the housekeeper's kitchen. He suspected that, from behind her dirty net curtains, she spent days and nights in unprofitable surveillance of his own uncurtained window. "Slack Alice," Roger Donnington, his colleague and flatmate, had dubbed her. "Face that would stop a coal barge."

One autumn Monday, he got up after a restless night to a humid, muggy London. The flat's tiny bathroom had no window and the electricity was off. Shaving by candlelight was a slow operation because he had to keep moving the candle as he traversed each cheek, and it was difficult to get any light at all beneath the chin without risk of singeing. He had long owned an electric razor, a present from his mother, but it had never left its box. The idea of using it had always felt like a concession to something, perhaps a luxurious and corrupting modernity. It was irrelevant now, anyway, because he had used the battery for his radio. Calling an electrician to restore mains power had, so far, proved too great a concession for either him or Roger.

The milk and butter in the powerless fridge smelt rancid. Someone would have to throw them away, sometime. He made toast in the gas stove, covered it with Marmite and drank black tea. He tidied the bed-clothes on his double mattress on the floor, put on his light suit and flicked a tie free of the clothes crammed on the hook on his bedroom door. Before leaving he knocked on Roger's door. Roger had his own mattress in the sitting room, with the television at its foot. Charles had got in late the night before, so had no idea whether Roger was alone or accompanied. There was no answer. He knocked again, louder. "Okay?" he called.

Roger's groan became a cough. "Okay."

It was not to be a normal day at the office, though few were at that time. He was glad of that: secret service seemed so far to provide the advantages of bureaucratic employment—security, purpose, compan-ionship and, though he might not yet have admitted it to himself, the pleasing consciousness of service—without the monotony he assumed to go with office life. He wouldn't need his bike that day, so left it propped up against the bedroom wall.

The best features of the flat were the front door of the building and the curving staircase, both of a size and grandeur to give an impression of spaciousness and opulence within. It had been cheaply converted into flats during the 1950s and 1960s and already the additions seemed older and more worn than the house. The plaster was cracked, paintwork faded, doors warped and skirting boards had parted company with their walls. The door of Charles's flat was tucked beneath the bottom turn of the staircase, so that stepping from it into the entrance hall was literally to enter a bigger and brighter world.

Out on Queensgate, he turned left towards Hyde Park after a deliber-ate glance across the wide street to check that his car was undamaged. The rush-hour traffic was heavier than usual, perhaps in anticipation of further wildcat strikes on the Underground, and the delay in crossing the Cromwell Road gave him the pretext to look about as if seeking a quicker way. He did the same at Kensington Gore, then walked behind the Albert Memorial and into the park. He walked unhurriedly, trying to establish a regular but not purposeless pace.

He looked back around again before he crossed the Serpentine Road and took one of the footpaths to Marble Arch and Speakers Corner. Anyone following would have to keep well back, or ahead or to the side, but then close quickly before Charles entered the Marble Arch subway.

Presumably they would have car as well as foot surveillance, and radio. A car team might become a foot team when they needed to close, but to do that the cars would have to loiter in the busy Park Lane or Bayswater Road, which was never easy.

Once in the subway and reasonably sure he was out of sight, he broke the rules by looking behind without an obvious reason. None of the figures in the park was hurrying. No puffy, sweaty man or woman suddenly appeared at the top of the steps. Perhaps they were waiting in Queensgate for Roger, if they were there at all. They might have a long wait.

In Oxford Street he made for C&A, where he bought two pairs of black socks. It was cooler in the store and he loitered a while among the suits, before taking a back street to Marylebone Station, walking slowly with his jacket over his arm. At the station he bought a day return to Beaconsfield. The newsagent had sold out of *The Times* because the printers had gone on strike during the night, leaving only the early editions available. There would be time to find one later. He settled for the previous week's *Economist*.

He knew the forty-minute journey. Whether or not they were following by car, they would have to put at least one watcher on the train with him. If there were any "they." He read until the approaching Chilterns countryside gave reason for glancing about the carriage. It was tempting to get off at one of the small stations before Beaconsfield to see who got off with him, but that was cinema stuff. The trick in evading surveillance, they were told, was not only to get away but to give the impression you weren't looking for surveillance because you were innocent of anything that would merit it. At Seer Green, the last halt before Beaconsfield, he glimpsed a Ford Escort in the car park with Russian diplomatic number plates. He saw it too late to get the number but was sure enough of its origin. They were supposed to report all such sightings.

At Beaconsfield a grizzled, grey-haired man wearing jeans and incongruously polished brown shoes got off with him. Charles walked unhurriedly up the station approach, pausing to look in a shop window at the top. The man crossed the road and became engrossed in an estate agent's window. Charles continued his walk, turning left towards Old Beaconsfield, with its stockbroker Tudor avenues, neo-Georgian mini-mansions and moguls' houses of the twenties and thirties, with large unseen gardens and new Jaguars and Rovers in swept gravel drives. The low cloud had thinned enough to permit weak sunshine.

7

He strode purposefully into Hughes's, the Mercedes dealership. The forecourt was lined with polished secondhand saloons described as "nearly new," with their distinctive vertical headlights and squared-off, no-nonsense styling. Beige seemed the most popular colour, followed by red. To one side was a trio of elegant sports models with their dished roofs and thick, rounded leather seats. Immediately outside the show-room was a luxurious new S class, gleaming silver and easily the biggest car there. Charles paused by it before entering the showroom and wandering with what he hoped was critical detachment among the new cars within.

A salesman sat smoking at a desk with a telephone, a notepad, a Mercedes brochure and a copy of *Glass's Guide,* the trade price list. He had rubbery features and crinkly dark hair. Charles watched through the window as Brown Shoes crossed the forecourt to the older saloons. His back was to the showroom but he could probably see it in the car wind-screens. The salesman took two long pulls on his cigarette before stubbing it out and slipping *Glass's Guide* into his desk drawer. He rose and came over to Charles, his features now composed into a rubbery smile. "Can I help, sir?"

"I'm thinking of buying a car."

"Just what we like to hear, sir. Mercedes, I take it?"

"Could be."

"Anything you'll be wanting to trade in?"

"No, I'll pay cash."

He made himself the ideal customer, accepting a cigarette while they discussed models and prices over coffee. The salesman was happy to talk residual values but became vague when asked pointed questions about trade prices. Brown Shoes studied the sports cars on the forecourt. They walked round the new cars in the showroom, then outside to the one and two year olds nearby. Brown Shoes crossed the forecourt to the older saloons, still with his back to them. Charles gave the impression that cost was less important to him than style and comfort, that he might be inclined to wait for the new mid-range model, that he would probably look in on Jaguar, BMW and Rover dealerships, with a possible nod in the direction of Volvo. There was the family to think of, and Volvo seemed to make a great thing about safety, which no one else did. Unless, of course, he allowed himself to be wooed by the new S class. That would presumably be even more solid and long-lasting than a Volvo and he particularly liked it in silver.

"You look every inch a Mercedes man, if I may say so, sir," the salesman said as they shook hands and Charles pocketed his card. "Love to see you in one."

Clutching his brochures, Charles carried on towards Old Beaconsfield. He had provided anyone watching with a reason for his visit and himself evidence, in the event of questioning, as to what he had been doing. He had ensured that the man in the dealership would remember him. He had also created time and space to spot surveillance.

It was not far but few walked the busy road. They might have a team of cars on him but, Brown Shoes having remained on the forecourt, he was sure he was the only walker. In an Old Beaconsfield tea shop he lingered over more coffee and ate shortbread, reading his magazine and listening to the conversation of two mothers with children at the same school. They were discussing a third whose marriage had broken up, whose mother was dying and whose child was ill.

"I didn't like to ask too much," said one. "She looked so awful, as if she might burst into tears at any moment. White as a sheet."

The other nodded. "Dreadful for her. Of course, those highlights she has don't help."

No one else came in. Surveillance would have been briefed to identify anyone with whom he had even an apparently accidental encounter. They would have had to put someone, most likely a couple, in the shop with him. He ruled out the mothers, who had been there for some time. Had it not been for Brown Shoes, he'd have been pretty sure he'd left them—if they were on him at all—in London.

Charles was approaching thirty, a supposedly vigorous age; the year in which a man might feel he entered full estate, experienced but forward-looking, fecund and purposeful. Instead, he spent more time musing upon the past than anticipating or shaping his future. This was partly why he had chosen Beaconsfield for what they called his dry-cleaning run. He had been brought up not many miles away and had spent a short time there on an army methods-of-instruction course in a former prisoner-of-war camp. His memories of that period were vivid. He was fitter then, going for hard daily runs through the beechwoods after hours in the classroom. It was a cold autumn with woodland carpets of crisp red, yellow and golden leaves and lung-fulls of frosty air. He was keen, always running in army boots, pack and webbing, drawing a rifle from the armoury to make it harder. He wasn't sure now why he'd done it so intensively. The approved military purpose—fitness—was part of it, but there was always something else—a craving for solitude amidst the very public life of the army, an escape from daily occupations, or from thought. Whatever he was running for or from, he felt better for putting himself through it. He didn't run so much now, nor so hard.

Old Beaconsfield was much as he remembered, little more than a single main street with some quaint shop fronts, oppressed by traffic but still, beneath lowered eyelids, possessed of a reserved charm. It had been in that very tea shop that he and Janet, his then girlfriend, had agreed to part. Theirs had been an affair in which tea shops featured prominently. It had started in one in Oxford before he joined the army and had begun to come apart in another in Belfast, where she had visited him during his single afternoon off in four months. He wouldn't have been surprised to hear that she now owned one. It was what she often said she most wanted to do, as she became a solicitor.

As lunchtime approached more customers came in and Charles ordered soup and bread. There was still no hurry and he was reluctant to break his semi-trance. As Roger said, Secret Service beat working for a living, so far. Roger, he imagined, would by now have made himself at home in some London drinking club, pouring drinks down a sequined cleavage and thinking to hell with surveillance. Unless the cleavage was the surveillance.

The journey back to London showed no further sign of surveillance. He took the now-functioning tube to Trafalgar Square and walked along the Strand to the short road that led down to the Savoy. He was fifteen minutes early. "If you're on time, you're late," he remembered their trainer, Gerry, saying as he glanced up at the Upstairs restaurant over-looking the main entrance where the cars turned. Someone had said it was good after a play or film, and not too expensive. He would recce it later.

An hour later he lowered his bone china tea-cup to its bone china saucer, using his left hand and without taking his eyes from the early edition *Times* he had picked up in Beaconsfield. If he had not found it he would have had to root through dustbins for an old one, since the instructions were that he had to be reading *The Times*. He lowered the cup as precisely as possible, appearing to read but concentrating entirely on the movement. One of his father's eccentricities had been to practise using his left hand in anticipation of the stroke he claimed was his destiny, and which was statistically most likely to paralyse his right side. In fact, death, when it came so prematurely, took both sides at once, in a heart attack, while he slept.

Cup reached saucer dead centre with a faint chink. The tearoom, quiet when he arrived, was beginning to bustle. He was now the only solitary, the others having been joined by their guests. He had considered ordering for two but his instructions—to await a contact who had his description and would give the password—did not indicate whether there was to be a meeting, with a discussion, or just a message quickly passed. He studied the faded opulence of the room, with its golds, blues and reds, the sumptuous but tired sofas and armchairs, the table legs that had been knocked a few times too many. In the middle was a grand piano and a harp. A man wearing a white jacket and an auburn-haired woman in a long black dress had arranged music sheets and sat at both as if about to play, then disappeared without a note. The tea-takers, mostly female, had paid no attention.

He folded the paper and looked around, transferring it from one hand to the other. The self-consciousness involved in deliberately appearing to be about to do what he was about to do made every action feel unconvincing. No one in the room looked a likely contact, not even the stocky, energetic man who so resembled the man who had first interviewed him for the service that Charles was tempted to ask him to take off his jacket to see whether he was wearing the same gold arm-bands. He certainly wore a similar spotted bow-tie. Charles wondered whether he would ever himself attempt a bow-tie. Perhaps you had to be forty to get away with it. It would help to be florid.

A waiter was working his way round, pausing now at a table of two women and two smartly dressed little girls who giggled amidst jokes and cake-crumbs on the sofa. One of the women was paying. Charles would soon have to decide finally whether to pay and go, or order more, or just go on sitting. The woman who was not paying got up and headed for the Ladies'. Charles took out his wallet and waited. He would pay, take one more swing through all the public rooms, recce the Upstairs restaurant, then go. Since he had not been briefed on what was to be conveyed, a missed meeting seemed no big deal.

"Excuse me, but you're not a friend of David Carter's, are you?"

He stood too abruptly. "Not exactly. I'm his cousin."

It was one of the women with the children, the blonde one he had seen make for the Ladies'. She stood before him, smiling with a mixture of shyness and determination. Her diction was perfect but her accent foreign. "Perhaps you were at his wedding in France?"

"I was, but I don't think we met." The recognition phrases over, it was now up to him to direct the meeting. "Won't you sit down?"

"I really haven't time since we are just leaving. But perhaps you could quickly tell me if you've heard from them."

As they sat Charles shook his head at the approaching waiter.

She was smiling at him again. "I think you must have spilt something."

He looked down at his trousers. "My tea, a while ago. Stupid of me. I hadn't noticed. I was experimenting."

"Experimenting?"

He smiled back. "Another time. Have you a message for me?"

The hum of the tearoom was sufficient to make overhearing difficult but not enough to compel raised voices. With two fingers pressed coquettishly against her cheek, she glanced at the ceiling as if trying to recall a date, or a name, or a shade of colour. Her eyes were grey-green, her skin slightly olive and her eyebrows well-defined and dark, despite her apparently genuine blondeness.

The waiter was still nearby. "Now let me see, I think it was"—she paused until the waiter had moved on—"the message is for Eric."

Charles nodded and leant forward. He could not be seen to take notes.

"Please tell Eric that Leonid could not make the meeting on the twenty-seventh because the committee has been in continuous session about new developments in the project. Following the last experiment it was decided to reinforce the tubes and further delay ignition. Eric will know what this means." She laughed and pushed back her hair, as if they were engaged in social chit-chat. Her mannerisms and tone were middle-class southern English; her accent and careful diction, he suspected, were Eastern European. He remembered that he would have to describe her clothes: calf-length dark skirt—called a midi?—shaped around her hips, looser at the bottom; polished brown boots, square-toed; cream roll-necked jersey, tight fitting. All a little warm, perhaps, for a muggy day, but in autumn you never knew. He was looking again at

12

the way her eyebrows lifted slightly at the corners when their eyes met, briefly. She looked away and went on.

"And so please tell him that Leonid thinks he will be able to meet next month as usual but two days before the usual date and that the currency for the last month had not reached his 24029609 account before he left so can Eric please ensure that it does this time." She paused. "Okay?"

"24029609?"

"That is correct."

There was another pause. The pianist had returned alone while they had been talking and, seated at the piano, began to play a single note, repeatedly, in slow time. Charles had been vestigially aware but had not heeded it until now, when he saw that she, too, was listening. It was slowly, softly done, the single insistent note becoming insidiously, then openly and finally triumphantly dominant as the tearoom chatter gradually fell silent before it. Cups were returned to saucers or held suspended. People looked at each other, then at the expressionless pianist sitting very upright, one hand in his lap. Tension increased as other sounds fell away. Waiters stopped, trays in hand. The pianist began slowly to vary his note. Incrementally, caressingly, he built up into a lingering, aching rendition of *Lili Marlene* that flowed and swelled to its fullest and then, at its height, declined as slowly and hauntingly as it had begun into the single note that started it.

When it ceased there was applause and cheering. The pianist bowed several times, grinning, the waiters started and the room was filled again with voices and movement. Charles caught her eye once more. She held his gaze, as if they had shared a private joke in company, then she stood and put out her hand. "It has been very nice to meet you again. Please give my regards to David and Avril when you see them."

He let the women leave before he paid, then spent some time in the Gents' so that he left a good twenty minutes after them, forgetting about his proposed recce of the Upstairs restaurant. From the state of the Strand, it was clear it had been raining hard. There were puddles on the broken and uneven pavements, the gutters ran with water and the rush-hour traffic was worse than usual. He walked briskly along to Charing Cross, where he bought shaving soap and a toothbrush, then headed across the concourse to join the crowd moving onto platform one, but slipped away before the barrier, down the steps and into Villiers Street. From there he made for the Embankment Underground station, where

13

he waited on the east-bound platform for a Circle line train, hesitated as if opting for the District line then, with an obvious last-second check of the destination display, boarded as the doors closed. He got off one stop later, at Westminster, and walked over Westminster Bridge to the south side of the Thames. A breeze rippled the brown water and an unexpected burst of afternoon sun glinted on the wet road and flashed in the windows of St. Thomas's hospital.

Charles maintained his brisk pace. He made no notes but mentally rehearsed the salient details, confident that he had the account number because he had trained himself over the past few months to remember telephone numbers after repeating them aloud to himself, once. The secret was to give them mental rhythms. A bus had broken down on the far side of the bridge, in the middle of some roadworks on the roundabout, halting traffic in all directions. As he picked his way between the clogged vehicles, he remembered Gerry telling them that a Russian spy had been discovered in the round building in the middle, which housed London's driving licence centre. The agent had used the records to help the Russians identify people they were interested in, and to help build up legends for Russian agents working under cover. There had been nothing of it in the papers, which heightened Charlie's pleasure in knowing it.

He continued under the Waterloo railway bridge towards Century House, which towered above Lambeth North tube, but before reaching it he turned left into Lower Marsh where the street traders were packing up for the day and a lorry was spraying the narrow wet road with yet more water. It was a thriving street in a poor area, cheap and dilapidated but always busy. You could get anything there, they said—anything—minus the wrapping. A little over half way along was a door near a cut-price clothes shop with a polished brass plate announcing Rasen, Falcon & Co., Shippers and Exporters. Charles pressed the bell and turned to face the pane of darkened glass let into the wall at the side. When the door opened he stepped through into a short hallway with another door and a uniformed guard sitting behind a raised ledge to the side. He showed his green pass.

The guard nodded. "Last one back, sir." He pressed a button to open the second door.

Charles went upstairs to a lecture room at the back of the building.

All the windows had blinds down and the dozen desks were mostly occupied by his fellow students bent over papers or slowly tapping the keyboards of heavy grey Olympia typewriters. They were writing up the results of the exercise. The only one to look up when Charles entered was Gerry, their instructor, slumped over the podium in his shirtsleeves and making pencil notes which he kept crossing out. The film screen was unrolled and blank behind him.

"Welcome, Carlos. Late lunch?" Gerry altered or invented names for everyone.

"Late agent."

"Agents are never late in Exercise Tabby Cat. Never accidentally, anyway." Gerry grinned and pushed his oversize glasses up his nose. Approaching forty, he had unruly fair hair, an expressive, good-natured, prematurely lined face and a generally dishevelled appearance. "Better crack on with your write-up. We've got the moving pictures soon. Big treat. You've missed tea."

Charles went to his desk. The worst part of exercises was the write-up. It was supposed to be concise and properly divided between factual account, intelligence product—if any—and opinion and recommendation. It was supposed to contain everything important and nothing unimportant, with the proviso that some unimportant things might later turn out to have been important.

"Never weary the busy A officer reader," Gerry often told them. "Action officers are dealing with at least twenty other cases apart from yours and they don't want to read about sunsets in deathless prose. At the same time, when your case goes bottom up and the proverbial hits the fan, as is not unknown"—he would grin and push his glasses again—"you will be the first to be blamed for not having told the A officer something which at the time he did not want to know."

When Rebecca, the training course secretary, entered, the students—all men between their early twenties and early thirties—looked up. "Message for Charles," she said, smiling more confidently now than in the early days when she used to blush through her suntan as they all looked at her. "C/Sov wants to see you a.s.a.p."

Controller/Soviet Bloc was in charge of all Soviet and Eastern European operations.

"Found you out already," called Roger, from the far side of the room.

"Wants more sugar in his tea," said Christopher Westfield, a plump former merchant banker who was said to have taken a salary cut of three quarters when he joined.

"Probably disgusted by your anti-surveillance precautions," said Gerry. "Becky, please politely convey to C/Sov that Carlos will sprint over to Head Office as soon as he has finished here, which will be some time after six. Meanwhile, let's be having your write-ups soon, gentle men." He rubbed his hands as he separated both words. "I'll be having some more tea." He and Rebecca left the room.

Charles looked across at Roger. "Is that mine?"

Yawning, Roger held up the bottom of his tie and considered it. "Possibly. Probably. Shirt, too, maybe. All my own teeth, though."

Desmond Kimmeridge, a former cavalry officer known, thanks to Gerry, as Debonair, glanced at the tie. "I should let him keep it if I were you."

Gerry returned rubbing his hands. "Right, that's it. Finish your write-ups later, in your own time. Meanwhile, *mes enfants*, we have a film show. Windows and blinds fully closed, please, for the Secret Intelligence Service's very own Keystone Kops. Probably all of you thought you were under surveillance at some point during this morning's exercise, and you should've specified times and places in your write-ups, with descriptions of surveillants. Perceived surveillants. Imaginary surveillants. None of you was, you see, except one. Cheaper that way. Let it roll, Becky."

After a couple of false starts and the usual teasing, Rebecca coaxed the cumbersome apparatus at the back of the room into action. Charles watched himself enter the Savoy, briefly looking straight at the camera concealed in the window of the Upstairs restaurant. Next he was seen reading his paper and drinking tea, replacing his cup without looking and, to guffaws from the audience, spilling some. Then he was seen talking to the blonde foreign woman, his exercise "agent," which provoked ribaldry. Finally he was shown walking briskly away from the Savoy.

"The team was with you all the way back here," said Gerry, "and for a while before you reached the hotel. They picked you up in the Strand."

"Rather they'd picked up the girl," said Christopher.

Charles tried to recover a little of his pride. "But I spotted the chap in brown shoes in Beaconsfield. And the Russian Embassy car at the station before."

16

"Nothing to do with us. You were on your own in Beaconsfield. Co-incidence, chance, like most of life. Make sure you report the Russian car, though."

"The man was behaving oddly. He followed me most of the way."

"No accounting for taste," said Roger.

Gerry shook his head. "Look around you and the world is full of people doing odd things. Cross my heart, cut my throat and hope to die, Charles, there was no surveillance on you until you reached the Strand. Then you had the full works until you got back here. The team reckoned your approach to the meeting looked reasonably natural except that your walk was a touch too deliberate, too slow. Let's watch you arrive again—Becky, thanks. Here, see. Most people are walking as if they're trying to get somewhere. You're not. We'll spare you the hotel shots again but they reckon your body language and so on was okay except that you obviously relaxed after about half an hour, as if you were no longer look-ing, no longer alert, no longer seriously expecting anything. The sur-prise encounter with your agent was handled well, they said. Looked very natural. Probably because it was a surprise. But afterwards you shot off from the hotel like Buster Keaton speeded up—there, you see, com-pletely different walk. Much brisker, much more purposeful, eager to get back before you forget it all. Looking forward to doing your write-up, I daresay. And clearly no longer looking. Not surveillance aware." Gerry emphasised the words with his fist on the podium. "Serious point, this, for all of you. SV teams reckon they can always tell the difference between—say—a KGB officer approaching a meeting, brush contact, emptying or filling a DLB—dead letter box—or whatever—and one who's just done it, because afterwards he's relieved and his pace quick-ens. Remember that, gentle men. Do not let it happen. Whenever you're doing any operation you should walk at your normal pace throughout. You probably don't know what that is. Well, get to know it. Measure it. And always, always, give anyone watching an obvious reason for your being wherever you are. One day the lives of your agents may depend on it. And the rest of you remember that Carlos got clobbered this time, so it may be you next. Or Carlos again, who knows. But in case you think you've got clean away with it, we've a further surprise for you. Okay, Rebecca?"

Rebecca went out into the corridor and returned leading a line of ten men and women, several sheepishly grinning. "Gentlemen, your agents," Gerry announced with a flourish. "Come to tell each of you how you performed from the agent's point of view, no holds barred. Nothing they say will be used in evidence against you"—he opened his arms and grinned—"yet."

Charles grabbed an extra chair and pulled it to his desk as the blonde woman approached. She carried an expensive-looking brown leather jacket. Her smile was very slightly crooked, he now noticed. "I'm so sorry to have kept you lingering over your tea for so long," she said. "I was told to give them plenty of time to try out their fancy new cameras. Apparently the one that gave the best results was the old-fashioned briefcase sort used by the man at the table on the far side, opposite you."

Charles hadn't spotted him. She spoke quietly and, against the general hubbub, he had to concentrate on what she was saying. Twice, even before she was seated, she had pushed back her hair. Her accent was educated southern English. "You've lost your accent," he said. "And your little girls."

"My borrowed accent. My husband is A1, desk officer for London operations. We were in Prague. The children were not borrowed, though. But office wives are, for this sort of thing."

"It was very convincing."

"Not to anyone who knows."

"Do you speak Czech?"

"Shopping Czech—queuing Czech, I should say. Menu Czech."

There was a pause, filled by the noise and laughter of the others. The loudest laugh was Gerry's, as he went from desk to desk. They looked at each other for a moment before speaking. "That pianist," Charles said.

"I know. It was wonderful. So simple. And so dramatic."

Charles knew he should resist staring so directly. She crossed her legs and glanced down at the square toe of her polished brown boot. The leather jacket on her lap creaked softly. "I'm Anna," she said.

"I wasn't sure whether I was allowed to know you as anything other than Mrs. A1. I'm Charles Thoroughgood."

"I know, Gerry briefed us all. I'm supposed to tell you how you did. So embarrassing." She smiled again.

"Was I that bad?"

"No, no, you were fine. Very good, very natural. There's nothing else to say, really. There'd be more if you were bad. No, it's just—you know—the necessary pretence of these necessary games."

"Fun, though," Charles said, hopefully.

"Oh yes, fun, of course."

Gerry shambled over and laid his hand heavily on her shoulder. "*Eh bien*, Anna, how did student F perform?"

"Student F was brilliant, Gerry. Best yet."

"But he's only your first."

"Second."

"Absolutely, spiffingly, world-championly brilliant? Remembered everything, no muffed lines, no use of his own name, no feet in his own mouth or on your toes?"

"Not a foot wrong anywhere."

"Great. I still long for you, Anna. You know that?"

"I'm so pleased, Gerry. I thought the wait must have wearied you."

"Never. Tell Hugo I'll step into his shoes tomorrow."

"I think he knows that. You tell him every time you see him."

"I mean it. Well done, Charles. Don't forget the write-up." Gerry moved on to the next desk.

"So funny to think of Gerry in charge of all you babies," she said. "He and Hugo joined together. It's hard to take anyone seriously when you've trained with them."

Charles thought she was about his own age. "You did the course as well, then?"

"No, but we were already married so I used to hear all about it and go to the parties and so on. Then when we got our Sovbloc posting we did the enhanced tradecraft course—spouses, too, you see, and the office pays for all the child-minding—and Gerry was on it because he was going to Warsaw."

"I didn't know he'd been in Warsaw."

"He hasn't. His marriage broke up. You had to be married for a Sovbloc posting, you see. I'm not sure you do now."

"I think you do."

"You're not, are you?"

"No."

"Better get a move on, then, if you want to join the Sovbloc mafia." She stood abruptly, as if prompted, and held out her hand. "And I'd better get a move on to pick up my children. They've had to be kept busy for the office's benefit, too. It's nice to have met you. Well done."

"Thank you for making it easy. They seemed very well behaved."

He had to repeat himself amidst the scraping of chairs as others stood to go. He wanted to say something else about the pianist, but hesitated too long.

"They won't be by now." She too hesitated as if about to add something, then said "'Bye" and walked quickly away.

Head Office was a 22-storey 1960s office block well situated for terrorist attack. The IRA campaign was a fact of everyday life but Middle Eastern terrorists, spawn of the Arab-Israeli conflict, had recently become active again. As everyone pointed out to everyone else, the building's proximity to Lambeth North tube made for easy reconnaissance and escape, the petrol station at its foot would enhance secondary conflagration, while the ramp leading down to the underground garage, and the nearness of run-down council flats, might have been designed for a car-bomber. It was, however, a light and cheerful building in which every office faced outwards, though the lifts frequently broke down and carpenters were forever moving walls and doors as offices were enlarged or divided according to the flux and reflux of bureaucratic life.

This contributed to the building's rabbit-warren feel, which was enhanced by the fact that each floor tended to be occupied by those working in the same area or controllerate, with most offices small and individual rather than open-plan. The to-ing and fro-ing that this involved, and the ease with which everyone could be discreetly indiscreet, contributed to each floor developing its own atmosphere. As in the Foreign Office, it was traditional to enter closed doors without knocking, though it was a serious security breach to leave unlocked any empty office with papers out. It was known to the overseas stations as Gloom Hall.

Students under training had little cause to visit it, so Charles welcomed the excuse. HO was the repository of secrets, the seat of mysteries, the source of power, mother and father to stations throughout the world, of which the curious display of aerials on the roof were the only outward reminder. Also, it seemed always to be sunlit and filled with attractive girls who knew things forbidden to the students.

C/Sovbloc and his empire were on the twelfth floor. The controller was a stocky, closely packed man with a beaky nose, iron-grey hair and gold-rimmed glasses. His speech was precise and rapid and his blue-grey eyes rested with disconcerting immobility on whomever addressed him. He gave an impression of contained energy, with nothing wasted or superfluous, and he had a formidable reputation for operational achievement, discipline and discretion. His suits were discreetly expensive and the toe-caps of his Oxford shoes had a military polish. He was rumoured to have equal seniority with the Chief, in terms of grade, and to have taken no leave for more years than anyone could remember. He was known as Hookey.

The twelfth floor was quieter than others, particularly floors such as the African or South American which tended to take on aspects of the areas they dealt with. Too many of the Sovbloc offices were occupied by the custodians of great—it was assumed—secrets, and too many of the doors were kept closed for there to be any obvious liveliness. Hookey was said to have forbidden any officer to have readable papers on his desk in the presence of anyone who had no right to see them. Even the outer office occupied by his secretary was closed, which was probably unique in the building. His inner office was in the corner overlooking Waterloo Station.

Controllers' secretaries were reputedly dragons, there to protect controllers and secrets and keep distractions and trivia at bay. But C/Sov/sec, a bespectacled woman in her forties who wore a sensible tweed skirt, smiled and breathed no fire when Charles introduced himself. "Hookey is expecting you. Please sit down." The chair she indicated was one from which he could see nothing of what was on her desk. She stood in C/Sovbloc's room with the door open so that she could see him the whole time.

When ushered in Charles had to resist the levitational impulse of his right arm, due not only to the slow growing out of army habits but also to the sense of authority emanating from the brisk figure beyond the polished desk. There was nothing on the desk save three telephones, black, grey and red, a buff file and a notepad, both of which Hookey closed as Charles entered. They shook hands.

"Tea, coffee?" asked Hookey.

"Tea, thank you." His reply felt unfinished without "sir."

Hookey asked his secretary, Maureen, for two teas and closed the door. "Who was your commanding officer in the army?"

"Peter Wallace. I believe he's now a full colonel in the MOD."

"He is. Interesting appointment."

Charles was never quite sure how to react to mention of his former CO, whose name provoked varied responses. "Not a natural one for him, I'd have thought." He smiled.

"Not natural, perhaps, but people sometimes succeed surprisingly well at what does not come naturally to them. It's a question of application. Because it doesn't feel natural, they try harder, and so do better. Have you ever noticed that?"

Put as a question, it still felt like a rebuke. Charles was easily made to feel guilty where the CO, as he still thought of him, was concerned. He was a man he both admired and judged hard, much as he suspected he might have his late father, had he known him under similar circumstances. Indeed, he remembered his father defending the CO against his no doubt intemperate attacks when home on leave. "He's right even when he's wrong because he's the CO and you're a subaltern," his father would say with irritating finality. "You're a soldier and a soldier's duty is to do his duty, and that's that." Charles was the serving soldier, but his father's war record inhibited him in such arguments.

When Maureen brought in the teas Hookey asked her to ask A1 to look in in five minutes. The door closed, he leant forward with his elbows on the desk, his hands clasped and his cup and saucer planted carefully before him as if forming an evidential object. His blue-grey eyes, so far from being windows on the soul, gave the impression of having no time for such frivolity.

"When you were at Oxford, before the army, you knew a Russian postgraduate student, Viktor Ivanovich Koslov, who was there for a year. The Russians permit few students to study in the west and those who do are closely monitored. It was not clear why Koslov, who was neither a scientist seeking militarily useful information nor, as far as we knew, an intelligence officer seeking recruits, was permitted. Undoubtedly, though, he would have had some sort of intelligence brief, if only to report on students and others he knew, such as yourself. You did not know him well but you were friendly enough when you came across him, much as you might have been with anyone else in your college to whom you were not close but who was sufficiently personable. You reported your acquaintance fairly fully during your positive vetting interviews before joining the service. Your longest conversation with Koslov was when one day you walked back from the Schools building with him and into hall for lunch."

Charles remembered the pale, quiet man with sandy hair and freckles, fluent but careful English and amiable but guarded manner. He seemed solitary without being obviously lonely; Charles could not remember who, if any, his friends were. He was doubtless more mature than most undergraduates yet had about him an apparent naïveté that led people to treat him as if he were in fact less mature, and in need of looking after. Hookey gave the impression of knowing more about him than was in Charles's PV reporting.

"You probably don't know that Koslov is now in London, at the Soviet Embassy, where he is one of the second secretaries. He's been here some time and his posting is due to end soon. So far as the records show, he is straight MFA—Ministry of Foreign Affairs. Neither his pattern of behaviour nor his traces in our own or MI5 records suggest any reason to identify him as KGB. It would be very unusual, too, for anyone who had spent such a period in the west to become an intelligence officer, unless he had exceptional influence. Nevertheless, I have my own private doubts, the reasons for which I won't go into now. Suffice it to say, that I am very interested in Mr. Koslov."

Hookey sipped his tea.

"What no doubt you also know is that it is difficult for us to operate in our own names in this country, since our Foreign Office cover when in London is normally not sufficient to withstand operational exposure, as in theory it should be when we're attached to embassies abroad. Also, the Foreign Office is wary of the embarrassment that could arise from own-name operations against foreign diplomats serving in London. Under normal circumstances, therefore, we could not consider using you in any operation against Koslov here in the UK. Ironically, because we could do so anywhere else in the world, including Moscow—but not in the very place where it is most natural for you to be. But never mind that." Hookey's lips suggested a smile, for the first time. "Circumstances are not quite normal. Firstly, we are even more interested in what the Russians are doing here than we were, especially as we believe they are reconstructing their operational base in this country following the expulsion of the 105 intelligence officers—actually, 104, we got one wrong—a couple of years ago. Secondly, we are very interested in Koslov himself. He is married and accompanied by his wife, Tanya, as they have to be for postings here. Also, as usual, they have had to leave their child behind in Moscow, as a hostage." Hookey pronounced the last word very distinctly. "According to surveillance and standard intercepts on the embassy, it seems a reasonably successful marriage, at least if lack of open hostilities and the fact of survival mean success in marriage." Again, there was a suggestion of a smile. "Except for one thing: Koslov has a relationship with a prostitute. This is of course highly unusual in a Soviet official serving in a hostile western country. Koslov knows the penalties but has visited the same woman at least twice. She lives in Belgravia and he was first seen visiting her by an off-duty member of MI5 surveillance who happened to recognise him. She thought he was acting oddly, so prolonged her shopping and followed him to the prostitute's door, got close enough to see which bell he pressed and reported it. MI5 put him under surveillance for the next two weeks—they thought he might have been up to something professionally as opposed to privately nefarious—but with no result, and no indication that he suspected or looked for surveillance. They concluded he was either very professional, or very lazy, or very clean. Then, on the evening of the last day they could spare for him, he visited the lady again, whom by this time they had identified."

Hookey returned to his tea, obviously expecting no response yet. The window behind him offered a view of rush-hour trains creeping reluctantly in and out of Waterloo. "The case—as it is already being termed, though it isn't one yet—has been much discussed, as you might imagine. Traces on Koslov showed up your acquaintance and we concluded that, if there is to be a case, it should be built on that, provided you are willing." Maureen put her head round the door to say that A1 was waiting. Hookey nodded. "Bring him in."

A1 was a balding, energetic, forty-ish man who wore a double-breasted suit with a red lining which flashed as he turned. His handshake was pointedly firm and his smile as welcoming as if he had known Charles of old and greatly enjoyed meeting him again. The neat triangle of handkerchief in his top pocket matched his spotted tie.

"Hugo March," he said, holding on to Charles's hand and standing very close.

"I've just met your wife." The statement, though factual, felt like a deceit because of what Charles did not add.

"Ah." Hugo's eyebrows lifted and his mouth opened wide, but he said no more and they sat down.

"Hugo has details of the prostitute," Hookey continued, with no pre-liminaries. "Obviously, we need to talk to her in order to discover what's going on and whether she would help us recruit Koslov."

"Lover Boy," interjected Hugo. "He has a code-name now."

Hookey's slight nod conveyed acceptance without approval. "His behaviour is that of a risk-taker who is willing to break the rules. That does not mean he is disloyal or disaffected, but it is a necessary condi-tion if ever he is to spy for us. We need to establish whether his behav-iour has any significance beyond the personal. Whether or not it does, we want him to know that we know about it. Because of his background, he would naturally assume that we would use the information to black-mail him—"

Hugo March's laugh was more of a bark. "Too right."

"—which of course we would not," continued Hookey quietly, look-ing at Charles. "This service does not use blackmail, partly because most of us would find it repugnant and partly because, unless you control the environment within which your target operates, as in a totalitarian state, it is rarely effective for long and is never a guarantee of loyalty. The anal-ogy often used is that we would not push a man off a ski-slope in order to break his leg, but we like to keep close behind him so that if he does fall we can offer help, and then make it easy for him to repay us, if he wishes."

The lecture was obviously for Charles's benefit. He had heard the same analogy on his course.

"And just as we would not normally ask you to approach Koslov in London, so we would not normally expect the officer who is to approach the target also to approach the access agent, the prostitute. Again, things are different in this case. MI5 itself, our own London stations and the joint sections we operate with MI5 are short of operational officers and currently have their hands full"—his eyes shifted briefly to Hugo—"and have no spare capacity. Also, if it were to be successful, we would wish knowledge of it to be kept extremely tight and would not wish to involve in the earlier stages more people than was absolutely necessary. You therefore have two tasks, if you accept them. Firstly, to talk to the pros-titute, discover whatever she can tell us about her client and establish whether she is prepared to help us talk to him. Secondly, to re-introduce yourself to Koslov, find a non-threatening way of letting him know that we know what he is up to and establish whether his behaviour means that he is prepared to be aberrant in other ways."

Hookey sat back and took a pipe and tobacco from his desk drawer. "So much for strategy and background. Now, are you prepared to do it or does the fact that you knew him—or any other aspect—trouble you? I should add that you'll have to do it in your own time because you can't duck out of your course. Indeed, we don't want them to know anything about it. So it could put paid to your private life for a while."

It had not occurred to Charles that his knowing Viktor could be problematic, morally or in any other way, but Hookey's question made him wonder if it should be. Perhaps he lacked moral imagination. He tried to recall his impressions of the quiet Russian, listening within himself for echoes of awkwardness or unease about exploiting the relationship, such as it was. Exploitation was what secret service involved, as the man with arm-bands had been keen to stress at his first interview. The prospect of a real case excited him. As for his own private life, he had joined expecting Jesuitical devotion and had been mildly disappointed when Gerry told them that most people in Head Office clocked off at six.

"I'll do it," he said.

He returned with Hugo March to his office on the sixth floor. "Hookey's a great man," Hugo said in the lift, "but he seems to do most of his work out of office hours. Never goes home himself and doesn't expect anyone else to."

"Is he married?"

"Yes, his wife's a—er—can't remember. She does something. Doctor, or something like it. Not that there is much like it, apart from vets, I s'pose, and she's not a vet. I don't think." He laughed in Charles's face, standing very close.

Hugo's office, smaller than Hookey's, also had a view of Waterloo Station, and he cast a surreptitious glance at the crawling trains. He had a wood and leather desk to which only officers of grade 4 and above were entitled, and the usual grey, combination-locked security cabinet. Three plastic desk trays, also grey, marked "in," "out" and "pending," were piled high with papers, files and telegrams. Other papers, such as pink Head Office notices and lists, were scattered beside them. There were two black telephones, an open copy of the PAX book, the red, spring-clipped Head Office directory marked Top Secret, a photograph of Anna and the two girls and, on the blotter, a fat, expensive Mont Blanc pen. On the coat-stand by the door was a military-style British Warm overcoat. Charles had one in the loft of his mother's Buckinghamshire house where, in immediate post-army reaction against his own military past, he had dumped everything.

Hugo put the wooden clipboard on the desk. "Just as well no notes needed," he said. "Forgot my pen. Wouldn't look good, eh? Hang on a mo' while I ring home, say I'm running late. Won't be popular. Dinner party." He picked up the phone, frowned, put it down, then riffled through one of his trays until he found a clutch of papers held together by a bulldog clip, which he removed before passing them to Charles. "There's your lady. Not bad, I thought. Excuse my removing the clip. There's an office-wide shortage, endless pink notices about not hoarding them and sending spare ones back to stores so they can send them out again. I keep any I find in a drawer. Very handy." He picked up the phone again and dialled.

The black-and-white photograph showed a neat, dark-haired woman wearing a belted light raincoat and carrying a patent-leather handbag. She was turning towards a door and had just taken a key from the open bag. The photograph was probably taken with the sort of briefcase camera used to such good effect on himself that day. The accompanying papers, mostly MI5, described her as Claire Camber, born thirty-seven years ago in Orpington, Kent, operating now as a "masseuse" under the name Chantal Jeanneau.

Hugo's conversation with Anna was brief. "Darling, I'm late. No, I won't. In a few minutes. I'm with a chap who says he knows you. Charles. He didn't say. What? Okay. 'Bye, darling." He put down the phone. "She says if you're the Charles from this afternoon you did very well and she's sorry she had to rush off. I don't know what that's all about. Sounds like a message from the lady you're reading about there." He laughed.

Charles began to explain his exercise meeting with Anna.

"I see, I see," said Hugo. "Forgotten she was doing it. Good exercise, that one. Chap called Whippett—known as *the* Whippett, of course—splendid operator, hopelessly out of control, charming alcoholic—got into frightful trouble for chatting up the policewoman who was playing his agent and taking her to bed in the hotel for the afternoon. They both missed the wash-up. Frightful stink. The Chief had to lunch the Chief Constable. General sense of humour failure all round, except for the Whippett and the rest of the course, and Training Department, and most of HO, come to that." He laughed, shaking his head.

"Nothing like that happened in the Savoy this afternoon."

"Then Personnel posted the Whippett to Bangkok, of all places. Went completely off the rails. Went native in about six minutes. Started turning up at embassy functions with bar girls. Moved one in with him. Or two. Got up the ambassador's nose and had to resign in the end. Now running his own bar, apparently. Pity. Very talented operator. Goes to show." He nodded several times. "Forgotten Anna was doing it today, to be honest. Bit much with six coming to dinner and the children to get to bed. Just as well I couldn't get home early. Wait till you're married."

They returned to what Hugo called the matter in hand. He would be desk officer for the operation and, since it was on their patch, would have to keep MI5 informed. Hookey would be in overall control. Charles would start by recruiting Mme. Jeanneau. She had had a French husband and spoke reasonable French, retaining a French accent when speaking English in her professional life. No doubt for business reasons. Charles would have to approach her under alias and not let on that he knew Lover Boy. They would cross that bridge when they came to it. The tricky bit would be letting Lover Boy—Hugo clearly relished the name—know that Charles knew her, and therefore about him and her, without her knowing. If Lover Boy were ever to be recruited, it would be best that she didn't know about it.

Hugo began clearing his desk while speaking, locking all papers and the PAX book in his safe, checking for loose papers on shelves and window sills, beneath the phones, beneath the desk, in his litter bin and finally locking away his brown confidential waste bag. Then he put on his coat and stood before a mirror, smoothing his thinning hair. "You could be on to a good thing with little Chantal," he said. "Not bad, is she? Not sure the office would pay all your expenses, though."

It was only as he watched Hugo's reflection that Charles noticed something he had been vestigially aware of, and obscurely unsettled by, for some time: Hugo had a slight, intermittent facial twitch, a rapid wink that was gone before it was properly seen.

"Hookey's a great man to work for," Hugo continued when they were in the lift. "Good experience so early in your career. But he's ferocious on security. He's run some of our biggest cases and was one of the chaps who unmasked Blake or Philby, whichever one it was. Understandable to be concerned about security, I s'pose, but it can go over the top a bit sometimes. I came under him, of course, when I was in Prague. Wouldn't let me sneeze without telling me when and how to do it. Maybe it was me he didn't trust."

They went out through the revolving doors into the windswept litter of Lambeth. Head Office's creation of its own wind and micro-climate was a frequent joke. Hugo referred to it. "Oh, and Anna," he added, before turning up towards Waterloo. "Anna says you must come to dinner some time."

"Thank you, I'd like that," said Charles, trying to ignore Hugo's wink.

CHAPTER TWO

R EMEMBER, THIS IS your second line of defence," said Big Tom, the wiry, diminutive former paratrooper and SAS sergeant who taught unarmed combat. He was so-called to distinguish him from Little Tom, his towering ex–Royal Marine SBS colleague who did guns and bombs. "The first line, and the best unarmed combat manoeuvre of all, is the hundred-yard dash. Don't get into a fight in the first place. Fights are dangerous and nearly always unnecessary. You might get hurt. It's sensible to avoid them, not dishonourable. But if he grabs you and you can't get away, or if you've got to protect someone else, this is your next line of defence."

The course disposed themselves on the grass in the bottom of the dry moat at the Castle, the south coast training establishment. It was sunny with a light breeze and a few seagulls wheeled above. Beyond the rim of the moat was the Solent, glittering in the morning sun and busy with shipping. Beyond that was the Isle of Wight, where it was just possible to make out a red tractor crawling up a steep ploughed field. Everyone in the moat looked on with anticipatory relish as Desmond Kimmeridge was chosen by Big Tom as his guinea-pig. Desmond, tall and self-deprecating, took languid hold of Big Tom's shirt.

Big Tom smiled with exaggerated pity. "Listen, Debonair," he said, his Welsh accent heightened for effect, "you're supposed to be trying to head-butt me, not seduce me. A little more aggression, if you please."

After a couple more attempts and some scoffing, Desmond was persuaded into a satisfactory simulacrum of aggression, sufficient for Big

Tom to demonstrate how to break the attacker's grip. He first shrank and sagged as in terror—a tactic which, he explained, invoked an unconscious weakening of the attacker's grip—then exploded into action with a loud shout and a swift upward and outward thrust of both arms, breaking Desmond's grip.

"And if he doesn't run away after that, you do," he concluded. "Right, choose a partner."

"Mind my shirt," said Christopher Westfield as he and Charles paired off. "It's the only clean one I've got left till I get home."

They were interrupted by Rebecca calling from the top of the moat. "Head Office wants Charles. Can you come and ring a.s.a.p." Castle dress was casual until evening, and she wore blue jeans and a white T-shirt. The sea breeze lifted her dark hair. Her suntan, acquired on a recent overseas posting, seemed to have deepened since they'd been at the Castle.

"Tell her Christopher wants Rebecca," murmured Christopher.

"Sorry to spoil your fun," she said when Charles joined her. "You seem to be much in demand by HO. It was A1 who rang. What's it about?"

"Need to know." The phrase was used at them a dozen times a day. He smiled. "It's really my address book they want."

She left him alone in her office. Hugo was crisp. "You're on for tonight. Your lady is seeing our friend this afternoon but in the course of arranging it she mentioned she was free this evening. You can see her as a new client. We've booked a hotel room in a suitable name and company. Your next train leaves in an hour and five. Come to my office."

Charles joined Rebecca outside on the battlements. She was leaning against the stone wall, smoking and watching the aircraft carrier HMS *Hermes* proceed magisterially out of Portsmouth Harbour. A distant sailor waved. She waved back.

"Friend aboard?" asked Charles.

"Need to know."

"Where's Gerry?"

"Probably in the mess." She gazed at the carrier. Her features were regular, her dark eyes widely spaced, she was always friendly and had a ready smile, but there was also a reserve, a sense of something held back.

Her seeming preoccupation at that moment with something unknown, possibly something suggested by the carrier, made being with her restful rather than, as might have been expected, disconcerting. The battlements were wide and deep and Charles leant against the wall beside her, gazing at three nineteenth-century forts far out in the Solent. He was excited by what he was going to do but, for the moment, preferred not to think of it. There was no hurry. Rebecca pulled on the last of her cigarette and flicked the butt into the sea. "D'you need to see him?"

"They want me to go up to town for the night. I assume I'd better clear it with him."

"They've already spoken to him in general terms, saying you might be called upon, but not for what. I'll tell him while you pack your toothbrush."

"No need. I've got two."

"What a clever intelligence officer you're going to be, Charles."

Late that afternoon he sat on the edge of the king-size bed in his room in the Park Lane Hilton, his hand still resting on the phone, his eyes on the yellow autumn leaves of the plane trees in Hyde Park. It had been easy, yet—as he was coming to expect—his heart thumped as if he had done something difficult or dangerous. He had rung and introduced himself as Peter Lovejoy of Gordon and Partners, an off-the-shelf alias and company name. Chantal had been recommended to him as a masseuse and he wondered whether she was free to join him for dinner at the Park Lane Hilton that evening. As anticipated, mention of an expensive hotel produced a willing response; she agreed in convincingly French-accented English, sounding like a courteous and efficient receptionist and stating, without his asking, her fee for dinner and what she called "private massage" afterwards. It was substantial. If the treatment extended beyond midnight, a further fee would have to be negotiated. They agreed to meet in the Roof Restaurant on the twenty-eighth floor. It was just as well he had taken the full cash float offered by Hugo's secretary.

By seven thirty the restaurant was beginning to fill. Unlike the Savoy, there was nothing faded about the Hilton's opulence. The burgundy seats were plush, the tables had a black satinwood veneer and the lighting was unobtrusive. The West End was laid out below and almost all around, as if solely for the benefit of diners. As when leaning against the battlement with Rebecca that afternoon, Charles was content to watch without participating, prolonging the state of suspension. His eye was soon caught, however, by the dark-haired woman, quite heavily made up, pausing by the maitre d' as he checked his list before ushering her over. She was younger and taller than he'd thought, with her hair let down to shoulder length, a tight black skirt, white blouse and a short red jacket. He stood and they shook hands.

"Sorry I'm a few minutes late," she said in unaccented English. "A client over-ran."

"A professional hazard, I imagine."

"Not just over-running. You can factor that in to your timetable. But it's everything else as well. They want you to be mother confessor and Lord knows what else. I could write a book on clients and their problems. Perhaps one day I shall."

He made to pour her some water but the bottle was taken from him by the wine waiter. While they agreed aperitifs—she chose champagne and he, with an inward twinge over his expenses claim, followed suit—he puzzled over her dropping her French accent and talking to him, a supposed client, about clients. Was it possible that this was in fact another exercise into which he had been tricked? There were rumours of that sort of thing on the course. Was the solitary man some tables distant, with a clear line of sight, filming them?

"Of course, in my field the law makes it worse," she said. "Interpretation is all. Your legal and client problems must be of a different order?"

"Probably, though I daresay there's some overlap." What, he wondered, could she know of his profession when he hadn't told her anything? Was she confusing him with someone else? "D'you you see many of your clients here?" he asked, taking his cue for directness from her. Hugo had recommended the Hilton because she had a regular arrangement there with a visiting American chief executive.

She shrugged. "One or two of the bigger ones, though generally I try to get them to come to me. Makes for a quicker turnover."

Such frankness made the whole thing easier. He could leapfrog several stages. "My own firm has an interest in one of your regulars." Her raised eyebrows were encouraging. "In your—his—pillow-talk, to be precise."

"Pillow-talk? What do you mean?"

Protection of her clients was presumably a natural reaction. "We'll pay for it, of course," he added.

"What on earth are you talking about?"

At that moment the maitre d' hurried over, leaving another woman by his desk. His brow was furrowed. "Mr. Lovejoy?"

"Yes?" Charles tried to sound unconcerned.

"Mr. Kilroy, surely?" queried the woman, sharply.

The maitre d' theatrically smote his forehead. "Ah, my mistake, my stupid mistake. I am so sorry. Very, very sorry."

Mr. Kilroy was the only other solitary man in the restaurant, and it was he whom she had come to meet. She left with one curious, offended glance at Charles and was ushered to the other table by the maitre d', his apologies showering like a meteor's tail behind her. He then hurried back to his desk and brought over a second woman, still in a welter of self-abasement. The wine waiter appeared as she and Charles shook hands. "Champagne?" Charles asked, dismissing from now on any consideration of his expense account.

"Merci, monsieur." She was shorter and older than her predecessor, presentably dressed in a mauve suit, though her gold necklace and earrings were large and gaudy. She laughed at his doctored explanation of what had happened. "I am so sorry," she said. "I should not have been so late. I was—what is the expression?—over-run?"

Charles smiled, as he had a few minutes before, remarking that it was hard to regulate business when you were self-employed. Always too much or too little.

"You work for a big corporation?" she began.

He described the multifarious international activities of Gordon and Partners, impressing himself with their range and variety. She was attentive and flattering, her dark eyes fixed on his and a smile in perpetual readiness. Her sustained determination to please was effective despite its brittleness. Had he been what she thought, her ready sympathy and her questions—none seriously probing but all seeking answers which it might please him to give or which she could use to praise him—would have made for an easy, undemanding, self-indulgent evening.

It was less easy to get her to talk about herself. She seemed unused to it; presumably most of her clients preferred to talk about themselves. After the champagne and a couple of glasses of wine, she said as much herself, after asking how old he was. "Most of my clients are middle-aged and married. They want to talk about their marriages and their jobs as much as they want anything else."

"Their wives don't understand them?"

"No, really, sometimes they don't, I think. They want to relax, these men. They have pressure in their jobs, pressure from their children, pressure from their wives who are always wanting something." She shrugged and smiled. "Women are always wanting." She was divorced, she told him, and maintained two children at boarding school. "It makes work in the holidays a little difficult." Her French accent fluctuated slightly.

He glanced at the woman who had first joined him, now talking happily to the older man. Lawyers, perhaps; maybe she was being head-hunted. "Perhaps she was after all a colleague of yours," he said, insincerely.

She gave a cool assessing glance. "I don't think so. But I think he would like it if she were."

He felt they were now sufficiently relaxed for him to be frank, or at least as frank as he was permitted. Pitch her in the restaurant, in public, Hugo had advised—provided there was decent table separation—rather than in his room afterwards because then if the whole thing went pear-shaped she couldn't claim there'd been any monkey-business. Hugo barked and twitched at the thought.

Charles leant forward across the table. "Claire, there's something else I want to tell you." His use of her real name was calculated. She looked at him without expression. "I don't work for the company I was telling you about. In fact, I work for the Secret Service. I'd like to talk to you about one of your clients. Just talk, that's all. We'll pay the same fee as for a massage."

This time it was real, his first recruitment pitch, subject of many lectures and much speculation. The frankness was liberating; the effect, to judge by her open-mouthed stare, striking.

"Is everything all right, sir—madam?" The maitre d' stooped over Charles's shoulder, hands clasped in supplication.

"Fine, thank you."

"I am so sorry for the confusion earlier."

"It's quite all right. Don't worry."

"I was confusing Lovejoy and Kilroy."

35

"Of course, yes. Mistakes happen."

The maitre d' looked across to the other table, rubbing his hands. "The lady, she is happy now, also."

"Good, I'm very glad."

Claire stood. "Excuse me." She picked up her handbag.

"This way, madam," said the maitre d', ushering her towards the Ladies'. He was followed by Charles's silent curses. He debated with himself how long he should wait if she didn't reappear and imagined the politeness with which his humiliating failure would be received in Head Office. Everyone would eventually get to hear about it. Putative agents who fled from him at first contact would become part of office mythology, like the Whippett and the policewoman.

"Bet you thought I'd done a bunk, didn't you?" She reappeared from behind, speaking now in the unmistakable accent of outer London. "I nearly did. Thought you might be the police but then I reckoned this isn't the way they go about it and I didn't want to leave you in the lurch, 'specially in a nice place like this." She sat and looked at him, then smiled and touched his hand with her fingers. "Listen, love, if you die with a look like that on your face, they won't wash your body."

He grinned. "I look miserable when I'm happy. My features relax and make me look more serious than I feel."

"Tragic, I call it. Anyway, so long as you don't want me to kill no one I'll do anything you like with them. All the usual services. What about another bottle?"

They took coffee in the lounge, where he told her that he wanted to talk about a client of hers, a Russian official called Viktor Koslov.

She raised her eyebrows and resumed her French accent. "Peter, you are not wanting me to seduce someone? How disappointing."

"Another time."

"Maybe tonight, monsieur. You had better be careful." She dropped the accent. "No, but who did you say? I can't think of any client called that."

Charles described him. She insisted she had no Russian clients and for a while he thought it possible that the office had misinterpreted Koslov's relations with her; that it was indeed an intelligence relationship, but one in which she was his client rather than he hers. If that was so, she was bound to go on denying it. They were getting nowhere.

Eventually he had to tell her that he believed she had seen Koslov that afternoon.

She looked puzzled. "You don't mean Erik? He's from Finland."

"Is that what he told you?"

"He's Finnish. He's in timber. He's rich. He showed me photos of his huge house in Helsinki and of reindeer. He's a nice man, Erik. He's fond of me. He's one of my sugar-children, the ones I'm trying to grow into sugar-daddies to look after me in my old age or if I have to give up work. Every girl needs one. More than one. But you're not having me on—he's not called Erik and he's not Finnish?"

"Absolutely not." This assertion was an act of faith. It had happened that surveillance had got the wrong man. "He's a Soviet diplomat and he's not rich."

"Cunning little sod." She stubbed out her cigarette. "So you've been following me around, have you, to see who I see?"

"We were following him."

"Serve him right. What about another packet of Stuyvesant? It's got me going, this has."

Either Viktor's deception, or his relative poverty, irritated her and she became happy to talk. She described him as polite, educated, intelligent, typical of real Scandinavians she had met. She greatly valued politeness and consideration in her clients, rating Germans the best and Iranians and Japanese the worst. Erik treated her as a mistress and had at first been embarrassed by paying her—not reluctant, but embarrassed as if for her sake. She had got him over that and now they made a bit of a joke of it, with her allowing him to please and surprise her by giving her more. He was generous in that way, especially given that he wasn't really rich after all. He had no odd habits, special requests or perversions. In fact, he was a good lover, keen, considerate, controlled yet straightfor-wardly expressive. "Like when you see a really good tennis player on the telly," she said. "Nice style, everything as it should be."

They had met through her occasional early morning walks with her poodle in Hyde Park and Kensington Gardens. She did it more often later in the day, for business reasons. "A dog is a help. It attracts attention and people think you're not in a hurry, so they stop to pat it."

"Gives you a reason for being there," said Charles.

"Yes, and it's easy to get into conversation. I've had some good clients that way." She didn't normally expect business on her early morning walks, which were for her own and the dog's sake, but she saw this same man once or twice and they were soon on smiling and nodding terms. One day he stopped and patted her dog and asked its name, which was Lucy. After that, they talked a little whenever they met. This had happened over some months. It was during this period that he told her he was a Finnish businessman.

"What did you say you were?" asked Charles.

"Masseuse. No point in beating about the bush."

"Did he realise what you meant?"

"Not at first, no. Later, when he did, he was a bit cast down. I didn't see him for a fortnight. Then when I did he said he'd been at home on holiday with his wife. P'raps he was."

"Where did he say he lived?"

"Other side of the park. I never asked where, or his phone number, or anything like that. Not professional. It frightens them. He used to ask me a lot about which hotels I went to, how much they cost and so on, but when I told him he could come to my flat if he liked, he didn't, not for weeks. And when he did he was very nervous, too nervous, you know. He just had tea and went."

"Did he say anything about it?"

"He kept saying he couldn't tell me what a big step that was for him. Kept saying it. I s'pose he couldn't."

An unauthorised visit by a Soviet official to the home of a westerner, especially that of someone who had picked him up in the park and who would be assumed to work for the British security organs, was more than a decisive step. It was disaffection and rule-breaking of a sort that could have ended his career, at least. Unless, of course, Koslov had other motives. "And after that you became lovers, or he your client, or however he saw it?"

"Not straight away. I didn't see him for a while. And then all in a rush."

"Did he pay you from the start?" Russian officials were lowly paid and meeting Claire's rates must have been a struggle.

"Not at first. I wanted to encourage him, you see. That's the sugar-child bit. I thought he was nice. I still do, cunning sod though he is." She lit another cigarette. "You're not in league with the income tax, are you?"

"No."

"And the KGB aren't going to duff me up or anything if they find you're on to it?"

"No. Has he ever mentioned the KGB or anything to do with intelligence?" She shook her head. "Or has he ever asked you to do anything unusual?"

"I told you, he's very straightforward like that. Not like some of them, wanting you in plastic wrappers and whatever."

"I mean, has he ever asked you to find out anything for him, or get anything, or get to know anyone?"

"Can't think of anything. He doesn't ask questions much. Nor does he like being asked a lot, either. But I do sometimes, just to tease him." She smiled.

Others joined them in the lounge and he ended the evening counting out her money in Park Lane. She agreed, as if it were a mere matter of course, to report on Koslov. He tried to hand over the wad of notes surreptitiously, without the doorman seeing.

"Taxi home?" she asked, once the notes were in her bag.

He took out his wallet again and handed her a pound note. "Keep the change."

She grinned and waved the note at the nearest cab.

Avoiding the doorman's eye, he went straight to his room where he made his own contact notes on Hilton paper. There was no need now to stay the night but the room was paid for and the large wide bed looked greatly preferable to his mattress on the floor in Queensgate.

"I hope you are not lonely in there tonight, monsieur," she had said with a smile as she got into her taxi, theatrically holding out her hand to be kissed.

CHAPTER THREE

COLIN NEWICK, FORMERLY a novitiate monk, touched his glasses before speaking. "No, but it was an unequivocal set-up by Gerry. Heartless. 'Pick up a stranger in a bar,' he said. 'That's all you've got to do. Get his identifying details without his realising you're doing it and without him getting yours. It's a bit ritzy, the bar in question, so look smart.'"

As he touched his glasses again he caught Charles's smile. His habit had been mercilessly highlighted when he was interviewed on film by a former ambassador during an exercise. "Don't you start," he continued. "You haven't even got specs. What makes it worse is that everyone who has has started doing it back to me and then I can't help doing it even more. It's contagious, like walking alongside someone with a limp. Wait till you need glasses."

Charles ordered two more beers from Harry, the Castle barman. They were in the mess before dinner on a Thursday, normally a good evening because Friday was effectively a half day and the forthcoming weekend was free, with no exercise.

Colin described how, in a velvet jacket borrowed from Desmond Kimmeridge, he was directed to the roughest and least ritzy of dockland pubs. There he was rebuffed and all but set upon by men he tried to speak to until he feigned toothache, got the publican to recommend a dentist and spent the rest of the evening hearing the tale of woe that constituted the publican's life history. "Got all his details, though," he said, "in spades. More than I wanted. But it was rough, that place. I'll get Gerry back somehow. Make him think I'm having a raging affair with French Kisser."

French Kisser was Gerry's nickname for a girlfriend acquired during his recent posting in Paris. Revealing neither her real name nor her nationality, and vague on other details, he chronicled with morbid pleasure the decline of their cross-Channel relationship. His ambiguous jocularity made it impossible to know whether he was putting a brave face on something he couldn't stop himself talking about, or simply found it an entertaining conversational football.

"You're lucky you missed that exercise," said Colin. "They're bound to clobber you with something later. Ian Clyde got the wrong pub, of course, missed the minibus back and lost his notes. This world should be grateful he gave up medical practice. The next should notice a drop in arrivals."

They were joined at the bar by Rebecca. All the men were in suits and that night she was the only woman. She wore a pleated tartan skirt and and her hair was newly washed and untied. Charles and Colin briefly competed to sign her drinks chit. Charles won.

"On condition you let me buy a bottle of wine with dinner," she said. "It's awful here otherwise. No one ever lets me buy a drink."

"Maurice Lydd might," said Charles. Lydd, a smooth and genially plump former journalist from Glasgow, was already known for his prac- tised sharpness in the matter of expenses.

"Actually, he did."

"Apparently he keeps a bottle of whisky in his room so that he can come down with a glass already in hand and avoid the danger of having to buy a round if he goes to the bar," said Colin. "Of course, Rebecca's problem would fade away if we had women on the course. Gallantry would become too expensive. Why don't we recruit female intelligence officers?"

"We do," said Rebecca, "in theory. Apparently, we used to quite a bit after the war and SOE and all that, then they had a run of disasters and stopped. Arabs wouldn't speak to them, couple of nervous breakdowns, one ran off with a target, usual sorts of thing. So they decided to recruit only from within. Which is why we have a sprinkling of senior women and a shortage of younger ones coming up. But they've decided to start recruiting again, according to Personnel."

Colin looked about. "Where are they, then? Can't find any, I s'pose. Don't know where to look, or something pathetic."

"Why don't you apply for the intelligence branch? You're a graduate, aren't you?" Charles asked. "Unless you're put off by us."

"When I can be a secretary and do a job like this, looking after all you babies and reading your files and knowing all about you and no other woman in sight? I wouldn't have anything like this access to you if I were one of you. I'd have to be much better behaved."

"You've been disappointingly well behaved up to now, so far as I can see," said Colin.

"Change your optician, Colin." She smiled. "No, I've sort of half thought about bridging but I'm waiting to see how the course pans out, to see if I like it. I might hate it. Meanwhile, I think I can put up with being the only woman around. I'm not about to burn my bra over it."

"What's this about bras?" Christopher Westfield joined them, slipping his arm around Rebecca's waist. "G&T, while you're about it, Charles. Ice and lemon." He turned to Rebecca. "We'll have to call you Need-To-Know. It's all you ever tell us about anything. But will you tell us when we really do need to know?"

"Depends, Chris. What d'you think you need to know?"

"I need to know if you'll be my exercise wife in a little plan I'm hatching for Danish Blue. I need a wife to support my cover."

Danish Blue was a travelling exercise for which they were having to prepare their own legends, routes and itineraries. There was intense suspicion that unpleasant surprises were to be sprung on them.

"You'd better ask your non-exercise wife about that."

"Can't. She doesn't need to know. If you don't agree I thought I'd ask Gerry if I could borrow French Kisser for a few days."

"You're welcome to French Kisser."

"What's she like? Have you met her?"

"No, but I've heard enough about her."

Harry rang the ship's bell for dinner. Despite the Castle's military origins, a preponderance of ex-naval staff made some of its traditions nautical. Thus, although the mess was not a wardroom, its bedrooms were cabins; the parade ground was not a deck but leaving the Castle was sometimes described as going ashore. The ship's bell, taken from a Second World War destroyer, had been donated by an early post-war course.

Charles and Colin sat either side of Rebecca. Gerry, who was late, took the last empty place opposite. "All done?" he asked her. She nodded. "Great stuff. You missed a good exercise yesterday," he told Charles.

"So I hear."

"Don't worry, we'll arrange a nasty surprise for you later, won't we, Becks?" He laughed.

"I've a bone to pick with you," Rebecca said quietly to Charles.

The phrase had uneasy resonances from childhood and youth, when it was used by parents and teachers to presage something more serious than the playfulness suggested. The last time he had heard it was on his father's lips, when his father had learned that Charles was—against all expectation—joining the army, but not the Royal Engineers, his father's corps. His father had used the phrase jocularly but beneath it, Charles realised, there was some hurt. "What?"

"You shot me."

"Not you. Just your picture."

They were taught elementary two-handed instinctive shooting with standard Browning 9mm pistols by Little Tom, the towering ex-Marine.

"Makes a break from sitting on your bums and listening," Gerry said.

The morning of Charles's return Little Tom had inserted a full-faced picture of a smiling Rebecca amongst the films and stills of armed men they had to hit. Everyone had withheld fire except Charles, who had shot her in the mouth and left eye.

"I thought I was meant to."

"No one else did."

"It was a manifestation of secret desire."

"Not a very nice way of showing it."

"Sorry."

"Little Tom says you've used a Browning before so I suppose you're allowed to show off."

"Well, that was in Belfast. A place apart. Seems a long time ago."

After dinner there was a case history concerning a senior Soviet bloc official who had survived undetected for thirty years as an agent and whose career was crowned by his secret exfiltration and retirement, along with the latest diplomatic ciphers. Charles sat near the back with his pipe—a habit he had recently affected partly because of a sense that he lacked habits—unlit. It reminded him of Hookey's unlit pipe during their discussion. Perhaps the lighting of pipes whilst working was a sign of boredom and disengagement, something you didn't do if you were stimulated. Roger, he noticed, notoriously prone to postprandial drowsiness, had left his cigarettes open but untouched.

The story was told by the last of the agent's many case officers, a tall, saturnine, good-looking man, now in Personnel. At the end he read extracts from the agent's comments on his handling over thirty years. The most serious criticism was of the frequency of changes of case officer, mostly dictated by the bureaucracy of postings and careers rather than by the demands of the case itself, which was undeniably important.

"On the one hand," concluded the case officer, "there's some truth in the service's dictum that no agent should be considered properly recruited unless he or she accepts handover to a new case officer, demonstrating that the relationship is by then with the service rather than the individual. Nor should any agent dictate someone's career. On the other, an intelligence service which gives greater priority to its own administrative tidiness than to its casework is arguably not fully serious."

Fully serious or not, Secret Service was turning out, Charles reflected, to be a pretty good choice. He enjoyed the course and liked the people, while the work so far had given him no cause for the excited unease he'd felt before his first interview. People he knew who'd gone into business or other professions seemed more routinely exploitative and unscrupulous than this. It answered, in fact, with everything he'd liked about the army—patriotic endeavour in a cause in which he could believe, a sense of belonging, the subtle satisfactions of service—but without the detailed domination and invasiveness of military life. Now, in the intelligence world, he felt he was at the heart of the Cold War. He did not think of himself as extreme or aggressive but he'd always had a desire to seek out the front line, wherever it was; a desire to be there, and to be able to feel later that he had been there. He sensed the same in some of those around him.

They were let off soon after lunch on Friday. Charles was to spend the weekend at his mother's house in Buckinghamshire and he looked forward to the leisurely drive in the Rover he had inherited from his father. It was the big P5, the ministerial Rover with the thirsty V8 engine and enough wood and leather inside to furnish a London club. "The drawing room on wheels," his father had approvingly dubbed it. Charles kept meaning to exchange it for something more suited to his age, pocket and unaccompanied status, but there had been little time for looking around. Anyway, it had been his father's.

"Going all the way in that?" asked Desmond Kimmeridge, whose two-seater Mercedes was parked nearby at the edge of the parade ground.

"About five or ten miles. Then the AA pick me up. You?"

"House party in Shropshire, with prospects."

"Who?"

"There's only one and she's very need-to-know. Hope you make it."

"Hope you do."

Desmond grinned as his car hood slid silently down.

Conscious of the amount of washing he was bringing home, Charles stopped in Marlow to buy flowers for his mother. His sister, Mary, was also to be there and, as it was the first he had seen of her since her engagement, he bought her some roses. There was a good tobacconist near the florist, so he bought an experimental tin of Balkan Sobranie and an unnecessary new pipe, his third since the course had started. He felt agreeably relaxed and alive, with the light-heartedness that comes of youth, health, independence, financial sufficiency, a sense of purpose and as yet no burdensome responsibility.

His widowed mother had remained in the family home, a 1920s house off a track in the Chiltern hills behind Marlow and Henley, backing westwards over the child's-picture-book Hambleden valley. His parents had bought it soon after the Second World War. His father, a surveyor, insisted that good houses of the twenties and thirties were the best of any period, combining Edwardian spaciousness, detail and craftsman-ship with better understanding of materials, heating and plumbing. "Georgian for damp elegance," he would say, "Victorian for freezing solidity, but these have warmth and dryness as well as grace and space. As places to live in, you can't beat 'em."

His father's presence in the house was still palpable. His deerstalker on the peg behind the scullery door, the boot-puller he had made outside it, his study, his shed. It was impossible to be in the house without recall-ing his passion for every detail of it, his devotion to the garden, his meticulously maintained tools, his local knowledge, his beechwood tramps with successive spaniels. Charles often wondered what he would have thought of his son's new occupation, had he told him. Probably

45

there would have been no need; it had been an old friend or former col-league of his father's—his status always unclear—who had first men-tioned the office to Charles and it was unlikely he had done so without his father's knowledge. His father had spent many years as a government surveyor and after his death Charles had discovered that much of his work was connected with building or altering secret establishments. He might even have known the Castle. Charles had told his mother, though not so far his sister, who, like the rest of the world, was supposed to think he was in the Foreign Office.

His mother's hair was uniformly grey now, and her delicate, wrinkled features were suffused with an anxious goodwill that seemed to be increasing with age. During dinner on Friday conversation was en-tirely about Mary's planned wedding. Charles contributed one or two suggestions—unadopted—while keeping to himself reflections on how much of this there would be over the next six months. Then, he sup-posed, there would be years of baby-fuss. Still, happy engrossment was generally a good thing and his future brother-in-law had seemed pleas-ant, so far as he remembered. He was a lawyer in the same City firm as Mary.

"Where did you say David was this weekend?" he asked as they settled with their coffees before the beech-log fire.

Mary stared. "David? I haven't mentioned David. I've no idea what he's doing."

"James, he means," said their mother quickly.

David, Charles remembered, was the previous boyfriend.

"Don't you dare confuse them when he's here," said Mary, her eyes darkening with indignation. "I don't see how you could, anyway. They're so totally different."

Charles was still well adrift. "Of course they are, I know. Can't think why I said David."

"It's about time you got another girlfriend, isn't it? So long as she's not like the Awful Alison. I think we should vet her first."

"I'm working on one but she's married, with children."

"Oh no, Charles," said his mother.

"Better that than have your own with the Awful Alison. Imagine." Mary shuddered.

He discovered later from his mother that James was "in the City" and that they had met, twice, when Mary had had friends down.

"Ah, so there were others there."

"A whole lot of them came down for lunch and you all went for a walk afterwards, leaving me to clear up. Except that you didn't because you went off to see Alison."

He remembered the weekend now. It hadn't been Alison but another girl he'd never mentioned. He still had no memory of James.

On the Saturday he cleaned and tinkered with the Rover, then resumed his slow sorting of his father's shed, which had gradually and unspokenly become his own. Hidden behind a hedge at the back of the double garage, the shed smelt of wood, engine oil and musty overalls and was crammed with tools, spanners, screwdrivers, awls, hammers, vices, clamps, pumps, hoses, braces, brushes, drills, oils, solvents, fuel cans and old batteries. Whisky flake pipe tobacco tins contained screws, nails, nuts, jubilee clips, car lightbulbs and anything else that would fit. Many of the carpentry tools were old enough to have value but Charles would no more have sold them than his father's photographs. The shed was infused with his father's presence and Charles's intermittent sorting— little more than a process of picking up and handling things before replacing them in a slightly different order—was part mourning and part adjustment. He felt he was both preserving his father's inheritance and making it his own.

In late afternoon, beneath dark unbroken clouds, he went for a run. He loved the patchwork quality of the Chilterns, with their towering beeches, hills, valleys, sudden declivities and surprising vistas. Little Switzerland, his father used to call it, invariably adding that it was just about as expensive. He still ran in army boots, slithering in the chalky mud of logging tracks, his breath like gouts of steam. The last part of the run was across a ploughed field back up the hill, the clinging mud weighing on his boots, his heart thumping and his legs so leaden it was impossible to think of anything but keeping going. When he reached the top the clouds parted across the Hambleden valley and the sun briefly touched the hills. He faced the view, gulping air, hands on head to lift his rib cage from his lungs.

He didn't feel he was running for or from anything now, but still he kept doing it. Physical exhaustion was gratifying; it took him out of himself, out of everything. Nevertheless, he had given himself a purpose in running that day, and had failed. He had meant to decide during the run whether to ring Rebecca and suggest an early dinner on Sunday evening.

The thought had been hovering throughout the drive from the Castle the day before. He didn't have her home number but the office switchboard would connect him. Dinner on Sunday gave focus to the weekend and was more relaxed, less a declaration of intent, than dinner on Saturday.

But he had not decided. He suspected it was contemplation of the event rather than the event itself that he enjoyed. He wanted something to look forward to but, otherwise, why was he taking Rebecca to dinner? The others, if they found out about it, would assume he was making a play for her, as might she. And as he might, indeed. Or might not. He decided to decide during his bath, while watching the glow of sun ebb from the room. He next decided to decide with a cup of tea in his hand, telling himself he did not actually have to decide until his hand was on the phone. While making the tea he reflected that he would normally have described himself as decisive.

His mother came into the kitchen. "Oh, Charles, I forgot to tell you. Someone from your office rang when you were out. They want you to ring back."

"Who?"

"I wrote it down. Where did I put it? It's not by the phone. I think I thought I'd better hide it."

"Man or woman?"

"Here it is, by the Marmite. I knew Marmite would remind me, you see, because you were bound to want some. A man called Hugo March. Here's his number. He didn't say what it was about and I didn't ask. He sounded very important—well, at least, he sounded like that. You know what I mean. You don't come across many Hugos nowadays."

The study extension was more private. He shut the door. "Hallo?" Anna's voice had a slight catch in it as she pronounced the "h." "Hugo's out, doing his duty with the girls. He won't be long." There was a slight pause. "It's nice to speak to you again." He asked how her midweek dinner party had gone. "You must come one week," she said, "if you're not too busy. Though I'm sure you've got many more exciting things to do."

"I'd love to." He felt now that he had been decisively right not to ring Rebecca.

Hugo returned while they were talking. "Fancy a run?" he asked.

"I've just had one."

"Have another at six thirty tomorrow morning in the park. We've just

48

learned from Chef that Lover Boy is going for one. Ideal chance for you to bump him with no one else about." "Chef" was the name given to the telephone intercept material. "We need to have a chat first about what you're going to say and so on. No chance you could come round here tonight, I s'pose?"

"Fine."

His mother was resigned to work taking priority over dinner. He promised he would be back that night or the next day.

Hugo's house was a substantial chunk of Wandsworth Edwardiana, three-storied, high-ceilinged, with a neglected front garden and stained-glass door. The hall was cluttered with childrens' toys and shoes. Hugo twice tripped on a large doll while ushering Charles in. "Anna, for goodness' sake!" he called. "She's upstairs putting the children to bed. Be down soon. Drink?"

They drank dry white wine while discussing what Charles should do. Lover Boy's usual route was a slow jog in a wide circle, nothing too taxing. Charles would intercept him and feign surprised recognition. It would be a success if he could get him to exchange addresses and telephone numbers, a bonus if they actually arranged to meet again. That was unlikely, on first encounter, and Charles shouldn't push even on Lover Boy's address if he sensed reluctance. They could always contrive another encounter.

"It goes without saying you mustn't hint at his girlfriend or anything. This must appear a completely fortuitous and unthreatening encounter, nothing he need feel uneasy about reporting to the embassy security officer, because he will report, if he's got any sense. They'll suspect provocation, of course, because that's their job, and anyway they're like that, and the other way round in Moscow it would be, of course. Well, it is here, of course, this time, but normally it wouldn't be, if you see what I mean. Anyway, what we must hope is that they'll let it run long enough for us to show him that you know what he's up to. Then you can talk on different terms, if he wants. Or not. Nothing lost if he doesn't and no need for Foreign Office clearance at this stage since we're not making a pitch or doing anything that could result in a protest."

After making an appropriate number of protests, and Anna an appropriate number of disclaimers about the meal, Charles stayed for dinner. It was spaghetti bolognese.

"We have proper lunches at weekends," said Hugo, "so it's always something like spag bog in the evening. Did you do much First World War in the army?"

Hugo viewed military service as primarily a course of study. He was an authority on the First World War, though he preferred the term "enthusiast," and while Anna cooked he showed Charles his books. He was wearing cavalry twills, sports jacket and tie, which Charles interpreted as an expression of identity with earlier generations until Hugo mentioned that he had been to Saturday Mass that evening.

"It's good for the girls," added Hugo, as if asked to explain. "Gives them the possibility of choice later. They enjoy it. They like dressing up. Anna doesn't. Go to church, I mean. Likes dressing up." He laughed abruptly, standing very close.

Dinner was in the kitchen at the back of the house, which had been two rooms. Looking for something to compliment without exposing his domestic ignorance, Charles chose the pine table.

"Deal," Hugo corrected. "That's what more honest, less pretentious generations called it. It means any cheap white wood, which usually happens to be pine. The whole pine business is a wonderful example of something old dressed up as something new. Fashion, that's all."

"Fashion maybe but at least it's a cheerful one," said Anna. "Better than the earlier fashion in houses like this for painting everything brown."

"Not the kitchen table. That would have been plain and scrubbed daily by the lady of the house."

"By her scullery maid, more like."

"True. It would be nice to have staff again."

"Then you'd better get another posting."

Hugo poured more wine. "Not that we'd have been eating in the kitchen. Earlier generations would not have understood our mania for the vernacular, for exposed brickwork, unpainted wood, paying vast sums for places where animals lived and calling them mews houses and living in them ourselves and all the rest of it."

"We could move into the dining room if you prefer," said Anna.

Hugo put his hand on Charles's arm. "Talking of which, there is a wonderful table in there. Bet you can't guess what it is. Come and see." He stood, wiping his mouth with his napkin.

Anna put her hand on Charles's other arm. "Hugo, you can't. He's in the middle of his meal. Why don't you wait till we've finished?"

"Won't take a second. Come on."

Anna's mouth set firmly as she looked at her husband, but she said nothing. When Charles caught her eye she raised her eyebrows and smiled her crooked, shy smile. Its crookedness made it seem personal and beguiling, a secret shared.

The table was a handsome oval leaf with turned legs. "Mahogany," said Charles.

Hugo was delighted. "Very understandable mistake. Very understandable." He clutched Charles's arm, blinking rapidly. "Experts have made it. Actually, cherry. Most unusual, isn't it?" They returned to the kitchen. "I was right, darling. He got it wrong."

"Darling, you are clever."

Charles left later than intended and drove back across the river to South Kensington. He had meant to ring Roger and warn that he would be back at the flat, since he suspected use of his room when he was away. He heard the noise of the party as he approached the building. When he opened the flat door he found a man he didn't know pinning a woman against the wall and urging her that it wasn't very far. They both held empty glasses.

"It is far," she said, staring into his eyes.

The man shook his head. "It isn't far."

She nodded. "It is far."

The atmosphere was thick with candle and cigarette smoke. There was music and dancing in Charles's bedroom. His bike was in the hall, with coats over it. The tiny kitchen was crammed and there was more music from Roger's room along the corridor. He knew two of the people in the kitchen, David Brooke and Alastair Devauden, young postgraduates from the course.

"Where've you been?" shouted David above the music. "We've been looking for you."

Roger came out of his room, smiling and sweating, drink and cigarette in one hand. He laid the other on Charles's shoulder. "Sorry about this, old chap. Bit impromptu. Some people I was at university with pitched up. Wasn't planned. I'll clear your room. Have a drink."

"Don't worry, I'm going back."

"Seriously?"

"Just dropped in to get something." Charles was annoyed; he liked Roger but resented invasion, although he didn't really mind driving back to his mother's. The woman who had been arguing by the door pushed past them both, pursued by the man. It was the sort of party he had always hated, yet, in his student days, would always have attended. Saying "no" became easier with age. Now, he was more grateful that he had an alternative than concerned to show his annoyance. There was also the consoling secret of what he had to do in the morning. "Really, that's all I came for."

Roger's eyes shone with drink. "You're a rotten liar, Thoroughgood, but thanks. I'll get it cleaned up tomorrow. You'll be able to eat off the carpet. Promise."

Darkness crumbled into gloom the next morning and the drizzle felt like a permanent condition of life. Charles's mother and sister had been in bed when he returned the night before and were still there when he left. It was still not properly light when he reached London and sat in the car in Queensgate. Lack of traffic made him notice how dirty and run-down everything was, from the uncollected rubbish on the pavements to the cracked and peeling paintwork of the buildings and the few, slouching young men who dragged themselves along in purgatorial gloom. This, too, seemed a permanent condition of life. London was becoming a Third World city. He imagined the flat filled with post-party detritus. The only good thing about the morning so far had been the pleasure of the uncrowded drive; his father's old Rover, emblem of a better-mannered world, had quietly ushered him into the city.

As soon as it was properly light he jogged up Queensgate. There was already a surprising number of joggers and runners, many wearing smart tracksuits and grossly over-developed plimsolls called trainers, which were becoming fashionable. Others wore natty shorts and competition vests. So far from blending with them, his muddy rugby shirt with the number 12 hanging off, baggy shorts and army boots which looked absurdly large for his legs made him feel laughably conspicuous.

"You won't have any surveillance with you," Hugo had said. "You should be able to find him easily enough in the park. Won't exactly be teeming with runners at that time of morning and it'll be immediately obvious if he's with a colleague, in which case go home. If we put a team out to help you we'd have to pay overtime."

It may not have been teeming but at any one moment there were a dozen runners in view, more as time went on. They ranged from the knock-kneed and wide-elbowed—the two seemed to go together—to serious-looking people in Olympic look-alike stripe and overweight middle-aged men who ran at a pace somewhat slower than they walked. Viktor—Charles had to make a positive effort to think of him as that rather than as Lover Boy—generally jogged within Kensington Gardens but sometimes strayed farther into Hyde Park. Charles had to pursue the widely scattered runners in order to confirm that each was not Viktor, and soon covered a good deal more ground than most. His legs, though not actually stiff from his hard run the day before, felt heavier than normal. By the time he approached the slight, neat-looking figure with short fair hair and little-used bottle-green tracksuit by the Round Pond, he felt nothing of the desired surge of energy for the encounter. He yawned, a nervous reaction that used to afflict him before army parachuting and gave a misleading impression of relaxation. Quite suddenly he felt he had barely enough energy to put one foot before another.

He was almost sure it was Viktor running clockwise around the pond, slowly, a genuine jog rather than a run, gazing at the water. Charles headed anti-clockwise, hoping that Viktor would not break off for the Soviet Embassy before they met since that would involve a too deliberate-looking, and perhaps exhausting, chase to overhaul him. "By the time I caught up," he imagined reporting, "he was too near the embassy and I was too exhausted to speak. We exchanged glances. I think he recognised me."

As they drew closer he became more certain of Viktor's neat controlled figure and of his almost delicate features, hardened by a suggestion of order, purpose, discipline. He reminded Charles of a self-conscious and newly promoted young army officer, a subaltern made early captain and adjutant.

They closed with surprising rapidity over the last few yards. In Charles's imagination the actual encounter had become infinitely postponable by another day, hour, minute or second. He would always have time to reconsider what exactly he was going to say just before he said it. When it happened it was like military parachuting: you found yourself through the open door and out into the slipstream while still trying to anticipate, leaving your fear behind because there was no longer time to indulge it. As in the course exercises, he fell back on what he'd mentally rehearsed then put aside because he was sure he could improve upon it.

"Viktor?"

They both stopped. The grey eyes, though not fearful, were alert and wary, as if it had been one of the park squirrels that had spoken.

"Viktor—I'm sorry, I'm not quite sure of your surname—Korlov? Koslov? Koslov, yes. We were at Lincoln together. I'm Charles Thoroughgood." He held out his hand, knowing how difficult it was to refuse a proffered hand. Viktor took it passively, saying nothing. "Lincoln College, Oxford. Four or five years ago. We used to talk sometimes."

"Yes, Charles, I know you. I am surprised. This is a very great coincidence." His diction, precise and deliberate, was slightly slurred by the attractive liquidity of his native Russian. He looked only a little older, but firmer, than when Charles had known him.

"What are you doing here?" Charles asked.

"I am a diplomat with Soviet Embassy in London. I am second secretary. And you? What are you doing? Do you live near here?"

"Another coincidence. I am in the British Foreign Office, but I've only just joined."

"Yes, another great coincidence." Viktor's smile, though not unfriendly, was as careful as his manner. "Which is your department?"

"I'm awaiting assignment. I'm still on the induction course. Perhaps it will be Hawaii, who knows? Or maybe Moscow. Though I have no Russian."

Viktor shrugged. "It is no matter. You would learn it."

"It would be nice to see you again. Perhaps we might meet, if you are allowed."

"I have to seek permission."

"Of course. May I ring you? Have you a telephone number?"

"You must ring Soviet Embassy."

Charles had a Foreign Office number he could use but Viktor seemed conveniently incurious. Charles was already elated; an agreement to meet again was the most he could realistically have hoped for. "It won't be a problem for you if I ring?" Hugo had told him to say that, since it could represent the beginnings of joint conspiracy.

54

Viktor shrugged again. It seemed that shrugging was part of his conversation. "It is not a problem. Why should it be?"

"Of course not, no. I just didn't know how things were in your embassy, that's all."

"It is not a problem."

Charles's legs were lighter on the run back across the park. He thought about showering and changing in the flat, then decided it would be wiser not to see it. He considered, too, driving to Hugo's house, but instead set the Rover's Viking head towards the M4. His mother was up when he reached home.

"It's unlike you to run early in the morning," she said.

He was brimful with his achievement and would have enjoyed describing it to her. He was already persuaded that it had the potential to be a great case. Russian penetrations—real, long-term, heart-of-the-bureaucracy penetrations, not peripheral pinpricks—were notoriously hard to come by. He lingered with Mary for an hour after breakfast, by the end of which he was also persuaded he remembered James.

That afternoon he walked with his mother down through the woods of Pheasant's Hill to Hambleden and back up the valley through Skirmett and Turville to Fingest. "The essence of England walk," his father used to call it, invariably adding that it was sad that the essence was now so untypical. The skies had cleared and for Charles, that late-autumn afternoon, combining the rural and domestic idyll with excitements in London made him feel he was at last breaking through to the sort of life he had long imagined himself living.

CHAPTER FOUR

T HE TELEPHONE WAS answered, as before, by a woman whose English was a parody of deliberation. "Please . . . wait."

The wait was at least as long as that during his first vain attempt to ring Viktor. He was in Hookey's office, seated at the side of the cleared desk and using a telephone with a Foreign Office number. Hookey was slumped in his high-backed, swivel armchair, his head and nose barely above his desk, smoke curling gently from his pipe. He stared expressionlessly at Hugo, who sat with papers and clipboard on his crossed legs, frowning and making lists with his fat Mont Blanc pen.

Eventually the woman returned. "Please, your name again." There was another long pause. "Mr. Koslov is not available."

"Would you please tell him I rang?"

"Who is ringing, please?"

He spelt his name for the third time. For the third time, she repeated it back to him, then the line went dead.

Hugo scribbled a final note to himself and looked up. "That's clear, then. Either he's reported it and the security narks have warned him off or he hasn't and he's hiding from you. Question is, whether we try one more time or whether that would look too much like the pursuit it is. Don't want to provoke a protest from the ambassador or get him into trouble."

Charles was disappointed. The case seemed to be slipping through his fingers, yet he still believed in his impression that Viktor was willing to meet.

"Not necessarily." Hookey spoke with his pipe in his mouth, causing it to jerk up and down and turn the rising smoke into irregular puffs of Morse code. "They often take time to decide. They could be asking Moscow for traces of Charles, to see what's known about him. They dislike being bounced into decisions. We'll try one more time, and once only. More would be suspicious. But leave it a week."

"Exactly," said Hugo. "They're bound to trace. Give it a week." He straightened one leg and pulled carefully on his trouser crease.

"Meanwhile," Hookey continued, "see the tart again. Ask her more about what he feels for her, what the relationship is so far as he's concerned. We've no real idea of that and it could be crucial to the case. Also, make sure she goes on being nice to him. We don't want her to drop him now she knows he's not rich. And, Hugo, make sure MI5 are kept informed."

"No, but they are, very much so. They're in the loop. In the loop." Hugo nodded as if the phrase pleased him. "It's in the middle of their patch, you see, the Soviet Embassy here. We have to. And I think we should."

"Yes, thank you," said Hookey quietly.

Charles returned to the typing room on the first floor where a dozen or so young men and women were picking their way through a training programme under the sharp-eyed supervision of a large, bejewelled woman who moved ceremonially amongst them. The students were of a mixture of grades and departments but all intelligence officers, like Charles, were supposed to be able to type. Some on his course had joined early for "special training," only to find that rather than the arts of disguise, assassination, sabotage, secret writing or seduction, they were given typing and language training. Charles and others who had not joined early had seemed likely to escape instruction altogether until Hugo hit on the idea.

"We need a reason for your visits to HO that won't broadcast to the world that you're doing a case for us," he said. "Catching up on typing training should be perfect. And to ensure that it's not you alone I'll ask Hookey to get the head of training to fix it so that everyone on your course who hasn't had it gets hauled across for the odd hour in their lunchtimes and that sort of thing." He grinned as he adjusted his tie in his office mirror. Bureaucratic manipulations gave him pleasure. "You'd be pretty unpopular if they knew it was all for your benefit. Strikes me we sometimes spend more time working out how to keep our secrets from each other than from the enemy. But typing's jolly useful, you'll find." He summoned his secretary for dictation.

There being no privacy in the training department, finding somewhere from which to ring Claire that day was not straightforward. Hugo's office couldn't be used because there was a meeting in it, his secretary's couldn't be used because she was expecting a call and Hookey was too important to bother. Eventually, Hookey's secretary evicted two young officers from their office, which meant they had first to lock away their papers and then stand in the corridor while Charles, after due apologies, made the call from behind their closed door. After that, talking to Claire was straightforward: of course, she would love to have supper with Monsieur Lovejoy and, yes, she thought she could manage that night but it would have to be late because she was tied up—"if you see what I mean"—until nine. He was to call for her.

The flat had been reasonably well cleaned after the party, which suggested that Roger must have had female assistance. Charles's bike was undamaged and his mattress appeared not to have been danced on, or too obviously subjected to anything else. His arrangement with Claire, though, meant that he couldn't go that evening with Roger and others to a wine bar in Battersea that someone's sister had opened. Wine bars were spreading. Charles had talked about them with Roger. They liked them. Charles had even said he felt they were his spiritual home, or something equally pretentious. Now, confronted with the unexpected offer, he could not immediately say why he couldn't go.

Roger laid his forefinger alongside his nose. "Say no more—NTK, need to know. All this spying business is getting to you, Charles. Especially this new case you're on."

"What case?"

"You tell me. No, don't—NNTK, no need to know. But everyone knows you're doing a case for HO. It's obvious, all these disappearances. Either that or it's a bit on the side, knocking off someone's wife. But I defended you. That's not our Charles, I said—too honourable." He poured the last of a bottle of white wine.

"An affair would be a good cover for espionage," said Charles. "Need for clandestinity, absences, no explanations, odd hours, secret telephone calls and all the rest. And the other way round, of course." Mentions of extra-marital affairs seemed to have proliferated since the image of Anna had been in his mind.

"Espionage itself is a sort of legalised illicit affair. Gives people a kick. Partly why we do it." Roger sipped his wine and pulled a face. A former university chemistry lecturer, he seemed neither to demand nor to expect very much of life, coping with it on intellectual tick-over, the motor within rarely extended. He had the easy generosity of the lazy clever, and an attractive, good-humoured pessimism. "D'you fancy Rebecca, by the way—given that she suffers the disadvantage of being unmarried?"

"No—well, yes, in a way. Not seriously. Why?"

"I don't. Everyone else seems to, especially that prat, MacLydd. He'll be there tonight. Can't leave her alone, always in and out of her office, always trying to chat her up when no one's around. I'd make a move myself just for the pleasure of screwing him up if it weren't against my principle."

"You have a principle?"

"Just the one. Never shit on your own doorstep. Amazing how often people disregard that."

"I'd assumed it was ambition with MacLydd. Trying to ingratiate himself and find out what's going on."

"Same thing. Desire and ambition are in him most determinedly commingled. That's not bad, is it? Shakespearean, nearly. But he'd fancy a bus if it had influence." Roger lit another cigarette from the candle on the table. "Bloody candles bloody stink. In the good old days everything must have stunk of candles and shit inside and horseshit and shit outside."

Without his having done anything in particular, Maurice Lydd's unpopularity with his fellow students had grown daily. It was visceral. Despite being congenial and capable, with a prompt smile and no record of offences against anyone, and despite the fact that his meanness with money was not actually so much greater than that of many people, he gave an impression of relentless self-seeking. He was either unaware of his effect on people or too thick-skinned to care. When there was nothing going on that might further his interests he was agreeable and undemanding company, yet Charles always came away from conversation with him feeling obscurely compromised. Others felt the same.

59

Roger emptied his glass and ran his hand up and down his face. "Better shave, I guess. Rebecca kept staring at me this morning and I naturally assumed she was overwhelmed by desire until she asked why I was shaving only one side of my face. It's that poxy little candle in the bathroom. How do you do it?"

"I hold the candle in one hand and move it across. S'pose we ought to do something about it." Neither had yet attempted to get an electrician, partly because it would have meant taking a day or half a day off to let the man in, something that Slack Alice did not see as part of her duties. It now occurred to Charles, however, that, if his case continued, it might be a convenient excuse. "I'll get someone in to fix it," he said.

The sitting room in Claire's flat was small and warm, richly coloured, cluttered with knick-knacks and old black-and-white or sepia family photos. It wasn't obvious that they were hers. The cushions were freshly pumped-up. It felt to Charles like being squeezed into a furnished tea-cosy.

She put on a short black coat that looked expensive and impractical. "If you agree, Pierre, perhaps we go to the place over the road. They know me there and they will look after us. *Très agrèable, n'est pas?*"

"*D'accord.*"

She exaggerated her accent. "Only, you know, it is necessary I speak like this all the time because that is how they think I am."

It was a Greek restaurant, moderately busy. Claire was welcomed effusively and they were shown to a corner table at the back, candle-lit like the one he'd just left in Queensgate. The waiter gave Charles a knowing smile as he unfolded his napkin.

"They like you here," Charles said.

"I bring them business. Sometimes they bring me some. Also, in my profession, it is useful to have friends nearby."

Meals with Claire, he was to learn, were never short and always expensive. He had the impression she ate out, or in any quantity, only when there was someone to feed her. She ordered a large *kleftiko*. Wine, he learned, had to be red, plentiful and look expensive.

The picture she painted of Viktor was fuller but essentially the same: a nice man, charming, considerate, interesting, with no obvious political or intelligence agenda and no sign of security concerns beyond an understandable reluctance to meet in public. That was the case with many of her clients.

"Yet he's lying to you about who he is."

"If you're not having me on." She had dropped her French accent.

"And presumably lying to his wife."

"Goes without saying."

"And he goes on seeing you. Why? Sex?"

"He loves me." A dribble of juice ran from her lip.

"Has he said so?"

"All the time. He's very passionate. Quite a little romantic." She dabbed at the juice with her napkin. "What you looking at me like that for? You think he must be cross-eyed or something?"

"Not at all, I was just trying to reconcile—"

"He's not the first, you know. He's not the only one, either."

"I'm sure he's not. Nor the last."

"I can pull a man when I want. I don't have to walk the streets."

He poured more wine. "I was just trying to reconcile his loving you with his lying to you."

"Act your age, Pete. Just because you love someone doesn't mean you can't lie to them, does it? I'd be out of clients if it did." She sighed as if it were an old argument between them. "And what about you? Aren't you in love?"

"No."

"Noo." She mimicked him, laughing. "You'd better watch out, dear."

The rest of the evening was spent talking about her—her marriage, her divorce, how she had become a "masseuse," her children and their private school, difficulties with clients and the Inland Revenue. There were, Charles learned, grades and strata within her profession as in his; she regarded her own niche as the respectable top level, viewed nightclub hostesses as sad cases and looked with disdain upon the girls in Shepherd Market, while for the street-walkers of other regions she had no words, only contempt. On the way out Charles was winked at by the waiter. He escorted her to her door and waited while she struggled with the keys in her handbag. It took her three or four attempts to get the right one in the lock. He heard her stumble on the stairs.

Although it was past one in the morning, he walked back to the flat to clear his head, then made notes for the write-up he would have to do after his typing lesson the next day. It was nearly three when he retired to his mattress on the floor. They were to have an early start in the offices of

61

Rasen, Falcon & Co. in Lower Marsh, with the morning on HO paper-work procedures and the afternoon on encipherment.

"You and I are the class dunces," said Desmond Kimmeridge. "More a surprise to you, perhaps, than to me. Guards officers are supposed to be thick. D'you know the one about the man who wanted a brain transplant? Rejects one from a brain surgeon for a hundred thousand, another from a rocket scientist for half a million. Eventually, he's offered one for a million. Belonged to a Guards officer. Why's it so expensive? But, my dear sir, it's never been used. All right, never mind. Gerry says we're slower than everyone else and less accurate, despite our messages being shorter. Bottom of the class."

It was mid-afternoon and Charles's torpor was deepening. The columns of figures and letters comprising the one-time pad manual encipherment system meant less the longer he looked at them. Theoretically unbreakable, unless either pad fell into enemy hands or was repeated, it was a cipher to be concealed within another, computer-generated cipher, also theoretically unbreakable. The course was divided into pairs to practise encoding and decoding.

"Was he annoyed by the facetious message?" asked Charles.

"French Kisser came out as Trench Litter. Better than French Letter, I s'pose. I fear he's fundamentally unembarrassable. Doesn't mind what anyone says about him. He sentenced you and I to another message each of at least twenty groups." He bent his head conspiratorially, close enough for Charles to smell his after-shave. It was slightly reviving. "Between you and I, I think it's no bad thing to get a reputation for being bad at these things. You're less likely to be asked to do them. Same with photography and Edwina. If I were alone on station I'd probably take an axe to Edwina."

Edwina was an obsolescent cipher machine maintained as a back-up system on many stations. They were all supposed to be able to use it. "So long as they don't suspect it's deliberate," said Charles.

"Little chance of that with you and me, I fear. Unlike our brace of young classicists. Or Maurice Lydd. He's doing pages of immaculate stuff. I bet he's cheating."

He and Desmond also did badly in clandestine photography at the

Castle later that week. Desmond was caught by MOD police while taking supposedly secret photographs of a submarine in Portsmouth dockyard, while Charles's attempt to develop and print a film using the hand-in-box equipment issued to stations without darkrooms resulted in thirty-six blank exposures. He minded much less about this than about the lack of progress with his case. He thought he had reconciled himself to a long haul but after a week of hearing nothing further from C/Sovbloc or A1 he began to feel unreasonably like a favourite who had been dropped.

The week following was spent wholly in London. A silver-haired lady who lived in Eaton Square and looked as if she might have been fashioned from finest bone china headed the forgery section. Her voice was soft, polite and persuasive, and she was explaining how she became a forger when Charles was called from the room by Rebecca.

"Sorry, but someone's been ringing your official number, your Foreign Office one. A1's got the message and wants you to go over to HO a.s.a.p. Exciting life you lead."

"Not as exciting as it sounds."

"You don't have to tell me that."

Half an hour later he was again with Hugo in Hookey's office, with its backdrop of slow trains and its interior of pipe-smoke.

"They've obviously traced you and decided you're clean," said Hugo. "That's good."

"All we know," said Hookey slowly, "is that after delay your call was returned. Koslov"—Hookey rarely called him Lover Boy—"very likely did report meeting you. He'd be foolish not to. And they probably have traced you, in which case they've probably assumed—rightly in your case, wrong in others—that because you were in the services you must have joined us, not the Foreign Office. Why they should agree that the cultivation, as they probably and correctly see it, should continue—if that's what he's ringing to say—we don't know."

When Charles rang back Viktor sounded as if he were reading from a prepared text. "Charles, I am very pleased to speak to you. I am sorry that my busy work has prevented me from replying sooner. But now I am free to arrange to meet if you would like."

Charles imagined him under instruction and speaking before an audience, as he was himself. He felt closer to him, as if they were two victims conspiring together. It was, after all, their relationship that was being traded upon, certainly by one side, probably by both. "I should be delighted to meet, Viktor. When would suit you?"

"At any time for me. Please choose."

Charles chose an evening, since dinner was likely to be more leisurely than lunch. "Where would you like?"

"Please. It is your city."

Charles suggested South of the Border, a newly converted warehouse not far from the Young Vic. It was cheerful, not too expensive, with good table separation.

"Great, we're in business," said Hugo afterwards. "Can't approve of your choice of restaurant, of course. Too close to HO. You should've thought of that. Anyway, too late now."

"We're in business but what sort?" asked Hookey quietly.

"Only one way to find out. Charles will know on Wednesday."

"Perhaps." Hookey put down his pipe with a wintry smile. "Come and talk about it beforehand."

"Yes, do, with me, too," said Hugo.

On the day of the dinner Charles took the afternoon off, ostensibly only in order to let in the electrician but also to allow himself to relax and prepare, without the risk of being kept at work because an exercise over-ran. The electrician took only as long as it took to remove a well-cooked mouse from a junction box. The call-out fee was substantial and the unfamiliar light showed up a lot of dust and dirt.

He booked an early table, as Hookey had said the Russians in London often ate early, and gave himself time to go by cab or tube, hoping that Viktor would drink a lot. He bought an *Exchange & Mart* to read on the way, since, without disloyalty to his father's Rover, the feline Mark 11 Jaguars of the 1960s were again featuring in his automotive daydreams during lectures, where they were joined by a 1950s Bristol 405 sometimes parked in Queensgate. It was not for sale but its swooping curvaceous lines haunted him like the memory of a woman glimpsed. When approaching something that needed thought and energy, he welcomed distraction.

As he was about to leave, the phone rang. He hesitated; he would have left it but feared it might be a cancellation. It was Mary, his sister.

"May I come round?" Her voice sounded small, a sign that there was something wrong.

"No—I mean, yes, later. I'll come to you. I've got to work now."

"At home? At this time?"

"No, I've got to go out to meet someone. Someone from work."

"So it's social, you mean." Irritation revived her.

Charles tried not to sound the same. "No, it's an official dinner. Diplomatic."

"At an embassy?"

"In a restaurant. What's the matter, anyway?"

"Nothing's the matter."

"It sounded as if there was."

"No. Anyway, you're busy. I was just going to say that Peter is going to sell his flat."

Charles floundered. He was sure Peter wasn't the fiancé, but he'd been wrong before. He didn't recall any discussion of flats.

"If you're interested," she added.

"Oh yes."

He struggled on, hoping to pick up clues by her responses. She was referring to a discussion they'd had months ago about a friend of hers who might sell his flat in the fashionable Boltons area between Chelsea and Kensington. It would be at the very limit of what Charles could afford but he had to buy it, she had told him then. It was ridiculous that he threw all his money away on rent when it could go into a mortgage that would get him on the property ladder. Happy in her small house in Battersea, a timely purchase, she pursued opportunities for her brother with a zeal that touched him, but which he never matched. He would get round to it one day, he told himself, and went on thinking about cars.

"He's not sure exactly what the price will be but if you're definitely interested he won't put it with agents until you've seen it, so you'd be able to get it for less because he wouldn't have to pay the agent's commission," she said.

"Tell him I am, definitely."

"You haven't seen it yet."

"I don't need to. You have. I trust your judgement. But I must go now."

"The other thing is James," she said, reverting to her small voice.

She was no longer sure that her engagement was a good idea but was unable, or unwilling, to say precisely why. Charles interrupted to say that he would call round after his dinner. She urged him not to, unless he really wanted. By the time he put the phone down he had ten minutes to get to Waterloo. He ran out of the flat and jumped in the Rover.

He need not have. For half an hour he sat alone at his upstairs corner table, circling cars in *Exchange & Mart* which he had no intention of buying. Most of the time he watched the door, the stairs and the people at nearby tables, regretting his choice of somewhere inconvenient to the Soviet Embassy and not easy to find. At least there was no one he recognised from the office, though that should not have been a problem since they were not supposed to acknowledge each other in public. It was apparently fairly common for Russians not to turn up for meetings, nor to offer apologies or explanations afterwards unless asked.

Viktor appeared, unobtrusive and smiling, during one of the brief periods when Charles was not looking. "I am sorry to be late. I was trying hard to find the restaurant. I was looking in the streets behind the Old Vic but then I remembered you had said the Young Vic. And then I found it. I am sorry."

His grey suit looked cheap and did not fit well, his silver tie was thin and too tightly knotted and the cuffs of his white shirt slightly frayed. His charm apart, it was hard to see him as a plausible wealthy Finnish businessman. They talked at first of Oxford acquaintances and then of their own lives since, without either probing deeply. Hookey had warned that most communist officials of any nationality would answer one question, and generally a second, but would shy away at three in a row. Viktor asked few questions and so, anxious that the dinner should not appear too much an interview, Charles volunteered whatever of himself he felt might reasonably have been asked. He did, however, establish that Viktor was a member of the Party.

"We like Party members," Hookey had said, with a smile. "For one thing, people often can't get valuable access unless they are. The Party controls everything, including the KGB and the military, although at the higher levels they're all interpenetrated. It's the whole *nomenklatura* business. For another thing, a good deal of information is distributed internally via the Party cells during their interminable meetings and if you can penetrate one cell you can sometimes discover a lot about what's going on in the rest of the hive."

The only subject to which Viktor returned unprompted was Charles's bachelorhood. "You have never met anyone you wanted to marry?"

"I suppose not."

"No one?"

"There was one girl—well, two, I suppose—I could imagine marrying, but not yet."

"My wife has her work to do in the embassy but she misses our child."

"And Chantal?" Charles wanted to ask, but it was too soon. The marriage theme had potential, since Viktor's interest in Charles's uxorial state was perhaps a concealed way of talking about his own, but he needed help with the menu. His English was easily good enough but he was reluctant to decide, gratefully following wherever Charles led. The house red, leek and potato soup and steak and chips seemed likely to appeal more to him than the less familiar Spanish or Mexican dishes. Charles kept trying to imagine the diffident, cautiously friendly man across the table as the ardent lover Claire described, the man who dared both to love and deceive her and to deceive his wife and his security authorities. Also, surely, himself, where she was concerned. But the only moment of unease was when Charles asked, with a casualness that sounded unconvincing to his own ears, whether Viktor had had to get permission to meet. He knew the answer but asked in order to see where the subject might lead.

Viktor's blue-grey eyes were steady but watchful. "Of course I asked for permission. It is practice for a diplomat."

"Was it difficult?"

"Should it be difficult? It is normal for officials to meet."

"I just wondered whether our knowing each other already made it more or less difficult."

"It made no difference, I think."

The noisy group some tables away became suddenly noisier. Charles remarked on them. Viktor looked across. "Two of the men are German."

"Do you speak German?"

Viktor nodded slowly, as if his thoughts were elsewhere. This was the nearest he had come, Charles realised, to answering any question with a straightforward yes or no. Either he answered with a question of his own, or he made a statement. Charles suspected he might himself have succumbed to what Hookey had warned against, the professional vice of being too focussed, too direct in leading the conversation. Too much concentration on questions you wanted answering, or on answers you sought without wanting to ask, could mean that you were never relaxed enough to listen. He was in charge of the conversation, which was as the training urged, but sensed that his determination might reduce what he was in charge of to something that merely fitted his preconceptions. Viktor, who had asked almost nothing, remained somehow free.

"I read German better than I speak it," he resumed, still nodding to himself. "Recently I read a German novel, Thomas Mann's *Doktor Faustus*. It is a very great novel but very bourgeois and therefore not well known in my country." He smiled. "Do you know this book, Charles?"

Charles did not.

"It is for me the greatest exposition of the Faust theme. I am fascinated by that, you see, and I have read every example, I think, even your own Christopher Marlowe's in Elizabethan English. But Mann's is the greatest for our century. Is it also in English? Are you allowed to read it?"

Charles smiled at the teasing. Viktor spoke on the Faust theme and its appeal for him throughout coffee, with an energy and conviction far removed from his earlier diffidence. Charles was happy to relinquish his sense of directing and controlling their meeting until afterwards, when they stood outside on the pavement, still talking, and he had to decide whether to offer Viktor a lift back and how far to push for the next meeting. "Your aim should be to come away with an agreement to meet again," Hookey had said. "That's all. A date might be a push too far. Be easy with him. Try to find a reason for meeting again, apart from liking each other's faces. One that he can give to his own people. Part on easy terms."

"Let me give you a lift back," Charles said.

"May we walk?" Viktor buttoned his raincoat.

"Well, yes, but it's quite a long way."

"I mean, around here. I am ignorant of this part of London and should like to see the river which must be very near. Also, I should like to continue our very interesting conversation."

"So should I. Let's walk." Briefly, Charles felt himself to be on the receiving end of a too-directed passage of conversation, but brushed the thought aside. He led the way along a back street parallel with the railway, then under one of the railway arches where a small workshop rebuilt old Citroen Light Fifteens. There followed terraced streets of nineteenth-century railway workers' cottages, one of the quiet secrets of central London, still undiscovered and with only one or two houses renovated. There were corner shops and a pub, a quiet, pleasantly dingy place of faded brown and cream paintwork which Charles used during his few solitary lunchtimes. They crossed Stamford Street and headed slightly downstream of the new National Theatre, along partly cobbled streets which shone with recent rain. Then they were among dark abandoned warehouses, overgrown bomb sites and temporary car parks now decades old. The river was very near but it was not clear whether there was a way to it through the warehouses. Charles spotted a dark narrow alley between two tall crumbling buildings which appeared to lean dangerously towards each other. At the end of the alley he could see the lights of the far bank of the Thames. "The river's this way."

They stumbled in the alley over unseen rubble. The end was dark up to head height and he feared a wall, but as they got closer he could see steps. "Up here," he said, with unjustified confidence.

Viktor chuckled behind him. "This is a good place for murder, Charles."

"We wouldn't be the first, I daresay."

From the top of the steps they had a full view of the river. It was low tide and the lights of the far bank were reflected in the pools and glistening mud of the littered foreshore. A set of wooden steps, rickety and partly rotted, led down to it. They could see and hear the traffic on the Embankment but where they stood, only a couple of hundred yards away, was darkness and dereliction, with grass and weeds growing from blackened brickwork and a large rusty iron derrick and platform projecting ominously above them. It was the foreshore that, differently configured, Shakespeare would have known. Trusting to Viktor's fondness for literary reference, Charles remarked on it.

Viktor nodded. "May I ask your opinion, Charles, as to whom you believe to be the most typical English writers? Not the most famous, or the best, but the most typical."

Charles pondered aloud. Chaucer? Ben Jonson? Dr. Johnson? Jane Austen? Trollope? Scott, the Scottish voice of English romanticism about Scotland? Galsworthy? Wells?

"Yes, yes," said Viktor eagerly. "You are confirming my theory. You see, I never before had the chance to ask an English person about this question. My theory is that the greatest writers—Shakespeare, of course, Milton or Dickens—are often not the most typical, even if they are chosen to be representative. They are different. This is true for all nationalities. People regard the greatest writers as essential and typical but they are not both. They speak for all mankind, not only for part of it. People say Tolstoy and Dostoyevsky are typically Russian but they are not. Of course, they could not be anything but Russian—they are essentially Russian—but they are not typical. Chekov or Gogol are more typical. It is the same for some people who are not writers. We might regard them as typically English or Russian, and they may be essentially so, but they are also more than that. They are for all the world."

The last phrase echoed from Charles's lectures. It was an old story, at least as old as Lenin, the Soviet communist appeal to international brotherhood, the implicit link with the emotional tradition of Christianity. National divisions are destructive and obsolescent. Help us to help mankind. Tell us your country's secrets. It had worked powerfully on western liberal intellectuals, Lenin's "useful idiots," and had been deployed to great effect ever since in the recruitment of agents throughout the world.

Viktor's expression of the sentiment in this context indicated, he thought, how it permeated their culture. "Shall we take a chance and go down?" He pointed at the rotten wooden steps.

"I will go where you go, Charles."

There was enough light to pick a way between pools, driftwood, plastic containers, old iron, bottles, bits of rope, fridges and bicycle frames. No boats moved on the river and in its eerie isolation the foreshore felt years rather than yards away from the public life of the city. The incoming tide lapped incessantly and a rat scuttled from beneath an empty milk crate back to the darkness of the river wall. Charles had read that you were never more than about three feet from a rat in London. Maybe it was six feet, or sixty.

He was not concentrating. Viktor had said something about Charles's father but it could not have been what Charles thought. "I'm sorry?"

Viktor stood beside the Thames, the lights showing one side of his pale face. He was turned towards Charles and speaking slowly. "I have been asked to tell you that we owe you, your mother and your sister many thousands of pounds for the work your father did for us. Of course, he never told anyone and it is a surprise for you and your family. He was one of the Englishmen we were talking about. A patriot for mankind, for all the world, not only for his own country. He did not want money from us but we kept it for him, all that we would have paid him for his years of work. It is in Moscow. We honour our debts and we would like you and your family to have it. We think your father would have liked that. But we must discuss with you how to get it to you, since we do not wish to get you into trouble, in your official position. This is what I have been asked to say to you, Charles."

A breeze had got up and the water lapped more rapidly. The rat, or another, crept back to the crate. Charles stared at the ripples. Of all the questions he might have asked, he chose the one that felt most safely academic. The office would like it. "Who asked you to say this?"

"Our people in Moscow."

"Your people?"

"Yes, Charles. My people are like your people." His tone was gentle.

"How do you know that?"

"Charles, I think we both know the game we are playing." His smile stopped as he looked at Charles.

"Tell me again," said Charles.

Viktor clearly knew the files and spoke with well-rehearsed confidence. Charles's father, he said, had been serving in Germany with the British Army's Royal Engineers at the end of the Great Patriotic War. He had earlier served, as Charles knew, with distinction in North Africa and Normandy. The sufferings of the people he had seen had made him determine to continue the struggle against fascism wherever it appeared. He had reasoned that the one country most likely to do this was the one that had suffered most from fascism and which had a strong ideology with which to oppose it, unlike the capitalist west which was contaminated by it. Having been allied with the Russians as a soldier in their victorious struggle against the Nazis, he had therefore volunteered to continue to help them in the struggle for peace and justice during the years that followed. He had shared with them the knowledge gained during his work on British establishments and embassies during all the following years, until his sad and unexpected death. His work had been of great value and the Centre had been sorry to be deprived by death of the opportunity to thank him for it. Now they wished to convey their gratitude and the money owed, but they realised that the British authorities would regard his work as merely spying and would make trouble for Charles. He would probably lose his job. But the Centre knew that Charles's father had worked in secret not to damage his country but to safeguard mankind, and they did not wish Charles to suffer for it. They wanted to discuss how the money could be transferred to him or to his family, or whether he would prefer them to keep it—until later, perhaps. Meanwhile, it was certain that no one would ever know what Charles's father had done, so Charles had nothing to fear from Moscow.

"I can promise you that," Viktor said.

Charles felt as if his stomach had been taken out, leaving a chasm beneath into which he would fall endlessly as in a childhood dream, if he let himself. To keep going he had to concentrate on what was before him, staring into Viktor's eyes, not trusting himself to look away. It was like skating not on thin ice but on no ice; momentum was all.

"This is a more professional evening than I had appreciated, Viktor."

Viktor nodded, taking it as a compliment. "It is an obligation upon us all."

They had every detail of his father's overseas assignments, their dates, durations and purposes. There was no doubt they knew it all. At the time Charles did not even try to reconcile what he had heard with his memories of a man he had thought of as an ideal—perhaps, as Viktor would have it, an essential—kind of Englishman, modest, conscientious, loyal, patriotic, concerned to do things properly, whether it was securing an education for his children or putting up a shelf, and as honest as the day. He postponed thought; the implications were too great to be thought about then, though they could be felt.

He managed a smile that felt like a grimace. "But what makes you think I share your profession, Viktor?"

"Because that is what the Centre told me. They know. Perhaps your father told them. They sent you this." He took an envelope from his inside pocket.

Charles put it straight into his own. It felt like a concession to look at it now. "He died before I joined the Foreign Office," he said, emphasising the two last words.

The emphasis was lost on Viktor. "Perhaps it is because you were in the British Army."

"It doesn't follow." He was beginning to believe in the façade of his own composure. There was even some relish in anticipating the security branch tooth-sucking in Head Office when they learned that he was Sovbloc Red already, within months of joining. It would be a pleasure to administer shock, almost a revenge for his own. Virgin covers were painstakingly and expensively protected for as long as possible, especially for anyone interested, as he had been, in a Sovbloc posting. That was to assume, of course, that he had enough of a career left after this to merit any posting anywhere.

He still clung to Viktor's eyes, as to a rope thrown to him in the river. Viktor returned his gaze with more sympathy than if he had looked upon him solely as a quarry, but still watchfully, with cool assessment. Charles admired that; that was right, as it should be.

He broke off and walked back towards the wooden steps. Some were missing, others wobbly. "Be careful," he warned. "Tread on the ones I tread on." Acting as if he were responsible for Viktor was a minor re-assertion of authority. At the top they paused and looked back at the river.

"You will think about it, Charles?"

Pride forbade any display of concern. He sensed he was regaining the upper hand. They were the *demandeurs* and Viktor was no doubt under pressure to return with an answer. "Think about what?"

"How you would like us to pay you the money." The brute fact hung in the air between them. Viktor was nervous now. "We can meet again to discuss it."

"Perhaps we should do that." Charles went decisively down the steps on the landward side.

Viktor remained at the top, his face in shadow. "Charles—I—am sorry for you. I am sorry to be doing this."

"Is this what they told you to say or are you becoming less pro-fessional?"

"Yes, and yes."

Viktor refused a lift, preferring to return by tube. Charles walked with him to Waterloo. They talked about football. Viktor was a keen Liv-erpool supporter. "It is permitted to support capitalist football teams," he said. "But not if they would play against Moscow Dynamos." He smiled but his expression when they shook hands was resigned. "I am sorry, Charles. I like you. I hope we go on meeting anyway, you know."

"Don't worry, I know it's not personal." No more than one soldier killing another on the battlefield, he thought, but he felt he was gaining strength by giving reassurance and wanted to show no resentment. "It's not your fault. Exploiting friendships is what we all do."

Charles drove slowly to his sister's house. He was probably over the alcohol limit but didn't care. He felt invincibly sober, as if life from now on held no alternative. His watch told him they had spent three and a half hours together—important for the write-up—but already he could sense his own history being rearranged into before and after this event, already he was looking back on his life up to three and a half hours ago as a state of innocence. Yet still he withheld thought, his mind hovering, uncommitted, in suspension. It was not yet digestible. It couldn't be processed. It was not only his memories of his father that would need rebuilding, but his sense of his own past. For the time being the way to keep going was to do just that, to keep doggedly going, one foot in front of another, like running up a ploughed field. It was also what you did after a bomb had exploded beneath you, as he knew well from Belfast. You simply carried on, clinging to routine, procedure, reassembling anything around you that was still recognisable.

He rang twice on Mary's door before noticing that there were no lights behind the curtains, but then the hall light came on. He did not relish spending half the night listening to her problems with her fiancé, but it was preferable to the alternative. It did not occur to him to tell her about their father; she did not even know what he himself did.

The door was answered by a tousle-haired man wearing a towel. "I'm Mary's brother," said Charles. "I said I'd drop round."

"I'm James, her—you know—we're engaged. She's asleep. D'you want me to wake her?"

"Just tell her I called. Sorry to disturb you. We have met, haven't we?"

"Think so. At your mother's house. Can't remember when, I'm afraid."

"Me neither. Well, sorry to have bothered you."

The man held out his hand and they shook. "Don't worry. It's all right. See you sometime." He grinned. "Well, quite a lot, I guess."

He would be all right, Charles thought as he turned the Rover onto Battersea Park Road towards the wine bar where Roger and the others were spending the evening. Through the steamed-up windows he made out plain wooden tables, candles, potted plants and ferns. The traffic held him up outside, conveniently because he was still undecided whether to go in. He wanted the distraction of company, but not much company. A man wearing wide flares and with long dark hair straggling over his Afghan coat walked in with a very tall girl whose mohair covered

74

her mini-skirt and who was otherwise all bare thighs, boots and spangles. Must be freezing, he thought. While the door was still open Gerry and Rebecca came out, putting on coats. She wore a white woollen hat and threw a long white scarf around her neck with an extravagant gesture. Gerry shuffled into a voluminous old duffel-coat. They were laughing. Charles moved on with the traffic. He didn't feel up to being merry.

Nor did he want to be alone, yet. He drove to Hugo's Wandsworth house. Hugo had said to call round afterwards, if there was time and if he were satisfied there was no surveillance. He had forgotten about surveillance, but no one turned in the street after him, or came the other way. There was no need to talk about it tonight, of course; nothing would change overnight. But the urge to talk about something—anything—was strong.

He made out Anna's form through the stained-glass door as she came down the hall. Her eyes widened. "Charles."

"I'm sorry it's so late. It's probably too late. I should've rung—"

"You don't look well. You look tired. Come in."

When she said it, he felt it. "Perhaps I am. It's just a—I was going to talk to Hugo. But it can wait till tomorrow. I needn't have bothered you. Sorry."

"Hugo's out. Come in."

"Just tell him—"

"Charles, come in." She spoke sternly, with a smile. They went through to the kitchen. He declined a drink, so she put on the kettle. "Hugo's playing war games at the house of a fellow commander-in-chief. He won't be long."

She asked no questions. She would know all about need to know, better than he since her Sovbloc posting with Hugo could well have involved her in casework more delicate and risky than anything he was likely to do in London. She picked up a cup from the crowded draining board and dried it with the tea-towel, holding it close to her body. When she had dried the second cup she stood holding it in the cloth and facing him. "Are you sure you're all right?"

He nodded, feeling quite suddenly that he couldn't trust himself to speak.

"Sit down," she said gently.

"I'm okay standing." His voice sounded gruff to his own ears.

"You're making me nervous."

He sat at the kitchen table and watched as she dried saucers and tea-spoons and made the tea. Observing the lift near the ends of her dark eyebrows, the way her blonde hair was pushed back behind her ear on one side, the profile of her cheekbone when she turned, the faint, doubt-less hated, crow's-feet on her olive skin and the deft, unselfconscious movements of her small hands made it easy to imagine what it would be like to be obsessed. He had never been obsessed. Was this how Viktor watched the woman he knew as Chantal? Viktor obsessed, or Viktor in love, was something else he could imagine more easily since their walk by the river. Did Viktor feel the movement of an eyebrow as a sudden catch in his heart? Was a detail, an accident of physiognomy such as angle of cheek in relation to eye sufficient to banish all other thoughts from Viktor's head whenever he noticed it? Was it for something like this that Viktor risked marriage, career, liberty?

"Penny for your thoughts," she said with a smile, as she put tea-pot and biscuits on the table and sat.

It was a phrase his grandmother used often when he was a child. "Deal. I was thinking about deal."

"Not cherry or mahogany?" She put a black tea-cosy over the pot.

"Your question reminded me of my grandmother. She also used to use one of those."

She sighed. "I'm a bit of an old tea-cosy myself, I'm afraid. At least, I feel I'm becoming one."

"No, you're not." His voice felt gruff again. It was strange to feel his voice out of control. Why should the voice be affected? "This evening I learned that my father—" It came in a rush, taking him by surprise, but a sudden tightening in his throat stopped him. Saying it would change it. So far it was private, something that, however corrosive or overwhelm-ing, could be assimilated and dealt with privately. Saying it would give it a public existence, what in Viktor's world they might call an objective reality. It would be part of history, public property, something for others to play with, yet every twitch on the wire he would feel in his heart, like the movement of an eyebrow.

She was looking at him, her elbows on the table, holding the pot by handle and spout.

"Sorry," he said. "I can't—not now. Another time." It was difficult to go on. It was absurd, what words did. Ridiculous, stupid.

She put down the tea-pot and put her hand on his. "I could see there was something wrong the moment I saw you. It was written all over your face."

"Sorry to burden you with it." He held her hand. Her grip answered his. His own reactions astonished him. He had to breathe deeply to get the words out.

"You haven't. It's not a burden, whatever it is." The front door opened. She gave a brief squeeze and removed her hand. "Tell Hugo everything or nothing. Whatever you feel like. We can talk another time."

She left them. Over tea, then whisky, he talked to Hugo for an hour, describing everything, including the riverside walk, but omitting all mention of his father. "He was interested in my family background," he said, "but I didn't volunteer anything."

"Quite right, quite right. Make them work for it. He's probably been told to do a pen-picture of you. They like to know about the family in case there's any angle they can get hold of. Don't suppose there is in your case, is there? Nothing you know of? Good. We must remember, though, that he's on paper as MFA, not KGB. It's Hookey who seems so convinced otherwise. What was your impression?"

"I think Hookey may be right."

Hugo frowned, twitching a couple of times. "Hookey isn't always right. No one's perfect even in the office. But from what you say Lover Boy's responses and interests do sound more like those of an intelligence officer than a diplomat. Interesting if true, as the Foreign Office always says." He laughed. "Now, your write-up."

Hugo considered aloud whether Charles should report by minute, memo, note for file or contact note. He seemed happier with the bureaucracy of casework than with casework itself, and Charles was content with the distraction. He had not lied directly. He was still postponing. And if the Russians didn't tell anyone, as Viktor had promised, what difference would it make to the world? None, except that he would spend the rest of his career living a lie. But was it true, or were they making it up? That was something he had to know; had to, and the only way to learn more was to talk about it to Viktor again, and perhaps again and again. Thus would the first lie become a second, and so on. Lies never came singly.

So far, he told himself, he had not lied. But then he recalled a remark of his father's, made long ago. "The essence of a lie is the intent to deceive." They were walking above Turville, near the windmill, his father wearing a cap, buttoned-up sports jacket and scarf. It must have been winter. Charles was still in the army and it must have been sometime after he had returned from Northern Ireland, because that was the context, a Belfast inquiry or inquest. They had paused by a stile and his father had tapped the top of it with his blackthorn as he emphasised each word: "The essence of a lie is the intent to deceive." Well, he should know all about that, if Viktor were to be believed. But what status did the precept have in the mouth of a man living a great lie? Did it have greater weight because spoken by an expert on the subject? Was it given added edge by bitter self-knowledge? Or was it rendered worthless on the lips of one who didn't—wouldn't—see what he was doing as lying, preferring to see it as service in a just cause?

It was only when undressing back at the flat that he remembered the envelope. At the time he had pushed it into his pocket, determined to concede nothing, to rise to no bait, to expose not even the vulnerability of interest, but it weighed in his pocket as he hung his jacket. He shut his bedroom door and, squatting on the mattress on the floor, opened it.

For the next few days he went through the motions: got up, went to work, did what he was told, sustained social intercourse. His preparations for Exercise Danish Blue passed muster, for the time being. In lectures he asked no questions and in exercises got away with the minimum. He forgot things—pens, keys, numbers, designations, arrangements. All the normal, everyday activities and routines, previously accomplished without thought, now required effort. He kept putting off his write-up, though Hugo pestered him for it because he wanted it on top of Hookey's in-tray when Hookey returned from an overseas trip. Charles was glad Hookey was away. It prolonged postponement.

Inside, he was dazed, picking his way through rubble. Among the missing was his sense of himself. His father, the man he thought he knew, had gone for good, of course. All his memories, the background from which he had grown so unquestioningly, now meant something different. His new knowledge entailed the construction a new man, a much less fatherly father. But it was also his own self—he, himself, the "I" he had used with such confidence because taken so completely for granted—that was missing. Or could not be put into action, which was perhaps the same thing. He should move on, he thought—he was not, after all, his father, something of himself must surely be left—but he could not bring himself to re-engage in anything. And the past was now robbed of all possibility of nostalgia.

He wanted to talk, and not to talk. He wanted most to talk to Anna, but he couldn't do that without talking to the office. It would be an unfair burden on her, no matter what she said. And if he did tell the office, how would they react? So much in his family, his background, in the whole inclination of his past had led to the sort of service he sought to perform. By confessing he might lose it all. By not confessing, he would kill the meaning of it.

Twice he started his write-up and abandoned it. The third time, staying late in the lecture room after the others had gone, he did it in one go and took it to Hugo's secretary for typing the next morning. Misleading on paper was different, he found, to misleading in speech: easier, on the one hand, starker on the other. The brief account contained no untruths but the spaces between paragraphs seemed like chasms when he read it through. He heard nothing from Hugo and for two days more mechanically continued with the course. It was hard to make anything matter. Near the end of the second day Hookey's secretary, Maureen, rang to ask him to drop by when lectures finished that day. No hurry; Hookey would be there until late.

The outer office was empty and the door to Hookey's ajar when Charles arrived. The inner office was lit by the subdued light of a desk lamp rather than by the usual harsh strip lighting. Hookey was slumped in his swivel chair, side-on to his desk, reading a file. His hook nose and stubby pipe were reflected in the rain-blurred window. The pipe was a straight-stemmed Lovat with a short, shouldered mouthpiece, the sort designed by Lord Lovat during the Second World War to fit in his battledress pocket. They had been Charles's father's favourite.

Hookey put the file face down on his desk. All three of his trays were empty but there was one paper on the blotter before him, Charles's write-up. "Might be wise to shut the door," said Hookey quietly, picking up the paper. When Charles was seated he took the pipe from his mouth. "Your account, which I received from Hugo, who seems pleased with it, is more interesting for what it does not say than for what it does. Now, I won't pretend to know what it does not say but I'm damn sure it doesn't say it, if you see what I mean." He held up his hand. "Nor am I asking you to tell me. Not yet. Often in this office what's not put on paper is more important than what is. God knows, I've kept enough things from files myself. That's why no history of this service could ever be comprehensive. But there is one thing more important than anything we might choose to record or not record. That is truth. The truth has to be told to someone, sometime. It almost always is in the end, anyway, so better tell it to the right people in good time. In an organisation in which deception is an essential tool, it is equally essential that we should be honest with ourselves. Never lie to the office. That is the great thing. Once you do, you're lost. Everything is skewed from then on. And if the office is not honest with itself, it is lost. Professional deceit demands clarity of thought, and clarity is impossible without honesty. This is as near to an institutional religious creed as we have. Honesty is the first and last quality one looks for in an intelligence officer." He leaned forward and tamped down his pipe. "That's my sermon, Charles. I'm not saying any more. Up to you now. Eh?" He raised his eyebrows as the match flared in the bowl.

Charles hesitated, not through indecision but through the self-indulgence of prolonging a life-changing choice, or so it felt. He had sensed all along that he would tell Hookey but knowing that he could still choose not to, even now, was the source of a novel sense of power, like contemplation of an act of revenge that would be utterly self-destructive. He did not luxuriate in it for long. "Viktor told me that my father was a KGB spy," he said.

Hookey slowly shook out his match and sat back in his chair, saying nothing.

The next morning photographs of Charles's father were spread across Hookey's desk. The envelope had contained two dozen. The earliest showed him in Berlin after the war, wearing battledress; others, dated in pencil on the back, were from the ensuing decades, in various countries where his work had taken him. He was open-necked and smiling in India and Thailand, fur-hatted and duffel-coated in snow-covered Sweden, pin-striped in Geneva and New York, tweed-jacketed and corduroyed in Rome, in shirtsleeves and—unusually—sunglasses in Mexico. Charles had very familiar memories of the wartime, ex–Royal Navy duffel-coat that his mother had tried vainly for years to get rid of. Worn and threadbare, it had retreated to the security of the shed, where Charles had found it after the funeral, along with old brogues, tweeds and hats, all stubbornly British, doggedly unfashionable. The coat was there still, and Charles often thought his father should have been buried in it. Such things, more even than the fact that he had never heard his father utter anything remotely sympathetic to the imposition of international socialism, made it still harder to credit that he had systematically, deliberately, over many years, let—as he himself would have put it—the side down.

Yet it was impossible not to credit the story told by the photographs. Ranging from soldierly youth to middle age, mostly black and white but with some of the more recent in colour, they comprised an incomplete but fundamentally accurate itinerary of his father's travels, and were taken with his obvious collaboration. Some also showed his father with another man—thickset, crinkly-haired, with broad peasant's features and a broad grin—who appeared, from a couple of pencilled inscriptions, to be called Igor. His father's case officer, presumably, though that would have been a work name, not a real one. From the same inscriptions, it appeared his father's KGB code name was Builder.

"They often choose code names which reflect the subject," Hookey had said when Charles told him the night before. "Odd, given their security mania in other respects. We'll check out Igor."

They had talked until late the night before. Once embarked, it was easy, with no tightening of the throat, no effort to control himself. He talked quickly, as if describing someone else's case, the task itself compelling a distancing perspective, a temporary adoption of other eyes. Hookey showed no surprise. His questions were like a doctor's, in that Charles felt that his answers were being fitted into a body of knowledge and a context unknown. He had no sense of the significance of what he said, only that it was significant.

At the end Hookey said he would like to go over it again in the morning. Hugo would have to be told, partly because he would have to provide cover for Charles's absence from his course. "I can only imagine what this must be like for you," Hookey said, "and I can only urge you to keep with it, wherever it leads. Recognition of reality is the beginning of wisdom and understanding, and we've got some way to go yet. See me at any time, say anything, ask anything. It's a bit late for you to find yourself an attractive dinner date and plenty of wine tonight, but that's what you should do from now on. Every night."

Now, the three of them sat looking at the photographs, the images that had haunted Charles, night and day, since he had first seen them. The early ones, showing his father in battledress at about his own age, had a suggestion of raffishness that was new. Either Charles had never noticed it before or his new knowledge gave every image a fresh edge. In the later ones his father was more familiar, not only in his clothes but his stance and expression, yet he still seemed subtly and radically different. He had acquired the glamour of unknowability, a strangeness emphasised rather than masked by such homely items as the duffel-coat. It wasn't only that he was in unfamiliar locations; it was as if he were photographed with another woman, wearing clothes his wife had given him. It was only now, as Charles sat staring at them with the others, that he realised he had always assumed his father to be somehow more innocent than himself. In need of protection, almost. It was his own innocence that angered him now.

This unpredictable anger, directed either at his father or himself and coming and going like bouts of nausea, had made it easy to face Hugo. When they met in his office that morning, anger made Charles feel careless of anything Hugo said about not being told. He almost looked forward to a show of indignation and the chance to display his own indifference.

Instead, Hugo was subdued and slightly embarrassed, as if confronting someone recently bereaved. "Hookey briefed me," he said, before Charles said anything. "I'm very sorry. How absolutely awful for you."

"It's quite all right." Charles felt he must sound absurdly stiff. "I mean, these things happen."

"Do they? Do they? Not often, I hope. At least, not in this service. Thank God." He stood and came round his grade 4 desk, holding out his hand. They shook hands in silence. Hugo twitched and sat again. "But we must not let emotion run away with us. There are arrangements to make. We have a duty to be impersonal."

"Quite, yes." Charles sat.

"But I must say." Hugo leaned forward, his elbows on the desk, hands clasped and face turned to the wall as if he couldn't bring himself to look at Charles. "How—how absolutely awful for you."

"Thank you. I hope you didn't mind my not mentioning it before."

"Of course not. Quite understandable." Hugo nodded at the wall. "Your own father. Awful. Absolutely. Never known a case like it."

It was a relief when they finally addressed what Hugo referred to as the logisitics of the enhanced security perimeter now to be constructed around the case. Charles's course was told he had been summoned on some urgent positive vetting inquiry concerning someone else; he was said to know one of the referees. It would take all day and, PV-ing being always a confidential matter, he should not be asked anything about it. Hugo made neat notes on his clipboard and then led the way into Hookey's office.

Now, during the long silence while Hookey slowly refilled his pipe, Charles let his mind float over all he had said, aware that he had yet to give thought to his mother and the effect on her. She would be devastated; it would be like his father dying all over again.

"There are four aspects," Hookey resumed, without any preliminaries and without looking up. "Firstly, the story the KGB has told. Is it true and how should we handle it? It will have to be investigated and, although we can do a certain—perhaps a considerable—amount ourselves, we shall have to involve MI5. Espionage alleged to have been committed by British subjects is formally their patch. This will almost certainly limit our freedom in deciding how to respond since what is for us an operational case becomes part of their espionage investigation. Secondly, we—"

Hookey jumped up, his chest and stomach showered with ash and sparks after he had bitten too hard on his pipe. He brushed himself down vigorously. "Serves me bloody right. Pipes are like bikes: they can be managed with no hands but it's better with one."

Hugo laughed, Charles smiled. Hookey's use of the plural was another reminder that the personal was becoming public, but Charles's unease was mixed with relief. His anger had faded again and it was good to feel he was not alone, that it was not only his responsibility; although he still felt that he alone would bear the consequences.

Hookey abandoned his pipe. "Secondly, we should consider how this affects the case we were trying to build up. What do we do with your friend now that he has taken us by surprise? Back off, carry on as planned or look for a way of turning it to our advantage? I've no need to tell you which I prefer, so long as we're allowed. Thirdly, since this is likely to take up more of your time than anticipated, Charles, Hugo will need to brief your course officer and secretary—not the whole thing, of course, general terms only—and get them to help with providing you with cover so far as your fellow students are concerned. Fourthly, there is the very important question of how it affects you personally, your family and your career. As for the latter, don't worry. Do not worry. You may think it's bad for your PV-ing status and a disadvantage being Sovbloc Red—but we'll see you all right. It's more the effect on you personally that we have to keep an eye on."

"You're certain it's true?" Charles asked.

"Pretty much." Hookey looked straight for a few moments, as if Charles had said something unusual. "They're certainly capable of fabricating the whole thing and as such it would be an ingenious ploy. Quite apart from the possible bonus of recruiting you, which is of course their aim. Putting money in your bank account is the first step, worthwhile simply for the disruption it causes. Not to mention tying up some of our limited investigatory resources and distracting our attention from real cases. But I've never known them do anything quite like this before and my hunch is that they wouldn't try to play this card here in London right under our noses, risking protest and expulsion, unless they really held it." He continued to watch Charles carefully. "It may seem unfeeling of me to discuss it as a kind of game like this, but that's what it is, albeit a game with consequences. I'd like to pat them on the back and say, well done, boys, nice try, now let's talk turkey. That's what I would like you to be saying to your friend—appreciate you were given no choice, old boy, but no hard feelings, you did it well. Tremendous feather in your cap if it works, life-long difference to your career. Of course, I can't accept but I like you and I want to help you. We could between us make it appear that I have accepted, I could get you information that my people would permit but which would seem like gold dust to yours. And in return you could help me, confidentially, of course. See what I mean?" Hookey raised his eyebrows. "Play it back at them. But all that's for later, if at all. We'd better concentrate on the immediate."

"The investigation," said Hugo. He wrote the word in capitals on his clipboard and underlined it.

"Yes, Hugo," said Hookey. "Start with Martha. All things in this controllerate begin and end with Martha."

Martha was a tall woman of around sixty with pendulous spaniel cheeks, an effect heightened by dangling black cord tied to her glasses. The glasses were elaborate, her lipstick and nail varnish thick and very red. She held a silver cigarette-holder theatrically in one hand and with the other wrote rapidly on a small card with a thin gold pen. The window was open but her small office was still thick with cigarette smoke. Behind her were three grey security cupboards, their drawers open and crammed with filing cards.

Hugo's manner was obsequious. "Martha, may we bother you for one tiny moment?"

Her brown eyes, alarmingly enlarged by her glasses, looked at him without expression and took no cognizance of Charles at all. "Go away, dear, I'm dreaming." Her voice was deep and throaty.

"Oh, sorry, we'll—"

"Don't be a twit, Hugo. You don't think I'd turn you away when you have a young man in tow, do you? I don't meet too many these days."

Her hand, when Charles shook it, was heavy and passive. "Tell Auntie Martha all about it," she said.

Hugo explained that they wanted to identify Igor, though not why, showing her the photographs and rough dates of his known travels. She looked for a long time at the photographs. "It won't be easy, I'm afraid. You'll have to give me time. Difficult." She looked at Charles. "In more ways than one, I daresay. I'll ring you, dear."

"Real character," Hugo said, the door barely closed behind them. "Knows everything that is known about Russian illegals. Igor's almost certainly an illegal, or at least a natural cover officer, because they wouldn't use an officer under official cover and attached to an embassy to follow your father around the world. Look odd. They'd use someone under natural cover with a reason for travelling. If Igor can be i/d'd we'll be one important step closer to confirming what was going on. And if anyone can do it, Martha can. That was one of Stalin's pens she was using." They were going down the stairs to his floor and he paused while his stomach hardened and his lips compressed. "Said to be, anyway. Only she and Hookey and the Chief know how we got it. Thing is, whether your mother was in on it with your father, or not. She's got quite a past—Martha, I mean. SOE in Norway, mistress to a squadron of

Polish pilots who all got killed, that sort of thing. Since then a hundred years of illegals." They had reached his office door when a hand-bell rang loudly from near the lifts back along the corridor. Hugo fumbled hastily in his pockets. "Gosh, the trolley. Got any money?"

Charles mechanically handed over a pound note and Hugo ran without a word along the corridor. Men and women issued suddenly from doors and clustered round a trolley of sandwiches, cakes, sweets, biscuits, chocolates and soft drinks that was pushed out of one of the lifts by a cheerful girl. Charles remained outside Hugo's locked office. It had not occurred to him that his mother might be involved. Hugo's casual reference showed how obvious the possibility would seem to others. The thought filled his head like the sound of the hand-bell a few seconds before.

Hugo reappeared with sandwiches, crisps and a can of fizzy drink that Charles associated with children. He fumbled for his keys. "Pay you back when I get to the bank. You're not a trolley man, then?"

"Never seen it before."

"'Course, you don't have one in training department. Essential in Gloom Hall. Keeps us all going, except for those killed in the rush." He opened the door and laid out the food on his desk. "We'd better decide what to say to Gerry and Rebecca and then I'll have to draft something for MI5. Also for the Foreign Office, just to keep them informed. Though maybe we don't have to tell them yet. Perhaps we should. Not sure. Have a seat."

Charles remained standing. "I hadn't thought about my mother being involved."

"Always more angles to these things than you think." Hugo opened his sandwiches.

"Perhaps I should ask her."

"I should wait a while, if I were you."

"Why?"

"In case she was. Is." He bit into cheese and pickle, his earlier sympathy evaporated now by the excitement of having angles to consider, complications to be pointed out, difficulties to be discovered. "Have a crisp. You'd better get on with your revised write-up. Funny, I had a feeling the other one was a bit, you know, economical. Would've said something if Hookey hadn't jumped in first. Now I can base my draft on your revision. We shall probably have to open a top secret annex to the file." He swallowed and looked pleased. "I shall do a minute."

Hugo liked minutes. He wrote a number during the next few days, careful, often lengthy documents, drafted, worked on, redrafted, encased in layers of security protection and subject to restricted handling procedures. Addressee lists were drawn up, reduced, expanded, debated, modified and discussed, all in the interest, he explained, that Charles's secret was known only to those who really needed to know.

"Rest assured that no one—absolutely no one—will hear anything about this unless they really need to. Quite apart from the security considerations, it would be awful for you personally if it became a subject of office gossip. Personnel will let us know if there's so much as a whisper."

"Personnel will know about it, then?"

"They need to."

"People say they're the leakiest part of the office. Source of most gossip."

"Not on something like this."

Gerry and Rebecca were briefed to give weight to the PV investigation cover to explain any absences on Charles's part. Rebecca, Hugo said, had had a Sovbloc posting before her last and was used to this sort of thing. She was quite a favourite of Hookey's, he added, with a wink that might have been deliberate.

"Carlos, mein Herr," Gerry said when Charles returned to the offices of Rasen, Falcon & Co., "you must say if there's anything we can do to help, with the others or whatever. Anything."

"Thanks, I shall."

"Becky will type your course work for you."

"No she won't," said Rebecca. "I've got enough on my plate. Anyway, the others would realise and it would look odd. But I'll do anything else for him."

Gerry's pliable features became an elongated question mark. "Rrreally, Rrrebecca? I never knew."

"You'd be surprised."

"More than," said Charles. "I'd be delighted."

"So long as you promise never to call me Becky."

His occasional absences passed without comment. The others were either surprisingly tactful or had enough to keep them busy. There was a wearying succession of paper exercises, with much typing, as well as the usual lectures and case histories. Subjects of gossip went rapidly in and out of fashion and for a day or two it was Rebecca and Gerry who held pole position.

"I reckon they're bonking," said Desmond Kimmeridge over tea and biscuits. "All this French Kisser talk is a cover. Don't you think, Charles?"

Charles pictured them outside the wine bar in Battersea. "Could be. Not sure."

"Sure you're not reading your own desires into others?" asked Christopher Westfield, his mouth full of biscuit. "You're jealous, Desmond."

"Of course I am. Fervidly. I'd rather she fancied me. Wouldn't you?"

"As a married man, no. But yes."

"We all do, you see. She's our mother-figure on the course. Oedipus and all that. We subconsciously want to kill Gerry, too. Meanwhile, one has to do what one can to console oneself elsewhere."

Christopher nudged Charles. "What about you? Strikes me you need something to go with that old heap of a car. Better still, something that doesn't go with it. Something better, younger anyway."

"Not much doing at present."

"So Roger says. He says you've never brought a woman back to the flat but that you've started sloping off mysteriously. She married?"

It was a useful suggestion. "Something like that."

Christopher nodded and swallowed the last of his tea. "The world is full of married women."

The next topic was a plot to kidnap Maurice Lydd during one of the final exercises at the Castle. His questions designed to draw attention to himself, his assiduous cultivation of important lecturers and the fact that he usually got off early because of his shorthand and speedier typing annoyed everyone.

"The plot," said Ian Clyde, behind a fog bank of cigarette smoke, "is to nab him on Exercise Finder, the one before the course dinner. Apparently, it's a routine filling and emptying of—of—what are they called?—DLBs, thank you. Delivery—I mean, dead—letter boxes. In the dark, you see. We work in pairs, one finding and filling it, then instructing the other by telegram on how to empty it. Simple, really, don't know why we're bothering. Alastair saw the plan on Rebecca's desk when she was on the phone. So whoever's paired off with Golden Balls will instruct him on where he has to be and when and we'll be able to nab him."

"How?" asked Charles.

"Bag him. In a diplomatic bag if we can nick one large enough. Then bring him back, making ourselves sound like the KGB or IRA or something, and empty him onto the mess floor."

"Why?"

"Because he's Lydd. Always so infuriatingly pleased with himself. Thinks he's got golden balls. Main worry is we won't be able to nab him because he's so bloody greasy."

When he next slipped away, Charles was taken to MI5 in Gower Street by Hugo. "This justifies a car," Hugo said. "There's a bag-run over there, anyway. We'll cadge a lift."

In all but the hottest weather Hugo travelled with his British Warm, brown trilby and heavy rolled umbrella. He carried all three down in the lift, putting on two while they waited in the basement garage.

"New Ford specially for you today, Hugo," said a man in overalls, wiping his hands on a rag. "No misbehaving in it." He looked at Charles. "Not that there's much to tempt you this time."

"What d'you mean, this time, Don?"

The exchange provoked hearty laughter. When the car and driver appeared from the workshop at the back, Hugo took off his hat and coat. "Great character, Don," he said as they drove up the ramp. "Been around about a hundred and fifty years. Used to be the Chief's driver in about 1806. All sorts of derring-do in Europe, post-war. Likeable villain. Get on his right side and he'll look after your own car here. What do you drive?"

"Rover."

"Good."

"Quite an old one."

"Better. Now, the chap we're going to meet, Bernard Kent, one of their top people, hates us. There are a few fuddy-duddies over there who do, just as we've got a few cowboys who hate them, but there really isn't much of that sort of thing now, if there ever was. Though you do come across it now and again, in both services. Regrettable, silly, all fighting the same wars, serving the same interests, after all. Not much of it, fortunately."

Charles nodded.

"Though, I must say, they are as a whole pretty dour and stick-in-the-mud. Terribly territorial. And some, like Bernard, just can't stand us. You'll see."

Charles did not see. Bernard Kent was a big, pale, quiet man occupying a director's office with a long, highly polished table. He was unsmiling but his manner was not unfriendly. Charles's write-up and Hugo's accompanying letter were on the table. "They're putting you through the wringer on this one," he said as they shook hands, then paused while his secretary delivered coffee and biscuits. "The important thing from our point of view, as from yours, Charles, is of course to establish whether what is said about your father is true. That's going to take some time. The secondary question is to decide what it tells us about the man you call Lover Boy." There was an edge of distaste to his voice. "It appears from what you say here that he straightforwardly avowed his KGB provenance. Very unusual thing to do in a western capital, especially here where they know we're pretty ruthless at kicking them out. We must be very sure before we re-categorise him. This sort of thing affects a man's entire career throughout large parts of the world, postings, visas, everything, whether he's aware of it or not. And you say he hasn't tried to recruit or use the prostitute?"

"No."

"So it's a private initiative? He's going off the rails?"

"Seems so."

"Foolish boy." At the end Bernard summed up the main points, dutifully noted by Hugo. "As you're doubtless aware, Charles, this now has to be a Security Service investigation," he concluded. "I must therefore ask you to do nothing more with Lover Boy until we've got somewhere with our enquiries. That may, as I said, take some time. Meanwhile, please come over if there's anything you want to discuss or if there's anything"—he hesitated, choosing his words—"from your family background or from your memories of your father that you think would have any bearing on it, either way. It's bound to be a difficult time for you, at home and at work. I hope your future won't be too much affected. Good luck with your course."

In the Gower Street foyer Hugo once again put on his coat, adjusted his suit and shirt cuffs and positioned his hat. "See what I mean?" he murmured, his back to the guards.

"Not really, no. I thought he was quite friendly. I can see he could be formidable, though."

"Well, he put the kibosh on our operation for a start. That's not very friendly."

"But from their point of view—"

Hugo nodded. "Exactly. Got it in one. That's the trouble." He stepped purposefully and immaculately onto the street and looked about proprietorially, forgetting his umbrella.

Charles collected it. "It's very heavy. What's it made of?"

Hugo didn't answer until they had crossed Gower Street and were heading briskly towards Tottenham Court Road. "Swordstick."

"It's a swordstick?"

Hugo nodded, looking firmly ahead. His trilby was the only one in sight and walking with him made Charles as self-conscious as if he had been wearing it himself. However, possession of a swordstick gave Hugo an almost romantic appeal. "Are they legal?" Charles asked.

"Depends what you do with them."

"Didn't the first chief, the original 'C,' have one? Take it on operations and so on?"

"That's not why I have one. No delusions of grandeur. In fact, not even sure I'd want the job if offered it. Life-long headache, if you ask me."

"I'm sure. But why do you—"

"Happy with my pension and a CMG, if so honoured. Or an OBE. More often earned despite its unjust reputation for being Other Buggers' Efforts. Doesn't come up with the rations, which Call-Me-Gods generally do."

There was another pause while they waited to cross the Tottenham Court Road. "No, but you never know," Hugo said, when they reached the other side.

"You never know?"

"When you might need one."

There was another pause. They were heading down the road but it wasn't clear whether Hugo had privately decided they should walk back to Century House or whether he was on his way to another meeting somewhere else and intended, if he had thought about him at all, to leave Charles at the door.

"What's she like, this—er—Chantal?" Hugo asked.

Charles described her.

"One of the troubles with the office," Hugo continued, "is that as you get more senior you get less fun. You drive desks, not cases. How long's she been on the game?"

Charles became uncomfortably aware that Hugo turned frequently and closely towards him, as if seeking visual confirmation of agreement. Charles widened the gap a little.

"And how much—you know—does she charge for a quickie?" Hugo asked. "Not that I'm interested, mind." He barked sharply and turned again. Charles realised now that he was checking his reflection in the shop windows they passed.

"I'm not sure about a quickie. Less than a night's rate, presumably. I'll ask."

"Not that I'm interested, as I say. Quite happy with present arrangements. I was thinking of a pub lunch."

"Well, I daresay she'd—"

Hugo barked again. "I mean for us, you nitwit."

Lunch was crowded and noisy. They had to stand. Hugo talked about the German spring offensive of 1918 while Charles pondered the mystery of what Hugo called his "present arrangements." It was not easy to imagine how he and Anna had come to be joined together; it was neither easy nor pleasant to imagine they still were.

After lunch they found Martha in Hugo's secretary's office, her imposing presence and her refusal either to say what she wanted or leave plainly irritating the secretary.

"Love one, dear," she said, sitting heavily when they got into Hugo's room.

Hugo was seeing to the hanging of his coat and hat. "D'you mean coffee, Martha?"

"'Course I do. Run out down there. Why else d'you think the mountain would come to Mahomet?"

"We'll get you some. Charles."

"Please."

Hugo hesitated, then left the room. Martha chuckled. "If that was deliberate, I take my hat off to you. But I see from your face it wasn't. He wasn't asking you, dear, he meant you to get it."

Hugo reappeared, looking cross. "Somebody will bring it."

Martha eased her chair closer to his desk. "Hugo, you kill me every time I think of you. Did you know that? Never mind, dear, don't trouble your head about it. You'll never understand why. Now, let me lay my cards on your grade 4 table."

She laid out half a dozen densely written filing cards, three with photographs of the same man. "Your man Igor. Here he is, see: Igor Smoletsky, Ministry of Foreign Trade, or so he tells the world. Identified intelligence officer by the Danes, on the basis of his behaviour pattern and contacts—my guess is they had a DA alongside him—and suspect IO according to the FBI. Not his real name, of course, but the one he most often travels under." Her long red fingernail separated three of the cards. "These are dates and places of his known travels. I take it that's what you're most interested in." Her dark eyes, magnified by her glasses, rested on Charles. "I'll leave these with you so you can check them. But I must have them back by close of play. Pain of death. Promise?"

"Cross my heart and hope to die," said Hugo.

Charles could see at a glance that Igor was the man photographed with his father, and that some at least of their travels coincided.

"Directorate S, no doubt," said Hugo. "Illegals support officer."

Martha's jowls wobbled as she shook her head. "Not for my money, not their pattern. Nor our old friends and opposite numbers in the First Chief Directorate, either. No, I think your man here is Second Chief Directorate, the KGB equivalent of MI5. If the case that interests you began on Russian, or Russian-controlled, territory, then 2CD might have done it and kept it to themselves ever since, without telling their overseas brethren in FCD, or the Illegals directorate, or the GRU or anyone at all. Or perhaps only bringing them in later when they needed help. My guess, given Igor's age and his travel pattern, is the case goes back a long time, that the agent was an occasional rather than a frequent traveller and that Igor was always his case officer. That would be most unusual in the other directorates. Must have been an important case."

Hugo was taking notes again. "That would explain why none of our defectors had ever heard of it, or anything like it. They're all FCD,

Directorate S or GRU, the sort of people we have contact with. Next to impossible to meet the 2CD, let alone in recruitable circumstances. Martha, you've done in a day what MI5 reckon it will take them weeks to do."

"Not all my doing, dear. Theirs too, though they don't know it yet. I talk to my opposite number, Doreen, every day. We do each other favours. You'll get your official answer from MI5 as soon as they get round to asking Doreen."

"So there are two Marthas?" Hugo laughed and blinked.

"One's enough. Make the world lopsided otherwise. She's half my size, Doreen. Poor girl. Seems to put up with it, somehow." She laughed throatily. "But back to business for a moment." She looked again at Charles. "It's not for me to enquire beyond what you choose to tell me but I couldn't help noticing a certain family resemblance in the piccies you showed me and I have to tell you that if you sought confirmation that someone was doing something, this circumstantial evidence is the firmest you'll get short of outright proof. There are lots of coincidences in spying"—she put one heavily ringed finger on each of the cards in turn—"but not this often, not this many. Yet what they were doing may not be quite, or all, you think. Remember that."

"I think you know rather more than we've told you, Martha," Hugo said.

"Just remember what I said, dear."

Charles drove down to his mother's house on the Friday night, following an early pizza with a former girlfriend who was soon to get married. Most of his friends appeared to be in, or moving towards, that state. Wedding plans and discussions merged in his mind. It didn't trouble him not to be part of it. In fact, it suited him that his sister Mary would not be at home that weekend, not only because there would be less wedding talk but because he wanted his mother to himself.

The pizza lasted longer than intended, though, so the evening chat he'd hoped for with his mother was no more than twenty minutes by the fire. She was already in her dressing-gown and drinking her Ovaltine. She talked of Mary's wedding.

"She says you're buying her friend's flat in the Boltons," she said.

"I haven't seen it yet." He was supposed to have rung to view it.

"I do think it would be a good idea if you could. It's a nice area and it's time you had somewhere."

"Yes, no, I shall." It had been more on his mind to leave a note on the windscreen of the Bristol 405.

After she'd gone to bed he reopened *Middlemarch,* which he was attempting for the third time, but soon got up and went to his father's study at the back of the house. It was almost a shrine, filled with the furnishings of his father's life—the books, the Fribourg & Treyer pipes, the blotting pad and heavy glass inkwells, the school ruler, the tweed jacket with worn leather elbows hanging behind the door, the ancient Windsor chair, the polished brass 25-pounder shell case filled with walking sticks, the First World War bayonet-cum-poker in the hearth, the battered spectacle case and many other inanimates, all articulate of his father's presence. The presence would fade, of course, and when the memories that preserved it were themselves extinguished such inanimates would be the only relics, by then unrecognised.

Meanwhile, it still smelt of his father, a combination of tweed and corduroy, logs in the fire-basket, pipes with tobacco left in the bowls. Charles had changed nothing, had not scraped out a single pipe. Now, as he surveyed it, leaning against the oak door he had closed behind him, he imagined sweeping it clean, scourging it, removing all trace of the man. But his imagination baulked at explaining to his mother. He took a few steps around the room, picked a blackthorn walking stick, felt the smoothness of the battered spectacle case, ran his fingers down the sleeve of the jacket. Did such things now stand for something different, or had they never stood for what he thought they had at all; or were they, at some level he could not imagine, compatible with the new truth after all? Was it possible that the man he thought he knew well could have been a continuum, not a fractured vessel? Was it possible to have been what these relics represented, and to have done that?

He pulled out the Windsor chair and sat at the desk. The rain tapped at the windows. With the curtains undrawn, he could see the water-blurred reflection of himself, pensive, sitting as his father might have sat, and becoming more blurred, like that image. If there were ghosts, he thought, let it be now; a sign would be sufficient, anything.

The wind buffeted the windows and the intermittent musketry of the

95

rain became fusillades, perhaps like those that had prompted Edward Thomas's reflections on such a night of the fate of "soldiers and poor, unable to rejoice." Could this be why his father had done it? A sense of compassion, of mission, perhaps as pure in its origin as it was divorced from its consequences? Communism had always done well out of compassion. Yet for his father never to have shown the slightest inclination or sympathy must have been a consummate performance, almost schizophrenic. Every believer, surely, over years and decades, would betray something to someone; they all had, the well-known spies, Philby, Blake and so on. All had confided or given clues; and Viktor had described it as an ideological recruitment.

He stared again at his reflection and resisted the urge to draw the curtains. He was a sniper's perfect target and since Belfast he had found it impossible to relax before uncurtained windows at night, even though the darkness bred only rain in the Hambleden valley. And nowadays the poor could keep dry.

What had he really known of this man, that other blurred reflection who had sat at that desk? They had been open with each other, he used to think, up to a point, nothing too personal. Neither had wanted that but both—he used to think—shared a tacit understanding that they could be if need be. That's why little had been said. They discussed things, issues, nothing nearer. It was comradely, based on the assumption that intimate sympathy was there, if called for. Well, it hadn't been, it now appeared. If he had called for it he'd have got only its simulacrum. No matter how helpful or restorative that might have been, it could not have been real because his father was deliberately, systematically, routinely betraying him, his mother, his sister, almost everyone he knew, and all they stood for. And now he was beyond reach. Charles understood that the past was past, of course, but until it included death he'd had no feel for its finality, for the cold absence of possibility.

He picked up the worn old penny by the inkstand. Britannia had faded around the edges, the head of George V was recognisable but his name worn away. The date—1918, the year of his father's birth—could just be made out. His father had always carried this penny. Charles found it when emptying pockets by the still-warm body in the hospital, as recommended by the nurses. He had meant to pocket it himself but it seemed too blatant an act of possession; now, he thought, he had been too nice. He tried to recall all he could of gathering his father's effects but could remember nothing that he might now recognise as contact arrangements, odd numbers, notes, concealment devices. Few agents trusted everything to memory. The more he considered such practicalities, with the rain still beating against the windows and the room colder now that the heating had gone off, the more his emotions were dissolved and rendered down into a sub-strata of granite. He would be cold, hard, unremitting, just—considerations of the office, MI5 or whatever notwithstanding—in his mission to establish the truth. As he let it take hold it felt like a liberation. When he stood he pocketed the penny.

His mother was pleased by his Saturday morning offer of a pub lunch after a little gentle shopping in Marlow or Henley. After a breakfast walk, without taking one of his father's sticks, Charles tried to remember Gerry's lectures on preparing for agent meetings. Have a clear aim, a reason for meeting, know what it is you want to come away with; if you can't state your aim in a sentence, don't put the agent to the risk of meeting. Think of everything, every reaction, however unlikely, everything that could go wrong, however unwelcome. Have a response to hand, no matter how trite or temporary, because it's bound to be better than blankness or panic. There was an office superstition to the effect that if you anticipated a disaster it wouldn't happen, as in a sense it didn't, because if you had a way of coping, things tended not to go seriously wrong. The corollary of this was that what scuppered you would be something you hadn't thought of—the sudden death of the agent in your hotel room, for example—and so you chased your tail in ever-decreasing circles trying to anticipate ever less likely scenarios. Supposing it was you that died, Roger had asked, provoking laughter. It had happened, Gerry said. A case officer had died in a safe house in South Africa, during the meeting. The lesson of that was not to carry anything that would compromise the agent.

Remember, too, that the agent was also a human being, who had a life outside spying. As should you, if you were sensible. Let the agent see that you were human. Be professional at all times, but show that you have a soul, a heart, some humour. And, finally, having thought of all this well in advance, forget it. Don't go to the meeting with your head bursting with all you intend to say, since you might not then attend to what's before you. Empty your head, relax, do something different. So long as you had thought of it, it would be there when you needed it, would come when bidden.

So he thought as he prepared for lunch with his mother, treading the sodden footpath down and up through the woods, past the convent and back across the fields towards Frieth. Only by thinking of it in this way could he contemplate asking the unaskable: Did you know Dad was a spy? If you didn't, how could you not have? Were you—are you—one too? What can you remember about people he mentioned, trips he took, things he brought home from work? Did he ever mention Russia, or communism, or spies? Did he ever say anything about a nest-egg?

The office—and particularly MI5—wouldn't approve, of course. The investigation was at a very early stage and warning his mother, if she did turn out to be involved, would be tantamount to sabotage. Even if she were it would probably not end in court, yet he was determined that, if she had anything to say, she should say it first to him. She was his mother. This, he would argue in his defence, was why he had done it. But what really drove him, he knew, was a combustible mixture of shame and pride, the determination that it was his case, that he would fix it— whatever that meant.

When he got back from his walk he suspended further thought by taking an axe to the beech logs in the woodshed until it was time to drive to Marlow. The town was busy and after minor household shopping his mother toured the several small, expensive ladies' dress shops. She was always saying how very good they were, and how opulent everyone seemed to be these days. At least, in Marlow and Henley. She shortened the inspection of one, though, because of Charles's yawning.

"I wish you wouldn't make it so obvious. You're as bad as your father."

"I can't help it. It's shops. As soon as I go into a shop I start yawning."

"Unless it's a bookshop or a car showroom."

"Or a pipe shop now. Why don't I go over there and you come and get me when you've finished."

She bought herself a green silk scarf in the autumn sale and they drove up to Fawley on the far side of the valley, where there was a pub in which they were unlikely to meet anyone they knew. They were early enough to take their pick of the tables. The fire, recently lit, flamed and crackled.

"I do wish I could get ours to go as well as that," she said. "Your father could but he approached it as civil engineering. I was never allowed to touch it."

"It should be better now I've split the logs."

"I thought that's what you must be doing. Thank you, dear."

They ordered ploughman's lunches, she with white wine and he with Guinness. He had decided to question her over lunch, and in public, because a meal was a useful distraction, something to be doing while other things went on. Being in public made it harder to retreat into emotion.

"I was trying to remember when you and Dad bought our house," he began.

"Before you were born. At the end of—no, just after—the war. We had no money, of course—hardly anyone did then—and although houses were cheap you still couldn't get them if you didn't have any. At the same time there was a tremendous shortage of housing because of all the men coming back from the war and getting married and wanting their own places rather than living with their in-laws, which is what most people used to do and still happened very often. In fact, we did to start with—well, we had ever since we were married in 1943, whenever Dad was on leave. We lived with his parents in Bristol first and then with Nanny and Granddad in High Wycombe. We were living with them for quite a long time after you were born."

"But how did you get the house?"

She dabbed her lips with the napkin. Her eyes always shone with interest when she looked back. "Oh, it was such good luck. Well, luck and your father's friendly persistence. It belonged to a widower, Colonel Capper, who was a miserable old stick or so it seemed, but he'd been badly injured in the first war. He always limped and his face was sort of sliced off on one side, just tight skin. Horrible. Not his fault, poor man, but no one seemed to like him except your father. He got to know him because we often used to come for walks out here and if Colonel Capper was in the garden your father would stop and talk to him. At first, you see, he still used to wear his army greatcoat—saving his demob one for best—and Colonel Capper had been in the Royal Engineers in the first war and I think that was how they got talking. After you were born your father used to come out here more often by himself and I think they must have talked about the house because I know he told Colonel Capper that it was the sort of house we'd love to have if ever we could afford one. And then one day he came home and said Colonel Capper was going into a home in Marlow—no, Henley, because that's where we used to forward letters—and he'd like us to buy it. Can't say I blame him. It seemed an enormous sum of money, far more than we could afford, but somehow we did it."

"But how?" His father always refused money, Viktor said, but Charles had to know. "More wine?"

"Just a small one."

Life was in its fullness for her then, Charles thought, when they were both about his own age, perhaps younger; but really older, in the ways that mattered. Early responsibility saw to that. "But how did you raise the money?"

"I can't remember the details. We got what seemed a huge mortgage, I know that, but your father had a good job so that wasn't such a problem as the deposit. No one in the family had any to spare and I know he had to scrabble around a bit, a lot. I think the bank was helpful and I think he had to sell his old car but that couldn't have raised much and he probably spent it all on his motorbike and sidecar." She looked thoughtful, clutching her napkin in her lap. "I'm sorry, dear, I really don't know. I must have known at the time but I really can't think now. It was so long ago. I expect it will come to me."

Charles tried to look at her as if she were not his mother, an ageing widow who these days sought to hide her scrawny throat. That afternoon she was thoughtful, relaxed, a mother contentedly talking to her son, happy above all, perhaps, not to be alone. His parents' marriage had been good, whatever that meant. It had survived, anyway, and although there were arguments he remembered no terrible scenes, no violence. Except, he now recalled, when he was very young. He was playing in the hall and heard his father shouting at her in the kitchen. At least once he had heard them both shouting when he and Mary were upstairs in bed. He had put his head under the bedclothes, crying. Mary had slept through it. For some years after that, whenever they so much as argued, it made him feel sick.

They had been faithful, so far as he knew, and there was no doubting her grief when his father died. Naturally they would have had secrets in common, as marriages must, and secrets from each other, as people must. Now, however, it seemed that widowhood suited her; at least, she didn't complain, though neither did she rejoice. It was as if she had simply acquiesced in it, neither finding in it a release, nor pining. She probably longed for grandchildren, but probably didn't dare mention it. Not to him, anyway.

Looking at her, listening to her, he couldn't believe that she concealed a great secret, had shared his father's great lie and was now living it alone. He could believe in a certain credulity, perhaps even a willingness born of loyalty to be duped on certain terms, but not in her guilt, not in a sustained, active, calculated double life. She could achieve that only by forgetting one half of her life, he was sure. Yet the thought of it ate away at him.

Afterwards, driving slowly along the lane behind a tractor, he asked, "Did Dad ever mention having anything to do with what I do—intelligence—while he was in the army, or afterwards?"

"Spying, you mean?" Her expression was vague and unconcerned. "Well, only on the fringes, I think. He had to talk to security people. Quite a lot of his work was secret, you see. But he never said much about it. I don't think it worried him. I mean, I don't think he ever had anything to do with microdots or secret rays or whatever they use. Much as he would have relished all that, I'm sure."

The tractor gathered speed and threw up clods of mud. Charles dropped back. "Who did he talk to, then?"

"I don't really know, I never met any of them." She sounded no more concerned than if they were discussing his father's parish council duties.

"But were they—did he ever actually say who they were, these people?"

"Well, MI5, isn't that what they call themselves? I think that's what he once said they were. Or maybe it was MI6. I don't know why they have these numbers."

Of course, his father would have to have talked to MI5 about his work in the secure areas of embassies and other establishments. He would have talked to the branch—was it C Branch?—responsible for physical security. He would also have had to talk to the office, or at least to stations overseas. This would have greatly enhanced his access, in KGB eyes, and provided convenient cover, so far as an unsuspecting wife was concerned, for agent meetings.

He went no further. If his mother were dissembling, then her reactions suggested a deception too deeply and determinedly buried to be yielded up to her son on the way back from the pub. But he couldn't believe she was.

It was with the sense of a burden eased, if not lifted, that he sat down to watch the rugby international that afternoon. England were due their annual slaughter by the Welsh and the game soon settled into the familiar pattern of Welsh verve and inspiration versus a stolid English scrum, adequate but uninspired half-backs and talented but neglected three-quarters. Wales had just scored from an early penalty when his mother put her head round the door.

"Your office on the phone."

It was one of the operators. "Mr. Thoroughgood? The office here. We've just taken a call on a special line for Mr. Peter Lovejoy from Chantal. Please could he ring her. Does that make sense?"

"Yes, fine. When did she ring?"

"About two minutes ago. She wouldn't wait while we got Mr. Lovejoy and wouldn't leave a number."

"Was it urgent?"

"She didn't say."

He returned to the television in time to see England score an uncharacteristically fluent try. Perhaps they were going to make a game of it after all, but they would have to manage without his support. He did not have Claire's number and knew it was not in the directory; she resembled, perhaps in more ways than one, a London club, in that her location was known only to those who needed to know. Her file was in Hugo's safe. Copies of his contact notes, which would also have had her number, were in his own safe in training department. To ring the duty officer and give the combination number over the phone meant that it would have to be reset a.s.a.p. by the safe-holder. There was no alternative but to go in.

"Agents are our *raison d'être*, our delight, our pride, occasionally our downfall, sometimes a headache and often a plain bloody nuisance," Gerry was always saying.

He listened to the match on the car radio. It was fifteen-all with ten minutes to go when he parked near Waterloo and walked back along the Cut to Rasen, Falcon & Co., where the security guard had to be lured from the television to let him in. His safe clanged open after his third attempt at the combination, echoing along the empty corridors. He went into the course office and sat at Rebecca's desk to ring. There was no answer. He went down to the guards' television in time to see Wales convert their third try, this one in injury time. His second call was answered.

"Pierre!" she exclaimed. "It is so nice to hear from you."

"You rang," he said.

"Ye–es." She paused. "Of course I would like to see you, *ma chérie*. Thank you. You can buy me dinner tonight if you wish."

"Of course."

She laughed. "That's what I like to hear."

"Has anything happened?"

"Not exactly but it might. I shall tell you about it."

When he replaced the receiver he saw Rebecca leaning against the door, watching. She wore jeans and a sheepskin coat, with a long bag slung over her shoulder. He stood. "I thought I might get away with pinching your desk for a minute on a Saturday afternoon."

"Normally you'd be welcome to it but I've come in to catch up. You lot have been producing so much I've got behind."

"Someone—an agent—rang and I didn't have her"—he hesitated, having meant to say "his"—"number, so I had to come in all the way from Buckinghamshire."

"Never mind. Queen and country. Hope it was worth it."

"Not sure it was." He watched as she expertly spun her combination lock. "I shan't be in your way, I'm just going. D'you want any tea or coffee?"

She smiled. "Not unless you stay to have some with me. In which case coffee would be lovely, thanks."

When he returned with it her desk was covered by trays and papers. He tried not to look at the papers as he handed her the coffee.

She smiled again at his ostentatious scrupulousness. "Are things going all right? With the course, I mean. Combining it with a case that no one's supposed to know about can't be easy."

"Not a problem so far. People don't seem very curious."

"And the case?"

"Creeping along."

"They can take it out of you, these things, especially when they involve you personally."

Perhaps she'd been briefed further than he thought. "It's manageable. Weekends don't go according to plan, though." He shook his head at her arched eyebrows. "Not that I'd planned anything exciting. Gerry coming in?"

"Shouldn't think so. Isn't there a rugby game or something?"

"I wonder if French Kisser watches rugby."

"Plays it by the sound of her."

This told him nothing about her and Gerry. "Hookey's quite a character, isn't he?"

"He has his enemies. Speaks his mind and doesn't suffer fools." This time he raised his eyebrows and she shook her head. "I don't mean I'm an enemy. I think he's great. I loved it when I worked for him, though I didn't see much of him. But he treads on toes wherever he goes."

"Not yours, though."

"He wouldn't notice."

Later, in the Greek restaurant, Charles sat at the back table he and Claire had shared before. The restaurant was busier this time. She appeared with a big, painted smile and wore a tight, sleeveless red dress with a black shawl. She had a handbag but carried her cigarettes and a gold lighter in her hand. Her large ear-rings wobbled as she kissed him twice with extravagant display.

"I am so sorry I am late, *chérie*. I hate to be late. It hurts me here, you know?" She put her hand on her heart. "Makes my heart go, especially when it's you."

"That's the anticipation of wine."

"You are so unromantic, you English." She smiled as he filled her glass. "But you know my needs."

She had suggested the restaurant because her children were at home. She then talked uninterruptedly and disconnectedly about their school, her former husband, other mothers and the iniquities of local parking regulations. He thought she might already be slightly drunk; perhaps was drunk when she rang him. Once her entrance was over—she plainly liked entrances—she dropped her French accent, resuming it only when the waiters were near.

"What was it you wanted to tell me about?" he asked eventually.

She put her hand on his arm. "Peter, love, I hope I'm not messing up your evening with someone else, am I? Spoiling your chances on a Saturday night?"

"Not at all. It was going to be an evening at home with my mother."

"You don't expect me to believe that, do you? Anyway, it's nice of you to say so." She lit a cigarette. "No, but what it was—apart from the pleasure of your company—was my friend you're interested in. He was round this morning. Thought you'd like to know."

"That must have been awkward, with the children at home."

"They're used to a bit of coming and going. But it was him, you see. It's not like him to turn up unexpectedly. He was in a bit of a state. Mind you, so was I, dragged from my beauty sleep by passion in a tracksuit."

"What did he want?"

"Not what you're thinking, or not mainly that, anyway. Not that he was going to get much of it, either, the way I felt. No, what he wanted was to tell me he may be sent home—transferred, he called it. His company—ha ha—might want to send him back to Helsinki, he said. They were waiting to hear about some reaction to something, if something worked or didn't work, I don't know. Anyway, he had his knickers in a right twist about it, so I thought you'd like to know. Was I a good girl?"

"Very good girl." She could, of course, have said it all on the phone, but he didn't want to discourage enthusiasm.

"And can I get paid for seeing him, even though it wasn't a normal session?"

"You can. Normal rate. Did he say anything else?"

"Just the usual about how much he loves me, can't live without me, if he threw everything up to stay here with me would I love him for ever and all that."

"He actually said that?"

She nodded. "And there was me dying for a fag and a coffee after a hard night, couldn't hardly speak and the kids with the telly on full blast and him pouring his heart out. It was awful."

He made her go through it word for word. The anguished Viktor she described differed so radically from the Viktor he knew. But the thing was that a KGB officer appeared to be considering defection. That, he was sure, would get them going in Head Office, unless it was simply a neat way of winding the affair down on Viktor's part without giving her any reason for resentment. He had offered to bring money "for the children" next time, she said.

"When will that be?"

"Dunno. He'll ring. Soon, I s'pect. Where's that other bottle?"

"I haven't ordered it yet."

Her eyes widened. "I was sure you had."

"You can be sure I shall."

"You're a real gent, Pete."

He made her quote Viktor's actual words. Note-taking was out of the question so he had to concentrate, drinking little. Her speech and mannerisms became more exaggerated, her emphases overdone or wrongly placed. Fortunately, people at nearby tables were too busy with each other to notice how loud she was becoming. When he was satisfied there was no more to learn he changed subject. "You had a hard night last night, then?"

"Hard, late and rough. With my minister. He likes his bit of sado-masochism. I have to drink myself silly to get through it. I keep meaning to hand him over to a girlfriend who doesn't mind that sort of thing but I don't have to go very often and he pays well."

"What sort of minister?" Charles assumed frocked priests or em-purpled prelates.

"Hills, the government one."

"The minister of defence?"

"Yeah, the politician. I'd rather he was a real soldier, proper general with medals. I like uniforms."

"What do you do with him?"

"Kinky stuff, domination, leather and whips, you know, all the gear. This younger man comes for me in a car and we go to this flat in Pimlico. I'd been seeing him for some years before he became a minister. P'raps that's why it's not so often now. He's busier."

Charles briefly pictured to himself the jowly, porcine, self-important fifty-year-old with the unfortunate high voice quivering with delight at the not-too-harmful lashes on his ample buttocks.

"To be honest, I'm getting past the kinky stuff," she continued. "All that acting up. I never did like it much. Give it me straight, any time." She smiled. "You can if you want, you know. Special favour, no rates."

He took her hand and kissed it theatrically. "I should like that very much. It's forbidden while we're professionally engaged, as it were, but the day we're not—"

She pouted and blew a kiss across her wine. "Very quaint, Peter. Let me know when the need arises."

Afterwards he saw her to her door across the road. She was unsteady on her feet and took his arm. "The press would pay a small fortune to know about your romps with the minister," he said. She must have thought of this.

"Yeah, but him being minister of defence he'd get your lot or the commandos or something to bump me off, wouldn't he?"

She was serious. Reminders of how Secret Service was often thought of were salutary, but illusions could be useful. "You'll be all right," he said. "Just keep quiet about it and pass him on to someone else. Give them the problem."

"You'll look after me, will you, Pete?"

"Of course I shall."

CHAPTER FiVE

REBECCA'S CRAMPED OFFICE in the Castle looked across a narrow lawn to the mouth of Portsmouth Harbour. It was dusk and the wind rattled the wooden window, draughts lifting the corners of papers on the desk. Red and green lights betokened distant small vessels, while fast-moving banks of white lights, high above the water, announced large ferries. Below the battlements, out of sight, waves surged upon the shingle.

Charles sat at her desk holding a bulky secure telephone with buttons in the handset. It was attached by a fat wire to a wall-mount on which were red, green and white lights, and two more buttons. Rebecca wedged herself between the desk and the wall, waiting to press the buttons. The system, called Bournemouth, was cleared to Top Secret. When Charles was summoned to talk to Hugo "in Bournemouth" Rebecca had discreetly vacated her office but he'd had to call her back to show him how to work it. The printed instructions had no effect.

"That's because you picked it up first," she said. "It's always more trouble than it's worth, this thing. It makes everyone shout."

There was a cackle, followed by the operator's voice again. "Ready to try again, caller. Going to Bournemouth now."

The white light came on. Rebecca's finger hovered over the button. "Charles?" It was Hugo's voice.

"Yes."

"Charles?"

"Press your button," whispered Rebecca. "He can't hear you unless you're pressing it."

Charles pressed. "Yes, here now. Can you hear me?" There was a pause, then a chorus of whales in mourning. "Hallo?"

"Release the button," whispered Rebecca. "You can't hear him while you're pressing."

Charles released the button. An unknown civilisation, deep in interstellar space, sent its last despairing radio signals.

"Now he's not pressing his, the fool," said Rebecca.

The red light flashed once. "Charles?"

"Yes, I can hear you."

A rain forest parakeet gave its alarm call. "Bloody thing," said Hugo, clearly.

"Hallo, I can hear you."

"Bloody thing."

"Hallo. Hallo." Charles felt his voice rising.

"That any better?" asked Hugo.

"Yes, I can hear you."

"Can you hear me?"

Rebecca began to laugh.

"It's okay. Go ahead." Firecrackers exploded.

"Going over!" shouted Hugo, as if abandoning ship. A green light came on.

Charles put his hand over the mouthpiece. "What does he mean?"

"Press your button. Not yet. Only when you want to speak."

Charles pressed. The silence on the line was restful. "Hallo," he said. The silence continued. He released his button.

"—anything," said Hugo.

Charles pressed again. "Say again all before 'anything.'"

Hugo was strangled. Screech owls applauded. Finally he said, very clearly, "Bollocks." Lights flickered and the line went dead. The telephone on Rebecca's desk rang. Grinning, she handed it to Charles.

"—happened there," Hugo was saying loudly. "Out of date anyway. Every link bar this one has been replaced by Blackpool. Is your comcen still open?"

Rebecca nodded. "Yes," said Charles.

"Fine, I've actually got a telegram drafted containing what I was going to say, anyway. I'll send it. Make sure they don't close till you've got it."

"Much easier to have done that in the first place," said Rebecca. "You'd better get back to your exercise. I'll bring the telegram to your room when it comes. Hugo's unreal sometimes."

"Aren't we all?"

"There are degrees."

Exercise Finder was a straightforward dead letter box exercise in which each student had to find and fill a DLB with a roll of film, then send written instructions on retrieving it to another student who would himself have filled one for the first, and so on. Filling had taken place during the afternoon, emptying was to take place after dark. It was the exercise during which Maurice Lydd was to be kidnapped.

Rebecca bought Hugo's telegram to Charles's room while he was typing instructions for Christopher Westfield, his pair. It was in a Top Secret brown envelope. She bobbed a curtsy. "Will there be any reply, sir?"

Roger, wearing a bath towel, put his head round the door. "I'd keep this open if I were you, Rebecca. Give us a shout if he tries anything. You know what he's like."

"Not sure I do. Mind your towel."

"Shit. Sorry."

It was the first real telegram Charles had seen. The top page was taken up mainly by arcane communications and distribution symbols but from the rest he learned that Viktor had rung him at the Foreign Office. Charles was to ring back from a call-box, after six when Viktor would probably not be there. Charles was to leave a message saying he was away on a management course and would be in touch when he returned next week. There was still no word from MI5 as to when they could proceed but there had been a swift MI5 reaction to Charles's revelation that a government minister was one of Claire's clients: it had sent them into spasm and they had asked that Charles have no further contact with her, pending consultation. Thus, commented Hugo, an offensive operation had become not only a counter-espionage operation outside SIS control but also a political hot potato, which meant that operational decisions would have to take second place to security and political issues. Charles would obviously be disappointed and frustrated, particularly in view of his personal interest. He should discuss with C/Sov who would be attending that night's course dinner, as would Hugo. He should not, of course, discuss with anyone else.

"Bad news," said Rebecca.

"You know about it?"

"Someone had to take it off the cipher machine and they didn't want to indoctrinate the Castle secretaries into the case and you're not allowed in the cipher room because you're a student, so that left me. Hugo will retrospectively indoctrinate me when he comes down tonight, he says. Sorry. It's obviously a very personal case."

It was actually a relief that she knew. "And Gerry, presumably?"

"No, only in general terms, like me before." She pushed the door to and sat on the end of the bed. "What will you do, now that they say you can't do anything?"

"I haven't thought yet."

"You won't do nothing, will you? I can't imagine you doing nothing, just letting it lie."

The remark felt like a vote of confidence. "You're right. I'll do something."

She looked at him for a moment, then smiled. "You can do something for me, too. Tell me what's going on here, with the others. There's a plot, isn't there? I hope it's not going to be Roger wearing his towel during dinner or anything like that."

"Nothing as bad as that. Need to know."

"Are you sure I don't?"

"Fairly."

"Liar." She stood. "I'll take your instructions to Christopher if they're ready."

The news of the freeze on his case was a heavy weight, carried within. He felt he moved more slowly, and his thoughts circled it like satellites round some sombre planet.

Nonetheless, he set off confidently on the exercise. He was proud of his public lavatory DLB. The film in its plastic container floated in the cistern. Christopher had only to lift the cistern lid and flush for verisimilitude; he would have an obvious reason for being there, it was easily accessible and completely private.

"The beauty of this exercise," Gerry had said, rubbing his hands, "is that it exposes you to the strengths and failings of your colleagues, just as your agents will be exposed in far-off climes. All it takes is a modicum of thought and common sense. That's why it's usually done badly."

The DLB Christopher had chosen was almost, Charles thought, as good as his own. It was beneath a church pew, easily reached by one who knelt to pray. People prayed less often than they went to the loo, but never mind. He had also received, secretly, the DLB instructions for Ian Clyde, one of the kidnappers, in which the film canister was wedged into the woodwork of one of the sea-defences along the coast. Charles was to empty it for him while Clyde and two others lay in wait for Maurice Lydd in the remote corner of a naval sports field. Lydd had been told he must appear as a jogger, wearing a tracksuit.

Christopher's church was easy to find, but locked. There were no lights in the porch, so he couldn't see whether there was a notice identifying the keyholder. He had little time, anyway. Christopher should have realised that churches were often locked these days. The nearby cottage probably held the key and he could have asked, but chose not to. The agent he was supposed to be would not want to expose himself to possible identification. As Gerry had said, all such arrangements took was a modicum of thought and common sense. It would teach the ever-confident Christopher a lesson. Anyway, it was only an exercise and, compared with his frozen operation, it was irrelevant.

He took a taxi from the ferry terminus to the deserted yacht club on the beach west of the Castle. The club was no marina, just a building housing an inshore lifeboat and a lookout area, with a dozen or so yachts drawn up on the beach. The tide was in and wires tinkled and rattled in the darkness against metal masts. There were lights across the Solent on the Isle of Wight and road lights a quarter of a mile or so behind, across the golf course. The intermittent beam from a beacon on top of an old fort was enough to see by. There was no one around.

He crunched across the wet shingle towards the third line of old posts and beams on his right. Starting with the first post, which rose only a couple of feet above the piled shingle, he had to count five down towards the sea, then stand on the lower beam to feel on top of the post a shallow hole with the canister stuck in it.

At high tide, however, the seaward posts were covered and there was water washing over the beam between four and five. Typical of Ian Clyde, he reflected. Once again, all that was needed was common sense and a little thought. This time, however, he decided to make the effort. He didn't want to return completely empty-handed. Holding on to the top beam, he walked along the lower as far as the water, then lifted his legs and tried to go hand over hand, as in a gym, to the fifth post. What would he say he was doing if accosted? Practising acrobatics? Trying to drown himself the hard way? Winning a bet? The beam was wet with spray and his hands slipped as he swung his legs towards the post. He was lucky not to go flat on his back in the water, getting his feet down to the lower beam just in time. The sea sloshed around his ankles. He gave up.

Drowning while clearing a DLB was the sort of thing Hugo would worry about, he reflected as he trudged back across the shingle, shoes squelching and wet trouser bottoms clinging to his legs. Hugo would doubtless carry flippers and snorkel in his briefcase. His father, he thought, would have enjoyed this sort of thing, just as Charles would have enjoyed discussing it with him. But his father would have emptied KGB DLBs. Yet again, memory was poisoned. There were moments—whilst shaving, listening to the radio news, tying up his shoes, in the midst of conversation—when he was seized by spasms of hatred for the man who had done this. It was the sharp, lightning hatred born of intimacy, short-circuiting all his carefully constructed rationality and detachment. There had been moments like this in adolescence when he was gripped by an intense, visceral distaste for the man across the table who slurped his soup and left drops clinging to his grey moustache, while talking happily on. There was a guilty pleasure in giving way to them.

He walked back along the coast road and stopped at a call-box. This time the phone was answered quickly. He gave his name and asked to leave a message for Mr. Koslov.

"Moment." The operator stressed the second syllable.

"Hallo, Mr. Koslov speaking."

This was unexpected. Charles sensed a mutual nervous tension as they introduced themselves. "Are you all right?" asked Viktor.

"Very well, thank you. Are you?"

"Thank you, I am well. I was wondering if we could meet again, you know."

"Of course." Viktor's "you know" sounded self-consciously casual. Charles said he would ring again to make a date when he got back from his management course. They were correct with each other, aware that every word was being recorded. Although meetings had been forbidden, this much had been sanctioned to maintain the semblance of normality. "And you, Viktor, are you all right?" He echoed Viktor's phrasing.

"Yes, I think so, thank you."

"We'll talk."

"I hope so."

He walked quickly back towards the Castle. Those few words proved the catalyst for his decision. He would resign and pursue the case independently. As a personal quest there would be no forbidden areas, no security or political constraints. He would get at the truth himself. The office may not like it but they couldn't stop him; he would be breaking no law, telling no secrets. Viktor held the key to his father's—and now, he felt—to his own past. Viktor, never less than professional, had an existence apart from his job and had let it show during their conversation. Viktor was a man he could talk to. And the key to Viktor was Claire.

"Thanks a bunch, old son." Christopher Westfield's hand lay heavily upon Charles's shoulder. "Great idea. Nice, insalubrious, public brick shit-house, just the sort I love to patronise and which you obviously associate with me. Only one problem: locked daily at five p.m. Notice on the door, for those who can read."

Christopher had come in just as Charles finished describing the inadequacy of the church DLB to Gerry and the others. Gerry was displeased; none of them had chosen well and Clyde, Lydd, Brooke, Newick and Devauden were not back. Everyone wanted to bathe and change for dinner and he was not inclined to wait any longer, now that Christopher had returned to add to the depressing catalogue of incompetence. Charles kept quiet about his wet shoes and trousers.

The course was nearing its end and it was a formal black-tie dinner that night with a number of guests apart from Hookey and Hugo, who had brought Anna. The bar was full. Hugo's glance at Charles was pregnant with undisclosed meaning but he continued talking to others. Anna stood by his side, her detachment emphasised rather than modified by her expression of polite interest. She had not seen Charles. It was an opportunity to examine her features more carefully than when talking to her. "Faces in those days sparked/The whole shooting match off," ran Philip Larkin's poem.

"Where are the missing four from the exercise?" asked Rebecca. "It's perfectly plain you're all up to something so you might as well say what it is. Even Gerry's noticed now."

"Is he angry?"

"Gerry doesn't get angry about that sort of thing."

Christopher pushed his way through. "They've got him. They're on their way." He grinned at Rebecca.

"Got who? What?" she asked.

His decision made, Charles felt as detached as Anna looked. He couldn't see her now because Christopher was in the way. Apart from attempting to empty Clyde's DLB, he was having nothing to do with the horseplay. It reminded him of mess jinks in the army, in which, now he thought about it, he had probably participated more than he would have confessed. Desmond, too, seemed to regard it without much enthusiasm, studying the various plaques and maps on the wall rather than gossiping and intriguing with the others.

There was a commotion from the far end of the bar near the door. The four captors, in jeans and tracksuits, half dragged, half carried a very large white sack with "HM Diplomatic Service" printed across it in black. It was tied at the top.

Rebecca pulled at Charles's sleeve. "Charles, tell me, what's going on."

"Nothing to do with me. You'll see soon enough."

People laughed at something one of the kidnappers said. The visitors looked on a little uneasily, the more senior the more uneasy, except Hookey, who turned away, smiling, to get himself another gin.

"Well here's Maurice Lydd anyway," said Rebecca. "With his drink already, so he must've come straight from his room."

Lydd, smiling as nearly always, had slipped in behind the kidnappers, and was looking on.

"Oh, Christ," said Christopher. "Then who have they got, the silly buggers?"

The bag was untied and, with a cheer, the four tugged at the corners and emptied onto the floor a tousled, tracksuited man with short fair hair and freckles. The bar was silent. He got to his feet, pugnaciously facing up to his audience. "What the bloody hell's going on?" he demanded. His voice was loud and confident, suggestive of one who was accustomed to using it. "Who are you lot?"

Ian Clyde started to say something but stopped. Gerry stepped forward, holding out his hand. "It looks as if there's been an embarrassing mistake," he said. "A prank that went wrong. I'm Gerry Welling, we're all civil servants and as stage one of our mammoth apologies I'd like to buy you a drink."

The man hesitated, then took Gerry's hand. "Peter Chester, captain, Royal Marines," he said quietly.

"Splendid, splendid. C-in-C Portsmouth dined at this table only last week. Now, what will it be? Drink the place dry if you like. And when you're ready I hope you'll help decide on a fitting punishment for the perpetrators." He turned to them. "You'd better get changed fast, you lot."

It emerged that Lydd had run across the wrong rugby pitch, while, at the right time and in darkness, the unfortunate captain had run across the right one. Lydd was pleased with himself. "It wasn't exactly anti-surveillance but I had a sort of hunch," he told Desmond. "I was uneasy about that particular pitch. It was in a dark corner of the field with no obvious way out. Though I daresay I could have out-run them." It did not seem to occur to him to question why he should have been picked on.

"Why weren't you at the wash-up?" Charles asked.

"I got back late because I decided to check that the DLB I'd laid had been properly cleared, which it had. A well-chosen site, though I say it myself. What about yours?"

Dinner was delayed. The Marine captain, after several gin and tonics, regretfully declined the offer of a place at table and the loan of a dinner jacket. He had a wife at home, who must be assuming he was doing a half-marathon, as he sometimes did. Normally he ran first thing in the morning but he had been getting lazy of late, so it served him right, almost. Perhaps an appropriate punishment for the miscreants was that they should join him for his 6 a.m. run every morning the following week? He was reasonably fit and should give them a run for their money. Gerry thought this splendid and conceived an equally splendid addition: both miscreants and the rest of the course, since they had all known about it, should pay for all the drinks that night. When eventually the now-garrulous captain was helped into a Castle car he was given a noisy farewell by the party of MOD civil servants on a management course.

As they went into dinner Christopher pulled Charles aside. "Hope you don't mind, but I've switched our places around so that I'm next to Maggie and you're next to that prat Hugo's wife. That okay?"

Maggie was an attractive, outspoken, widely travelled woman of around forty who had lectured them on office procedures and paperwork. She had started as a secretary and was now a senior general branch officer.

"Very much your ears only," Christopher continued. "Married man and all that."

"Does Maggie know about this?"

"Not yet."

Charles took his place next to Anna, who was talking to a Head Office visitor on her other side. He read the menu, rearranged the silver cruets and watched Desmond trying to overhear Gerry's earnest conversation with Rebecca. Hookey nodded briefly from behind the candelabra while talking to the Director of Administration, the most senior guest.

"How did this happen?" asked Anna, turning. "Did you switch places?"

"No, the other chap did."

"It was rather presumptuous of you."

"No, really, he did. But I didn't make much effort to stop him."

"Anyway, I gather things have come to a full stop with your case, for the time being, anyway. Hugo told me about it. He shouldn't have but I think he assumed you'd already told me yourself, more or less. I hope you don't mind. It must be more than upsetting for you. I'm sorry."

"I'm thinking of resigning."

She looked at him, her eyes unsmiling now. "You shouldn't let the office and its business take over your soul. It can, you know, from the best of motives. Most things turn out to be not as important as they seem. Even espionage. Sometimes especially espionage."

"It's not that, it's the personal elements. The truth about my father. Resigning seems the only way to resolve it, now that the whole thing is put on ice."

"I can understand that but don't do anything in a hurry. There's always more time than you think. Hugo resigned once. I know it's hard to credit but he was desperately concerned they were going to use the reporting of one of his agents in such a way that it might compromise the agent. So, after a night of torment and darkness of the soul he handed in his resignation letter the next morning. Then he found the story had broken anyway and the information was common knowledge so he had to crawl back to the head of Personnel and pinch it from his in-tray. Typical Hugo, always doing what turns out to have been the wrong thing for what might have been the right reason."

"Don Quixote?"

"Inspector Clouseau, more like."

The Director of Administration, tall and balding, gave an after-dinner speech in which he predicted no foreseeable end to the Cold War, an increase in the intrusiveness of the European Community, Hong Kong as the major British issue in the Far East, with South Africa and Rhodesia as major preoccupations in Africa, Brazil as the main factor in South America and the Middle East and Ireland as continuing insolubles. Oil was the joker in the international pack and at home the petrol shortages of a year or two ago could become a regular feature of life. Internally, the service had to invest in new communications technology and would look to employ more women and coloured people. PV requirements had hitherto made recruitment of the latter difficult but this would ease as the parents of younger generations tended to be born here. The Chief himself was very keen on seeing more black, brown and yellow faces. Maggie was particularly vigorous in her applause at the end, with Christopher, next to her, joining in belatedly. Maurice Lydd clapped longer than anyone else.

There was no lecture or case history that evening and the bar was crowded and noisy. The kidnappers' accounts of their escapade were already beginning to diverge, Lydd talked earnestly to the Director of Administration, his podgy face taking on the masked weightiness of a seventeenth-century Dutch political portrait, while Hugo lectured Hookey, who stared into his glass and said nothing.

"Room 2, Gatehouse," Hookey rasped, clutching Charles's arm as he squeezed past. "See you there in ten minutes."

"Bloody disgraceful," said Hugo a moment later, in lowered tones. "All that horseplay before dinner. Sort of thing that gets the office a bad name. Right in front of the D of A, too. I bet he's furious. Won't do much for Gerry's career. Though I admit he's done enough damage to it himself in his time. Just as well it was a Marine and not some local councillor or busybody. Reprehensible, I call it." He stood very close, twitching rapidly. "Eh?"

"A bit silly. No harm done, I daresay."

"Not the point. Sort of thing that makes me despair of the service."

.　.　.

The Gatehouse was built of massive stones and straddled the entrance from the moat. A flight of unlit stairs led up behind the guardroom into a brick passage evocative, in its utility finish, of the Second World War. Hookey's large bed-sitting room faced across the parade ground towards the sea. He was in an armchair by the gas fire. There was whisky on the table, to which he pointed while lighting his pipe. "God, what an awful evening. Bloody glad to get out of that, aren't you? What I hate about coming down here. All that heartiness. Like the army, don't you find?"

"I don't mind, as long as I can get away from it."

"I do. Well, perhaps I didn't so much, then. Joined in a bit more, I s'pose, but I never really liked it. After Anzio"—he exhaled a landmine burst of pipe smoke—"I was evacuated, wounded, not badly, fortunately. But when convalescing I found base life so awful I fiddled my way back to the battalion early. Persuaded the medics I'd get better quicker at the front, with something to do, if you've ever heard such rubbish. Fool that I was." He coughed. "Stopped another packet twenty-four hours later, more seriously that time. Never saw the battalion again after that. Sit down."

Charles sat with his whisky and took out his own pipe.

"Delighted to see you smoke," continued Hookey. "You shouldn't, of course, but it's important to have at least one vice. Never trust people with vices you can't see. They've got worse ones. I shouldn't smoke as much as I do, of course, but what with the war and all that, I thought what the hell. Most of my friends were killed and I should've been. Felt I've been on borrowed time ever since, so I've done what I liked. And said it, too, which causes more trouble. Now this latest development of yours has really set the cat among the MI5 pigeons." He laughed. "London tarts, KGB officers, government ministers, their idea of a nightmare. Huge bloody joke to us, of course, because we're dealing with that sort of thing all the time overseas. But for them it's shades of the Profumo scandal and all the rest of it right in their backyard. You can imagine what the press would make of it, especially if your tart chose to tell her story. MI5 would end up being accused of spying on our own ministers. They always are. Last thing they'd dream of doing. They'd much rather the Russians did it, and kept it secret so they don't have to arrest anyone. Spy cases always cause problems for them—why didn't they catch 'em before, how many more are there, does this mean that MI5 itself is penetrated and all that rubbish. They'd much rather just know about and record it—monitor it, they call it—and kick a Russian out now and again. Anyway, as I think you know, they've formally asked that you—we—break off all contact with both your KGB friend and his topsy. That means killing the case. How d'you feel about it?"

"I don't like it. I want to get to the bottom of it."

"Hoped you'd say that."

"To be honest, I'm thinking of resigning and continuing as a private citizen. I want to find out exactly what my father did."

"Are you now? Are you?" Hookey spoke musingly. "That would be a pity. A loss, both for the service and you. Perhaps even a serious loss, eh?" He raised his eyebrows and laughed briefly again. "MI5 would be in a frightful stew, terrified it would all come out, but I can't see any way you could be prevented. It may be wise to wait, though." He leaned forward, his elbows on his knees and one hand splayed, as if to tell off his fingers. "MI5 have asked that we suspend meetings with your two friends. Fine. Unless we have an overriding reason to continue, we have to respect that. But what if we can take the case to the next stage without any meetings? After all, the next stage, if I remember rightly, was to be crucial: to show Lover Boy—whose nickname will be changed if this case ever comes to anything—that we know about his girlfriend, and to judge from his reactions whether he's recruitable. If he is, you see, we're in a different game altogether, because recruiting him is an infinitely better way of finding out all about your father than a long-winded investigation. And we can probably get him to drop the tart, so MI5 can go back to sleep on that one. We recover our aggressive initiative rather than watching with creeping paralysis as the case gets closed down around us."

"What do we do—telephone him, write to him or what?"

"No, no, dear boy, nothing as unsubtle as that. Any actual communication would be construed as a meeting. Mere casuistry to pretend otherwise. No, what I have in mind is simpler, a more defensible piece of casuistry. In order to show him we know what he's up to, we don't need to say anything to anyone. All we need do is let him see that you've seen him with her. Not a word need be—indeed, must not be—spoken."

"And what then?"

"We watch to see if he goes on doing it. Coming from where he does, he will assume that we would use the information to blackmail or entrap him. If, knowing that we know, he goes on seeing her, it's fair bet that he's prepared to talk. He may even get in touch with you, in which case we can argue that you should respond. If he does neither, then we know he's battened down the hatches, doesn't want to play any kind of game, and MI5 can relax." He sat back. "Except on the matter of your father, of course," he added, making it sound like an afterthought. "Are you on for it? Eh?"

Charles was.

"It'll take some engineering. Lot of monotonous hanging around with surveillance on your part. But if you're prepared to delay your resignation—delay, that's all, I'm not asking you to change your mind— I shall tell—tell, not ask—MI5 that this is what we want to do and if they don't like it they can get their DG to take it up with our Chief."

"Do we have to tell them at all?"

Hookey nodded. "Once things have gone this far, and they're formal, there's no dissimulation. Disagreement, yes, but high-level dissimulation, no. Not in either service's interest."

Charles relit his pipe. The four matches in his tray contrasted with the single one in Hookey's.

"You're not tamping down properly," Hookey said. "It's got to be firm but not so tight as to disrupt air-flow."

"If Lover Boy does carry on, are you sure we'll be allowed to continue?"

"Well." Hookey sat back and stared at the ceiling, pausing with the unhurried confidence of those who do not expect interruption. "We could make a much stronger argument for doing so. You see, there is another element to this case." He looked down his nose at Charles. "What I am about to tell you constitutes formal indoctrination. I'll get you to sign the papers later. You must never so much as hint to any living soul that we possess this sort of information. If you do, it will not be a case of your deciding whether to resign but of your immediate resignation, like it or not, eh?"

Charles nodded.

"We know from a reliable and extremely delicate source that for some years the Russians have been burying secret caches in western countries. More on the Continent than here, but recently here too. They could be used to conceal anything from small nuclear devices at the alarmist end of the scale to arms and explosives for use in sabotage operations during the run-up to war, to agent comms, to alias documentation for anyone on the run or needing a new identity for whatever reason. Anything they damn well like, in fact. Some of those on the Continent we believe to contain radio transmitters and explosives, though we know less about those here because we've only fairly recently broken into this end of it. It is called Operation Legacy and locating and filling the caches is the responsibility of the KGB's Directorate S. It is probably their agents— Illegals, infiltrated here under natural cover, usually having little or no contact with the London Residency—who would use them. We are very keen to know where these secret sites are and what's in 'em so we can neutralise and monitor them. Now, in a highly hostile and difficult environment such as this country—which, since the 105 expulsions, is how they see us—Directorate S probably needs help from the Residency, and my hunch is that this is where your friend comes in. I reckon he is probably the Illegals support officer, tasked with operational support of these delicate Directorate S operations. That would account for his behaviour pattern differing from that of his KGB colleagues. There's usually not more than one per residency and no other possible candidate has been identified. If he is, and if he were recruited, he could give us vital information about these things. As you might imagine, MI5 are as keenly concerned about it as we are, to put it mildly. Even our minister of defence might keep his trousers on for this one."

It was easy, too, to imagine how useful a recruited government surveyor might have been in selecting sites. "But could Lover Boy have been my father's case officer in England? I mean, he's my age, and my father—well, he might—"

"Doubt it. You've seen yourself that his looked like a 2CD case with a 2CD case officer who followed him around the world. He might have been handed over for local running here but didn't Lover Boy give you the impression that what he knew of your father's case was drawn from a written briefing from the Centre? That suggests that he was not the case officer and that they never met. But he may have had a supporting role without necessarily knowing who your father was until they told him after he'd met you. You'll give it a go, I hope? Good. More whisky."

· · ·

122

It was late when he walked back to the mess. Through the windows facing the rose garden he could see a few survivors propped up at the bar or slumped in chairs, talking, no doubt, the inevitable shop—who was posted where, how so-and-so of all people had been made controller, whether it was true about old what's-his-name and his secretary. Not wanting to be dragged in, he crossed the garden to return to his room via an outer door. The night was mild, with almost no breeze, and a half moon shimmered on the Solent. He recognised immediately the figure leaning against the battlements.

"I thought you must have gone to bed," said Anna.

"I've been with Hookey."

"What did he say to the news of your leaving?"

"He said to wait."

"As I said to Hugo when he thought he was going to. Sometimes wish I hadn't."

"You don't like being an office wife?"

She turned towards the sea. "I'm not sure whether it's being a wife I don't like, or whether it's being married to the office. Both have their compensations, of course."

"Did you know you were marrying the office?"

"Oh yes, right from the start, from before he joined. The office is the great romance of his life, not me." She folded her arms on top of the wall and rested her chin upon them. "It's so beautiful, isn't it? There always seems to be more weather here. I don't know why we don't all live by the sea, all the time."

"Get a posting to a sea-port."

"I'm not sure I could bear another three years as an embassy wife. All those coffee mornings, those interminable bridge evenings, those dreadful dinners for people you'd never dream of talking to, just because they might be useful or because you owe them. I suppose it's the same with any job that's at all political. And having to be nice to the head of chancery's awful wife who's forever trying to queen it over you. All for the sake of your husband's career. And the school fees. We might be better off in a beach hut in West Wittering."

"So it's a toss-up between which of us leaves what—or who—first?"

She straightened and pushed back her hair. "Oh, it's not that dramatic. I shouldn't complain. I go through these moods sometimes, like everyone else. We're very lucky, really." She glanced at the bar window, where by now only Hugo and a couple of others remained. Her mouth set firmly. "I think he's had enough shop. They won't have talked about anything else, not a thing. When you think of all there is in the world to talk about—and they just go on about each other. D'you know why I'm down here? Because I'm talking to a spouses' course tomorow about being a diplomatic spouse *en poste*. They'll probably all leave."

They were standing closer now. "How did you meet?" he asked.

"Me and Hugo?" She laughed as at a joke. "In a pub the first time, with a lot of others. Then at a charity ball. He was the only man around who didn't seem all wishy-washy and overcome by flower-power and all that. Also, he could dance. It may surprise you but Hugo's a good dancer. Ballroom, of course, nothing informal for Hugo. I love it too but you hardly ever meet a man under fifty who can do it. Now d'you mind if I ask you a personal question?"

"So long as it's not about my dancing."

She indicated the pipe and tobacco pouch he was holding. "Why do you smoke that?"

"Well, I like it—that is, I sometimes like it, other times it makes me dizzy. It's an acquired technique and taste, I suppose. I'm not very good at it yet."

"But why acquire it?"

"I wanted a habit. Other people have habits. I didn't see why I shouldn't, so I thought of this. At least it's not cigarettes or morris dancing. And my father smoked one. I took it up after he died."

"I'd have thought that might now be a reason for not. Anyway, it doesn't suit you. You're not old enough."

"It doesn't lend me gravitas?"

She smiled. "What do you want with gravitas, Charles? What are you trying to be? You still cut your hair as if it's the fifties. You'll be going for walks with a tweed hat and stick soon. You don't have to be your father. Not yet, anyway."

"I do walk with a stick. And I have a tweed cap. Both his. Nostalgia, I suppose. I like nostalgia."

"Keep that for your old age. You should be doing things now about which you can feel nostalgic then, when it's too late for anything else." She took a step away. "I'm sorry. Who am I to lecture you on your life? Especially with what you must be going through. I was shocked when Hugo told me but not surprised, if you see what I mean. Not that I knew your father, of course, but I sensed that something intimate was wrong with you, something horrid—and made worse by other people talking about it like this. Time I dragged the other half of my own life off to bed."

"I'd talk about it all night."

She smiled and shook her head. "Yes, but we can't, Charles. Can we? Sadly. Very sadly. Sweet dreams. 'Night."

He watched until the door closed on her, then turned and faced the sea. A few minutes later the lights went out behind him, but he remained, leaning in the battlements where she had leant. Farther along the wall, someone lit a cigarette.

CHAPTER SIX

URING A WET rush-hour morning a week or so later a London bus hit a car which hit a drunk, causing traffic to back up in all directions from Notting Hill Gate. Drivers were ill-tempered or wearily resigned, the hunched pedestrians morose and indifferent. Charles sat in the back of a Ford Cortina parked in Pembridge Square, off the Bayswater Road where it led past the Soviet Embassy. The mild exhilaration consequent upon being part of, and apart from, the workaday world, had faded. *The Times* was now refolded on his lap as he watched congregations of starlings in the bare plane trees. Conversation had lapsed and the only human sounds were the occasional crackling, staccato announcements over the VHF surveillance net, such as "Red Four Two off. Out." Jim, the driver, rested his arm on the door and stared straight ahead. Sue, in the front passenger seat, read a paperback. Charles opened one of the windows a little. It began to rain again.

Charles no longer paid any attention to the people walking past. At first, everything had been interesting; now, there was only waiting. The high spot of the morning had been when two drab youths had tried fiddling the lock of a newish but dirty and bird-spattered XJ6 Jaguar parked a few cars ahead. They ran off when Jim put his fist on the hooter.

"Would you have called the police if they'd broken in?" Charles asked.

Jim grimaced in the mirror. "Difficult one, that. On the one hand, we don't want to draw attention to ourselves. On the other, we hate seeing the bastards getting away with it. If it was serious we'd tell control to get on to the police and give them descriptions."

"You wouldn't follow them?"

"Not when we're on a job like this, no. Unless it was murder or something."

"Or they were good-looking," said Sue.

An hour and a half later, after the humiliation of his first-ever attempt at *The Times* crossword, a walk in the rain had become an exciting prospect. "Any chance of a stretch of legs?" he asked.

Jim looked at his watch. "You two have a cup and smoke. We'll park round the corner."

They went to a café with red plastic tables and a notice advertising breakfast all day. Jim parked across the road in sight of it and checked with control via a microphone concealed in the sun-visor. "You wired up?" he asked Sue as she and Charles got out.

She nodded. "No need to call, just flash us. We'll see you."

They sat in the window with frothy cappuccinos. The background music was non-stop Rod Stewart. She lit a cigarette and Charles, for the sake of doing something different, accepted one. "Is surveillance always as exciting as this?" he asked.

"Sometimes even more exciting. You can spend a whole week not getting out of the car. Targets drive more than they used to. That's why everyone's always keen on a bit of footwork, if there's any chance of it. Car seats make backache an occupational illness."

SV, MI5's surveillance section, appeared to comprise men and women in roughly equal numbers. Some of the men, such as Jim, were ex-soldiers with Northern Irish experience, while some of the women, such as Sue, were long-legged, attractive girls with the accents of Benenden or Rodean. Sue had been to the former, he discovered. When he surmised that she might have failed selection because her appearance would stand out in a crowd she accepted the compliment as a straightforward matter of fact, with no flicker of flirtation. Her blue eyes were curiously flat and expressionless.

"So long as you're not a dwarf or an absolute giant," she said languidly, "looks don't really matter. You can change them quickly, especially women, headscarves and all that. It's more a question of attitude and adaptability. The rest is training."

She shared a flat off Sloane Square with two other girls, who thought she helped run her sister's modelling agency, and did three twelve-hour shifts a week, though she was on call for some of the rest. She had no career ambitions, the pay was reasonable, hours flexible, company congenial and the work sometimes—present appearances apart—exciting.

"Passes the time till I find someone rich enough to marry me," she said.

"How rich?"

"Quite seriously rich. Enough for a generous alimony. I suppose he'd have to be foreign or someone in the City. Got any friends there?"

"I'll have a think. So long as you and I have a meal for every one I introduce."

"Okay." She smiled as she put out her cigarette.

"Meanwhile, if our friend doesn't come out to play, we sit here all day?"

"And half the night, and all tomorrow and the next day and so on if you're really keen, until he does. Then he'll probably be with someone or we'll lose him or we'll be hauled off on some higher priority as soon as he pokes his nose out of the door."

Hookey had done his work with MI5. Charles was to show himself to Viktor when Viktor was seeing Claire, but no words were permitted with either, pending the security review of the case.

"No words," Hookey had chuckled, "but sign language I leave to you. It wasn't mentioned."

They knew from Chef that Viktor was due to leave the Russian Embassy for some part of that day, so a team of four cars and ten surveillants was pulled off from watching the military attachés, who had been particularly active lately.

"One of their periodic obsessions with government buildings," said Sue. "Probably in response to some regular reporting requirement, we're told. They even send a KGB officer out to buy *Jane's Fighting Ships*. No doubt they stamp 'secret' all over it before sending it back to Moscow."

When they returned to the car Jim left them to have his cup of tea, after which the three of them sat in it until lunchtime, when each crew took a break in turn. They had to move around the area in order to avoid traffic wardens. Charles wondered how his fellow students were doing on Danish Blue, the extended overseas exercise, for which each had had to work up his own legend. Gerry and Rebecca had so arranged it that no one knew he was not on it; there was some suggestion he might have been going to Reykjavik. A week in Reykjavik was beginning to sound an attractive proposition.

The radio crackled. Sue and Jim went from a comatose state to rapid response while Charles struggled to catch up. Jim started the engine. "Just in time," he said. "That bloody warden's on his way back."

Sue noted and quoted numbers and nicknames, her voice procedure quick and precise with no trace of her earlier languor; a league above, Charles reflected, his own rusty army procedure. After a couple of minutes she turned to him. "Static Ops report Foxtrot Alpha heading west in the Ford Escort he normally uses. Red Four Two and Three are with him. We and Four are hanging back in case he's only gone west in order to do a U-turn. OPs also report three of our usual targets leaving at the same time, all mobiles. Could be a ploy to test our responses and frequencies, work out the call-signs we give them and so on. Or it could be that one of them's genuinely up to something and the others are providing diversionary cover, pulling us in all directions."

"Or coincidence," said Jim. "Your friend Foxtrot Alpha could be visiting the Foreign Office and there could really be Foxtrot Alpha else going on."

"How do you know they monitor your signals?"

"Lyalin told us when he defected, before we kicked out the 105. The Residency used to send people out just to check on their symbols and make sure they've still got our frequencies. We've got more secure comms since then, all this frequency-hopping and that sort of thing, but you have to assume they're advancing, too."

Charles was in mid-question when Sue cut him short. "Roger. On our way. Out." She turned to Charles. "He's definitely going west. We're joining the others."

The rain had stopped but the routes to Shepherd's Bush and beyond were still busy. "Where is he?" asked Charles as they approached the Shepherd's Bush roundabout.

"On the A40, still going west. You won't see him, we're too far back. Three's on him, Four's ahead and Two's—not sure where Two is—"

"Gone to the dogs at the White City, knowing them," said Jim.

"Given that you want to be put alongside him later," Sue continued, "we want to keep you out of sight, so we're hanging right back. If we go near him you'll have to get down on the floor—there's a blanket on the seat—but ideally you won't set eyes on him until you want to get out and be seen. We certainly don't want him to spot us."

Jim drove swiftly, making it look easy. Red Four Three and Four reported that Foxtrot Alpha was alternately speeding and slowing. This made him a difficult quarry, Sue explained, because anyone wanting to keep him in sight had to do the same, which made them stand out. It was a standard anti-surveillance trick, the sort of thing you did to check whether they were on you when you didn't mind them realising that's what you were up to. If you were trying to look innocent, of course, you couldn't draw attention to yourself in that way. But it was also the sort of thing people did if they were trying to arrive somewhere at a precise time, or if they weren't sure of their route.

As he left London Viktor did not take the first section of the new M40 but turned off, keeping to the old A40.

"What's the next place?" asked Jim.

"Beaconsfield," said Charles, before Sue could consult her map. "I was there recently on an exercise like this."

"Perhaps you can guess what he's up to, then, because it doesn't make sense, what he's doing so far."

"He doesn't often drive out of London," said Sue. "He may not be confident on motorways. Anyway, he can't go much beyond Beaconsfield or he'll be over the limit."

The limit was the thirty-five mile radius from London beyond which Soviet officials could not travel without permission, imposed in response to a similar restriction on British diplomats in Moscow.

"He might just get as far as my home, my mother's house," said Charles. "Perhaps he's going to call on me." Or perhaps he, or someone else, used to meet my father in Beaconsfield, he thought.

Foxtrot Alpha headed straight into Old Beaconsfield and parked near the tea shop Charles had used. Jim lingered before the town, waiting to be told where to park unseen. They were directed by Red Four Four to a spot by a small garage at the start of the main street, shielded by a white builder's van. Viktor was out of his car and looking in the window of a ladies' dress shop. One of the crew of Red Four Two, Julia, was already in the shop, in case he went in. A record of what he bought or, if a post office, where he sent letters, would be made. Two others had him under observation from outside.

The white van drove off. "We're in full view," said Jim. "Be ready to get on the floor if he comes this way."

Viktor was about a hundred yards ahead, walking slowly. He wore the suit he had worn when they dined. He crossed the road unhurriedly, looking in their direction but focussing on an approaching coach.

"He's either undecided or he's playing for time or he's not well," said Sue. "That's not his usual walk. He's usually brisker, more upright. Steps out, lifts his toes more."

"Or he's unhappy," added Jim. "You can tell if you see a target often enough, even tell if they've got a cold sometimes, just by their walk. I've not seen much of him. Sue's seen him more than me."

Viktor entered an antiques shop after gazing in its window. A woman's voice on the radio said that she thought she had been spotted and would have to pull out. "You go," said Jim, going on air himself to tell the others. Sue got swiftly out of the car and, with the aid of head-scarf, turned-up collar and shopping-bag, instantly became a passing shopper. Her eye was caught by something in the antiques shop window and she went in. She did not come out until after Viktor had left and driven off towards New Beaconsfield.

"Back to you?" she asked on the radio, while apparently doing something with her bag.

"Pick you up the other side of the roundabout," said Jim.

The other cars went with Viktor but Red Four One took the parallel A355 towards Amersham. "I think he's trying to buy a present," said Sue, when she was back. "Is it his wife's birthday? He was interested in all the knick-knacks until he saw the prices. Didn't speak and left without buying anything, which is less than I did. Look." She held up a miniature Spode cup and saucer. "Don't you think that's sweet?"

"All right for a thimble of gnat's pee," said Jim. "Couldn't get a decent cuppa out of it."

"Not the point, cretin."

Jim grinned as they cruised the quiet tree-lined roads while Viktor went to a florist in New Beaconsfield. They parked in an avenue off an avenue. Viktor bought roses. "Told you," said Sue. "Wife or girlfriend."

He then drove out of town in their direction, passing the end of their avenue and crossing the main Amersham Road as if heading for Chalfont St. Peter. They remained where they were, listening to reports of his slow progress which, once again, made it appear he was either looking for something or lost. He gave no sign of being aware of surveillance. Next he did a U-turn and left the road for the small, secluded station car park of Seer Green, the halt at which railway, beechwoods and golf course coincided. Red Four Four sought instructions: should they join him at the station in order to see what he did, after which they would have to be withdrawn for the rest of the day, or should they hang back?

"The car park's tiny," volunteered Charles. "I know it from the army. The wooded hill above backs onto the camp. I used to go for runs round here. He might know it, too. There was a Russian Embassy car parked there a while ago when I came through on a train, before the case started. I reported it but never heard anything. Anyone who follows him in will be blown."

"It's not so much blowing a car I'm worried about," said Jim. "It's more a question of what you think he's up to in there and whether he'll abort if he suspects surveillance or whether you want to try to get alongside him now in case you don't get a chance later."

They assumed Charles wanted to speak to Viktor. He did not disillusion them. As they passed the station, Red Four Two cruised the other way. "What about that golf club?" asked Jim. "Can we drive into it without being seen from the station?"

"Possibly, if we're lucky. Worth a try." Jim drew up by the verge.

"Better if someone foots it," said Sue. "Courting couples are less suspicious." She looked at the wet grass and sodden trees. "Except that we've all got the wrong clothes and shoes. Unless you've brought your wellies and golf clubs, Jim."

"Always forget something."

"I'm more dressed for it," said Charles. He was wearing jeans, blue Guernsey and a sports jacket, albeit with conspicuously polished army *veldskoen*. "I know the country here, all the paths and tracks."

"You reckon you can keep out of sight?" asked Jim. "Bit of a risk if you still want to get alongside him later."

"It should be possible to keep well back. We can let you know what's happening if Sue's wired up."

"I'm not going up there in these shoes," she said. "You're on your lonesome. Take a flat hat." She handed him a green tweed cap from the glove compartment. He had not brought his father's, having resolved to stop wearing it after what Anna had said.

"We'll risk a car in the golf club to cover the entrances and one of us will pick you up when he's gone," said Jim.

"Suits you," said Sue as Charles got out onto the soggy verge. "Bring a black Lab next time."

He crossed the verge and walked quickly through the trees until he could see the car park. The diplomatic-plated Escort stood out but there was no sign of Viktor, nor of anyone else. He advanced cautiously to the parapet of the railway bridge, his cap pulled well down. A train was coming, so he leant against the brickwork to watch. A black Lab and a stick would have helped. He maintained an imaginary debate with Anna on the subject of walking sticks and pipes. The train came but no one left and no one came on the bare platform.

He cut up the hill through the trees, keeping parallel to the track and stopping every so often to listen. The wet leaves that softened his footfalls would do the same for anyone else's. Glad of the exercise and with no serious hope of finding Viktor, he determined to walk to the top of the hill. He knew well enough what he would find there.

When he reached it he halted inside the wood, gazing across the open land of the army camp perimeter. There was a rusty, sagging wire fence and a broken stile for the little-used perimeter footpath. Beyond were the goal posts of the sports fields, a few huts and a dilapidated watchtower, remnants of the camp's wartime role. The only nearby feature was a neglected firing range for short-range weapons, with sandy butts and a high, pock-marked brick wall.

As Charles watched, Viktor walked out from behind the wall. He wore his bottle-green tracksuit, the trousers now mud-spattered, and looked in Charles's direction. Charles stood exactly as he was, breathing gently through his nose and trusting to stillness and the trees to protect him. Viktor's glance was general rather than focussed, as if he were trying to get bearings from the stile or estimate distance from the wood. Then he put his hands behind his head and began slowly bending and stretching, dipping from side to side. Next he jogged to the stile some fifteen yards to Charles's left. Charles knew he would be clearly visible from the track if Viktor turned to look. His only hope lay in continued stillness. He moved neither his head nor his eyes as Viktor squelched down the track and out of sight in his old-fashioned black plimsolls.

Charles followed downhill, keeping well to the side of the track. When the railway footbridge was in sight he stopped and listened. Hearing nothing, he walked casually to the bridge and leant against it in time to see Viktor, dressed in his suit again, roll up his plimsolls inside his tracksuit, put them in the boot of his car and drive off.

Jim and Sue turned into the car park at speed a few minutes later. "He's gone belting off towards the motorway," said Jim. "Different man now."

It was a rapid journey back to London and Jim had to do ninety to stay in touch. He speculated aloud about what Foxtrot Alpha might have been up to. Had he had a clandestine meeting, emptied or filled a DLB, recce'd something or been part of a plan, with the three others who had left the embassy at about the same time, to draw off surveillance? Or had he genuinely been using some free time to look for a present and go for a run? He did go for occasional runs, they told Charles, but usually in the mornings. The fact that something had happened excited them. It made the shift worthwhile.

"Now he's running for home as fast as his legs will carry him," said Jim.

"It may not be home," said Charles.

Viktor cut south onto the M4 via Slough, then crawled through the rush-hour traffic towards Belgravia. Charles told them where he thought they were going. "You'll need someone on foot before he parks so that we can see whether he goes into his girlfriend's flat. Also, there's a Greek restaurant opposite. Useful to know if it's open."

The crew of Red Four Three were on foot in Claire's street before Viktor reached it. There were no free parking places so he had to drive round to an adjoining street just, unfortunately, as Jim was entering it. "Down," said Sue sharply. Charles ducked beneath the seats. Viktor, protected by his diplomatic plates, parked in a residents' parking bay. They were past him before he got out.

A minute or two later they heard from Red Four Three that, clutching the flowers, he had been let into Claire's flat. The Greek restaurant was open but empty.

"He'll be some time," said Charles. "I'll go and sit in the restaurant window. We'll see each other when he comes out." The sight of himself sitting watching Claire's door should be sufficient to make the point. "It'll probably be a long evening. You can knock off if you like. I'll sit it out."

He didn't really anticipate a long wait because Viktor would have to account for his time, to his wife as well as to his colleagues. Yet he obviously felt he had time to visit Claire, which suggested that the afternoon's excursion had been official. He would doubtless say it had taken longer than it had. Charles wondered whether Claire had rung in to say Viktor was coming, as she was supposed to do. It must have been arranged, if it was arranged, before he left the embassy, since he had made no calls while out.

He bought a classic car magazine in the newsagent's, took a window table in the restaurant and ordered the first of a number of Greek coffees, medium sweet and with the consistency of silt. Later he supplemented them with pita bread and taramasalata. It was too early for dinner but he wanted to give the impression he would become a serious customer. His position was prominent, directly opposite Claire's door. If she came to it, or looked out of her window, she would probably see him; but there was likely to be no better chance of silently making the point to Viktor.

An hour and fifty minutes later her door opened and Viktor came out alone. He looked preoccupied, as if emerging from the dentist and feeling with his tongue for the absent tooth. Claire was not at her window. Viktor turned in the direction of his car. Charles hesitated between tapping on the window and going out, leaving his jacket over the chair to show that he intended to return and pay. Either could precipitate the forbidden conversation, but with Viktor at last within reach, he didn't care.

Before he could move Viktor looked directly across. Charles raised his hand, palm outwards, his elbow still on the table, careful now to show no sign of getting up. Viktor stood facing the restaurant, hands by his side. Charles lowered his hand and nodded, unsmiling. For a few seconds they stared at each other across the road. It was exactly as the office required: Viktor knew that they knew, no words exchanged, and Claire, to judge by her window, seeing nothing. Nevertheless, it was with relief rather than concern that Charles watched Viktor advance slowly across the road.

They would have the conversation he wanted and he could honestly say it was at Viktor's initiative, not his.

Viktor stood by the table, hands still by his side, ignoring, or just possibly not noticing, Charles's proferred hand as he rose. His features were pale, his manner controlled and quietly hostile. After a few moments, he pulled back the chair and sat. "So, Charles, what will you do to me?"

"Nothing."

"So why are you doing this?"

"To let you know that we know."

"Why do you do that, if you are to do nothing?"

"To see what you will do."

Viktor spoke quickly and quietly. The exchange had already taken them into new waters. They were talking now as professional to professional. Honesty was not only best policy; there was no point in anything else.

"And if I do nothing?"

"We do nothing."

A waiter laid cutlery before them and looked enquiringly at Charles. Charles ordered a bottle of retsina.

"Why do you do nothing?"

"We don't blackmail."

"But you will ask questions, knowing my secret. And you make sure that I know, like this. What is the difference?"

"The difference is that nothing will happen to you if you don't want to answer."

There was a pause. Viktor's tension lessened a little. "So, Charles, what do you want to know?"

"Anything you want to tell me."

He shook his head. "Please, please. They will have given you questions before you came."

"They did not. They did not even ask me to speak to you. But I know what their questions would be about."

"So why don't you ask me?"

"I'd rather talk about other things." The waiter brought bottle and glasses. Charles did not bother with the proffered tasting. He raised his glass. Viktor drank without comment. "Shall we move away from the window? She might see us."

"Why does it matter?"

"Or your own people might."

Viktor smiled with something of his former wryness. "Charles, I have taken so many stupid risks that I don't care about this one."

"Will you go on seeing Chantal? It must be dangerous for you. Your own people—"

Viktor drained his glass and shook his head. "It is not possible for me to talk about this question. Nor about my marriage. Anything else, external things, objective things, but these I—no. It is an emotional matter for me, perhaps like you and your father. You know, Charles, I am sorry for that. I had to do it but I did not like it and I thought all the time how I would feel if it had been my father. I am glad you have not taken the money, though it would have been good for me if you had. I can say this now. I hope we can be frank."

"Did he really do it? Is it true?"

Viktor looked puzzled. "I think so, yes. Well, it is certain as far as I know. I have never seen his file but the Centre sent a summary when I was ordered to respond to your approach. It was like other file summaries."

"And he was an ideological agent?"

"His sense of socialist reality was awakened by the struggle against fascism and developed by his admiration of the Russian soldiers of the Great Patriotic War—it was a phrase like that."

Charles refilled their glasses. "But was there anything in his own words about his motivation? Any quote from him?"

"I think there was not. It was a summary, you see."

"I can't believe it, Viktor. I can't believe that is really how he thought and felt."

"Maybe not. It is a standard sort of phrase. You see it in many files, especially files of cases that began a long time ago. You see, the Centre used to like to tell the Party bosses that its agents were ideologically pure and that they worked for political reasons even though they took money as well, most of them. Indeed, the truth was that the Centre was happiest when they did take money. At one time, though, it was necessary for the agent to have the correct ideological motivation in order for the case to be considered a complete recruitment, so case officers would often put it in the files when it was not always true. Or not always the only truth." He drained his glass again. "But you don't ask me about what he did."

Charles almost did not want to know. The thought was enough; detail later, perhaps. At the moment every word of confirmation was an arrow in his heart.

"You really, truly, as an English gentleman"—Viktor used the phrase without irony, as of a known quantity—"are not intending to take advantage of my situation?"

"No."

"You know, Charles, I can hardly believe that." He laughed briefly and paused, but Charles said nothing. "You could destroy me and have me sent home in disgrace and for punishment, but you don't. You could try to blackmail me into working for you, but you don't. So, what do you want of me? Why are you doing this? What is the point? Is it only that you want to know about your father? Or is it that—no, it is not, is it?—that you wish after all to be like your father—?"

Charles shook his head. The waiter came again to take their order for food. He knew Viktor must be taking a risk by staying out, but the risk was already embarked upon and it was becoming awkward not to order. Without asking Viktor, he ordered two *kleftikos*.

"What will you do about Chantal?" he asked again.

"What will you do—arrest her?"

"Of course not. She's committed no offence."

"Then you will make her report on me. You will talk to her and I understand what such talk would mean."

"We don't make people do things. We can't force anyone to help us. It's not like your service. People help us if they choose."

"You mean, only if they come to you and offer? You would wait for Chantal to come to you?"

"Quite often." He emptied the last of the bottle into Viktor's glass, recalling his father's dictum about the essence of lying and the bleak self-assessment that must have underlain that perception. "Does she know your posting must end soon?"

"She wants money—diamonds—to remember me by. She has become greedy. I can't do that, I haven't that money. I told her. And I do not want it from you. But nor do I want anything to happen to her. She is not a bad woman. I know what she does. I know that. But still I have feeling for her." He put his fist over his heart, almost as in a Soviet military salute. "Perhaps, Charles, you do not understand that?"

"I think I understand."

"That means you do not. Not really."

When the *kleftikos* arrived Charles ordered another bottle. He was probably slightly drunk but the effect would not come until later, when he had no need to concentrate. Viktor showed no sign of having drunk anything, and ate with appetite and indifference.

"And how is"—Charles hesitated over Viktor's wife's name—"how is your wife?"

"She will be very happy to be at home in Moscow with our daughter. It is very hard for her to be separated."

"And you?"

"I will be happy to be with our daughter again." He put down his fork. "Excuse me, Charles, you are not trying to persuade me to defect, I hope?"

"It never entered my head."

"It should have. You are a professional intelligence officer. You should seek to exploit every weakness, to learn everything about your main enemy."

"I meant that I had never detected in you any willingness to forsake your country and your family, so I had not thought of trying to persuade you." He poured more wine. "Anyway, I'm resigning, so my professional interest is limited."

"Why are you resigning? This is a serious matter. Why are you smiling?"

"I am resigning because of what you told me about my father. I have reported it and it has now become a security investigation. That will take a long time and will probably never tell me what I most want to know— why he did it, how, morally, he could have gone on doing it. Because of my father they don't want me to pursue this case—your case, you—but talking to you is the only hope of really finding out about it. I'd rather do that and leave than stay and not be able to do it. It would always hang over me."

Viktor pushed aside his plate and leaned forward with his arms on the table, assuming a ponderous formality that might, in other circumstances, have seemed funny. "Charles, may I say something to you? We

139

are enemies and friends. Perhaps we shall never meet again, perhaps we shall be friends for life. I am grateful, whatever. I hope we may continue as friends somehow. But there is something I have to say to you. I can be friends only with someone for whom I have respect and, since we are of the same profession, this includes professional respect. For you to resign for these reasons is bourgeois individualism and professional negligence. If you are serious, you must be above merely personal concerns. Your duties to your service and your country are more important. It is also negligent not to be more interested in what I have been doing here. I am not going to tell you, of course, but you should be interested, you should try to find out. It should not be for me to lecture you on this here, Charles, in your own country."

It would have been a grave error to smile. Charles inclined his head, and continued in Viktor's tone. "I accept what you say, Viktor. I argue in my defence only that in not asking you to tell me what you were doing I was paying you the compliment of assuming that you would not."

"You are correct."

"Even though I could argue that in some ways—one way—you are negligent of your duty, too."

"I have broken rules, I confess. I allowed my feelings and desires and my—my search for excitement to carry me away. Then I came to love her a little. Not completely, with all my heart, but enough, you know. She is not a bad woman. But when I go home from here I shall never do such a thing again. That is it. It is not like your resignation, which is for ever. And it is not like betrayal."

A sliding scale, Hookey had called it. Great sin was reached by many small steps rather than one big one, St. Paul had written. "Is that how Tanya and Natasha would see it?"

This time Viktor bowed his head. When he looked up his face was softer and sadder. "You cannot imagine, Charles, what your father was helping us with when he died. It was important. I would like to tell you but I cannot."

Holding his gaze, Charles decided to take the risk. They were on all fours with each other and there might never be another chance. Hookey might be angry but he would welcome the confirmation. If Viktor knew nothing, then nothing would have been given away. If he was involved as Hookey thought, then he surely could not report what Charles had said without explaining the circumstances. "What is the Russian for 'legacy'?"

The softness of Viktor's expression hardened. "If you know enough to ask this question, I think you do not need me to tell you the answer."

"We need to know whether it is happening."

"What will you do to Chantal?"

"I told you, nothing."

"Perhaps one day we will speak again but only if you are still in your profession." He stood abruptly and held out his hand. "The word is *'nasledstvo.'* Goodbye, Charles."

CHAPTER SEVEN

WHENEVER MARY HAD to repeat herself on the telephone, irritation made her speak faster. "Because, as I've said, he's away on business and his girlfriend who's my friend and who has a key, her mother's just been taken ill and she's got to go to King's Lynn, but she'll leave her key with Christina, the neighbour downstairs who's only going to be there during the middle part of today because she's doing up a cottage in Wales and she's expecting you to call. At the flat, that is, not in Wales, and no one's asking you to go to King's Lynn. Honestly, Charles, you seem rather dense this morning and not at all grateful for everyone running around on your behalf."

Charles, summoned naked from his bed by her early call, clung to the phone as if it were a rope on a rock face. "No, I am, very grateful, just not quite with it when I answered."

"Only if you don't decide today he's going to put it with the agents and it'll probably go like a shot and even if you did buy it it would be more because of their commission. Did you talk to the building society, as you'd said you were going to?"

"I'm waiting to hear from them."

"So you'll go today, then?"

"Could you give me the address again? Someone must have walked off with my bit of paper."

Shaving in the now fully lit bathroom, he tried to remember which building society she'd recommended. It was academic, anyway, since, if he were shortly to have no job, there'd be no mortgage. But the idea of buying a flat, especially if it was easy and he didn't have to go looking, was appealing. With Roger away on the exercise, having the existing flat to himself that morning was a novel pleasure. Having his own would be even better, albeit that his uncertain future made such a stake in life seem irrelevant.

Reporting to Hookey that morning was not easy, partly because he had to do so without Hugo knowing since Hugo was not indoctrinated into Legacy. For most of the morning Hookey was in meetings; budgetary and personnel matters took more time than anything operational.

Later, looking as if it had been a bad enough day already, Hookey heard Charles out with a minatory lack of expression. When Charles had finished he stayed slumped back in his chair, speaking quietly. "You did precisely what you were instructed not to do."

"Yes, though I didn't seek it."

"You allowed it to happen. You permitted it. I shall now have to explain to MI5 and to the Chief, whose backing I had to secure, that what I assured everyone we would not do, we have done. Are you still intending to resign?"

"Yes."

"That will make it easier. Speak to Personnel and draft your resignation letter soon." There was silence. "More importantly," continued Hookey, "we have to consider whether your gratuitous mentioning of Legacy will have compromised our knowledge of the operation, and therefore also the existence of a very sensitive source. I appreciate that you think Koslov won't report it because that might lead to his having to account for more than he wants in terms of his relations with you and the tart, but that's only an assumption. His professional concern, or his patriotism, might get the better of his instinct for self-preservation. Or he might disguise the circumstances. Or they might have already become suspicious of him—there are some indications of this, Hugo tells me, from MI5—and they might get it out of him. If any of those happens, it could be disastrous."

There was another silence. "I'm sorry," said Charles, "I shouldn't have done it."

"Of course you shouldn't. On the other hand." Hookey leant forward, clasping his hands on his desk and turning his head sideways, once again as if reading something from the wall. "On the other hand, now that you have—and if he does not report or confess it—it is possible to derive some encouragement from his response." He grinned at Charles. "His acknowledgement of the existence of Legacy, implicit in his response to your nicely tuned question, indicates to me that he is prepared to say more. Mention of secrets is like mention of sex between a man and woman: any mutual discussion of it is significant. If he is prepared to admit that he knows of this great secret, then I think he is prepared to say more. And his translating the word for you is a little like some floozie telling you she doesn't lock her bedroom door. After all, it would have been very easy to feign ignorance and cut you off stone dead. That, combined with his insistence that you are failing in your professional duty by not pressing him as to what he's up to—even though he says he wouldn't tell you—suggests that this is a man who wants to tell us—or you—something, even if he doesn't want to go the whole hog. He might even help us to monitor the progress of Legacy. Pity you're leaving, eh?"

He stared with eyebrows raised and the form of his grin still on his face. "Do you mean that if I didn't resign we might be able to continue the case?" asked Charles.

"I don't mean anything beyond what I've said. There's no question of MI5 agreeing to further conversations with either Koslov or his tart. Not on. Even less so now that you've possibly compromised Legacy. So if you still feel you should resign, do so. No one's forcing you, remember. Free for lunch? Good. Ask Maureen to book my club on your way out."

Charles felt he was being urged both to resign and not to resign. His instinct was to stay, his determination to go. Avoiding the lift, he trudged heavy-heartedly up to Personnel on the eighteenth floor.

Beyond a notice in the corridor which facetiously promised that anything that could be fixed, would be, he was received by Peter Sidley, the tall man of saturnine good looks and impeccable suits who chain-smoked small cigars and who had lectured the course on the case of the important Eastern European official. He was said to have an impeccable operational record and incalculable private income, having apparently never drawn expenses while head of station on his last post because he couldn't be bothered with the claim forms.

"Obviously, we wouldn't want to give your real reason for leaving," he said, "and we don't like the direct lie, so what if we say 'family reasons'?

That covers almost anything you want to suggest and is the sort of thing people feel inhibited from being too nosy about. At the same time it needn't be your fault."

Charles accepted one of the small cigars. "Sounds fine, except for my own family."

"Ultimately, that depends on whether MI5 will want to interview your mother but meanwhile I suppose you could consider disillusionment, dislike of the sound of embassy life overseas, need for more money, girlfriend who won't leave her job and whom you don't want to leave behind or whatever. Of course, there's no problem if you decide you do want to transfer to the Foreign Office and they like you enough to have you. There's a trickle each way and we've taken a couple of theirs recently so they owe us one. There'd be no need to say anything to people outside the office while inside we simply say you'd rather be a diplomat than a spy. The question remains as to whether what your father did—is alleged to have done—would affect your own vetting status. A department of the Home Civil Service might be easier from that point of view."

This businesslike acceptance of his resignation was disconcerting. "Wouldn't it have affected my vetting here, if I hadn't decided to go?"

"If you weren't in already you might not have got in, if this were known about. But since you are you wouldn't lose your PV certificate over it unless"—Peter smiled—"we wanted to get rid of you because of your appalling drink problem, monstrous incompetence or you were found to be a shirt-lifter. Then it could become an issue. But we don't, so it won't. You really don't have to go. Think carefully about it."

Others said the same. Martha, whom he ran into in the corridor outside Hugo's office and who made no secret of knowing about it already, stared at him through her enormous glasses. "Premature," she said, as if recalling a code-name. "You are acting prematurely. A perennial failing in this service. Shooting from the hip. Better wait until all the facts are known."

"But the important ones are."

"Not in my book, they're not." The trolley bell rang and the corridor filled with hurrying people parting around her. "You don't know why."

"Well, we think we do. It seems pretty clear—"

"Because we think we know we stop looking. That's another service

145

perennial. You'll be back, I daresay, before you're properly gone. Seen it before, dear." She moved through the trolley queue like a liner through harbour craft.

Hugo was searching for something in his overflowing in-tray. "Bit of a flap on. But speak." He barely looked up at Charles's account of his conversations. "Not surprised, to be frank. Do the same in your position. Family disgrace and all that. Nothing to do with you but you feel responsible. Quite rightly. Anna will be pleased."

"Pleased?"

"Takes a maternal interest in your career. Thinks you're not cut out for the service. Probably thinks nobody is. But she has a soft spot for people who harm themselves on principle. Likes that sort of thing. Did I see you coming away from Hookey's office earlier?"

"Yes, I was telling him."

"Not discussing the case? Because I should be included in all case-work discussions."

"No."

"Drop in again before you go. Ah. Found it."

Gerry and Rebecca were in their Rasen, Falcon & Co. office. "Pity," said Gerry. "I had a feeling something was up. Good luck with the family, whatever the problem is. Your merry men are doing well on the ex., on the whole. One or two bog-ups, but that's what it's for." He took off his glasses. "No, but I mean it, Charles. It's a pity. You'd have done all right. Have a good life."

Rebecca came out into the corridor with him. The place was scruffier than Head Office, older and more cluttered. A partially dismantled cipher machine was being pushed along on a trolley by two men in brown coats, heading for an unmarked door at the end of the corridor, beyond which none of the students had ever been. Charles and Rebecca had to squeeze against the wall to let it pass.

"It's very sad to lose you," she said.

"It's sad to go. I like the people, I believe in what we're doing, but I feel compromised, as if I compromise it—you." The words came in a rush and he checked himself. "But we can keep in touch."

"Have you told Anna March?"

"In outline. Hugo will fill her in, no doubt." He smiled. "Why do you ask?"

"Another time. We'll miss you, Charles. I'll miss you."

"We might have dinner."

"That would be nice."

"I'll ring."

Lunch with Hookey meant delaying viewing the flat he was supposedly buying, but Mary had said that the woman with the key would be there during the middle of the day, which he interpreted as until mid-afternoon. He wasn't greatly bothered.

There were people in Hookey's outer office when he arrived before lunch, including two anxious-looking A officers. "Bit of a flap on," said Maureen.

"There is on the sixth floor, too, according to Hugo. The office seems one big flap this morning."

"It's catching. I've noticed before. One floor gets a flap on and gradually it spreads to other floors, although the reasons for the flaps are quite unrelated. Maybe it's competitive, sort of demand for attention. Hugo's not in on this one, though I'm sure he'd love to be. Hookey won't be long. Believes that nothing in life should get in the way of lunch. I'd booked you into the Travellers but he said there were too many office and Foreign Office people there. The office's other canteen, he calls it. So you're going to Brooks's, one of his other clubs."

"How many does he have?"

"He admits to three, these two and Pratts, but I suspect more."

"Does he ever take you?"

She smiled. "Funnily enough, it does occur to him now and again, yes. Usually when someone's cancelled, but still. Or if he thinks it's my birthday, which he invariably gets wrong although I've put it in his diary in red ink and capitals." She was summoned by an irascible shout from within. "Here we go again. I'll tell him you're here."

As a controller, Hookey merited a car to take him to lunch. "Thing about office flaps," he said as they waited at the Parliament Square traffic lights, "is that everyone enjoys them, really. People love cock-ups. Ideally other people's, of course, but even their own provided responsibility is shared. It's the excitement."

He walked quickly past the bar in Brooks's. "We'll go straight in, if you don't mind. Danger of bores in the bar and I'd have to explain you. I had the misfortune to be in the army with the editor of *The Times*, who's there now, and because he still doesn't know what I do he thinks I'm a failed would-be ambassador and commiserates infuriatingly." He laughed and coughed. "One of the problems of an office career. Either they don't realise and think you're a Foreign Office failure or they do and think you're far more influential than you are and keep pestering you with things they think you want to know. Not a problem you'll have, of course, if you do as you say."

As soon as they were at their table a pink gin was put at his elbow. He took four or five seconds over the menu, ordering lobster bisque, roast beef and the club claret. Charles, not minding what he ate, chose the same. Like Viktor, he thought.

"What'll you do when you've left?" Hookey continued. "Have to do something. Young chap like you can't do nothing, even if you can afford it. Can you?"

"No."

"Foreign Office the obvious thing, of course. More postings, more high-status jobs, more self-importance, gratifying illusion of being re-sponsible for international relations, lots of important boring stuff like negotiating numbers of potatoes with this wretched Common Market. Wish to God that referendum had gone the other way. I seem to be in a minority of one in Whitehall on that. But if real diplomatic work is what you want you shouldn't be with us anyway. Postings apart, I'd have thought the Home Civil Service might offer more real jobs, interesting jobs. That's if you want government service at all. Perhaps you'd rather go to the City and make some money."

"I might if I understood what it is they do to get it."

"I agree. Baffles me. My brother's in it. Makes fortunes. Every Christmas I ask him what exactly he does when he gets in in the morn-ing and every Christmas he tells me and at the time I think I under-stand but by New Year I'm still none the wiser. Dreadful old boy network, of course. Not that that's necessarily dreadful. Way the world is, works on connections. Like the office. Journalism's no different. Maybe you should go for that. Maybe I should've introduced you to *The Times* man."

They took their coffee upstairs, sitting in the windows overlooking St. James's. "Best view in London," said Hookey. "Everything you need to know about life can be surmised from the human traffic below us.

Wonderful perspective, best justification for privilege there is. Perhaps the only one. Pity about the portraits, eh?" Charles began looking about him but Hookey allowed no more time for that than for menus. "Thing about our profession," he continued, "is that, apart from the enduring fascination with the foibles of human nature and the interaction between the individual and bureaucracy, the individual and ideology, the individual and power, and the occasional bit of excitement, there's the feeling that at the end of it you might, if you are lucky, have done the state some service. Peculiarly gratifying. Lot of people long to feel they've made a contribution in life. We're lucky. Not easy to find that combination in a single job. Port, brandy?"

"No, thanks."

"Don't mind if I do?"

"In that case brandy, please."

"Sensible fellow. Lunchtime drinking is a positive virtue. People treat each other better, helps the world go round more smoothly. It's like dancing, does people good. You don't dance, I s'pose? So few do now."

"Hugo does, apparently."

"How d'you know that?"

"His wife, Anna, told me."

"Well, that's something, anyway." Hookey seemed lost in thought for a while. Charles knew he should be on his way to the flat.

"I understand why you feel you can't remain," Hookey resumed. "It reflects well on your—your—what do we call it?—your sense of honour?" He stared at Charles with raised eyebrows. "That is, I sympathise with your reasons although I don't agree with the action. Whatever you might feel, and whatever I said this morning, it is not necessary for you to leave. You don't know the full story and you may very well be no better placed to discover it from without, as it were. It would be sensible to wait, eh?"

In his heart, Charles agreed, but he was reluctant to go back on his decision so easily. It was beginning to feel like an issue over which he had to prove himself. "It's not only a question of honour, or how I feel about it. Given the restrictions on what I can do if I stay in, I don't see how anything can emerge which would alter the fundamentals. And it is important to me to know exactly what, and why."

"Have you sent your letter of resignation to Personnel?"

"It's written but not sent. I've got it with me."

"May I see?"

Charles handed the brief letter over. Hookey put on his glasses and scanned it in a second or two. "I'm seeing Personnel after lunch. I'll drop it in for you."

It was a statement, not an offer. Hookey slipped it into his inside pocket. Charles had not yet sent it because doing so would feel like the point of no return for which he had not quite prepared himself. Its disappearance into Hookey's pocket was brutally final.

"Now," said Hookey briskly, leaning forward in his armchair. "I have something here for you." He waited while the waiter delivered a brandy and a white port, then took from his other inside pocket a bulky plain brown envelope. "This is part of a document written by your father many years ago. I shall lend it to you to take away and read. Don't read it here. I'm doing it because it may help you to come to terms with what has happened. It comes from a source of very great delicacy which I am not about to reveal to you and I want you to assure me that if anyone else sees it, if you show it to anyone—as you may feel you want to—you must convince them that you found it among old papers and diaries left in the loft by your father. It must not, under any circumstances, have come from or have been seen by us. Do I have your word on this? Cross your heart and hope to die, eh?"

Charles nodded.

Hookey sat back. "Good. Now, one other thing. If you do make contact as a private individual with Lover Boy—and you'll have to be quick about it because indications are he'll be going back in the next week or two—I beg you to remember Legacy. You may think it odd that I feel it necessary to remind you of it but Lover Boy's words to you about not neglecting your professional and patriotic duty strike a deep note for me, a resonant note. Not only do I think these are the words of a man who wants to talk, despite what he says about not talking, and that it would be worth pursuing him—were we permitted—for those reasons alone. Beyond that, what he says points to a truth about your generation and, if I may say so, perhaps a danger for yourself."

He paused, his hands clasped across his chest, his unlit pipe on the coffee table between them and his gaze on the sunshine and traffic of St. James's Street. "That is, the romantic elevation of the individual above all else, the cult of sincerity, the idea that if I really feel it, it really matters, the assumption of happiness and self-fulfilment as not only the natural state of mankind, but a right. I don't just mean all that E. M. Forster crap about betraying his country rather than his friend—which means betraying his friend's friends—but the insistence on validation by the personal, with the personal always coming first." He took up his port. "Now, of course, I'm an old buffer and I have to remind myself that I must seem to you like old buffers of the previous generation seemed to me when I was your age. But with this difference—they had been through the mill, the first war, as we had ours, whereas your generation has been blest with unbroken peace and unprecedented plenty. Good for you. We—which includes your father, it's worth remembering—knew ourselves lucky to be alive, fed, housed and in one piece, give or take a few loose screws. We were less inclined to rate the importance of anything we were involved in in terms of our own feelings for it. It's not that we were morally any better—you would have been us and we you if the generations were reversed—but the struggle for survival compelled us to look first to what your friend might call the objective realities of a situation rather than at the emotional consequences for ourselves, which come somewhat lower down the survival scale. This, essentially, is what Viktor was getting at when he was berating you for your alleged lack of professional concern. That's not because he's a good communist—believe me, there are very few real communists where he comes from—but because he was brought up in a country that stresses your duties to the state far more than what the state is supposed to do for you. He knows the importance of things like Legacy, he knows that the Cold War is not phoney. It has casualties even while it's cold—look at the Cubans and South Africans in Angola or at what's happening in South Vietnam now that the Americans have pulled the plug on their allies and left them with an army of occupation which gets all the support it wants from Russia and China. I won't go on about that. Makes me too angry. The whole thing was wrongly understood and wrongly handled from the start—and not for want of telling from us, I can tell you. But there we are.

"The point is, people like your friend understand all too well how easily the Cold War can get hot. They're serious about making it hot wherever and whenever they think they can get away with it. That's why they're so serious about penetrating bodies such as the National Union of Mineworkers. They look at the power cuts and three-day week and all the rest of it and the lesson they draw is that democracies are fragile and weak. Did you know that almost from day one of those mining strikes there was a significant increase in MiG-fighter incursions into British airspace? Testing RAF reaction times. And that almost from day one of the Northern Irish troubles they've had signals monitoring ships just outside territorial waters, logging our forces' personnel and procedures? So, for them, filling secret dumps with stuff that could be used to knock out NATO radar or worse is not just playing war-games for the sake of it, or norm-filling. They're doing it because they hope to use those dumps. Knowing that, your friend is understandably a little shocked at your casual, self-referential approach to it all."

He held up his hand as if to forestall a protest that Charles was not, in fact, about to make. He disagreed with nothing of the argument, but was surprised to hear it being applied to him.

"That said," Hookey continued, "I understand your reactions, I don't think you're likely to drown in self-pity and self-concern and I'm sure you won't neglect the broader picture when confronted with it. And I also think that your very obvious lack of pressure on Lover Boy might paradoxically prove your strongest card in recruiting him, whether you intended it or not."

"You want me to recruit him, then, when I've left?"

"Dear boy, how could I possibly say so? We are forbidden contact."

They parted in St. James's Street, Hookey for Head Office and Charles to view the flat. He was late, so took a taxi.

The driver frowned. "Tregunter Road?"

"Bottom edge of the Boltons." He hadn't looked it up in the A–Z and paid little attention as they headed along the Brompton and Fulham roads. He could feel the envelope in his pocket but didn't want to read it until he was alone. How Hookey came to possess something his father had written was a mystery which reading would presumably resolve.

Tregunter Road was a street of tall, mostly stucco-fronted nineteenth-century houses. He mounted the steps to one and was peering at the faded writing for the correct bell when the door was opened by a bustling woman of late middle age in an old Barbour, festooned with bags and riding tack, carrying car keys in her teeth and wearing a black, lace-fringed eye-patch that looked like a miniature bra. "You're not Mr. Thoroughgood?" she asked, challengingly.

"Yes, I'm very sorry to be so late, I'm—"

"Can't stop, awful rush. Keys in my pocket. This one." She turned side-on to him, moving one bag enough to expose a pocket.

"Let me help you with the bags."

"No time. Just fish them out. Delighted to have you as a neighbour. Come for a drink when I'm back. I'm the flat below you. You'll have to dig deeper than that. Hurry up." She hurried down the steps and crammed her tack and baggage into the red E-Type Jaguar parked outside.

Inside the large hall was a letter table and mirror. The stairs narrowed as they wound upwards, ending in a small landing off which were two doors, one to the woman's flat and the other to Charles's destination. Beyond that was an even smaller landing and a set of even narrower stairs with wobbly banisters. They led up into a final landing, giving on to a sitting room, a tiny kitchen, a passage, two bedrooms and a bath-room which faced the road. The flat had been an attic, the ceilings slop-ing with the roof-line. French windows in the sitting room led onto a small balcony overlooking a large rectangle of private gardens, secluded from the roads on all sides by similarly tall houses. The balcony was level with the tops of the plane trees. Charles opened a window and stepped out, startling a pigeon from a branch.

He walked again into each room. The flat was lightly furnished and lined floor to ceiling with empty bookshelves. He would buy it, he thought, whatever happened. He was in the mood for decisions, ges-tures, change. It made him feel better. Since first going to Oxford and throughout his time in the army he had lived from a single trunk. There was that, his bicycle—little-used of late—and whatever clothes he could find hanging for. His books were in his bedroom at his mother's. It would be an easy move; all except the bike would fit in the Rover. He would need plates, he supposed, teaspoons, chairs, boring things like that, but they could come later.

It was not a cold day and he returned to the balcony, sitting out in one of two dilapidated wicker chairs. Resignation involved a month's notice, so in one sense he was still employed by the office. That would mean he could complete the mortgage application with details of salary, refer-ences and so on without telling the lie direct. And then—well, then the rest of life, whatever that entailed. Until now phases of life had followed on one from another in a seemingly natural progression—school, uni-versity, the army, the office—like holes on a golf course. But now, for the first time, there were no more marker flags, no clear direction. The sense of progression that had been so much part of the natural order was suddenly not there. What was left was uncertainty, and not feeling part of anything, perhaps normality for the mass of mankind. The prospect was neither appealing nor stimulating.

Postponing further thought, he took Hookey's envelope from his pocket and began to read.

CHAPTER EiGHT

_____

THERE WERE SEVERAL photocopied A4 sheets of lined paper, covered in his father's precise, sloping handwriting. Staple holes and condition suggested they had been kept in an envelope or file. There had almost certainly been a covering sheet, or sheets, now removed. "Berlin 1945" was written at the top in pencil, in another hand.

"I sensed, really, that it was a set-up," it began, with no preliminary,

even as I was letting it happen. No young woman in Berlin had food, money, her own flat, decent clothes and shoes, make-up and nylon stockings unless she had somebody influential looking after her. Her eyes, too, were different. Most eyes here were hungry and fearful. Hers were watchful, but in an assessing way, vulnerable but determined. It was as if she was saying, "Here I am. You may not want me but this is it, this is what I have to do. So."

That was in the summer, of course, after the German surrender. For me it came after nearly a year of living in woods and fields, of fighting every hedgerow, ditch, canal or river. True, I had had seven blissful days back in Gloucestershire with Jean, whom I never wanted to leave again. But then it was back to the mud and mines of the Reichswald and bitter continuous fighting. Our division used more ammunition in that month in the Reichswald than any division in any month of the campaign. Nor was that all. We took the hard route from Normandy up through the Low Countries and into northern Germany. Not the easy path of flowers and girls and liberation through France, Paris and all the rest of it. Ours was the grim way, the Wehrmacht way. Every field, every copse, every ditch, every ruin had to be fought for. In those last months of war I never slept beneath any roof, saw any whole building nor any smile on the face of any civilian. They were sullen, resentful, beaten, scowling. "No Frat"—No Fraternisation—was the order, but there wasn't much temptation. They hated us. Most of the uniformed Germans we saw were either POWs or teenage corpses. The latter, I'm afraid, were of no more consequence to us then than lumps of wood to be heaved out of our way.

After the surrender I was plucked from the division and flown here to Berlin to help liaise in reconstruction with the other occupying powers. It meant a bed at last, with blankets (no sheets) and, once we got it going again, running water and electricity. All around were burned and blackened houses, streets full of rubble, gaping bomb-holes, opened-up sewers, stray dogs, rats and rampant weed. The people were like rats at first, too, furtive and frightened, emboldened only by hunger. They were terrified of being left with the Russians.

Rightly. To the Russians, reconstruction meant looting. It was systematic, it was their policy. Rape and casual shootings were mere incidentals, harmless diversions permitted to the soldiers of

156

the proletariat as a reward for relieving the sufferings of the fatherland. I had to work mainly
with the Russians, through interpreters, trying to
restore services where our zone bordered theirs.
It was pretty thankless, futile and frustrating,
but I suppose it's how they got on to me.

The interpreter I worked most with was Ivan Ivano-
vitch Rostok, a Red Army lieutenant from the
Crimea, or so he said. He was better than the others, not only in his English but in his attitude.
His instinct was to be helpful rather than indifferent or obstructive. He could not overcome the
suspicion, rigidity and lethargy of the system
within which he lived but he was more companion-
able than burdensome. I suppose he had to be, in
order to report on me.

Not that there could have been much for him to say.
He knew that I had married on my last leave before
D-Day but I cannot think of anything which would
have led him to report that I wanted to be unfaithful. Though I suppose we were all affected by
the anything-goes, grab-what-you-can climate that
came with peace. And after living in ditches and
shell-holes for months on end you can't help being
affected by whatever is clean, soft and feminine.
We never discussed sex or women, that I recall,
and we never socialised together when the bars and
so on got going again. Perhaps there was something
about the way I looked at women, or perhaps they
just thought it was worth a try anyway. It must
have been the same for him, too, I guess.

I met her—or, rather, she met me—one evening
at the Café Berlin that had reopened in our sec-
tor. I ate out whenever I could, mainly just to get
away from the army for an hour or two but also to

practise my German. There wasn't much choice of food but the city was beginning to pick itself up quickly. Human life is remarkably resilient. She simply came to my table and said, in careful English—I was in British Army uniform, of course— "Excuse me, may I share your table, please?" She wore a flowery summer skirt and a spotless white blouse. With her handbag slung over her shoulder, she could have stepped straight out of pre-war Berlin. She looked like no one else I had seen there.

I stood for her and as she sat she said, "I promise I shall not cause you disturbance. It is simply that if I sit at a table alone other soldiers of your army think I am wishing to meet them. I shall eat and read my book but you have no need to speak to me."

It came so pat, sounded so rehearsed. Then she smiled and said, "We shall look like a married couple."

Of course we talked. I was pleased, flattered, refreshed by her presence. She told me her name— Ulriche—and said she had been training to be a doctor until quite late in the war, when training was suspended. Her father was a well-known doctor, very influential, who would build up a good practise again when things got back to normal. Meanwhile he and her mother had escaped to Bavaria when the Russians came. They were still there. She had a boyfriend in the U-boat service but it was many months since she had heard from him. No one knew what had happened to his boat. She was lucky she could live in her parents' flat nearby. It was untouched, so far.

You know how it is when you think you have things under control. In fact, you do have them under control—you actually do—and therein lies the danger. Being aware of what is going on, you are confident of your power to stop it at any time. So you let it continue. You enjoy steering it. Then one day you realise it has acquired a momentum which means that, although you can still guide or steer it, stopping has become difficult. It has by then entered your past ineradicably. It has become part of you, part of your present. Now, even if you stop it dead, it will never leave you. So nothing lost by going on, you think. That's how you get caught.

I was a pushover, I guess. When we went back to her flat afterwards I still had no intention of doing anything. Because I knew I could say no, I was confident I could continue to enjoy the idea of it, the ever-present possibility, without the guilt of acquiescence. And I liked talking to her. I wanted her to go on talking. It was a long time since I'd talked to a woman.

It's curious that I can't now—I really can't—recall exactly how it happened. I have vivid memories of parts of it but no recollection of the sequence. It started on the sofa but how I came to be on it with her, and how—or who—moved from a position of no contact to contact, I simply cannot say. If we lived in times that believed in witchcraft, I'd have claimed I was bewitched. That might still be true but not wholly fair.

I spent most of that first night in her apartment. It was a high-ceilinged, turn-of-the-century place, with heavy faded curtains and solid dark furniture. My work meant I could come and go fairly freely, you see, but I had to be back for reveille. In fact, we spent a lot of time talking. Perhaps, during all those months of hard lying, the real deprivation was more of intimate companionship than sex, which was simply the obvious thing. I can't remember all we said, but we talked a lot and it all seemed so vital at the time.

I don't think I ever thought she was a prostitute by profession, but I had assumed that she would want money, despite her clothes and apartment. Every German needed money. She didn't mention it and neither did I, until I was buttoning up my battledress. I handled it badly, saying something like, "Can I give you some money?"

She was still in bed and just stared at me. "If you like."

I tried to appear light-hearted about it. "If you like, surely. Don't you need it?"

"Everyone needs money."

"How much?"

"Whatever you like."

I felt awful. If I put my wallet away it would look as if I was meanly trying to get away without paying. Yet if I paid it demeaned us both. "I hate this," I said.

"It is better if you pay."

"Better?"

"For you, Stephen."

It was the first time she had spoken my name. Tears stood in her eyes. I went to her. Afterwards she said, "Leave something. Just anything. It will be easier for you."

It was some time before I understood what she meant. In the meantime, I went back to her, and back, and back, as you know. Becoming obsessed is like being adrift in the sea. When you're in it up to your head you have no knowledge of how far or how fast you're being taken. Your horizon is too limited. You lack the perspective that the sight of land could give you. If you could see land you could measure your drift and appreciate what was happening. For a while, early on, I really did lose sight of land, but I had Jean's letters to remind me and, of course, my guilt. It wasn't that I ceased to love Jean. It would have been simpler if I had. It was more that this seemed something set aside from normal time, as if a whistle had been blown and this didn't count. Geography alters the moral compass as well as the magnetic, but really I always knew where true north lay.

Also, something about Ulriche was different. The intensity and release of that first night was echoed but never repeated. She remained keen but I sensed an underlying resolution, as if something took determination to go through with it. Not because she didn't want to see me. I shall never believe she didn't want that. Our times together and our talk could not have been faked. The whole affair was one long passionate dialogue. But she was having to steel herself to something else at the same time. Our only argument was about money. I'd said again that I hated paying her, hated her feeling she had to sell herself, yet at the same time if she needed financial help I was only too happy to give it. It was turning our lovemaking into a transaction that I didn't like.

"You must pay me," she said, "you must." When I demurred she turned on me with tears in her eyes. "Stephen, it is for you I say this. You must. It will help you to hate me."

"Hate you? Why should I want to hate you?"

She turned away. I could more easily hate myself than her, especially when I thought of Jean. When we parted that time I left her money on the table, as usual. It was an ornate occasional table in the sitting room beneath an oval nineteenth-century mirror. For a moment the mirror showed me, the money on the polished table, my hand on the money, and Ulriche, in her red dressing-gown by the fire-place, watching. I don't know whether she knew that was the last time we were to meet. I don't think she did, but she may have sensed it.

The next time I went to her flat the door was opened by a balding, thickset man in a heavy blue suit. Two other men were suddenly behind me. They must have been hiding up the next flight of stairs. "Major Thoroughgood," said the man, in heavily accented English. "We are expecting you. Very welcome. Please to come in."

Without anyone actually laying a hand on me, I was shuffled through the door. Sitting in one of the armchairs was another man in an identical blue suit, but he was younger, with dark curly hair. He was smoking a cigarette and seemed very relaxed. He introduced himself as Igor Smoletsky. "I apologise for this rude shock, Major Thoroughgood," he

said, in good English. "Ulriche has been transferred to other duties. We thought we should discuss with you how to handle this delicate
situation. Please be seated."

Well, the rest was predictable: the photographs of
Ulriche and me in the café where we met, the mention of others more compromising, the suggestion
that the English newspapers might take an interest
in this secret relationship between a British Army
officer and a communist prostitute, the tape
recordings, the effect on my military career and
my future of this unauthorised, undeclared, out-
of-hours, compromising fraternisation, the sad-
ness that would be felt by my pretty young wife
when she opened the envelope containing the compromising photographs.

In fact, I'm not convinced they had those compromising photographs, or not useable ones, anyway.
If they did, they would have shown me, just as they
played an extract from the tapes. I realised then
why Ulriche would always switch out the light when
we went to bed, claiming she liked just the
"romantic" light from the sitting room through the
half-open door. It was my second reason for gratitude to her. That, and her insistence on payment
because it would make it easier to hate her for
what she had done, and therefore recover more
quickly from the pain of it, were of course trivial compared with the overwhelming fact of her
entrapment and betrayal of me. Yet they were the
more touching because of that. It was, I guess,
all she could do, and it may have been why they
took her off what I suppose I must call my "case."
She never tried to get any sort of information out
of me.

Anyway, who was I to complain of betrayal? The shock of what was happening, my anger with Ulriche and with the Russians who were talking to me, my worries about what would happen were bad enough. But they were as nothing to my anger with myself and the shame and remorse which now accompanied my every thought of Jean. Remorse for what cannot be undone is a corrosive that eats at your heart and soul. Why cannot this be felt as piercingly at the time as it is afterwards?

During that first talk with Igor, though, it was practicalities I was most worried about. How to get out of my immediate situation came before deciding how to cope with the longer term. All sorts of things were going on in Berlin at that time and there was credible talk of kidnaps and killings. Were they going to abduct me and, if so, for what? Her flat was a few yards inside the Russian zone—something I haven't mentioned so far, which shows how little account I took of it at the time, since my work took me in and out of that zone every day and I had a pass for it. I could imagine myself the centre of a show trial as a spy. Admittedly, they did not mention anything like that but the situation was threatening enough and I had no doubt that the heavy mob was there to stop me making a run for it. Igor's calm recitation of the possibilities and consequences of disclosure was bureaucratic rather than bullying, like a lawyer wearily outlining court procedure, but the more truly threatening because of that.

I decided that the best way of getting away from them was to go along with whatever they wanted, then think about it afterwards. "What happens now?" I asked.

Igor shrugged and raised his eyebrows, which sent his forehead into corrugations. "It is up to you, Major Thoroughgood. I have described one set of circumstances. However, if you prefer, it is possible to avoid all that. All that is necessary is for you and I to agree to meet regularly and confidentially and to discuss frankly issues of mutual interest."

"What kind of issues?"

He offered me one of his strong Russian cigarettes. I don't know what they had in them but it was a relief to have something to do. "Military matters, naturally. The intentions of the capitalist powers in this city. Then it depends upon your future career. Almost whatever you do, if we achieve a good relationship and you are willing to help build socialism, there will be ways you can assist. So long as our relationship remains confidential and you are always honest in what you say. Then we can help you. We like long friendships. We can help you throughout your life."

Even then, almost despite myself and what he was doing, I had begun to like Igor. It wasn't that he set out to charm—he never did that, he had no need, he was sufficiently confident of his own strength of character and purpose—but more his imperturbable matter-of-factness. His quiet but unflinching recognition of reality gave him great strength. It is a most attractive quality when accompanied by a sceptical humour, which he had.

We agreed to meet again. We would use the flat, he said, because it was convenient for me, I had reason to visit the Russian zone, it was safe and, if I were forced to account for my visits, I could always confess to visiting Ulriche, but not mention that anything else had happened.

"What is happening to Ulriche?" I asked.

"Ulriche is well, nothing has happened to her but it is better you do not meet. Do not try to find out about her. I will tell you if there is anything to know."

As I stood by the door, next to the oval mirror, he added, with a smile that again creased his forehead, "And please be punctual for our meetings, Major Thoroughgood. We Russians are unfortunately not famous for our punctuality, but I am. If you do not appear I shall conclude you do not object to disclosures."

And that is how it started.

Charles sat while the watery sun left the balcony. The tops of the plane trees were busy worlds even in late autumn, but his mind was filled with his father's voice, at once familiar and new. This was his father and not his father, his father at about his own age, believable, forgivable, recognisable as an earlier version of the man he had known. The voice was moderate and clear, the voice of a patient, exact man, concerned to get things right. What was different was the expression of feeling in the first person, something his father rarely, if ever, did. Normally it was impossible to imagine his father as a young man but, strangely, it was his unusual directness that made him now so immediately believable.

What came after, though—the decades-long deceit—was less forgivable and less credible. The threat of blackmail would have weakened over the years because as the case went on the KGB would have had something to lose, too. Could it be that his father had simply got the taste for spying, as others did? The manuscript demanded a leap of imagination, but an achievable one. That first betrayal was easy—perhaps, for Charles, all too easy—to understand, but the sustained betrayal that followed made it impossible to respect the voice whose candour pleaded so eloquently for itself. Why had he gone on? Why? Charles asked the question aloud, addressing his father, with only the chattering starlings as answer. For the first time since the funeral, tears ran unregarded down his cheeks.

He left the balcony, closed the French windows and took one last look around the flat. He believed now that he knew why Hookey had given him the manuscript. He still had no idea how Hookey came to have it, but that would have to wait. The next stage was up to him. The woman below having gone, he kept the key.

CHAPTER NiNE

TWO NIGHTS LATER Charles was trying a new pizza restaurant near Queensgate when Rebecca walked in. "Found you," she said, with a triumphant smile. "Your phone's out of order. The office has been trying to get hold of you for a day and a half. They've rung your mother, knocked on your door, everything. It was me who said you never neglect yourself when it comes to food but can't be bothered to do anything, so you'd find some convenient trough."

He stood. "You know me better than I thought. Join me in my trough?"

"I shouldn't really, I had a big lunch." She sat. "Do they do small ones? Perhaps I could have some of yours."

"I'd rather you had one of your own. I could get hooked on pizzas."

"Spaghetti for me, then."

He'd been drinking wine by the glass but now ordered a bottle. Apart from one call to Mary about the flat, he'd spoken to no one for two busy, fruitless days.

"Have you found him yet?" she asked.

"Who says I'm looking?"

"Hookey. He summoned me and indoctrinated me into the whole thing. He calls me his 'runner' now. He wouldn't have done it if I hadn't worked for him before. He says Hugo thinks he's too important to do any running around and anyway he's not indoctrinated into Legacy, so doesn't know about it. Hookey asked me to ask if you've found Lover Boy."

"No joy. It's hard, mounting surveillance by yourself, but I'm getting fitter. I must've run over every blade of grass in Kensington Gardens. No sign of him or his car."

"Hookey thinks you should ring him. His contact with you is sanctioned and they might think you've changed your mind or something. You'd have to invent a reason why you need to see him, of course. Something he could say when he got back. MI5 might huff and puff but Hookey would say you're a free agent now, sort of. Out of control."

"It still puts Lover Boy at risk, though, and he may refuse to meet. Probably would. A chance encounter would be better."

"He's at risk anyway, Hookey says. His girlfriend's been trying to get hold of him. Wants her pay-off before he goes, Hookey thinks. She rang the embassy but fortunately she got his Russian name wrong and they put her through to one of the military attachés. Now he's got some explaining to do. But she might try again and then he'd be in serious trouble. That's why the office has been trying to contact you. They want you to stop her."

"But I'm not supposed to see her, either. Perhaps they should ask the minister of defence."

"Hookey says you've got to stop her even if you have to marry her yourself."

"It might be very expensive."

"Hookey says do whatever it takes and do it a.s.a.p."

"I'll go round in the morning."

"Tonight, he says."

She picked at her spaghetti. They talked of how the others were coping with Danish Blue. Alastair had got himself arrested in a case of mistaken identity in Copenhagen, there were worries about Christopher in Paris, Desmond had submerged into Florence like a stone in a pond, Roger was doing well in Vienna, Gerry was enjoying flitting about Europe and clearing up behind them.

"Is it true about you and Gerry?" asked Charles. "I feel I can ask now I've left."

"Me and Gerry?" She laughed. "Who says?"

"Speculation by new sources on trial." He thought for a moment. "F1, R3, A3."

"Frequent, irregular and with poor access just about sums it up.

Perhaps they've got the names wrong." She smiled. "And have you been in touch with Mrs. A1 since you left?"

"Should I have?"

"I was the other person in the rose garden at the Castle that night. I felt I couldn't leave while you were talking because you'd have thought I was listening, but I couldn't help overhearing. You want to watch yourself with her."

"So you were the unknown cigarette?" Charles couldn't recall any compromising words or actions. But tone and manner could say enough. "I don't know her that well."

"Dangerous lady. Anyway, it's time you went to see your other lady friend. Too many women in your life, Charles."

"On the contrary. None of them mine."

"Perhaps that's how you like it?"

He could make but not receive calls on the flat phone. There was no answer on Claire's number, which Rebecca had brought with her. He drove down to Belgravia, intending to leave Claire a note to call. He took his father's manuscript.

Claire's sitting room light was on. She came to the door in her coat and calf-length boots. "Thank God it's only you, Pete. I've just got back."

"You're expecting someone?"

"No, but you never know."

"Busy?"

"Worked off my feet, you might say." Something was awry with her make-up and her hair straggled. "You don't mind pouring us both some wine, do you, while I get these things off? Bottle in the fridge."

The fridge was empty save for a little milk, an unopened packet of butter and half a bottle of Spanish white. Charles could find no clean glasses, so washed two dirty ones, drying them with his handkerchief. She reappeared in a fluffy pink dressing-gown and matching slippers, her hair brushed and her make-up partially removed except for a smear on her cheek.

"I haven't seen or heard from him this week," she said. "I was expecting to but I know he's busy, rushing around before he goes. He's only got another few days, hasn't he?"

"You haven't tried to contact him?"

"No." She sipped the wine and pulled a face. "Bloody paint stripper. Who gave it to me? Unless it's my mouth. What about a cup of tea?"

"Good idea."

Charles kept the manuscript folded in his newspaper. He wanted Viktor to read it and had considered using Claire to get it to him. It would expose their connection but the sacrifice could be worth it. It also meant trusting her to say to Viktor only what he wanted her to say, but her lie about her telephone call was not encouraging. He was angry with her about that, to the point of disliking her for it. One more call could finish Viktor. But the important thing now was to get her safely off-stage. Showing anger would be self-indulgence. "Merely personal," Viktor might call it.

"Just as well he hasn't been round, really," she said when she returned with the tea. "Been one of those weeks."

"Bad week?"

She nodded as she drank. "You meet all sorts in this job. There are some pretty funny people around, I tell you. Not funny ha-ha. Nasty funny."

"D'you mean your minister?"

"No, he's just kinky funny, harmless. Last night I went to a client I'd never had before. He was staying in the Park Lane Intercontinental, it was fixed through the escort agency, all kosher, usual sort of thing. Then when I got to the room I found this thin little bloke in glasses, looking as if he couldn't knock the skin off a rice pudding, you know, and he stared at me and said, 'Take your clothes off.' Just like that, cold as charity. Watched me undress as if he was a hospital doctor waiting to operate. Then when I was standing there starkers, just standing because he didn't want me to do anything, he looked me up and down and said, 'I was promised a beautiful girl, not mutton dressed as lamb.' That got me really angry, right off me trolley, you know. 'Listen, mister,' I said, 'you're getting the best screw in town, take it or leave it. And the price has just gone up.'" She fumbled in her dressing-gown pocket for cigarettes.

"What happened?"

"He took it and paid up and I went. But it takes it out of you, that sort of thing, when someone looks at you and speaks to you like that. Then this afternoon I had this geezer who wanted to pretend he was raping me. I had to go to his flat and pretend to be a housewife in an apron and he had to have just broken in and chase me around and then have me from behind on the bathroom floor. Got knocked about a bit. I could do without all that."

Her fingers shook slightly as she lit a cigarette. Her skin was blotchy and the smear of make-up on her cheek now looked like cover for a bruise. "Perhaps you need a break," Charles said kindly.

She exhaled and nodded. "If I had the money I'd have a few months off in Cornwall. There's a bloke down there who wants to marry me— well, he will when I tell him he does—and then I'd be all right. I wouldn't have to work no more. Trouble is, I can't afford to stop working, what with school fees and all that. After all, it's all for the kids. That's why I do it." She looked truculent and near to tears, as if he had contradicted her. "That is why I do it, you know. For the kids."

The telephone rang. He sipped his tea, ignoring the milky lumps. She was suddenly welcoming and coquettishly French, although the call was brief. "It's him," she said afterwards, "Viktor. He's coming round now. He's in a call-box round the corner."

Charles put his cup and saucer in the sink and ran the tap. "He mustn't know I've been here. Find out when he returns to Helsinki, as he calls it, and anything about his movements between now and then. Try and arrange for him to call again at a definite time and don't press for money."

"Last thing I feel like now, seeing him. I want double time for this session."

"Okay. But don't press him for money. Promise? It's very important. Tell me about it over lunch tomorrow?"

"Providing you pay me for that, too."

She was squeezing all she could out of his need to get away quickly. That was all right so long as it enabled him to do what he planned. "Fine. Go easy on him."

After using the peep-hole to ensure that Viktor wasn't already at the door, he crossed quickly to the other side of the street, leaving it as Viktor approached the flat.

Around the corner, in the same street as his own, he spotted Viktor's car squeezed carelessly between a Mercedes and Jaguar. He sat in the Rover, weighing the pros and cons. He was some way from Viktor's and

172

facing the other direction, but he could see it in the mirror. It was not ideal and he wished he had a copy of the manuscript, but this could be his only chance.

He walked back to Viktor's car, stuck the manuscript beneath the windscreen wiper, then returned to his own. There was no one in sight and no obvious interest from any of the houses. If it rained he would have to go and buy something to get a plastic bag for the manuscript, but he didn't want to abandon his watch. Viktor was most unlikely to stay all night. He had probably been on another out-of-town expedition, combined with or covered by a run, and was tagging this unofficial element on to the end. The Residency would expect him to report when he got back, so he couldn't be too late.

Charles settled down to wait. He could read *The Times* by the street light but there were few pages that day because of more print union trouble. He resolved, as he often had, to carry a book with him everywhere, all the time.

From a movement in the mirror he realised he had missed Viktor's arrival. Viktor was standing beside his car, studying the pages he had taken from the windscreen. He broke off to look up and down the street, then returned to them. Then he slowly got into his car. He had been with Claire about forty minutes.

The Escort stayed at its acute angle to the kerb, front end jutting out. Minutes passed. Charles got out and walked back up the street. Viktor's head was bent over the pages, which he held towards the street light. Charles walked slowly past the Escort, but Viktor did not look up. He stopped with his back against somebody's gatepost, arms folded, clearly visible.

Viktor leant back in his seat and stared straight ahead, the pages resting in his lap. Charles continued to wait, wishing neither to intervene too promptly nor to miss his chance. Viktor did not move. Charles pushed off from the gatepost, approaching the Escort from behind. The driver's door opened. Viktor must have been watching in the mirror. Charles stopped.

"I thought you might like to see how it really happened to my father," he said. "I turned out all his old papers. He'd hidden it in the loft of my mother's house. So much for ideological motivation."

Viktor stared straight ahead. To say more might look like weakness, but to say nothing risked a competition in silence when his aim was to talk. He didn't know how much time Viktor had. "It's not very safe for you to talk here, like this. We'd be better walking."

Viktor got out without a word, handing Charles the document and locking his car. Charles led back down the road, away from the direction of the embassy. He handed Viktor the still-undiscarded tweed cap that had belonged to his father, and which he kept in the Rover. "You're less likely to be recognised in this."

Viktor put it on. "Very English."

"It was my father's."

"It should not fit me. He was a better man than I am. He had more excuse. He was in love with Ulriche, I think."

"You were not with Chantal?"

"I was in—I was in obsession with her. We did not talk like your father and Ulriche. Then I was in fear and confusion and despair. Now I am in prison."

"Why?"

Viktor's expression beneath the incongruous cap was mocking. "That is a question the camp guard asks the prisoners—why are you here to disturb me? Why must I bother with you? What is your offence?"

"I don't understand, Viktor. You'll have to explain."

"So there is something the great British Intelligence does not understand? I am proud to be it. When I am in my labour camp and my family is destitute, that will be comfort for me."

They headed through quiet streets towards Eaton Square. The background traffic of London, the humming of the hive, a reminder of the overwhelming indifference within which the abnormalities of life were lived.

"You know what she said, of course," Viktor continued.

"No."

"You wish to make me tell it to you, for your pleasure?"

"I don't know what 'it' is."

Every other uncurtained window in Lowndes Place showed a dinner party in progress. A chauffeur-driven Daimler limousine waited outside one. Viktor paused until they had passed it. "I tell you, then. I went this evening to tell her that this may be the last time I can see her. A delegation arrives from Moscow tomorrow which I have to accompany. I may have no time alone between now and my departure in one week. Also, I sense in the climate in the Residency a security cloud, something is going on and I must be more careful. One of the military attachés received a strange telephone call and people have become very formal with me recently. It may be that I am under suspicion. Two of the delegation are not usual trade officials. One of them, Rhykov, was sent to Paris two years ago to bring home a Russian official who was—how do you put this?—showing signs of possible reluctance. They drugged him. Unfortunately, he died because they gave him too much. This is a detail, you understand, not a problem. The other, Krychkov, is more senior. I have met both before. They don't like each other but I think they don't like me, either, Rhykov especially. Therefore, I had to tell Chantal that I may not see her again, unless I come to London again, and to give her a little present I had bought her. A little present for her but a big present for me, you understand. A necklace. Then, when I get—got—there, she was strange with me. I gave her the present and she looked as if it was nothing. But for me it was not nothing, it was a lot, I have been as generous with her as I can but I have little money and she does not understand that. Then, this time, I said, 'You should be pleased. At least you should thank me. It is to remind you of me, especially as we may not meet again.' And then she says to me, 'I do not need to be reminded of you. I shall always remember because you have deceived me. You are not a Finnish businessman as you told me, you are a Russian official from the embassy, you are KGB. I shall write to your ambassador and tell the newspapers what you have done if you do not give me five thousand pounds for a nice holiday for my children. You must give it to me before you go back.' And then when I tell her this is blackmail she is very angry and says it is what I owe her because I was her lover and a lover is supposed to pay for his mistress and I have paid only enough for her lunch and she has turned down other lovers who would pay her much more because of me."

Anger silenced Charles. In Eaton Square he led them right, towards Sloane Square. Viktor had been speaking quickly but now resumed more slowly, with his earlier bitterness. "But of course you know all this, Charles. She has reported to you. How could she know I was from the Russian Embassy? Now you have told her to do this so you can put pressure on me just like with your father. It is your revenge."

Charles stopped. "Viktor, I give you my word that I—we—are not trying to blackmail you. Chantal did this herself."

"But you have talked to her, you have told her who I am?"

"Yes."

"You knew she would do this."

"I did not. I told her to do nothing of the sort, to put no pressure on you."

"But now she has you can use it. You can say you can stop her if I spy for you. If I do not agree, you will let her do it. It means the same for me."

"I shall try to stop her. I think I can stop her. But you don't have to spy for us. Unless you want to."

"So I must say I want to and then it will be all right for me?"

"It will be all right for you anyway. You don't have to say anything."

"Why not?" He laughed. "Charles, this is funny, you know. I mean, it is not, not for me, not at all funny, but objectively speaking, you know."

Charles smiled. "I know."

"So why are we here, why are we talking? If you can stop her and you want nothing from me, I can go home."

"If you wish." Sloane Square was busy, with people spilling out of the Royal Court Theatre. Charles led them across into Kings Road. He wanted to keep walking and talking. At least among crowds they were less likely to stand out. The variegated population of Kings Road was perfect for that. "Of course it's true that there is something we should like from you," he said as they passed the Duke of York's barracks. "But only if you want to give it."

Viktor laughed bitterly again. "Charles, you are not talking to a virgin."

"Sorry."

"There is nothing I want to give you. I do not want to betray my country."

"Okay, that's fine."

"But I understand from what you say and the way you speak that you have not resigned? You are still in your service?"

"Yes."

"I am pleased about that. You have done the right thing. You are a professionally serious person again."

Charles led the way into an Italian café just past Shawfield Street, as if it were what he had been making for. They took a small corner table and, without asking Viktor, he ordered two cappuccinos. Viktor kept his cap on at the table. With that and his tracksuit, he could have been any of a thousand on the Kings Road seeking identity through incongruity.

"So the Centre lied to you about my father?" Charles continued.

Viktor shrugged. "Not really. No more than they lie to themselves. As I told you, it used to be important to say that people worked for us for love of the socialist revolution and your father probably agreed with whatever they told him after recruitment. They only left out the beginning in their case summary, that's all. This is a case of probably eight, ten files. A big lie to you, perhaps, but a small one for them."

"What did he do for you? What sort of agent was he?"

"If you are not blackmailing me, why must I answer such questions?"

"Do you love the socialist revolution, Viktor?"

He smiled. "Listen, Charles, you in the west know much about my country but understand little. We live on different levels simultaneously. Of course I love socialist revolution and of course I am the loyal Communist Party member. At the same time, no one in Russia cares a kopek for the socialist revolution and there are no communists in Russia. Because the Party is the Party, it is not communism. Only in the west do you find real communists. In Russia they would be in labour camps. The Party could not permit them."

"But you are happy to continue to serve it."

"It is what I was born into. Ask a fish if he is happy to swim in his sea. It doesn't matter if he is happy or unhappy, if he wants to swim and this is the only sea he has. There may be other seas but he is not in them, he has to swim in this one."

"You could change seas. You could stay here. You could defect. KGB officers are always welcome." The backwoods of Charles's mind echoed with Gerry stressing that no Russian official should be propositioned, or in any way urged to defect, without Foreign Office clearance. But they were well beyond that now and, anyway, private citizens could say what they liked to KGB officers. The one category of people who could not freely urge defection upon KGB officers were SIS officers, who were also the one category paid to do so. He was beginning to enjoy his freedom.

Viktor shook his head. "Even if I wanted, there is my daughter in Moscow. And I do not want because I love my country, I am a Russian patriot."

"You love the country that keeps your daughter hostage?"

"It is the sea I have to swim in."

"And you love the country that crushed the genuine people's revolution in Czechoslovakia?"

Viktor put his hand to his heart. "With my experience here, and with what your father wrote in his diary, how can you think that seeing fault must mean you stop loving?"

"Brandy? Shall we have brandies?"

"Why not? I am so late now, it is no difference."

"Late from what—another Beaconsfield reconnaissance?" Viktor's surprise was obvious. "I was there last time. In the woods. I saw you."

"Congratulations on your professional skills," Viktor said carefully. "As you were not there this time, I can tell you it wasn't Beaconsfield."

"Where do your people think you are? How will you explain when you get back?"

"I will tell them I took extremely elaborate anti-surveillance precautions. They approve of that. That is what I should have been doing when you saw me at Beaconsfield. There must be anti-surveillance before approach to target area. Only I went directly, more or less, as you know, so I would have time to see Chantal afterwards. That tells how unprofessional I have become."

They toasted each other in brandies, touching glasses. Viktor downed almost all of his immediately, leaving just a taste. Charles ordered two more. Any KGB officer who talked in these terms would talk more, given time. But time was what Charles lacked and, lacking that, he needed a key. Not knowing where the lock was, he couldn't choose a key to fit. He changed tack, focussing on practicalities. "With regard to Chantal, I will see her tomorrow. I shall get the money she needs to go away, make sure she goes and try to ensure that she stays quiet and doesn't come back for a long time. It's possible she might do something rash in the meantime but I'll try and stop that, too. It's vital that you don't attempt to see her. Can you give me your word?"

Viktor nodded. "It is not possible for me to see her, even if I wanted. Krychkov and Rhykov will be watching me too much. But if your service pays her for me that will put me in your debt for ever."

"We can't help that. We are not your people and Chantal is not Ulriche, to be ordered off-stage when it suits us. This is a free country, more or less."

"Poor Ulriche. Rich Ulriche, perhaps. Or dead Ulriche. I wonder what happened to her."

"Maybe you could look her up in the file when you get back to the Centre. Let me know sometime."

"So we have to stay in touch, do we? We have to have contact arrangements. This is the price, Charles?"

"No contact arrangements," said Charles emphatically, "no price. But it would be sensible, from your point of view, that we agree a mechanism for you to signal if, during your remaining week, you decide you are under suspicion and you want to jump ship—change sea—after all. Of course you don't want and of course there's your wife and daughter but if you're disgraced they're disgraced anyway and they'll see no less of you if you stay here than if you go back and do twenty-five years hard labour. And there's always the remote chance they'll be let out. Twenty-five years hard is about the going rate, isn't it, for those they go easy on? Penkovsky was shot, of course."

"Actually, Penkovsky was hanged, quite slowly. It was filmed. Sometimes they show it to recruits in GRU, to remind them of consequences. But he was a big important spy. He did enormous damage. I am not a spy. I have done no damage."

"If it suits them to believe you. There may be political reasons why it would suit them to have a big spy case, a show trial with confessions beaten out of you and your wife forced to give evidence against you by threats against your daughter so that they can once again demonstrate the iniquity of western special services." He could see that his words were hitting home, and he had a fleeting vision of Hookey in his position. Hookey would not pause, as he had, but would press on. "It's not just a question of one sea or another, Viktor. There isn't a moral equivalence. Ours has no end of junk and rubbish and rottenness in it but the one you're in is deliberately nasty, polluted and polluting. It spawns and swallows Ulriche and thousands like her. One way or another, your own little girl is going to have to make the sort of choices you make, or that Ulriche made. She too is going to grow up in a system where a love affair can be treason. They're hard choices—and we have it easy, I know—but they are choices. You're lucky you have them. Most of your compatriots don't."

"Your father must have thought his love affair was treason."

"My father was wrong. It wasn't. It was just against the rules. But what he did afterwards was wrong." Viktor's pale features were taut. Charles felt that the case had never been more in his control. It would have been a natural moment to ease off, to relax things and perhaps move on together in harmony; but if ever he was going to go for it, he should go now. "You may be in trouble, you may not, but every minute you've spent with me this evening makes it more likely that you will be. If there's even half a chance that you are, you should agree signalling arrangements so you can tell us whether you're okay about going back, or whether you want to talk, or whether you're being taken back and you want to jump ship. If the last, we'd have to intervene and grab you. It would be a major incident and we do it only if you and I agree a mechanism in advance. And there is a price. For this, on top of keeping Chantal quiet, there has to be a price." He was not at all sure that, even with the price, the office would agree. Foreign Office clearance would have to be sought retrospectively, which was always a problem. There would be fuss. Everything he said was unauthorised and he had no power of delivery. But if the price was high enough, and paid, there was a chance.

"So, Charles, blackmail after all," said Viktor quietly.

"No blackmail, Viktor. We will keep Chantal quiet anyway, whether you agree anything or whether you don't. I can't say you will never hear from us again but you will certainly never hear in circumstances that could compromise you. If you come abroad again, we would probably try and talk to you, to see if you have changed your mind. But if you choose to make no arrangement now, you can walk away tonight and go back to Moscow under no threat from us. If you want us to be prepared to help you, though, there is a price. That is not blackmail."

Viktor sat back, his second brandy untouched. "What price?"

"One question and one promise. You answer the question honestly and you keep the promise." Viktor said nothing. Charles gazed at the colourful, talkative, youthful crowd in the café. The profile of one of the women was slightly familiar.

"What is your question?" Viktor asked quietly.

"Look around you." Charles nodded at the other customers. "There are young people enjoying themselves like this in every city of the world, even in Moscow. And in several of those cities, or near them, your people are planning to leave your *nasledstvo*, ultimately so that these people could be threatened with incineration or with having their water poisoned or whatever. Operation Legacy is being prepared here, in London, now. You know the sort of tactics it's there to support. You are part of it. I don't want you to give me any details, any identifications of your people or agents. I just want to know whether you have found and prepared your sites, your arms caches or whatever they are, or whether you are still looking. That's all."

"And the promise?"

"That if you ever hear in future of any sites, prepared, planned or filled, you will let me know, no matter where in the world you are, for the rest of your life, even in your old age in Moscow. And that we agree a system of covert communication here and now."

"I can agree these things but how will you know I am telling the truth?"

"I shall have to trust you, as you have to trust me with Chantal."

Viktor stared as if searching Charles's features for his own decision. "I have a condition. That this agreement is between us personally. I am not your service's agent. I am not going to spy for them. But this thing— yes, this thing is important for you, so I will tell you." He sat forward with his elbows on the table. "It will not be easy for you personally, Charles."

"Tell me."

"My role in Operation Legacy, as you call it, is quite recent really. I knew nothing of it when I came here. Then I was told that we had an important agent who was doing secret work for another department—"

"Directorate S—Illegals?"

Viktor nodded. "And this agent was run from the Centre, he had no contact with the embassy, his case officer used to travel to see him. He was recruited by the Second Chief Directorate many years before but later he was given to Directorate S to run, and then us here in London in conjunction with them. The other officers here had no idea about him, only the Resident and me. He was your father, of course. He had done many things for us for many years but now he was doing unusual work. He was trusted and he had certain skills. His new task was to find places where we could bury radios, arms, explosives or documents so that Directorate S agents who had been trained in sabotage could use them at an appropriate time. There is at least one cache here already, an old one, found by another agent and filled before your father. Only the Resident knows where. But the Centre needs more and your father agreed to find them as his last task before retirement. The last time he travelled abroad he came secretly to Russia and a senior official presented him with the Order of Lenin. He was very pleased by that."

Charles thought he was getting used to the idea of his father's treachery, but he felt Viktor's words in the pit of his stomach. He was relieved that he did not have to speak.

"I never met him," Viktor continued. "Nobody from the Residency ever did. At first we didn't know who he was, only his code-name— Builder. The Centre would tell us what he had done, what stage had been reached, and what we had to do in support. My role at first was to only find dead letter boxes and pass the details to Moscow. They would be filled and emptied for him by someone else, I don't know who. Another agent, perhaps a visiting Illegal. Also, I was to check any site he found. He was ordered to find one close to the west of London. You have strategic military headquarters in this area for your navy and air force, as well as communications centres and the government airfield at Northolt. Also there is Heathrow and Chequers, of course. It is a sensitive area, but very accessible. In Russia you would not be allowed within five hundred miles of such places. You are too relaxed in England."

Charles nodded, his eyes on his father's cap, now on the seat beside Viktor.

"And because this site is for very delicate equipment the Centre sent your father some special instruments to test for damp and vibration and things like that. He found the site in the country close to London when he had some holiday—it was during Christmas—and could go walking and he put the instruments in immediately because it was not safe for him to keep them at home. The Centre had his message to say he had done this and describing the area of the site and his next message was to give the exact coordinates and directions. But then he died. So we knew only the area but not exactly where and what I have had to do is to try to find it."

"Hence Beaconsfield?"

Viktor nodded. "The Centre wants the instruments. We know the site is near the top of the hill, near where the footpath goes through the corner of the army camp, but I could not find it. There is no disturbed earth or any sign. And we cannot risk me or anyone going there too often. That is why I must go for my runs, you see, so that organs of British security will think I am just practising for the Olympic Games. And also the

Centre must find someone to carry on the work of your father. They do not like it being done from the embassy because of your surveillance. Since Lyalin defected, it is not so easy to operate in England. That is the truth, Charles, I know that." He smiled ruefully. "So, all this was happening when you met me in the park, as if by chance. Of course I reported it to the Resident and he reported to the Centre and they surprised us by saying you had a file. Well, it was not your own actually, it was an annex to your father's, but you have your own now, I think. And then they made an even more surprising request that I must see you again, tell you about your father and try to recruit you. Perhaps they wanted you to take his place in Legacy, as well as for other things, but until then we had no idea your father and the Legacy agent were the same person." He sat back and drank off his brandy. "Now, Charles, I think I have more than answered your question. What I have told you is worth more than twenty-five years. It is"—he drew his forefinger across his throat—"so now you must do your work with Chantal. You will not hurt her very much? Even with what she has done I would not like that."

"We'll pay her to go and keep quiet. Enough to make sure she stays quiet. She will not be hurt at all. We need to discuss signal arrangements, for the next week and after."

"And after for the rest of my life? You are serious?"

"Completely. Not only for Legacy, which you might or might not continue to know about, but for you. In ten, twenty years' time you might want to defect. We need a system that will get your message to us regardless of where I am or where you are. But for the next week it has to be, 'Help, come and get me,' or 'I want to talk,' or 'I'm okay.' We'll have to be right up on you. We need to discuss this delegation you'll be with. The Foreign Office must have their itinerary. Are they sticking to it? What about these other two you mentioned?"

Hostile intelligence officers, Gerry had said, were among the hardest to recruit, but the easiest to run. The language of covert communication was international, like the drills and disciplines common to armies. Viktor was an experienced and imaginative operator. "They trained you well," Charles said, when they finished, finding it tactful not to mention his own status.

"How can you say so after Beaconsfield? You know, I am ashamed about that."

They took a cab back, passing Claire's flat on the way. They both glanced at her window. "I wish you more than luck," said Viktor. "This has to work."

Charles stopped the cab before the street where their cars were parked. It was better that Viktor was not seen with anyone alongside his diplomatic registered car. They were together only briefly on the pavement. "So I keep the cap," said Viktor.

"Until."

"If."

Charles went to shake hands but Viktor ignored his proffered hand and stepped forward, arms outspread. They parted with a Russian bear-hug, cheek to cheek, and without further word.

Charles detoured to his car, giving Viktor time to get away. As he went to unlock it, the door of a nearby Volvo opened and a woman got out. "Message from Hookey," she said. "He's got some more brandy in his office. He'd like you to join him there. We'll take you, so you don't have to worry about drink and drive."

Charles stared. "Sue."

The girl from SV smiled. "You know how to corpse your old friends, don't you? Twice in that café you looked straight across at our table, right at us. I had to turn my back. Jim thought you were trying to tell us you'd spotted us. You hadn't, had you?"

"Not a slither. Hopeless. I was too busy discussing tradecraft to practise it."

"Just be grateful we weren't the Russians. There weren't any, by the way. That's why we were there, checking. Urgent request from your office. Better not keep the famous Hookey waiting any longer. Not that he ever leaves his desk, from what I hear."

CHAPTER TEN

A T LUNCHTIME THE following day Charles sat alone in an Argentin-
ian restaurant just off Covent Garden. This time he had a book,
intending another attempt on *Middlemarch*. His eyes read the same paragraph over and again.

"She must leave you feeling grateful, secretly delighted that she's getting one over on us, determined never to see us or the Russians again and
wetting herself with anxiety to get away," Hookey had said during the
early hours. "That's why she must believe it's a loan, not a gift, so that
she'll fear that if she gets in touch she'll be asked to repay. At the same
time she must believe that you're keen for her to get back in touch
because you want her to do the same with Lover Boy's successor, whose
reputation for sexual violence and high jinks has preceded him. And she
must be convinced that there is no point in even thinking of contacting
Lover Boy again, that he has disappeared into the gulag, unmentioned
and unmentionable."

They had talked for two and a half hours amidst the brandy and
tobacco fumes of Hookey's office, alone in the building save for the comcen staff, the guards and the duty officer. Hookey had made him go over
every word of his encounter with Viktor, twice. He had criticised their
signal arrangements, pondered how the thing should be presented to
MI5, noted the two delegation members Viktor had named, chuckled
at Charles's failure to spot the surveillance, congratulated Charles on
the Legacy news, chuckled again because MI5 had crawled over the
grounds of the army camp at Beaconsfield with toothpicks and found

nothing, speculated about the future and ruled that this was not yet a recruitment.

"There is a growing tendency in this service to count the conscious provision of intelligence as a recruitment. It isn't. As you should know from your course, an agent may be said to be properly recruited—and therefore be an agent—only when he or she accepts handover to another case officer, thus accepting that his relationship is with the service, not the individual. You have done extremely well with your friend but we're a long way from that, even if you do meet again this side of the Styx."

They spent the last half hour discussing in detail arrangements for the following week, by the end of which Charles felt drained and sluggish while Hookey continued with undiminished vigour and clarity. "Report to Hugo first thing in the morning, leaving out any reference to Legacy, of course. He can do all the paperwork. He likes that sort of thing. I'll square MI5 in advance at the appropriate level so that they'll know it has a Legacy context. If you think it's difficult to discuss it without Legacy, put in something else—Lover Boy thinking of defecting, for example. Point is, there has to be something bureaucratic to account for our continuing concentration on Lover Boy without widening the circle of Legacy knowledge. And I mean first thing. The rest of your day's going to be busy, like the rest of your week. I'll get the duty officer to ring Hugo at sparrow's fart and get him in. As for the elusive Beaconsfield cache, MI5 will have to look again. You should go with them. You might have an idea how your father might have thought. I'll fix it." He made another note, then clasped his hands behind his head. "Very useful, your resignation. Be hell to pay for all this uncleared, unauthorised activity if you hadn't. There'll be moderate hell anyway but not too bad because you're the scapegoat. Equally useful, though, that you're still on the payroll for your final month. Means I can still boss you around, eh?" When Charles left sometime after two Hookey relit his pipe and began drafting.

Charles now saw Claire approach across the street, tottering on high heels and wearing a tight, short, white skirt. "Darling," she said theatrically, attracting the attention of everyone in the restaurant. She kissed him extravagantly on both cheeks, then dabbed at the resulting lipstick smears with a tiny frilly handkerchief. When they sat she took a mirror from her handbag and repaired her damaged lipstick while he talked about the menu.

"I 'eard about this place," she said, rounding her mouth in the mirror. "I want to try them things that sound like Tampax."

Charles floundered for a while but eventually settled on *empanadas*.

"That's it," she said. "Sort of pancakes, aren't they? And wine?"

"Naturally. Of course wine. Always wine."

He had chosen the restaurant to get her off her own ground, to make things feel different and also, in the event of it going wrong, to ensure she was away from people she knew. She was much livelier than the all but crushed and exhausted woman she had been the night before, although beneath her shovelled-on make-up there was the stretch and strain of ageing, like a taut mask of skin drawn across her skull. Her eyes had a surface shine that blocked all depth or variety of expression. Her account of her forty minutes with Viktor the night before was anodyne: he was jogging, had dropped in to tell her he loved her and give her a necklace, would call again before he left, regretted he couldn't stay longer. She did not mention her money demand or her threat. Nor did she stop talking.

Charles waited until they were nearing the end of the first bottle. "I've got good news and bad news for you. Which way d'you want it?"

"The good, of course. Don't like bad news."

"The good is more money for you, much more. On top of what they're paying you, they agreed with my suggestion that because of all the good work you've done for us they should lend you the money to go to Cornwall and have the break you wanted. The timing's right, with Viktor going away—though we'll come back to him in a minute—and you can have a nice long break before getting stuck in to his successor, if you're happy to do that. It's a five thousand quid, interest-free, a no time limit loan and you don't even have to pay it back in money. You can pay it in time spent on our behalf with Viktor's successor. Does that count as good?"

Her eyes widened. "Peter, darling, you serious? As long as I like? What about the revenue—won't they get on to me if it's government money?"

"They won't know anything about it unless from you. If you talk about it, one way or another it's bound to get back to them. The bad news—"

"Don't spoil it now, Pete, I don't want to know."

"The bad news is that Viktor's successor, if it's who we think it is, has a bit of a reputation as a bedroom romper. Nothing you couldn't handle, I'm sure, but probably like those men you were telling me about. There was some trouble during his last posting with a girl in Mexico City, though nothing was ever proved. In fact, I'm not sure she was ever found. The CIA are still looking for her, so we might hear more and it may not turn out as bad as it sounded. Interesting to see what you think when you meet him."

She nodded.

"More seriously, though, is what's happened to Viktor himself. Apparently his own people had him under surveillance for most of yesterday, though we're not sure whether they were with him on his run when he called on you. Might have been, might not. Anyway, he didn't follow his usual routine this morning and the switchboard aren't putting any calls through to him. The only time he's been seen he was with a couple of security narks, minders who've just flown in from Moscow. They must have discovered something about him, whether that he's been seeing you or not, we don't know, but it could well be. Some of them were seen in Belgravia this morning, though not in your street. Could be coincidence or could be that they only have a description, no name or address."

"You mean they're after me?" Credulous fear kept her eyes wide and her mouth open. "What would they do?"

Charles shrugged. Her anxiety was so palpable that he felt briefly sorry for her; she was outside the service, someone to be used and carefully manipulated, then gently left when her usefulness was finished. An outsider. An outsider was what he was becoming. What she had tried to do to Viktor, however, and could still do, leant effortless conviction to his lie. "Don't know. Probably just identify you as part of their interrogation of him. But you never know with these people. It's just as well you're going away for a while anyway. No harm in lying low for a bit."

A naked man with a beard walked into the restaurant. There was laughter, a wolf whistle and some ragged cheering and clapping. He walked past their table to the far end, turned and walked back and out. Claire, who had lit a cigarette, watched him with unseeing eyes. "How soon do I have to go? When can you get the five thousand?"

"I've got it with me, in cash. Plus what's owed you. If you want to play safe start for Cornwall tonight." He wasn't sure whether she was so preoccupied that she hadn't seen the man or whether, for her, naked strange men were such an everyday occurrence that their appearance in public lacked the novelty it held for others. "Did you see that man?"

"London's full of nutters. Glad to be out of it, to be honest."

Charles nodded. Just as people went on eating their *empanadas* despite the naked man, so in Whitehall Operation Legacy would take its place among other papers filling the in-trays of bureaucrats. It would not disrupt weekends, golf, school sports days or dinner parties—except, perhaps, Hookey's. It was incongruity, he decided, rather than unreality that the naked man symbolised, the incongruity of everyday. Espionage was like that. He was developing a taste for it.

The money was in a parcel in a Marks & Spencer plastic bag. He got her to sign for it while they were still at the table. They parted in the street outside, she with a flurry of kisses and fervour, promising to return to London as soon as she could and to be in touch without fail, he with cautious assurances that all would probably be well, that the office would keep an eye on what the Russians were up to, that they weren't allowed to travel as far as Cornwall without permission and that he looked forward to hearing her impressions of the notorious bedroom romper, when she got into action with him. Pretence was mutual and successful.

Charles had imagined he would begin job-hunting the following week, but couldn't yet believe in himself doing anything else. The very idea of a CV was repugnant. CVs were inevitably dishonest and he disliked that sort of self-promotion. Perhaps he would try to transfer to the Foreign Office, if they would have him, which was doubtful. He didn't really want to do it and they would probably detect that. Without actually becoming bitter, he felt increasingly disaffected from everything. One morning he slept late, another he did not shave. He lunched with a couple of old friends, one from Oxford who was now an ambitious barrister, another from the army now doing well in the Treasury. He could barely manage that pretence of enthusiasm that is usually sufficient to engender its reality. Always before in life there had been something to go on to, but now all that kept him moving was his determination to get at the truth about his father, and that was not a welcoming prospect. Spasms of anger gave way to troughs of despair, which in turn gave way to a longing to talk to him, to have him there, to argue with him, to seek from him the reassurance that was no longer possible. He maintained a separate, consoling imaginary dialogue with Anna, too, but there was no future there, either. He advertised the Rover in *Exchange & Mart*.

Throughout it all, one part of his mind followed the itinerary of the Soviet delegation to the International Maritime Organisation, which Viktor was accompanying. There was surveillance on Viktor day and night whether he was on the streets or off them, in meetings, at home in bed, eating or interpreting. Every step he took outside Soviet premises was observed, every opportunity he had to signal distress closely monitored. The system he and Charles had devised was a traditional one involving chalk marks or stickers that closely resembled, Viktor had confided, the emergency contact procedure agreed with Charles's father.

"It has the virtues of simplicity and flexibility," Hookey had conceded, "but lacks plausibility for Lover Boy's precise circumstances this week. Where does he get his bit of chalk without anyone knowing and why does he carry it around in his pocket? Easy enough for an agent in your father's position but less so for a KGB officer operating from within a watchful residency. However, if he suggested it, he must think he can get away with it."

Viktor sent no signal indicating greater danger. The signal to him that the ploy with Claire had worked—a sticker in one of the glass panes of the telephone box nearest the main entrance to the embassy in Kensington Palace Gardens, easily visible from car or on foot—was made, and remained in place all week. There was nothing more for Charles to do but that did not prevent Hugo summoning him to review progress, as he put it. There were various contingencies involving fake car accidents, police roadside checks, prearranged slip-away points and, if things became desperate, bomb warnings, all designed to enable Viktor to escape anyone to whom he wasn't actually handcuffed. His wife, Tanya, was the main complication; he had no way of knowing in advance whether she would want to defect with him. He suspected not, because of their daughter, but didn't dare discuss it with her. The signals had to indicate that she was joining him, if she chose, but she would have only minutes to make up her mind and take in the instructions.

"I know it's all set up but I think it's worthwhile checking every nut and bolt of the arrangements daily in case we see scope for modification or find we haven't screwed everything down," Hugo said more than once, pleased with his metaphor. "I'm talking to MI5 all the time and of course it's their resources that are being stretched over this. They've had to reduce coverage of some high priority targets to maintain this round-the-clock business that you and Lover Boy cooked up between you. Of course, he's used to KGB SV resources, which are massive, whereas you're just inexperienced. I've explained that to MI5. Not surprisingly, they were pretty unhappy about your contacts with Mata Hari, given their firm request that we steer clear of her until they establish the truth of this ministerial business of hers. Very unhappy, actually. But I took Hookey's line that you were out of control, having resigned. They weren't very happy about that either, to be honest. Blackens your name, rather. What's more, it makes my life difficult, not knowing how to categorise you so far as expenses and the money you drew to pay Mata Hari are concerned. If you're still in the service it's one set of forms, if you're not it's one of several others depending on how we describe you. If we call you an agent I'll have to open an agent file for you. If we call you a registered contact it's something else again. Bloody nuisance. Anna sends love, by the way, and wants to know if you've found a job yet."

"There hasn't been much time."

"Better get on with it. Are you growing a beard?"

"No, I just haven't shaved." Charles was wearing jeans and no tie. He sensed, and enjoyed, Hugo's disapproval. Hookey, when they met briefly, ignored it, and was brisk and businesslike.

"An MI5 search team is going out to Beaconsfield this afternoon," he said. "I've told them to take you. Maureen's arranged for them to pick you up at your flat. She'll tell you what time."

They picked him up in a Cortina estate; two men, Mick and Jeff, both short and wearing jackets and ties. Mick was from London, Jeff from Leeds. They were pleased.

"Haven't had a decent rummage for ages," said Jeff. "Been all breaking and entry stuff recently."

"Last week's go at this place weren't a proper search," said Mick. "They told us the wrong bloody area, sent us poking about the officers' mess and all that. You reckon it's out on the perimeter?"

"I'll show you."

At the main gates in Old Beaconsfield they were waved through by a bored sentry on production of a single black and white MOD pass.

"Gets you in anywhere, this bit of plastic," said Mick. "Funny thing is, it don't mean nothing, really. Ordinary MOD passes are different, they just dish these out to us, but they look better than the real ones. Work with the police as well. Get out of gaol free cards, we call them."

They drove past the modern officers' mess, past the instruction wing where forces, Foreign Office and office students came to learn Russian, then on to the former POW compound itself, used now for drill and stores. "Straight on," said Charles.

"Right across the sports fields?"

"Well, round the edges."

A gaggle of young soldiers in red vests and baggy blue shorts ran reluctantly around the fields. It was a cold, still day and their exhalations hung in the air. Nets and corner flags were up on the football pitches. Someone shouted at the soldiers, who just perceptibly speeded up. There was always shouting in the army, Charles remembered. You got used to shouting and being shouted at. In modern civilian life, though, a shout was a shock. The camp recalled memories of his week or two there: the comfort compared with life in the battalion, the not too taxing course, the comically querulous commandant, tea with Janet in the town, the inebriated cavalry officer who had fired both barrels of his twelve bore into the newly decorated bar wall, either side of a shaken infantry volunteer. The commandant, sounding like a startled chicken, had fined him heavily.

The Cortina wallowed around the fields towards the wooded corner and the high wall of the pistol range, where they stopped. From the covered rear they unloaded spades, prods, probes, a metal detector and other acoustic devices. The two searchers put on blue overalls and wellingtons. "You'll get soaked in that long grass," Jeff told Charles.

Charles was soon wet up to his knees. They began in the wood, away from the area of grass that Viktor said he had searched already for signs of disturbance. Mick used the probe and Jeff the metal detector. The yield was two bits of old wire, a rusty fork, a small heap of 9mm bullet cases and a piece of metal that might have been from an old ammunition box.

Charles wandered off and leant against the shot-marked wall of the pistol range. He tried to imagine his father with his walking stick and small spade, the latter probably hidden beneath his duffel-coat, tramping about during the Christmas holiday shortly before he died. He would have sought somewhere easily concealed but easily found, not overlooked but not too far from the road, somewhere that a walker or jogger might reasonably visit, but which was generally unvisited. The exact site would have to be briefly and accurately describable in secret writing or in short-wave burst transmission. Ground disturbance would have to be minimal, and easily hidden. He tried to think of his father only as the practical man, the professional surveyor who might have stood where he did, looking about.

As soon as it struck him, it was obvious. He went over to Mick and Jeff and pointed at the butts. "Try there, in the sand."

The sandbank into which the bullets were fired was piled against the wall to a height of nine or ten feet, extending about twice that outwards at the base. The cardboard targets he remembered so well—scowling, slightly Asiatic, helmeted heads and shoulders, clutching weapons— would be on poles stuck into the ground at about five feet. Most of the bullets would go into the sandbank at about that height, some into the wall above, some into the sandy ground below.

Jeff was sceptical. "In there, with bullets smashing into it?"

"Down here, at the base," said Charles. "It's still sand, look, always churned up by soldiers' boots when they're setting the targets but no one shoots that low. Try it."

"Still be full of lead." The metal detector made a continuous noise. "Told you, full of lead. Spent rounds."

"Try the probe."

After only three or four goes they struck something hollow-sounding, not deep. Mick dug carefully and exposed the lid of a wooden box about one and a half feet square. He stood back. "Better call the technical team out to open it."

"Why?"

"Booby traps. Sort of thing they do with caches."

Charles hesitated. They knew nothing of his father and had simply been briefed to search for a Russian cache. "It won't be. This was just a trial run."

"They wouldn't do you the favour of telling you that, would they, the Russians?" said Mick. "You couldn't know unless they told you and if they did you couldn't know you could trust them. We ought to get the technical team. We always do on jobs like this."

The top of the box, thinly covered by sand and soil, seemed to grow more sinister under their gaze. The glumness of their expressions was comically emphasised by their overalls and boots.

"You stand behind the butts," said Charles. "I'll open it." They did not move. "You're quite right to be cautious. Normally I'd agree. But I've seen the operational plan. I know this one's harmless. You stand behind the wall while I open it."

"You sure?"

"Absolutely. But I'd feel happier if you were out of the way. It's standard ATO procedure." He had seen little of bomb disposal in Northern Ireland but enough to give him confidence to make his point. "Only one man exposed at a time."

The reference to standard procedure reassured them. "You'll call out when you've done it?"

"I'll describe what I'm doing throughout."

Once they were behind the butts he knelt by the box. Until then it had not occurred to him that it might not be what he was seeking. It could be anything, buried years ago, in the Second World War even; it could be booby-trapped. But the wood, when he dusted it off with his fingers, looked like newish softwood. His father had always had a few pallets stacked at the end of his shed, rescued from builders' skips. He used the wood for odd repairs or for fire-lighting. Charles eased his fingers down the sides of the box. "Lifting lid now," he called.

It came up easily, sand spilling into the box. Inside was a smaller cardboard box, filled with what looked like salt or sugar. There was also an instrument with a dial and some wires. He called for them to join him.

They came out from behind the wall, extravagant now in their enthusiasm. "We'll take the contents back to the technical lab," said Mick. "Got some foam in the car to wrap them in. Then Jeff'll dig the box out."

Charles thought. "I think it would be better to leave it for the time being, just as it is. Might be more useful here than in the lab." They looked at him as if he had suggested leaving buried treasure. "Might be better to watch and see what they do about it."

"What, concealed cameras, you mean?"

He hadn't thought of that, but nodded.

They took measurements and photographs, replaced the lid and covered it. It was easily hidden in the churned-up sand.

"KGB knew what they was about when they chose that place," said Jeff.

It was well after six when they returned to London but Hookey, as usual, was in his office. When Charles finished describing what had happened Hookey sat in silence, hands in pockets, chair swivelled so that he could watch the trains. "So your idea in leaving it untouched and intact is that we can then tell Viktor where it is so that he can go and find it, thus gaining kudos with his own people and being himself all the more grateful to us? Fine. And if we have no more contact with him before he goes and if he anyway hasn't got time to trot off and find it, we've lost nothing because the chances of their finding it in the meantime, particularly given their lack of success so far, are remote? Also fine. And it's for me to square it with MI5, presumably. Tell them we've left it unguarded, unmonitored, unexamined for anyone to stumble across if they're lucky enough. You hadn't thought of that, eh?"

"Not really, no."

"Not at all, you mean. But also fine. I'll do that." He faced Charles. "What you don't know are the results of further tracing on this delegation Lover Boy is bear-leading, particularly on the two he named. Alexei Krychkov and Sergei Rhykov both have security traces as long as the Limpopo. Didn't come up when MI5 first traced them in their own records, then with us and GCHQ, because the given names on the visa applications were slightly different. Had they been recognised, they wouldn't have got visas. As it was, the deception came to light only after their visas had been granted. They could still have been stopped then but the Foreign Office was reluctant because we've just won the most almighty argument with the Russians over their trying to reject one of our delegations to Moscow. To have done the same thing ourselves would have invited retaliation. Further tracing, prompted by your information, has confirmed it all in spades. They're both KGB, Krychkov Line K, the security narks. Not so sure about Rhykov. But they're here, so that's that."

"Checking up on Lover Boy?"

"At least that. Probably also to ensure he gets on the plane at the end of the week, as he suspects. On past traces, Rhykov may also have another role, something more operational. But it's not clear. Thing is, whether Lover Boy realises that this means he might face some nasty questions when he gets home. The fact that he hasn't signalled means that either he doesn't realise—which is unlikely—or that he does but thinks he can handle it, which is very likely mistaken. Question is, do we initiate contact in order to tell him?" He stared at Charles with theatrically raised eyebrows. "If we do, it could put him under yet greater risk. If we don't, it could be the long goodbye."

"Surely we do. We take the risk. We put it to him. We give him the chance to defect, again." For some days he had secretly hoped that this was what Viktor would do. It would bring the case to a conclusion, with all the appearance of dramatic success, and he would feel he had atoned somewhat for his father.

Hookey waved his hand dismissively. "I'll think about it. Meanwhile, I've got to talk to Hugo about something else. You can bring him up to date on the security narks, leaving out your Legacy business, of course. See me tomorrow."

Hugo, waiting in the outer office, was disagreeably surprised. "I thought Hookey was in an important meeting. Anything I should know?"

"Just that—"

"Wait here and brief me when I come out." He turned with a flash of jacket lining and closed the door.

Maureen made a face. "So reassuring to know that intelligence branch officers are selected for their people-handling skills. Cup of tea? You could be in for a long wait. Even his nibs finds it difficult to keep meetings with Hugo short."

Charles sat at the far side of his room with his tea and a month-old copy of the *Economist,* its lengthy circulation list still uncompleted. He looked at Maureen as she typed, making two carbon copies of each page. Hookey was rumoured to be a man of affairs. He was variously reported as being on his third marriage, having married his former secretary, and to be still on his first—but conducting an affair with Maureen. Charles would not have credited either when he had first met Hookey but now, without a word about women or affairs ever having passed Hookey's lips, he would have believed either. Or neither: it was hard to imagine Hookey having a personal life. The Green Book, the diplomatic list on Maureen's desk, would give the official story, but he did not want to look up Hookey in front of Maureen. The door opened and Hugo appeared, clutching his minute-board and still in full flow.

"So I info A20 and C/AF on the QT that if the potential OCP keeper is N/T in FX and FT we can recruit her before AV-ing provided we i/d her cohabitant *fnu snu* and don't go ahead with the proposed ACA/BCA role in Matrix. Should it be TS or S?"

"It should be a.s.a.p.," came Hookey's voice, drily. "Doesn't matter a monkey's how you classify it so long as you don't broadcast it half way round the world as you've just done."

Hugo closed the door with compressed lips, avoiding Maureen's smile. "Come on," he said to Charles.

They waited in silence for the lift. Hugo, frowning and with his lips still compressed, tugged at his shirt cuffs and tweaked his trouser crease. "Hookey says you've something to tell me," he said eventually. The lift arrived while Charles was explaining. Hugo held up his hand to silence him. In the lift was a young man with fair hair nearly to his shoulders and wide flared trousers. They stood in silence until he got out. "Can't stand flares and hair," said Hugo, when the doors had closed.

"Flares?" Charles was still wrestling with *fnu snu*, whom he now remembered as a ubiquitous figure in espionage: first name unknown, second name unknown. "I've never got round to them. By the time I catch up with a fashion it's moved on."

"Quite right. Now. Continue." They were standing before the closed door of Hugo's office by the time Charles finished. "I see," said Hugo. "Can't help noting that I'm always the last to hear of these things. Was there anything else?"

"No."

"Nothing at all?"

"No."

"I'm sure there's something being kept back from me in all this. Don't trust Hookey an inch." His hands moved from pocket to pocket. "Sovbloc mafia carries all this need-to-know business a bit far sometimes." He stepped along to his secretary's office, where there was a brief altercation, then came back and stood by Charles. "Very odd."

"In the door," said Charles, who had just noticed the key in the lock.

Hugo stared at it for some moments. Once in the room he walked to the window and stood facing out, his back to Charles, hands clasped behind him.

"I hope Hookey lets us contact Lover Boy," said Charles.

"My first security breach," Hugo said, without looking round. "You could breach me, of course. So could Angela, my secretary, or anyone else who saw the key in the lock and discovered the office was unoccupied with papers left out. But if you don't mind"—he turned, still with his hands behind his back as if facing a firing squad—"I'd sooner breach myself. It's more honourable. I'll report myself to Security Branch."

It hadn't occurred to Charles to report. "If you really think it's necessary. I'm sure it isn't."

"Of course it's necessary. Security is an attitude of mind. It's not something you can be keen on in principle and sloppy about in particular. Being secure means being particular, or it means nothing. I should be grateful if you would witness my report."

"If you really want. Why don't you—"

"I imagine you must have dealt with similar cases in the army." The telephone rang. Hugo's responses were monosyllabic. "That was Anna," he said, "on about our weekly dinner party tomorrow. Small affair this week. Rather lacklustre. Two people have dropped out. She wonders if you would like to come."

"Tomorrow?" He was to have a curry with Mary. "Thank you."

Fortunately, Mary was doing nothing that night, so the curry was brought forward. Roger was packing in the flat when Charles got back, since the course was being sent on leave immediately after Danish Blue. Charles's story of having been in Reykjavik was not put to the test. Roger was tactfully incurious, speaking only of his Viennese adventures.

"Spent an entire evening with the wrong Joe," he said, using the old SOE slang for agent. "Well, he wasn't a Joe at all, it turned out. Hungarian, you see. No English, hardly any German, no French, and me with no Hungarian. But the description fitted and he was carrying the right bloody newspaper. And of course he just went along with my recognition phrases because he couldn't understand a word I said and thought I was the police. I thought he'd just stumbled over his phrases because the office had briefed him to be incoherent with nerves. So I bought him dinner, briefed him as best I could and sent him on his way. Turned out the real Joe was in the upstairs bar." He wiped the laughter tears from his cheeks. "No idea who my Hungarian bugger was. Christ knows what he thought was going on. Must've reckoned every day was Christmas Day in the west. Gulped his dinner and scarpered as soon as the bill came, anyway."

He had had more success with a middle-aged Viennese woman he had met in a coffee-house. "Adds spice, doing it under alias. 'Specially with her in her undies and furs. Wondered afterwards if she was part of the exercise. You know, sent round us all to give us a bit of a lift. They're not that generous, Gerry says."

"She must've liked you, then."

"No accounting for taste."

The reason for the curry with Mary was to discuss how he would proceed with the Tregunter Road flat. For once, he felt at an advantage.

"You'll have it?" she asked. "Just like that? Don't you want to see it again?"

"No need."

"And the solicitors and building society?"

"All fixed." He didn't tell her he was soon to lack a salary and would have to get a tenant to pay the mortgage if he didn't get a job.

"And Nigel and the price—?"

"No problem. We spoke on the phone. I've got the spare keys still. He's happy for me to hang on to them."

"Aren't you having your own survey?"

"No."

"Nigel's girlfriend—he's moved in with her—said he hasn't done a thing about moving out, not a thing. He's awful like that, apparently. Just moved in with the clothes he wants and his books and won't lift a finger about the rest. You may find it difficult to get vacant possession with all his furniture and everything there."

"He's leaving it. Chairs, beds, sheets, teaspoons, clothes in the cupboards, milk in the fridge, curtains, flannels, everything. All included in the price. Saves him having to move it or get rid of it, saves me having to get anything."

Her domestic instincts—a fairly recent development since she had been a wilfully careless adolescent—were aroused, without her quite knowing which way to turn. "But d'you want them? Have you looked at them? Are they the sort of things you would like?"

"No idea but they're there, which is the main thing."

"Well, shouldn't you—shouldn't we—go and have a look, as you've got the keys?"

"Let's go now. Help yourself to anything you want."

"I can't if it's yours, or will be."

"That's never stopped you before. Treat it as your commission for finding it for me. There are one or two pictures you might like."

He was supposed to be on call in case Viktor signalled, and anyway was waiting for Hookey's decision on whether to initiate contact. When he was away from a telephone he had to ring in every few hours, and had to ring Rebecca in her office twice a day in case of further problems with his line. She also fielded any calls for him, pretending to be his secretary. "I'm learning quite a lot about you," she said when he rang in the following morning. "Who's Suzanne?"

"No idea."

"Come on."

"Oh—the building society girl. Who's your admirer, if not Gerry?"

"Need to know?"

"Yes, I do, actually."

"One day, Charles. Perhaps."

He travelled to Hugo's dinner by train because of a superstition that, having advertised the Rover, he was more likely to crash if he used it. He thus arrived last, underestimating the walk from the station. Anna answered the door wearing a long skirt and a tight white jumper.

"You shouldn't've, you really shouldn't," she said, accepting his flowers. "How did you know I love roses? Red, too. That's very flattering for an old married woman."

"But they're for you."

She took his arm to lead him down the hall. "I hope you don't mind but we've invited Angela, Hugo's secretary, as a pair for you. I know you've met her already and I don't really believe in gender equality at dinner parties but somehow when it comes to it my nerve always fails and I just do the conventional thing. And Hugo thought we should because we haven't had her round for ages. Not that I'm reluctant, not in the least, it's just that I didn't want you to assume I was matchmaking."

"Last thing I'd have thought of."

In the kitchen were two more bunches of roses—pink—still in their wrappers, which were the same as his own. She put his with them. The kitchen was in some disarray. "My fault for attempting a soufflé," she said, following his glance. "I should never do anything in which timing is critical."

"My fault for being late. I'll disappear."

"No, don't, I didn't mean that." She faced him, as if she were about to continue but thought better of it. He, too, was about to speak but hesitated. They laughed.

"Ah, there you are," said Hugo, advancing down the corridor from behind. "Come and be introduced."

Angela was slim and dark haired with a tense expression but a hesitantly friendly manner. The others were an office couple: Alastair, a stout, loquacious, balding man in his forties and his wife, Emily, a former office secretary with kindly features riven by anxiety.

The soufflé was a success. Conversation during it was mainly about cooking. Charles's attempt to look intelligently interested was made more difficult by the fact that, as usual, he finished well before everyone else, so had to do it for longer. The talk then was about people he didn't know.

"Not more office gossip," pleaded Emily, to a sympathetic glance from Anna as she cleared the plates. "Alastair used to talk about all sorts of things before we were married, since then it's been office, office, office. Can't you think of anything else? Try, darling."

"All right. Rugby."

"I'm going home if you talk about rugby."

"What about the latest Jacko story?"

"That's office gossip again."

Alastair ignored her and went on to describe how the man called Jacko was being awkward about leaving Nairobi. That reminded Hugo of the famous story about old Mucker Maclean in Tripoli. Alastair matched him with other stories about Mucker Maclean.

Angela got up to see if Anna wanted help in the kitchen, beating Charles to it. As she did not immediately return, he got up anyway. Anna was hurriedly putting poached salmon on plates. "It's terribly sweet of you," she was saying to Angela. "We can do it here instead of—potatoes there—letting people help themselves. The trouble with asking Hugo to help is that he interprets it as an invitation to take charge—assume command, I should say. Charles, go and sit down."

"Sure there's nothing I can do?"

"Well, yes, you can, actually. You can open some more wine. We seem to be getting through it rather. Unless it's just Hugo."

"Alastair's never exactly averse," said Angela.

Anna paused, pan in hand. "You know each other already? Sorry, I didn't realise."

"We were in Brussels together."

"So you know Emily too? How nice."

When Charles rejoined the others Alastair was defending office gossip on the grounds that "shop" was the preoccupation of most professions. The great thing in life was to have a few belly-laughs. There were more belly-laughs in his job—operational security—than if he had followed his brother into the Society of Actuaries.

Over the main course Hugo and Anna had a spirited disagreement over whether there was such a thing as pure intelligence, in the intellectual sense. Anna's father was an experimental psychologist. They talked over each other.

"You don't know what I mean," Hugo concluded crossly. "You won't listen. You never do."

"No one ever knows what Hugo means," said Alastair, laughing. "It's what makes conversation with him so intellectually challenging."

During coffee in the sitting room Hugo and Anna avoided addressing each other directly. Angela remained quiet. Hugo sat heavily next to Charles on the sofa. "Brandy?" His manner suggested an incipient moroseness, something not quite in control. "That's the great danger with the office," he confided. "Can become all-enveloping. Privilege to serve, of course, but important to have something else in life. Partly why I do my war-gaming. You got any outside interests?"

"Depends how you define them, I s'pose, I quite like—"

"You should find one. Otherwise you'll end up like—" He nodded lugubriously in the direction of Alastair. No one else was looking in their direction. "Agreeable colleague, sound officer, but nothing else in his life. Except—" He nodded again, this time at Angela.

"You mean—?"

Hugo's final nod was funereal. He had one eye closed.

Alastair was talking about Brussels, ignoring Emily's punctuating contradictions and qualifications. Angela was sitting upright in an armchair, trying to look part of the discussion but still saying nothing. Anna, perched sideways on the other sofa, was attempting to make Alastair's monologue more inclusive without appearing to wish to stop it. She interjected remarks, asked questions, appealed to the two women, glanced at her husband and Charles, was busy with coffees.

Hugo leaned over and murmured, "I have a good marriage. He doesn't. Luck of the draw, really. Plus what you put into it."

Anna came over with the coffee pot. "Come on, you two, what about a bit of audience participation?"

Charles sat up but Hugo remained slumped. "Brandy?" he asked again, out of the side of his mouth.

"No, thanks."

"Think I shall." He got up at the second attempt and went to a drinks table in the corner. Charles was about to join the others when Hugo returned and sat heavily again. "Thing is," he said. Charles waited. Hugo sipped his brandy and stared moodily at his wife. "Too many prima donnas."

"Prima donnas?"

"Espionage success, like military success, is nearly always a question of organisation. Of course, personalities play a part but they should never be allowed to dominate. We over-indulge the cult of the magical recruiter, like what's-his-name in Personnel who talked to your course about the Eastern European case. All very well. But."

"D'you think we'd better join the others?"

"Not that I've always been an angel, I admit." Hugo grinned complacently. "Bit of a bad boy myself. Once or twice. Not seriously, not like—" He nodded at Alastair again. "Can't keep off it. Welsh, you see."

"I thought he was Scottish."

"Welsh ancestry, far back. Always comes out."

Charles searched Hugo's face for clues. "I thought you said you were very happy with present arrangements."

"So I am, so I am. But having plenty of booze at home doesn't mean you never want a drink when you're out, does it?" He looked mildly indignant.

The telephone rang in the kitchen. Anna jumped as if she had been waiting for it. "It's for you," she told Charles when she returned. "The office, inevitably."

"For him?" Hugo struggled to sit upright.

203

"They're offering Charles a peerage."

"What?"

"About time, too," said Alastair from across the room. "He's been doing noble work keeping you awake, Hugo."

It was the duty officer. He had heard from the MI5 duty officer that the SV team on Lover Boy had reported that their subject had left the embassy alone for the first time since the delegation had arrived. He was behaving strangely and they had asked that Charles be told. His driving was erratic and now he was wandering on foot near the Thames with no obvious purpose but evidently dissatisfied and unhappy. He had taken no anti-surveillance precautions. They recommended Charles's presence, if possible. "No idea what he's up to," the duty officer said.

"Where are they?"

"Waterloo area, by the river. They can't spare a car to pick you up as they've only got two on him but I can send the duty car and driver if you're stuck."

"I'll get a cab. Where should I join them?"

"Wait one." There was a long pause. "Stamford Street, one hundred yards east of the Waterloo Bridge roundabout."

It was not easy to leave quickly because Hugo wanted a full explanation, *sotto voce*, in the kitchen. He seemed almost wilfully obtuse and Charles had to repeat himself several times. "But why do they want you?" Hugo asked.

"Because I know him."

"What do they mean, behaving strangely? What's he doing—exposing himself?"

"I don't know."

"What do they think you can do about it?"

"I won't know till I get there."

"Seems odd to me." Hugo looked sad and thoughtful. Oddity, in his lexicon, was a serious matter. "Does Hookey know?"

"Shouldn't think so."

"Very odd. I'd better talk to him before you do anything."

"And I'd better get there. You can get in touch with SV if Hookey has anything to say."

"I'm sure he'll think it extremely odd. Extremely. I'll ring him when I've dropped you off."

"Hugo, you can't possibly drive, you're drunk." Anna stood with folded arms in the kitchen doorway.

"I'll get a taxi," said Charles.

"That will take ages. You can't get them round here unless you ring for them. It's quicker if I take you."

"If I'm drunk, you are," said Hugo.

"I've had less than a glass." She took the car keys from a hook on the pine dresser. The others sat in silent disunity as they left, with Hugo standing in the corridor, frowning.

"D'you think it's awful of me to leave them all like that?" asked Anna, as she started the Austin Maxi. It was a wide car but they were close enough for him to catch her perfume. One of the Chanels, he thought.

"Don't answer," she continued. "It is awful, no matter what you think. But it's such a relief, I can't tell you. I've had to do it for years, week in, week out. Hugo insists. It's worse when you're abroad, of course. But this one was particularly awful. I'm so sorry. Real suet pudding evening. I don't think anyone wanted to be there. Damn these gears, they're so awkward."

"They've got a funny sort of cable link on this model."

"Oh dear, you're not a car bore as well, are you?"

"As well as what?"

She smiled. "As well as most of the men I meet. One thing you can say for Hugo: he's got not the slightest interest in cars. Where are we going, by the way?"

She drove quickly. Neither spoke. He tried to focus upon Viktor, to work out what he might be doing, anticipate every eventuality, but the silence was distracting. It was not an uneasy silence, but complicitous. Once he caught her eye in the driving mirror.

"Nearly there," he said gratuitously as they headed along Stamford Street from the Waterloo Bridge end. "I wish we weren't." His words hung in the air. She glanced at him but said nothing.

A Saab was parked in the appointed spot. She pulled up behind it, keeping the engine running. "Shall I wait for you?"

"You shouldn't. Anyway, I've no idea how long I'll be."

"Good luck."

"Thanks for dinner." As he opened the door he leant over and kissed her on the cheek. She made no response.

Jim, the team leader from the Beaconsfield trip, was in the Saab with a man and a woman, who was not Sue. Charles got in the back, next to the man. "He came out the embassy at a hell of a lick," Jim said. "Turned right where he shouldn't, driving careless, came over here, three times round the Elephant and Castle then up towards Borough, parked and wandered about as if he was lost, then back in the car and up this way, parking on double yellows behind the theatre, wandered about a bit more and finally went down this dark alley towards the river. We didn't follow him in because you'd know if a mouse was behind you in there, even though it is as black as pitch. No idea what he's up to but he looked ragged, uncertain, not careful and controlled like he usually is. Static OP is sure no one followed him out and we're pretty sure he's still down there. There's no other way out. Unless he's donated his body to the fishes."

"Is that what he looked like doing?"

"Looked pretty desperate to me, to be honest. Didn't you think?" The others agreed. "Don't know what you want to do with him, Charles, but thought you ought to know. Orders were, if in doubt, call you in. Sorry to mess up your evening."

"You haven't, don't worry. You did right."

"We can take you to the alley, the entrance to it. Rest of the team's on it now."

"I know it. I know where he'll be." Charles made his decision. "I'll walk down to it. If I don't soon come back it means I've found him."

"Want someone with you?"

"No."

"We'll stick around, anyway."

He walked around the bomb-site car park towards the river. Not far from the alleyway, where the road became partially cobbled, there was an abandoned, wheel-less Ford with broken windows and one door hanging open. The rest of the SV team were presumably in the car park. There was enough street light to make out puddles on the uneven ground of the alley; the crumbling, weed-infested walls on either side appeared to lean in towards each other even more than he remembered. The river wall at the far end was distinguishable as a darker patch of dark.

He entered slowly, looking down to avoid the puddles, and was still dry-footed when he reached the steps leading up the river wall. The sounds of lapping water, soft but distinct against the background traffic of the city, indicated that the tide was in. He climbed the steps carefully. The water was near the top of the rickety wooden stairs on the other side and two barges were moored close in. Empty and high in the water, they made an occasional dull boom whenever the current knocked them together. Reflections of the Embankment lights rippled and waved in the river. There was no Viktor sitting on the steps, staring into it, as Charles had confidently expected.

He felt at a loss, deflated, almost stupid. He had simply assumed that Viktor would be there, returning, for whatever reason, to that spot, there to—to what? Contemplate? Throw himself in, as Jim had suggested? The water was eight or nine feet deep at the edge, at least, and the bank shelved steeply farther out. The tide was still coming in, so the body would have been washed upstream. It took weeks for bodies to be washed downstream of London, since each incoming tide brought them seven-eighths of the way back again. If Viktor had jumped not long after arrival he'd have been in at least half an hour, so that was that.

But if he hadn't gone in, where could he have gone? The river wall of the upstream building was tall and unbroken. There were old windows high in the downstream wall, a former warehouse, but too high to be climbed without equipment. There was also the rusting gantry used for loading and unloading barges. He looked up. Below it was a wooden plat-form, incomplete and lop-sided, too far to climb, surely, but it was the only alternative to the river.

He called Viktor's name. There was no answer. Disappointment, and the silence, made him nervous. He called again.

"Hallo, Charles." Viktor's voice was flat.

Charles grinned with relief. He could see nothing but the bottom of the platform. "Where are you?" There was no answer. "Are you up there?"

"What is it to you where I am?"

"What are you doing?" Again, no answer. He leant against the up-stream wall, smiling to himself. "This is silly, Viktor. How did you get there?"

"I flew. I have artificial wings. It is new Soviet technology. But it is secret. You must not know it. Therefore, I shall jump into the river and drown myself and it."

"What are you doing up there?"

"I told you. Just now I told you. I am here to drown myself."

"Why?" A breeze got up and the moored barges did a double, sepulchral boom. "Why don't you come down and talk about it?" There was no response. "It's difficult, having to shout. People might hear us."

"What people? Anyway, I don't care."

Charles was no longer smiling. If Viktor meant it, the best thing was to summon the river police or fire brigade, or whoever dealt with these things. If Viktor drowned and Charles had summoned no help, he might be blamed. But if he did summon help the whole story would be bound to come out and the undrowned Viktor would be doomed. As usual when confronted by difficulties, he played for time. "Tell me why, Viktor."

There was another pause. "For my wife and child. I am killing myself for them. I am under investigation, I know that now. The two men I told you—"

"Krychkov and Rhykov?"

"You see, you know. You do not need me to tell you."

"Go on." He pictured Viktor squatting on the platform, arms resting on his knees, addressing the Thames. "Assume I am stupid, Viktor. I need convincing that it is not already your immortal soul that is talking." He thought he heard a chuckle.

"The reason of these two nice men is to make sure I don't forget to return to Moscow at the end of the week. They keep me very busy with the delegation. I can do nothing else, go nowhere else, see no one else. At least, that is part of their purpose. One at least is also interested in the anti-nuclear campaign here, which he supports. That is, the English anti-nuclear campaign, not the Russian, which does not exist. If it did he would not support it. As for me, I think the Residency has become suspicious and probably they think that all the times I was with Chantal I was doing something even worse, you know, like seeing you or your people. When I get home I shall be interrogated and I shall tell the truth. That is what most people do when they are interrogated because of what they do to you. But probably they will not believe me. What I have done is bad enough but for political reasons they may like to believe the worst and will try to make me confess to that. As you have said, I know their methods. Whatever happens, it is the end of my career, perhaps my life, and the end of my salary and pension for Tanya and Natasha. They will be poor and will be expelled from our nice KGB flat and have nowhere to live and no one will wish to speak to them. They will be contaminated for life.

"But if I kill myself first there is only minor investigation and Tanya will get the pension and privileges of being KGB widow. They will have a flat. You see, Charles, our system is very legalistic. If I am not investigated and convicted, nothing bad will happen. The KGB will not wish to report to the Party that they have another traitor in London like Lyalin unless they can show him admitting it and then shoot him, to show how watchful and vigorous is the Sword and Shield of the Party. So, because I have done this stupid thing with Chantal, it is better I die. It is my way to make up for it."

"Tanya and little Natasha might not see it like that."

"Perhaps not, but still it is better for them."

"I am sure we can help you."

"Thank you, Charles, but I know what that means."

"You're wrong. We'll help anyway, any way we can. There's no price."

The platform creaked and Viktor's pale face appeared over the edge, as if he were lying or kneeling. It was too dark to make out his expression. "Even if I was—were—inclined to accept your kind offer, it is too late," he said. "I have come out without permission. They do not know where I am. If I go back they will believe I have been doing something bad. It will seal my fate. So, you see, by coming here I have sealed my fate. For me, there is one way only now."

"Two ways."

"Of course, I was forgetting. I jump off forwards or backwards."

"Suppose you returned having found the site of the cache my father had found for them, the one at Beaconsfield. At least, its location. You could say you had a sudden inspiration, even a dream, about where it must be, and tonight was the only time you had to check it before you leave. And you went without asking because you thought you would not get permission to search again on the basis of a hunch or dream. But you did find it—I can tell you exactly where it is—so they will then think you were up to something good, not something bad. You broke the rules, yes, but with good results and you could say that this was what you were doing on all your other absences. It had become an obsession for you, but finally it got them what they wanted. And you might then be in less trouble when you go back to Moscow." Charles waited, prepared for rejection and ridicule. "Also—"

"You really have found it? Really?"

"I can tell you exactly where it is and describe the instruments inside. You could say you went out and found the box but thought you heard something, so covered it up and came back, not wanting to be caught with the instruments on you. You tell them where it is and later they can send someone to retrieve it and find you are a loyal Soviet citizen after all."

"Where is it?"

"Come down and I'll tell you."

"Tell me now."

Charles described it, quoting from memory the measurements from the wall of the firing butt.

"Not feet and inches," interrupted Viktor. "Nor metres. We don't measure like that. It has to be in paces, which a person can do without looking as if he is looking for something."

Charles translated into estimated paces, then, at Viktor's request, described again what was inside. "Not that you could see much in the dark. Would you have a torch?"

"I suppose so. It would be a risk."

"You'd have to. Have you one?"

He had, but he asked more questions before moving out of sight once more and not responding for a while. Eventually, he said, "Possibly I can escape with this ingenious plan, Charles. At least for now. But when I am back in Moscow I am not sure it will be enough. These men will not like to have come all this way for nothing. To say, he is innocent, we have found no guilty man, is a failure for them. They have to find someone."

It was this that gave Charles his idea. However fantastical, it might at least get Viktor down. It might do more. "There's another way we might be able to help with that. But this time you must come down first." There was no response. "Viktor?"

"In life, comedy holds the hand of tragedy. You have this saying in English, Charles?"

"Don't think so."

"It is not in Russian, either. But it is in my head at this moment. You see, I cannot get down. So I have to kill myself after all. Or wait for the river to diminish and be found here."

"How did you get up there?"

"I climbed along a ledge and then up the drainpipe before the river became so high. Now the ledge is gone. Inside these windows which have no glass there are no floors in the building, just a great pit, as if a bomb has been here. So there is no way inside."

It started to rain. Charles was reasonably confident that suicide was no longer a serious possibility, if it ever had been, though less confident of his claimed solution to Viktor's problems on returning home. There was no time to worry about that, though. He had to be got back to the embassy first, and fast. "Where is the ledge?"

"I told you, beneath the water. It cannot be seen now."

"How far down?"

"I had to go down several steps to climb onto it."

Charles took off his shoes, socks and trousers. He was getting used to wet feet, of late. His pants were dark blue, so wouldn't show up to people crossing either of the two nearest bridges, but his legs had lost most of their summer tan. Holding the top of the river wall, he took three steps down the wooden stairs into the river. He had expected the water to be cold but was unprepared for the strength of the still-rising tide, which pressed hungrily against his thighs. He felt along the wall with his left foot until he found the ledge. It was reasonably wide, about half as wide as his foot was long, but there were no handholds and he had to work his fingers around the edges of crumbling bricks. Once he had both feet on the ledge and finger-holds for both hands, he began to inch himself along. The rain fell steadily. "You know not what you are about to do for Queen and Country, gentlemen," Gerry would say at the start of exercises, rubbing his hands.

By the time he had got beneath the platform the rain was hissing in the water and trickling from his hair down the back of his neck. The river was over half way up his thighs and twice he felt that the current was about to take him. Gratifyingly, Viktor called out his name.

"I'm here, on the ledge, beneath you," he called back. "Seeing if it's still possible. Is this it, the drainpipe on the other side of your platform?" The large iron pipe felt reasonably firm, its heavy brackets protruding enough for a hand to be pushed between it and the wall.

"There is only one. You are coming to join me?"

"Certainly not. Just seeing if your route is still navigable. It is, but you'll get soaked up to your thighs unless you take your trousers off and throw them back to me on the steps."

"And if they don't reach you I return to the Residency and say I have found the cache site but somehow I lost my trousers?"

Charles smiled in the darkness. "Actually, it's better you do get them wet. The long grass would have soaked them and if you can say you slipped in a ditch, so much the better. I'll wait here if you can get back down the pipe. Hurry up. The river's still rising."

The drainpipe shifted under Viktor's weight and a small shower of mortar fell on Charles's head. Viktor came down hand over hand, knees bent and feet pressed flat against the wall. The last few feet were a barely controlled slide, ending just above the water. He wore corduroys and a jersey. Crouching, clutching the pipe, he looked at Charles and laughed. "What a wonderful photograph. The famous SIS and the famous KGB working together again, as in the war. But SIS caught with its trousers down. Like the old days, Charles? How is the river?"

"Wet."

Viktor lowered one leg at a time, feeling for the ledge. "You are right. Imagine we are both drowned. What a mystery for the security people. Shall we swim back? We are wet enough with the rain. Why not, Charles?" He let go with one arm and made a swimming motion. For a moment it seemed he might take them both into the river.

"Are all Russians mad?" asked Charles.

"All. But not enough Englishmen are mad. That is our tragedy and yours."

Back on the river wall, Charles dressed. One of his socks fell into the river. They both reached for it and missed. "I hope you can claim for it on expenses," said Viktor. "If I survive and we meet again I will pay you from KGB funds. We can afford it, I think."

"Better lose a sock than you, I guess. Were you serious up there? Seems rather an over-reaction to me."

"You have not seen what happens to people. You have no child. You are responsible only for yourself. Your life is easier, Charles. I was really considering it, for the reasons I told you. And I still have to face them."

The rain was steady and cold. They stood at the bottom of the brick steps, pressed against the wall while Charles explained his second idea.

Viktor was sceptical, dismissive at first, eventually conceding that it might help even though there would be no knowing for some time whether it had finally worked. Any distraction, anything to muddy the waters, was useful. "It is helpful that they dislike each other," he said. "Krychkov is senior. He is old Stalinist. He resents the new generation. Rhykov is younger and cleverer and shows it, which means he is not really so clever after all. He thinks Krychkov is stupid. He is right. Each would like to blame the other for anything but Krychkov has more influential friends, old Stalinists in senior places. And because of his background, and because he is stupid, he is always suspicious. So you must point your finger at Rhykov."

"What else might they be doing here, apart from looking after you?"

"I don't know for sure but it is connected with Legacy. The Resident has called for the file and he discusses it with them. Not with me. I am left out of Legacy now. Except for my surprising discovery tonight."

"Why do you think they became suspicious of you?"

Viktor shrugged. "Maybe I have been careless. Maybe someone saw me going to Chantal. Maybe someone just said something. It can be enough."

When they had agreed tactics, Charles insisted Viktor leave first. Viktor smiled. "Still you don't trust me. You think if I stay I might still jump into the river?"

"Why didn't you signal, if you felt you were in that much trouble? Defection is better than death, surely?"

"You know, there was a murder in a provincial town in Russia. The head of the state farm was having a relationship with the wife of the district Party secretary. They killed him, the Party secretary, so they could marry each other. But people became suspicious and they were arrested. At the trial they were asked, Why didn't you just leave him, divorce, go to another town? Why did you think the only way is to kill him? You know, they had no answer to that question. They had not thought of it. Divorcing and moving were not thinkable. It is the same for me with defection. Suicide is more common in the KGB."

"Well, if what we've agreed works, you won't have to consider either."

"If." Viktor held out his hand. "Good luck with Operation Compromise. I will not know you, I promise."

"But you will signal?"

"Wait and see. Yes, Charles, I promise."

Charles waited a minute or so after Viktor's silhouette had disappeared from the end of the alleyway, then picked his way back. Rain dripped from the buildings and spattered in the puddles. His shoe rubbed on his sockless foot. No one was in sight when he emerged. The slanting rain came now in blustery waves through the dim orange street lighting. He walked up to where Anna had dropped him and saw Jim's Saab in a side street on the other side of the road, facing him.

"Looks like he's on his way back to the embassy," Jim said through the half-open window. "The other car's on him. Thought we'd better hang about to see if he'd done you in. You look wet. Not raining, is it?"

"Sweat and sun-tan oil."

"Want a lift home?"

"Thanks."

"Unless you'd prefer to go with your girlfriend. She's still here—behind us, look." Anna's Maxi was parked about twenty yards up the road. Jim grinned. "We won't take offence. Think he'll be out again tonight?"

"No, you can knock off now. Thanks for calling me out. It was worth every minute."

Jim started the engine. "Glad he didn't top himself. We was praying he wouldn't. If he had we'd've had to spend all night with the police."

He waved them off and walked up to the Maxi. "You must be soaked," said Anna.

"I'll make your seat wet, I'm afraid."

"Me too if you stand there with the door open."

He got in. "I didn't expect you to wait. But I'm glad you did."

"It gives Hugo a chance to appreciate the joys of washing up. You'd better tell me where you live."

He gave directions, not mentioning that Roger might still be there. That would stop them talking. He described the flat he was buying. "I'd rather you dropped me—that we went—there. I'd like you to see it, if you've time. It's empty and I've got the keys."

"As long as we're not too long. But I still don't see how you can pay for it without a job."

"I'll go dishwashing, I guess."

The hall light was out, the switch not easily found. He feared they might meet the lady with the eye-patch, then that the flat owner might have fallen out with his girlfriend and, for once, be there. But everything was as he had left it. He showed her round, then opened the windows onto the balcony and stepped out. She leant against the door-frame, her arms folded beneath her breasts, the sleeves of her jumper pushed up. The light caught her blonde hair. Her arms were slender. The rain had stopped but the plane trees were dripping.

"Such beautiful scent after rain," she said, "even in London. Especially here, with this huge garden. You must buy it, no matter how many dishes it takes."

He kept his distance, leaning against the balcony. "There's a scene in *Anna Karenina* in which Karenin returns home and looks up to see Anna in an upper window, laughing and talking to someone invisible behind her, her arms folded and—unusually—bare. Her bare arms are suggestive of freedom, sensuality, intimacy with whoever is behind her. Someone called it the most erotic scene in all literature."

"I'd no idea you were such a romantic."

"Admittedly, Anna's lover, Vronsky, didn't do her much good."

"But you don't want to be a Vronsky, do you, Charles? Wife of a colleague and all that? I know it goes on but you wouldn't feel very good about it, would you?"

"No, I don't want to be a Vronsky. I wouldn't feel good about it. But."

"And I'm not married to a Karenin. I've no excuse."

She turned back into the sitting room and stood, arms still folded, facing him. He followed and put his hands on her shoulders. He could smell her hair now and feel her warmth beneath her jersey. He kissed her on the lips. She neither resisted nor responded. "It's no good, Charles, much as I'd like to," she said quietly, from beneath lowered eyelids. "I have two children, my marriage is not a positive misery, even if it's not much else. It couldn't—we couldn't—lead anywhere. You do see that, don't you?" She looked up, but did not move away.

He nodded. This seemed far from the game-playing temptress Rebecca had warned him against. "No matter what we feel—might feel—?"

"It's easier for you to feel. There are fewer consequences, fewer costs than if I feel, if I allow myself to feel. Your life is simple. You have no children."

215

"That's the second time someone's said that to me this evening."

She put one hand on his arm and stroked his cheek with the finger-tips of the other. "I don't mean that I wouldn't—don't—feel anything." She leant forward and kissed him, then broke off abruptly. "I must, must go. How will you—d'you want me to—?"

"I'll walk. I need a walk."

She paused at the door. "Perhaps, one day. When I let you do the washing-up. And when you've found your other sock."

He listened to her footsteps fading on the stairs and, distantly, heard the front door close.

CHAPTER ELEVEN

T HE NEXT DAY Charles shaved and resumed his suit for a meeting with Hookey in Brooks's. "More tactful to meet you here than in the office," Hookey said. "MI5 are touchy about your resignation. Seem to doubt it for some reason." He grinned. "So it's better you don't pop in and out of the office every day, especially my office which is mystifyingly construed as a nest of conspiracy and subversion. Then there's Hugo. He's increasingly convinced he's being kept out of something, unfortunately. Ought to know by now that this sort of thing happens all the time in the office. He could be indoctrinated into Legacy but the list is long enough already and he doesn't actually *have* to know, as things currently stand. We learned that lesson with Blake in Berlin. Saw all sorts of stuff he shouldn't've just by casually asking one of the girls if he could glance at what was being circulated 'when everyone else is finished with it.' I might have to arrange a posting for Hugo, something to distract him. But that's my problem. What's yours?"

Charles described what had happened, outlining his idea for what he called Operation Compromise. Hookey heard him out, then poured coffee. "And your friend agreed all this?"

"Yes."

"I daresay in his state he would be more suggestible."

"You think it won't work, then?"

Hookey raised his eyebrows. "No idea. It's far-fetched, awkward to stage-manage, chancy, but that's perhaps why it could work. Anyway, doesn't matter what I think. The die is cast, he's gone back, doesn't sound as if he'll jump ship or jump anything else in the near future. All we can do is give it our best and stick with him. Now, I've a little news for you."

There was a change to the delegation's itinerary. At the end of the week instead of London sight-seeing as proposed, they wanted to go to King's Lynn where Russian timber ships regularly docked. "Can't imagine they really want personally to convey fraternal greetings to their seamen, inspect dockyard facilities for their wretched ships and whatever, but so they say. I've my own ideas about that. Anyway, permission's been granted and they're going by minibus tomorrow. Bloody long journey for a day trip, but they're not taking the train because they want to spend the night in Suffolk on their way back. Place called Southwold, on the coast. D'you know it? Where I was brought up. Doubt that that's why they've chosen it, but you never know. Then they drive down to Stansted at sparrow's fart the next morning and fly home. I've discussed this with MI5, who've got a lot of other demands on SV at the moment, and we wondered whether a change of plan on our part might be permissible for the last couple of days. I wanted your opinion."

Charles's signalling arrangements with Viktor were planned to culminate at the airport as the delegation left. There, contrary to every other day of the week, Viktor was to signal positively that all was well rather than signal only if it wasn't. His cue was to be the sight of Charles. This positive signalling arrangement had been criticised as unnecessary, possibly inconvenient and therefore potentially dangerous by Hookey, but it was what Viktor had wanted.

"Now, airports are good places for snatches if he needs to be snatched," said Hookey. "We control the environment, can direct who is where and when and so on, but SV are very pushed and it means widening the circle of knowledge. Anyway, your new arrangements, your Operation Compromise, somewhat supersede this. As I recall, the original arrangement was that you would appear either at the airport or at some other convenient spot shortly before. Could that reasonably include dinner in the Swan at Southwold, where the delegation is staying?"

Charles agreed it could; what was important, under both plans, was that he showed himself. He felt it important for the future, too; what in arms reduction talks might be called a confidence-building measure.

"Good. Just as well you agreed because the Swan is a busy place and I got Maureen to book you in under your alias. So long as you're happy to do it on your own, with no SV to help out. Well, not quite on your own. Rebecca's booked in too, under alias. A couple look much more natural, even if you are in separate rooms"—he raised his eyebrows again—"and you'll need someone to handle the emergency comms just in case he signals he wants out. Phone is okay most of the time, of course, but it's bound to go through the hotel switchboard and if we have to act we'll be on to you throughout the night. Rebecca is trained on the Dogsbody emergency comms system and will bring a set with her. She'll have an office car and she's Legacy indoctrinated, as you know. Good girl, Rebecca. More useful on something like this than half a dozen Hugos. Just as well your course is on leave. She should put in for promotion. Try and persuade her. Meanwhile, your friend will have his missus with him, won't he? Interesting to see how they get on. Nice place, Southwold. You'll like it."

Hookey sat back, clasping his hands across his chest. "Bit early for a pink gin. Must stick to the not-before-noon rule or we'll all go the way of empire. No, but this Southwold excursion is intriguing. Most unlike Soviet delegations to make last-minute changes. Indecision is a national characteristic, flexibility isn't. Papers are full of this anti-nuclear demo at the Sizewell nuclear power station this weekend. Not a million miles from where you're staying. You know they're targeting nuclear sites, all these long-haired weirdos and earnest useful idiots. Useful to their Soviet paymasters, that is, though to be fair to them they've no idea they're in receipt of CPSU funds channelled by our KGB friends. Perfectly sincere, well-meaning people, most of 'em. Understand their point of view. Just wrong, that's all. It may be professional paranoia but I can't help wondering whether there's a link with the delegation's last-minute proximity. I wonder if they're planning some little drama, by way of a publicity stunt?" He slapped his thighs and stood. "Anyway, can't sit here gossiping all day. The bureaucratic process demands one's corporeal presence, if not one's soul. And you'll be looking for a new job, eh?" He laughed. "Bloody lucky if you find one that's as much fun as what you're about to do."

On the drive up to Southwold they passed indications of the scale of the forthcoming demonstration: road signs, a coach plastered with stickers, police patrols. The town itself, however, was small and relatively isolated, up the coast and well to the north of Sizewell. It evoked for Charles memories of family holidays in the 1950s though the 1930s might have been more appropriate. There were rows of terraced cottages built for fishermen and the workers at Adnams brewery, the town's only industries. Grander eighteenth- and nineteenth-century houses, many facing the sea across large open grass spaces, testified to periodic influxes of wealth. There was a small hospital, a school, enough shops for living, enough pubs for comfort and two bookshops. The dominant buildings were the Perpendicular wool church, the brewery and the red and white lighthouse. The Swan hotel offered modest grandeur and was comfortable, spacious, friendly and a little shabby, in an acceptably lived-in way. They had single rooms at the back.

"The best are the doubles at the front," said Rebecca. "I looked in. You look straight down the high street to the sea."

"It's only about a hundred yards from us at the back, anyway."

"I know but you can't see it."

"D'you want to move, then?"

"They're taken. Maureen told me."

"Perhaps they'll knock some walls down for you."

"They'll need a new floor if I drop this thing."

Dogsbody was concealed in an overnight travelling bag with a shoulder-strap. It was heavy. Meant to be slung over the shoulder as for a carefree weekend, it was dangerous to walk rapidly with it. Setting it up needed a sturdy table and privacy. Charles lowered it to the floor of the wardrobe in Rebecca's room, where she put her other bag on top of it.

"Presumably security branch would say you're supposed to have it with you at all times," he said.

"If security branch want to provide a pack mule, they can. Anyway, who takes a travelling bag into dinner? Especially one that would shatter all the glasses if you dropped it on the dining room floor."

After taking tea in the horizontal armchairs of the bow-windowed drawing room, they wandered through the town and along the sea-front. It was quiet, with no road near the beach, a row of well-anchored huts, grey featureless sea and no amusements to encourage trippers. To the south wind-blown dunes sheltered marshy flats dotted by horses and cattle. Beyond was the narrow harbour mouth and the rigging of fishing vessels. Beyond that, on the blurred bulge of the coast, was the grey mass of Sizewell. The Russian delegation was due at about six.

"Could Southwold be a Legacy site?" mused Charles. "Hookey suspects something. But why should they want one here?"

She leant against the rails. "Only if they didn't need to service it from the embassy. It's way outside the travel limit. They'd need agents to do it. Or visiting delegations." She looked at the town lighthouse which, in the fading light, had begun its leisurely flashing. "George Orwell lived here. Well, his parents did, he was here some of the time. He lost his virginity to the gym mistress at the girls' school we passed on the way in."

"Hookey was brought up here, he told me. Didn't mention his virginity, though. I wonder where they did it? Hard to be private in a place like this."

She nodded at the marshy flats. "Down there, according to the book I read. Shrouded in a cloud of mosquitoes, I expect."

"How long till the meeting?"

"Thirty-five minutes."

They wandered back along the promenade. "What happens to you after the course finishes?" Charles asked.

"I've been offered New York. No one's supposed to know, so don't spread it around." She looked seawards. "I'm trying to make up my mind about it. I'd like New York. It's also nice to be offered it so soon after my last posting."

"Something to keep you here, though?"

"You're not giving up on that, are you?"

"Worried about your future, that's all."

The high windows of the church caught and intensified the last of the daylight. There was no one visible when they arrived, twenty minutes before it was due to be locked. Rebecca remained by the open door, reading a pamphlet and watching the approach. Charles walked slowly through the limewashed luminosity towards the hourglass pulpit, his steel-tipped heels ringing with sedate purpose on the stone. Michael, the area Special Branch officer, was examining the carving on the choir stalls. He was a ruddy-faced, cheerful man who looked and sounded like a farmer.

"The hotel manager is an old friend, very helpful," he said quietly. "We've done him a favour or two over the years. Krychkov is in 26, Rhykov along the corridor in 27. This key will do both. Keep it till they're gone, then put it in an envelope addressed to the manager and leave it at the desk. Don't give it to him personally. Ring me if there's anything else I can do but only on the direct line. It takes a while to get out here, remember."

They walked in step up the north aisle, beneath the heavenly host. "Not often we're honoured by Russian visitors," Michael said. "Interested in just these two, are you?"

"Yes, pair of villains. We want to see what they're up to here."

"Well, my weekend's already gone for a burton thanks to this Sizewell business. I have to mark the register on the usual suspects, professional agitators on a day away from the mines. Could do the list now. I might be out of touch for some time but otherwise any distraction would be very welcome."

"I'll see if we can do anything."

Michael looked across at Rebecca. "Your service usually seems to do a pretty good line in distractions, if you don't mind me saying so."

At dinner that night they had a table near the door. The Russians— the six delegates, Viktor and his wife, Tanya, and an embassy driver— occupied two tables by the windows. Tanya was a short, dark-haired woman with a round, kindly face, who said nothing. Viktor wore his suit which, compared now with those of the delegates, looked relatively well-cut and sophisticated. The other men were all short, stocky and uneasy, either trussed in their suits or lost in them. Necks were evidently unfashionable in Soviet society, heads apparently hammered directly into shoulders or screwed in through nuts disguised as shirt collars. Krychkov, the oldest present, had a grizzled peasant's face that, in another life, might have been kindly. As it was, he looked dour and suspicious. Rhykov was younger, smoother and more rounded, as though the awkward bits had been sanded off. He, too, looked wary of his surroundings, but more interested.

"You can always tell Russians abroad," said Rebecca. "Not just their looks and their clothes but their uncertainty at table. They watch for someone to take a lead, even what to choose. Not used to choice, I suppose."

"Our friend is like that. Each time we've eaten he's had what I've had. Like me with Hookey."

"But how much more sophisticated he looks in comparison. That's a thing about KGB officers posted abroad. They're more western, better off, more experienced, they've seen more. It makes it more difficult for them when they go back, spouting the Party line and not believing it."

"That's what he said, more or less."

Viktor was not only more at ease than the others but evidently at pains to keep a fairly desultory conversation going, in which he was not much helped by his wife. "You can see why he went elsewhere," said Rebecca. "Was she attractive?"

"Not really, no. Well, presentable and, by comparison, yes, I suppose so."

"You never—"

"No."

"—asked him much about his wife."

"Perhaps I should've."

Viktor had his back three-quarters to them. He had almost certainly not seen them. There was a reasonable chance he would on the way out, or that it should be fairly easy to arrange in the drawing room over coffee. The signal required eye contact. Charles and Rebecca had to linger over dinner.

"Not sure you should leave it until afterwards," she said. "They might not have coffee, might go straight up to their rooms. And we can't guarantee he'll look at us on the way out. I think we should take an interest in the pictures."

There were large, rather sonorous portraits at the far end of the room. They detoured past them when they had finished their meal, pausing before each. "There is something of granny in her," said Rebecca quite loudly, standing before a heavily jowelled, unhappy looking lady in pink. "She always said we were descended but no one's ever checked."

"Wrong side of the blanket, knowing your family," said Charles.

"At least mine had blankets." She turned to face the portrait on the far side, looking straight across the Russian tables. "There's a resemblance there, too, you see."

The Russians looked at her. None paid any attention to him except Viktor, who sat facing them. Charles, his hand in his pocket ready, took out his handkerchief and briefly wiped his nose. "I'm not sure that's the same artist."

"Same family, I bet." Rebecca stepped adroitly round the tables without waiting for him, her skirt swinging, her eyes on the painting and the

Russians' eyes still mainly on her. Charles followed. As he passed, Viktor took out his handkerchief and dabbed his lips. Okay to go ahead? Charles had signalled. Go ahead, Viktor had replied.

"Told you," said Rebecca. "They're sisters."

"Time for coffee." Charles moved off.

Rebecca faced the picture for a moment longer, then turned, glanced directly at Rhykov, smiled slightly, raised her eyebrows as if to suggest helplessness, and followed Charles. Rhykov's surprise became a mute, embarrassed appeal as he looked at his colleagues to see who had seen. Their expressions were suddenly guarded, awkward. Krychkov stared from him to Rebecca, his features furrowed almost into a parody of suspicious disapproval. Viktor began talking to Krychkov, as if he alone were oblivious. Rhykov looked at his plate and toyed with his food.

They did not take coffee in the drawing room but had it sent upstairs to an elegant and deserted reception room on the first floor. "D'you think it was enough?" asked Charles.

"I was more worried about overdoing it, making it too obvious. I felt awkward about it, to be honest. Not sure we should go ahead with part two." She looked tense.

"I'm sure you did it brilliantly. Viktor says you have to lay it on with a JCB as far as Krychkov is concerned. Most hints are too subtle."

"You're the case officer."

Twice Charles went downstairs to reception, from where he could see through glass doors into the drawing room. The first time the Russians were not there but the second time they were. The room was crowded, with most seats taken. He went in and crossed to the newspaper table, in Viktor's line of sight. From the corner of his eye he saw Viktor take out his handkerchief and dab his lips again. He returned to Rebecca. "He says go ahead with part two."

She took off her jacket, took a scent bottle from her handbag and applied it liberally to her wrists and neck, lifting her dark hair out of the way. "I'm going to smell like a brothel. Are you sure this is really necessary?"

"It was his idea."

"I think he's a bit hung up on tarts."

Rooms 26 and 27 were in a short corridor of their own but Charles's room opened onto the carpeted corridor leading to it. He and Rebecca went to it and waited in silence, she in the armchair, he sitting on the bed. Her blouse was cream, her skirt the tartan and pleated one he had seen before. She looked composed now, and slightly playful.

They heard the lift, then footsteps and low voices, the seamless murmur of Russian. Charles watched through the keyhole as Viktor and Krychkov walked in slow, conspiratorial conversation down the corridor. When they had gone he nodded to her. "Give them a minute or two."

"What pretext has he used to get Krychkov up here?"

"He'll have told him he has worries, something he wants to confess in private. Sort of thing Krychkov can't resist. He'll say that his worry is that he thinks he's being targeted by British special services because he's seen us—the couple in the dining room—before, more than once. He might even have seen us at one of the functions the delegation has attended. He won't mention Rhykov but we hope Krychkov will make the connection himself and draw the right, i.e., wrong, conclusion. That's what they'll be talking about when you do your bit."

"You're quite, quite sure it's not overdoing it?"

"I'm quite sure that Viktor is sure it isn't. I trust his judgement. He says he knows Krychkov's type well, that he's like his father's friends. His father was a Chekist. He thinks that even if Krychkov suspects Rhykov is being set up by us, it'll be because we're seeking revenge for Rhykov's letting us down in a relationship he hasn't confessed. He says people like Krychkov got where they did only by being even more unreasonably suspicious than the next man."

She took a pink envelope from her handbag and sealed it. "You're absolutely sure it's 27?"

"Yes. Anyway, you can listen first." He checked the corridor. "Okay."

She took off her shoes and slipped out. When she reached the short corridor, which turned off at right angles down two steps, she paused, then stepped carefully down. She tiptoed to number 26, listened to the murmurs within, then bent and slipped the envelope beneath the door of number 27, leaving the corner showing. She straightened, gave two soft knocks on the door, then walked rapidly back to Charles's room.

"Well done," he whispered.

"Pity we can't see if it works."

"Listen." They heard a door open and indistinct voices. Through the keyhole he saw Krychkov's head show briefly round the corner. Charles turned and gave her the thumbs-up sign. "Well done," he said again.

"I'll have to have another bath to get rid of this scent. It's overpowering. My clothes will smell of it. So will your room."

"I rather like it."

"You probably like tartiness, too. Don't you prefer something more subtle?"

"I guess I must like the obvious."

"How disappointing."

"What about a walk along the front? Blow some of it away. So long as we get out without running into any of them."

"I'll get my coat and boots."

The empty envelope was Viktor's refinement of Charles's idea. Charles had suggested a compromising letter but Viktor argued that the absence of any letter was even more compromising. Rhykov would almost certainly open it and his story, if he reported it, of finding it empty would probably not be believed. An empty envelope was more subtly compromising than the more obvious contrivance of a letter of assignation. If he did not report it, he would be judged guilty beyond doubt by Krychkov who, with Viktor, would have seen it beneath the door. Any subsequent assertion that it contained nothing would not be believed. If Krychkov insisted on retrieving it before Rhykov saw it— Viktor would try to persuade him not to—its emptiness would still take on the sinister aspect of a signal.

"We have to trust him to know his own," Charles had argued to Hookey.

"But they can't always be trusted to get it right, or they'd never get into trouble. Anyway, you must go ahead now it's set up. Even if it does no positive good in distracting attention from Lover Boy and casting doubt on his accuser, it at least won't do him any harm."

The moon showed through broken cloud and a chilly, fretful breeze came off the sea as Charles and Rebecca walked the length of the promenade. "His wife didn't open her mouth except to eat," said Charles. "Perhaps she's found out about Claire."

"Or she's too frightened to say anything in front of those gorillas."

"Doesn't look a very cheerful marriage."

"Who knows what goes on in a marriage?" They continued beyond the promenade, trudging along the wet beach to the narrow harbour, a river estuary with a few cottages, sheds and a pub. "I think I shall take New York," she said.

"Sounds a good idea."

"As for what might have kept me here, it was an affair, as you doubtless guessed."

"Yes."

"With a married man."

"Ah."

"I finally realised he would never leave his wife."

"Some don't. Office affair?"

"*Fnu snu* as far as everyone else is concerned. I only mentioned it because—well, you meet so many girls like me in the office. They get around, have a nice time for a few years, go to lots of places, settle in none, meet lots of people, settle with none—or if they do try there are problems, as with mine. Another posting is always a convenient way out of an affair. And then one day you're over the hill, you're an office spinster, one of the old bags, no more postings, only admin jobs and playing bridge with each other or going to concerts in the evenings. They're nice girls, they've got such a lot to offer, but I don't want to end up one of them. Neither did they, I suppose."

"You could leave."

"True, but for what? You get bored with secretarial work after a while, even good secretarial work. I suppose it's the same with any job. But it's all I'm qualified for and if you're going to be a secretary then this"—she shrugged and looked from Charles to the sea and back—"is a better way of doing it than most."

"Bridge to another branch, get promotion. That's what Hookey thinks you should do."

"Less fun, though."

"So you still want fun?"

"That's the trouble."

The breeze had a spiteful edge to it now. Charles regretted not bothering with a coat, though he was in no hurry to end the walk. He was elated, and for most of the day had hardly thought about his father.

"And you?" she asked. "The lovely Mrs. A1? She can't be very cheerfully married, surely? Not to the awful Hugo."

"Is he that bad? An honourable man, in his way. Must have his good points." Defending Hugo made him feel as awkward as joining an attack upon him.

"But you wouldn't want to be his wife, would you? Anyway, that's not the point."

"Why did you warn me that Anna was a dangerous lady?"

"Not because I have anything against her. There's no gossip or anything and I hardly know her myself. But she's very attractive and gives the impression of not knowing what she wants, while wanting something. Dangerous for you is what I meant."

"I like her."

"Bit more than that, surely?" She smiled. "Funny we should both have our hearts elsewhere. Or bits of them."

"Bits" was about right, he thought. Anna was right, too: it was easy for him. And his father had been right when he wrote that geography moved more than the magnetic compass needle. Even the short distance from London to Southwold made a difference, he reflected, noticing how Rebecca's pleated skirt swung beneath her coat as she walked. She was an athletic walker. "Convenient if your married man was Mr. A1," he said.

"Dream on, petal."

They were back on the promenade when they saw the other couple coming towards them, both wearing coats, the woman with her collar turned up against the wind and the man with a cap on. Long before they could see their features, they knew who they were, but there was no avoiding them without drawing attention to the fact. The promenade at that point was a raised path above the beach, bounded inland by the garden fences of a handsome, stucco-fronted terrace. The other couple were arm in arm; Rebecca slipped her arm through Charles's. The moment it became necessary to simulate conversation he could think of nothing to say.

"What?" said Rebecca as they drew nearer.

"What?"

"I didn't catch what you said."

"I—have to confess, it was me sending you all those letters and those flowers. I've been obsessed by you since the day we met. I adore you."

"I assumed it was you because of the spelling."

"Do you forgive me?"

"So long as you don't stop now."

Each couple made way for the other, passing without acknowledgement. The cap Viktor was wearing was Charles's father's. It was part of their long-term contact arrangements, intended as a signal at overseas meetings, and wearing it when there was no need seemed dangerously frivolous. On the other hand, that was what you did with a cap. After they had passed Charles risked a glance back. Viktor, without turning, silently raised the cap, while his wife was looking at the sea.

They remained arm in arm until the hotel. The drawing room was clear of Russians. He waited in the corridor outside her room while she unlocked the door. "At least Dogsbody can stay where he is," she whispered, "and we don't have to get up at some ungodly hour."

"They're leaving before breakfast."

"Good. 'Night."

Charles experienced an unwelcome sensation of anticlimax. "Might seem a bit odd to the hotel that we're in separate rooms, don't you think? Unrealistic, unnatural, unlikely? Bad for cover? I was wondering whether there was anything we ought to do about it."

She raised her eyebrows, smiled and closed the door.

Later that night Charles was awoken from an uneasy sleep by a knock at his own door. He wrapped a towel round himself and opened it, thinking it might be Rebecca. It was Viktor, dressed in jeans and a jumper. He came in without a word while Charles locked the door.

"I had to ask for your room number," Viktor said. "It was a risk but we go early so no one will hear about it."

"Has something happened?"

"Only good things, so please do not look so worried." He threw Charles's clothes from the armchair to the bed before he sat. "You will need these."

He talked as Charles dressed. The smile and envelope had worked. Krychkov had greedily snapped up the bait, convinced that Rebecca was an agent of the organs of British state security who had lured Rhykov into a clandestine relationship. Charles, in whom he had shown remarkably little interest, was her minder. The envelope, which he was sure was from her because of her scent in the corridor, they had left untouched. Rhykov must have found it when he went to bed but had not reported it.

He would be interrogated about it on return to Moscow; they would get it out of him.

"All that is necessary to make his guilt certain is for your girlfriend's knickers to be found in his suitcase. She will oblige, I hope? She is your girlfriend, Charles? I am disappointed she is not here with you."

"Where does Tanya think you are?"

"She is asleep. Anyway, I leave a note saying I have gone for walk in the moon along the beach. She knows I am mad. She is used to it."

"Why am I getting dressed?"

"Because I have discovered something, a big thing for you. The reason the delegation is here. And tonight we have to do something. It is our only chance."

Viktor spoke rapidly, excitement adding facetiousness to his tone so that he sounded on the edge of laughter. Charles was wary, but his story was persuasive. Krychkov, cheered by the prospect of Rhykov's downfall, had become expansive, telling Viktor that Operation Legacy was the reason for the change in itinerary. He also felt confident in Viktor now, following his finding the Beaconsfield cache. There was, he said, a second arms cache, this one at Southwold, filled many years ago by an agent who was not Builder, Charles's father. It was operational and was to be emptied at first light the following morning by an agent unknown to the Residency, run from Moscow by the Illegals directorate. This agent did not know where the cache was and was to have been told by short-wave transmission but there were problems with his receiver, so the Centre had got a message to him via someone from a Russian timber ship in King's Lynn. The message told him that instructions would be left in a DLB in Southwold, which was to be filled by Rhykov.

"Where is it?" asked Charles.

Viktor raised his hands. "I don't know, I cannot help. Somewhere in the town because Rhykov filled it not long after we arrived when he went for a walk by himself. The agent was to empty it this evening. We have missed him. But"—he laughed—"what do you think, Charles?"

"I don't know."

"Guess. What has victorious Viktor done?"

"Tell me."

"Krychkov was so pleased to think that Rhykov perhaps is a traitor that he took me to his room again when he was going to bed and told me what I have said and got out his vodka. We drank. And again we drank. He thinks the operation might go wrong if Rhykov is a traitor and if it does it will prove it, he thinks. And then he has to go to the toilet because he is getting to be an old man and must often go there. And when he is in the toilet I see the wallet in his jacket pocket which I recognise is a wallet issued by the Centre with a secret part in it. I know this because I have used one. We have to hand them back afterwards but Krychkov is too mean and too important to buy his own so he keeps his all the time. So when he is pissing, which takes a long time because he is getting old, I looked inside it. In the secret part are the instructions for the cache. Because I am a well-trained KGB officer, I remember them. Afterwards, I go to Gents' downstairs by the bar and write down what I remember." He tapped his pocket. "It is here. We can find it and empty it before the agent if we go now. Then there is no mystery operation and Rhykov is blamed and Viktor, perhaps, is still a free man."

"I should go. It's too risky for you. If something goes wrong—"

"No, Charles, we go. I have directions. If I am not going, you cannot because you do not know where."

Charles argued but knew he would have to give in. Leaving Viktor in his room, he hurried through silent corridors to Rebecca's. It was gone half past two and there was still a moon. He knocked once, twice, three times, called her name softly then, fearing to wake others, tried the door. It was unlocked. He crept in, sat on the edge of her bed and touched her gently on the shoulder. "Rebecca, it's me, Charles, wake up."

She woke, and sat up quickly. "Thank God it's only you."

"Thanks."

She switched on the bedside light, rubbing her eyes. "I must look awful. Where—why at this time—?"

"Viktor's in my room. I'll explain. D'you always sleep in hotels with your door unlocked?"

"Depends."

He paused, but there was no time. He described what had happened. "So I guess we should wake up Dogsbody and tell HO." There was nothing in terms of SV or permission that the duty officer could organise in the time available but Charles's developing bureaucratic instinct was to report anyway, even though it made no difference to what they were about to do. Reporting provided partial cover against future criticism. "And if Viktor will give us the directions in advance HO will at least have a record of where it was in case it blows up or something."

"If it blows up it'll be only too clear where it was, won't it? D'you mind getting off the bed and letting me out?"

He stood. "Well, yes, but you know what I mean. I think we should at least tell them."

"See if you can prise directions out of Viktor while I get Dogsbody on air."

When he returned she was in jeans and jumper and sitting at the dressing-table with Dogsbody open before her. There was a keyboard, some switches, green and white lights and a quiet beep when she tapped. "London's up. The DO's been summoned to the comcen so he'll see it as it comes off the machine and can reply immediately. What do you want to say?"

He was not used to dictating, particularly when there was no chance of correction, and Rebecca typed faster than he spoke. It was important to make clear that he was informing, not seeking permission. When he had finished she pressed a button, typed a five-letter group, pressed the button again and sat back. "I've told them we're awaiting immediate response."

After a pause, the answer came quickly, with chattering and whirring from the machine. She tore off the page and handed it to him. Paragraph one simply "noted" Charles's proposal. Paragraph two asked whether C/Sovbloc and the Security Service needed to be informed at once or whether it could wait till early morning.

"If you say inform them now, the DO might suggest you wait for their responses. You know what HO is like, always on the side of caution," Rebecca warned. "If you want to do it, we just do it."

"Tell them to inform Hookey at 0700. He can decide what to tell MI5." He waited while she did it. "Would you mind coming with us to watch while we search, in case the agent turns up? It'll be vital to identify him, or at least his car. And there's no point in waiting here to communicate with London because there'll be nothing to communicate till we get back. And you probably wouldn't be able to get to sleep anyway."

She was closing down Dogsbody. "Do I look as if I need persuading? I've been dying to meet Viktor."

They left by the front door, telling the surprised night porter that they couldn't sleep and felt like a moonlit drive and walk, while Viktor slipped out the back. He hid under cover of the arch leading into the street from the rear car park. When they picked him up he squeezed himself onto the floor and Charles threw his coat over him. Rebecca drove, heading inland for Reydon and the A12. When they were out of sight of the hotel Charles pulled the coat off. "This is Rebecca. Tell us where we've to go."

Viktor leant between the seats to shake hands. "Good evening, Rebecca, I am delighted to meet you. You are much more beautiful than the paintings of your ancestors."

"Thank you, Viktor. That's more than Charles has said."

They drove for some minutes with the interior light on so that he could read his notes. His translation of terms such as road, track and path were interchangeable. When nearly at the A12 they had to turn round and head back towards Southwold, eventually pulling off the road just before the town where a footpath led through sandy hillocks and scrub down to the marsh.

"From the footpath sign," Viktor read haltingly, "we must take one hundred and fifteen paces along the path. On the right is a thorn tree. Go behind the thorn tree and walk fifty-six paces along the gully that leads down to the marsh. At the bottom is the concrete floor of an old building. Turn to the near left-hand corner of the floor and face the two willow trees growing out of the bottom of the bank. The distance between the trees is seven paces. The cache is half way between them." He looked up. "It is not far. I will read the rest when we get there."

"How? We have no torch."

"The moon is bright."

Rebecca parked the car some way up the road and rejoined them. She was to hide somewhere off the footpath in a spot that would give a view of anyone approaching and time to warn them. "Glad I brought my coat," she said. "I take it the office will pay for any damage or cleaning?"

"If MI6 won't, KGB will," said Viktor. "I will find a way. So, you see, you have to meet me again, Rebecca."

They found the thorn tree easily, from which there was a view back along the path. She would hide behind it and slip down to them if she heard or saw anything. "What about a spade?" she whispered. "You'll need something to dig it up with."

Viktor turned to Charles. "You see, Charles, women always make problems. It is same in KGB. That is why our officers are men. If she were not here we would not have this problem until we get there."

Charles was annoyed with himself for not having thought. Not that thinking would necessarily have produced one, unless they had broken into the gardener's shed at the hotel. "You two wait here behind the tree," he said. "I'll get the jack handle and wheel brace from the car. If we can't dig with them we might be able to feel where the box is and dig with our hands."

Viktor's febrile excitement recalled something of his mood during the escapade on the Thames and Charles was half prepared to find, on return, that he had been trying it on with Rebecca. However, she seemed relaxed and Viktor now seriously concerned with what they were doing. "This place is good," he whispered as he got up. "We could hear your steps before we saw you so Rebecca should have more time to warn us. And the earth is soft. I could dig with my fingers."

They left her and headed down the gully. The cracked and broken square of concrete at the bottom looked like the remains of a wartime gun emplacement or pill-box. The two willows loomed as dark masses against the night sky. They knelt between them, feeling the earth. The ground was grassy and uneven, softened by rain.

"Must be cows here," said Charles, wiping his hand on the wet grass.

"KGB cow. It marks the spot. The Centre thinks of everything."

Charles prodded with the screwdriver he had brought with the other tools. He soon felt something hard but not extensive; the screwdriver slipped off it.

"A bottle and a piece of metal pipe have been put above the cache to warn you when you are getting to it and to show if it has been disturbed," said Viktor. "The mouth of the bottle should face east with the pipe at right angles. We should dig now."

They peeled back the turf, then began the slow work of loosening the earth with the tools and scooping it by hand. "The agent will surely realise it's been interfered with before he gets to the box," said Charles.

"So much the worse for Rhykov." Bottle and pipe came out easily. "Dig carefully now. We must feel for a wooden board on top of a metal container. It has a hole in it for the handle of the container, which we must not move yet."

The moonlight was just sufficient to see by, now that their eyes were accustomed. "You don't need your notes for this?" asked Charles.

"I know this sort of container. We have used them in many other countries."

They paused when they heard a car pass. The only sound afterwards was the munching of nearby cattle. They exposed the board and lifted it carefully off, over the T-shaped handle which was like that of a tap. Below it they could just make out the metal top of the container, about a foot square.

"Don't touch," said Viktor. He took from beneath his jersey a battery and two lengths of wire which he attached to the terminals. "You see, I come prepared, even if no torch or spade. This is from my big personal radio that I bought, what you call ghetto-blaster. I hope the battery is strong enough."

"Booby trap?"

He nodded. "Molniya system. It means 'lightning.' I know this system. Screwdriver, please." He scratched the top of the container, then held one wire end above the scratched part and the other over the lock. "Now, listen carefully, please."

The cattle munched, a distant dog barked twice. There was a faint background murmur that might have been the sea. Slowly, Viktor bent and put the ends of the wires against the scratched part of the container top and the lock. "Did you hear something?"

"A click."

"Good. Me too. Now it should be okay." He put the screwdriver into the lock and banged sharply with the wheel brace. "That should be enough. These are cheap locks, for children really. Now, all we must do is turn the handle and lift the lid."

"You're sure it's disarmed?"

Viktor raised his hands. "I think so, yes."

"You only think?"

"If it is not, we shall never know. We can only know if we are right, as with the Christian belief in the afterlife. That is comfort for us. Would you like to turn, or shall I?"

Hookey's statement on the unlikeliness of there being small nuclear devices seemed less reassuring. The much greater likelihood of sabotage equipment—detonators, primers, explosives—was hardly more reassuring. "Look, if there's the faintest chance that it's not, it makes sense for only one of us to be here to do it. It could be double-booby-trapped. No point in both of us being blown up. The other should go back to Rebecca."

"Go, then."

"You go."

"After you, please, your honour."

"This is absurd, Viktor."

"You English are so sensible. You do not appreciate absurdity, therefore you are even more absurd than Russians who have better understanding of the value of life and death. High value or low value, what does it matter? Goodbye, Charles, it is nice to have known you." He bent quickly over the box and turned the handle, then slowly straightened and grinned. "Hello, again. Still here, you see. Life continues. How absurd."

Inside were two parcels wrapped in greaseproof cloth, one larger and heavier than the other. The smaller felt as if it contained more than one thing. Viktor held it up. "Documents," he said.

"How do you know?"

"I have filled such things myself, in other countries. Probably money, too." He took the heavier parcel. "This I am not sure but probably it is a radio." He unwrapped the smaller parcel with practised expertise, laying out the contents on the wooden lid of the container. There were sterling notes, a cheque book, driving licence, cheque card, passport and other papers which it was hard, in the moonlight, to identify. Charles could just make out the name Evans on the passport but could make nothing of the photograph. "Alias documentation," said Viktor. "Whoever is coming must need to change his identity, or disappear, or travel, or get a job somewhere interesting, or something." He was more careful with the other parcel, only partially opening it. "Receiver. Not one I am familiar with. Perhaps he needs it to overcome his communications problem."

It was a dilemma. The clear intelligence interest was in identifying the agent and the best way to do that was to note all they could of the documents, re-bury them and wait for them to surface in use somewhere; passport details would go on the watchlist at all ports and airports. But that would do nothing to ensure Viktor's safety, which needed a disturbed or empty DLB to reinforce suspicion of Rhykov. Charles peered again at the passport.

"It could simply be that the documents are becoming out of date," said Viktor, taking it from him and peering at it himself. "They must be replaced sometimes. Or perhaps they were for another agent who cannot use them and so this one is retrieving them."

Perhaps the original agent died unexpectedly of a heart attack, thought Charles. He looked at the man near him, keen, young, full of life. It wasn't a difficult dilemma. "We'd better take them. Come on, we haven't much time."

It took longer than they thought to replace the earth and its contents on the container and they then spent some minutes searching for the screwdriver. The sky was just lightening over the sea to the east as they made their way back to Rebecca, crouching behind the thorn tree. "All right?" Charles whispered.

"Frozen."

A car approached, slowed, reversed, stopped. "Up here." Charles led them farther up the track, away from the road and into the bushes. They crouched and waited, hearing nothing. After some time Viktor whispered, "I must not be long. I must be back."

There had been no opening and closing of doors, no footsteps. Keeping away from the track, they crept through the bushes towards the road. It was slow, frustrating and uncomfortable, also impossible to be completely silent. Eventually, they reached a point near the road some way up from the footpath sign. A Morris Minor van was parked by it, backed off the road. "Anyone got pen or pencil?" asked Charles. No one had. "We'll have to remember the number, then."

"What is he doing?" asked Viktor. "What is that thing in the window?"

"It's a courting couple," said Rebecca. "That's her leg."

"The agent won't come while they're here," said Charles. "This could be the saving of Rhykov. Not so good for you, Viktor."

"We could go and watch, then they would leave."

"He might have been already. We should get you back."

They dropped him beneath the hotel arch where they had picked him up. Afterwards, Charles discreetly unlocked the back door and let him in. There was no time for a parting because they heard the porter coming down the corridor, probably on his way to the Gents'. Charles grabbed Viktor's hand. "You sure you'll be all right? You can still—"

Viktor gripped him firmly. "I think so, I think so." He took the stairs three or four at a time.

Rebecca had set up Dogsbody. "We're up. London is waiting."

Charles reported the bare facts, plus the car number, adding that they would close down while they slept. It was gone six. "Not that we'll get much sleep now."

Rebecca yawned. "I shall, if I can ever get warm again. Join SIS and spend your Friday nights in a thornbush. Who'd have guessed. 'Night."

"'Night."

CHAPTER TWELVE

—————

CHARLES WAS AWOKEN early by noises in the car park below. From his window he watched the Russians board their minibus. There was confusion about their luggage, involving rapid simultaneous talk and gesticulation on the part of all except Tanya and Rhykov, who stood silently apart. Viktor, to judge by a repeated two-handed gesture as if he were holding down a blanket, seemed to be calming everyone. The radio news was of the possibility of further oil crises, of east-west confrontation in Angola and of the likely scale of the Sizewell demonstration. He bathed and went for a sea-front walk before breakfast.

It was Saturday and traders were already setting up their stalls in the small market square outside the hotel. There was a blue sky, a fresh breeze and high, puffy white clouds. A few people walked their dogs on the beach and a solitary elderly man, wearing a deerstalker and a long raincoat of the sort that 1930s motorcyclists were pictured in, stood barefoot in the surf, his trousers rolled up to his knees, his shoes in one hand and an open umbrella in the other. Charles had a faint memory of his father wearing such a coat at one time. Like all such memories now, it bubbled up unexpectedly and already tainted. He examined them all for a sign, a hint, anything that would help explain, but to no avail. It was like another bereavement, as if his father had died twice. Away to the south the sun glinted on Sizewell.

Nevertheless, some sort of conclusion had been reached in the early hours of the morning, some sort of line drawn. With luck, Viktor would survive, and Claire would stay quiet. MI5 would get on with their investigation. Anna would stay married to Hugo. And Charles would leave, his sense of honour—or self-myth, or pride, or all three—intact. It felt like an act of revenge, though it wasn't clear upon whom—his dead father, the past, unpalatable reality, the world in which this sort of thing happened? What was clear was that he alone would suffer.

Back in the hotel, he glanced into the dining room, saw no woman by herself, and was about to withdraw when a hand was raised at the far end. Sitting at a window table, near where the Russians had been, their features at first masked by the morning sun, were Rebecca and Hookey. Beside them was a bottle of champagne in a silver bucket.

"Been waiting ages," said Hookey. "Didn't want to drink a toast until you were here but we've ordered the full works breakfast for you. Stop hanging around and sit down."

The sun was bright on cutlery and clean linen. Hookey wore a ragged blue guernsey, a meticulously pressed pair of cricket flannels and polished brown shoes. He look ruddier than in London, and slightly nautical. Rebecca was laughing. A waiter appeared, whom Hookey called by name, and opened the champagne. "We still have a house here," explained Hookey. "Didn't tell you in case you thought I'd be snooping on you. And no, it wasn't the gym mistress in the marshes for me, I'm afraid, much as I'd've welcomed her. Bloody war saw to that, like everything else when I was young."

When the waiter had withdrawn he raised his glass. "Well done, both of you. We have useful information, some valuable alias documentation and a secret understanding with a young KGB officer. Not yet a recruitment, mind, but if he comes out again and we can get Charles alongside him, then I expect we shall. That depends, of course, on whether Charles decides to leave or stay after what I'm about to tell him." He raised his eyebrows at Charles and lifted his glass again. "Because the person we should really be toasting, and who would have relished this occasion, is my old and true friend, Stephen Thoroughgood, your father."

Charles was nonplussed. Rebecca watched him closely.

"Let me tell you a story," continued Hookey. "You remember I told you I stopped a packet in the war, twice, and after the second one never rejoined my regiment? Well, I was no longer A1 FE—Forward Everywhere—but I managed to wangle myself a secondment to the Intelligence Corps and ended up in a security outfit in Berlin at the end

240

of the war. Which, incidentally, after tortuous to-ings and fro-ings and the good fortune of running into a chap called Biffy Dunderdale—colourful character, now long retired and living in New York, been in the office since the First World War and knew the first chief, Mansfield Cumming—is how I wound up in the office. Anyway, it was when I was in Berlin—what's this, tea or coffee? Blast. Rebecca, be mother, will you—that I got to know your father. Our supposed allies and fraternal friends, the Russians, were giving us a lot of trouble already. Sort of thing you've seen in that document of your father's I gave you. Well, it happened just as your father described it, though there was a lot else afterwards, and his case officer for many years was the man Igor, whom he wrote about. Impressive man, good operator, excellent case officer really and still is, no doubt, for others. We know a lot about him—habits, career successes and reverses, family and extra-marital life, political beliefs, vulnerability to corruption, loyalties—because the agent–case officer relationship is not only often close but rather more two-way than we case officers like to admit." He pointed his knife at Charles. "Remember that, if you stay."

Hookey ate as he spoke, with frequent pauses. He paused again while the waiter poured more champagne. "Half a bottle of bubbly with breakfast every day—proper breakfast, not the sort of thing Rebecca's picking at—would set us all up, you know. We'd be nicer to each other, days would pass better, work would get done just the same." He wiped his mouth and waved at someone through the window. "Now, we know all this about Igor and much, much else, because of your father, Charles. No doubt you see now where I'm leading. Yes, he was blackmailed by the Russians in the way he describes, he was unfaithful to your mother—though never again, so far as I know—and he did become a Russian spy. And in his last year he did help them with Legacy—indeed, he was the lynch-pin of the UK end of that operation."

"You've penetrated the KGB and found out about him?" Charles asked. "You've known all along?"

Hookey spoke slowly and clearly, watching where each word fell. "We know because he was really our spy. During all those years when they thought he worked solely for them, when they tried and tested and eventually trusted him with some of their most delicate operations, he was a double agent, our double agent. From the start, from day one, the day following their blackmail pitch, your father worked for us."

241

Something coursed through Charles's skin, a suffusing warmth, like an extra blood supply. He felt he might be blushing.

"He did the sensible thing, you see," Hookey continued, "unlike some others. He reported it to his commanding officer the next day, came clean, told everything. Always the best thing to do. His commanding officer reported to the local int. and sy.—intelligence and security—detachment. That was me, or part of it was. I met your father later that same day. I liked him and trusted him. Also, what he said tied in with agent reporting we already had about a number of similar honey traps they were trying at the time, one of which fitted your father's circumstances exactly. So I knew he was being truthful, wasn't holding anything back. I decided then and there that we should turn this round, play it back at them. It had to be done from the start, you see, to be really effective, because if you got on to it later there were nearly always problems, things you didn't know, differences the other side noticed, difficulties about getting the right sort of chickenfeed for the agent or whatever. 'Course, to react that fast I had to do it without clearance and seek agreement retrospectively, but that was my problem. Been doing it ever since." He chuckled. "I became, and was proud to remain, your father's principal case officer through the decades that followed. Most unusual, even irregular—we don't usually do these things as thoroughly or as well as the Russians, DA cases especially—but it was one of the very best long-term DA cases that MI5 have ever recorded. I say MI5 because, strictly speaking, it became their case—British official, run on British territory—and they're very territorial about these things. But de facto control always rested with us, with me. So, when your friend Viktor sprung the surprise on you that he did, telling you about your father, we had to do some quick thinking, eh?" He grinned.

"Fortunately, I'd already done it, some of it. Everything we knew about Legacy came from your father—he was the delicate source I referred to—and when he died I not only lost a good friend but our radar screens went as blank as the Russians'. The kit they'd given him he'd handed over to us, of course, and after we'd examined it we gave it back to him to conceal when he found a site. Naturally, he'd have consulted us on the site and we would have monitored it. But, as you know, he found it over Christmas and died before he could pass on the location to us, or to the Russians. That's why we were so anxious to monitor their progress in finding it and see what they were going to put in it. And we were equally anxious to find a source to replace your father, which is where your friend Viktor came in."

Hookey poured the rest of the bottle. "Seems a pity to stop here but I suppose another would be overdoing it. Not yet eight thirty, after all. Now, I won't claim the gift of prophecy but when our traces on Viktor showed that you knew him, and with my hunch that he had a supporting role in Legacy, I thought it possible—just possible—they might do something along the lines of what they did. It is not unprecedented. And if they did I thought it possible—no more than that—we might be able to use Viktor's affair to turn it back on them in rather pleasing parallel with your father's case. Important differences, of course, and no blackmail by us. Not directly, anyway. But I knew if I said anything to anyone about this there'd be flutterings in the hen coops for ever and a day and nothing would get done. So I just let it run and waited. And it all worked out, as you know.

"Except that your resignation was never a part of my planning, you'll be pleased to hear, and when that came up I had to decide whether to tell you all or whether to let you resign in ignorance, taking the chance of being able to salvage things later. I chose the latter partly because your resignation actually made things easier, bureaucratically, partly because I hoped that, being your father's son, you would remain loyal and helpful—as you have—and partly because I feared you might not play your part with Viktor with sufficient conviction if you knew that's all it was, playing a part. Not that I expected you to blurt out anything you shouldn't have but if you were to establish the sort of relationship with him that you have, there needed to be a genuine emotional engagement on both sides, not just the simulacrum of one. We can all feign emotion, of course, but it's deeply wearing after a while, dries out your heart. Believe me, I've done it. And from all we knew of Viktor, for him to like and trust you enough to entrust his life and future to you by accepting your help, he had to feel that you had been put through the wringer just as he had.

"Meanwhile, knowledge of your resignation made things so much easier internally and with MI5, with their worries about the tart and her minister and about our knowledge of Legacy coming to light. They were much happier that you should live the rest of your life thinking your father was under investigation and that we should make no attempt to recruit Viktor, for fear of revealing anything. Fortunately, everyone lost sight of the fact that your letter never reached Personnel." Hookey took Charles's letter from under his seat and handed it to him. "You can tear it up or keep it as a memento or what you will, but if you still want to submit it you'll have to stick it in the bloody post."

Charles bristled with questions born of relief, surprise and a quite unexpected anger that grew in proportion to his relief. "You knew, all the time?" he asked, superfluously, because he wanted to hear it said.

Rebecca smiled encouragement but Hookey was unsmiling. "Yes."

"You—"

"Put you through the wringer, rather, as I said."

"Does my mother know about it?"

"He never told her, given the way it started. But she knew he had working contacts with intelligence and security people. She just didn't know about the extracurricular bits. He was an extremely conscientious agent, your dad, very hard-working. I think partly he felt it was in expiation for the beginning, though he didn't need to. It was very understandable. Lots of people had experiences like that and he did the right thing. But I think he always felt guilty with regard to your mother."

There was much that Charles wanted to say, if only he knew what it was. "What happened to Ulriche?" he asked. It wasn't quite that, but it would do for the time being.

"I've a feeling your father did talk to Igor about that, when they got to know each other. It's in one of the early volumes of the file. You can read them all if you like. I'll tell Maureen to let you have it. It's a very long file. Come and talk again then, if you're still with us." He held up his hand for the bill. "I very much hope you will be. Will you?"

"I don't know."

"Too soon to say, eh? Bit of a shock. I can see that." Hookey paid the bill. There was no softening of his briskness. "Got to take my wife into Norwich. Which reminds me. In my case it was the dunes in Walberswick, other side of the harbour, while on leave from battle school. Thought it was the only chance I might ever get. There's rather a good pub there, by the way. In fact, it was one of the barmaids who took pity on me. Excellent mussels for lunch if you fancy walking off your breakfast. Go along the beach to Dunwich. And stay here the rest of the weekend. I think the Queen can stretch to that." He stood and put his hand on Rebecca's shoulder. "Do your very best to persuade him, my dear, but if he won't listen, don't worry. I'm sure Viktor would be happy for you to take Charles's place." He nodded at Charles, grinned and went.

They sat in silence for a while. "Did you know?" asked Charles.

She shook her head. "Not the whole story, and not until just before you came in. He said, 'Charles is in for a surprise. His father was a DA working for us all along. He should be relieved and he will be when he gets used to it, but he might be angry at my deception. We might lose him.'"

"Did you know he was here, that he was coming this morning?"

"He said he probably would. Told me not to tell you." She lit a cigarette. "How do you feel?"

"Like laughing or smashing the place up. Well, no, not quite like that. It's hard to say." He stopped and made himself smile. "Anyway, no room for personal indulgence in our business, Viktor would say. Or Hookey."

She put her hand on his arm. "What do you think you'll do?"

"Don't know."

She went out after breakfast while Charles made notes for his write-up of the night before. There was relief in the process of writing and recording. He would have to do two versions, the full one for Hookey and one that excluded Legacy for Hugo. It took longer than he thought; much of his mind was elsewhere.

Later he found her sitting on one of half a dozen ancient cannon that faced the sea. She was smoking another cigarette. "You look like a Senior Service advert."

"Peter Stuyvesant, please. Bit more glam." She gazed at the sparkling sea. "Well?"

"Well what?"

"Have you made your decision?"

"Yes, I have. And the hotel couldn't extend us. Our rooms are fully booked. Then while I was at the desk someone rang in to cancel one of the larger rooms at the front. But it's a double, I'm afraid."

She took another pull on her cigarette, exhaling slowly. "Trust you did the right thing."

"I think so."

A NOTE ON THE TYPE

The text of this book was set in Ehrhardt, a typeface based on the specimens of "Dutch" types found at the Ehrhardt foundry in Leipzig. The original design of the face was the work of Nicholas Kis, a Hungarian punch cutter known to have worked in Amsterdam from 1680 to 1689. The modern version of Ehrhardt was cut by the Monotype Corporation of London in 1937.

Composed by Stratford Publishing Services, Brattleboro, Vermont
Printed and bound by Berryville Graphics, Berryville, Virginia
Designed by Robert C. Olsson